The

BOOK

of

LONGINGS

ALSO BY SUE MONK KIDD

NOVELS

The Secret Life of Bees

The Mermaid Chair

The Invention of Wings

NONFICTION

Traveling with Pomegranates
(with Ann Kidd Taylor)

The Dance of the Dissident Daughter

Firstlight

When the Heart Waits

The

BOOK

of

LONGINGS

SUE MONK KIDD

VIKING

VIKING
An imprint of Penguin Random House LLC
penguinrandomhouse.com

Copyright © 2020 by Sue Monk Kidd, Inc.
Penguin supports copyright. Copyright fuels creativity, encourages
diverse voices, promotes free speech, and creates a vibrant culture. Thank
you for buying an authorized edition of this book and for complying with
copyright laws by not reproducing, scanning, or distributing any part of
it in any form without permission. You are supporting writers and
allowing Penguin to continue to publish books for every reader.

Grateful acknowledgment is made to Springer Nature for permission
to reprint material from Taussig, H., Calaway, J., Kotrosits, M., Lillie, C.,
Lasser, J., *The Thunder: Perfect Mind. A New Translation and
Introduction*, published in 2010 by Palgrave Macmillan US,
reproduced with permission of SNCSC.

Map illustration by Laura Hartman Maestro

LIBRARY OF CONGRESS CATALOGING-IN-PUBLICATION DATA

Names: Kidd, Sue Monk, author.
Title: The book of longings / Sue Monk Kidd.
Description: New York : Viking, [2020]
Identifiers: LCCN 2019049624 (print) | LCCN 2019049625 (ebook) |
ISBN 9780525429760 (hardcover) | ISBN 9781984881380 (international edition) |
ISBN 9780698408197 (ebook)
Subjects: GSAFD: Biographical fiction. | Historical fiction.
Classification: LCC PS3611.I44 B66 2020 (print) | LCC PS3611.I44 (ebook) |
DDC 813/.6—dc23
LC record available at https://lccn.loc.gov/2019049624
LC ebook record available at https://lccn.loc.gov/2019049625

Printed in the United States of America
1   3   5   7   9   10   8   6   4   2

DESIGNED BY MEIGHAN CAVANAUGH

For my daughter, Ann
with all my love

I am the first and the last

I am she who is honored and she who is mocked

I am the whore and the holy woman

I am the wife and the virgin

I am the mother and the daughter

I am she . . .

Do not be afraid of my power . . .

I am the knowledge of my name

I am the name of the sound and the sound of the name

THE THUNDER: PERFECT MIND

Knock upon yourself as on a door,

and walk upon yourself as on a straight road.

For if you walk on that road, you cannot get lost,

and what you open for yourself will open.

GOSPEL OF THOMAS

Sidon

Tyre

PHOENICIA

Leontes River

Jordan River

Damascus

Caesarea
Philippi

Lake
Semechonitis

Capernaum

Magdala
Cana · Sea of
Galilee

TETRARCHY
OF
PHILIP

GALILEE

Sepphoris · Tiberias
Japha · Nain
Nazareth

olive tree

Mediterranean Sea

N

Plain of Sharon

Caesarea ·

Besara ·

SAMARIA

Salim
Aenon

DECAPOLIS

Jordan R.

Jabbok River

PERAEA

Joppa ·
Lydda ·

Jerusalem ·
Bethlehem ·

JUDEA

Jericho ·
Bethany ·

Dead Sea

Machaerus

Arnon R.

KINGDOM

Delilah
in
stone
trough

Gaza ·

En-gedi ·
Masada ·

IDUMAEA

NABATAEAN

0   25   50   75   100
Scale of Miles

Petra ·

Sinai

Ezion
Geber ·
Elath

Gulf of Aqaba

Liberated
lambs

N

to Samaria

later walls

Golgotha

Garden of
Gethsemane

Golden
Gate

TEMPLE

Herod's
Palace

Gennath
Gate

UPPER
CITY

Aqueduct

LOWER CITY

HINNOM VALLEY

Pool of
Siloam

Fountain
Gate

KIDRON VALLEY

Mount of Olives

Jerusalem in the Time of Jesus

SEPPHORIS

16–17 CE

i.

I am Ana. I was the wife of Jesus ben Joseph of Nazareth. I called him Beloved and he, laughing, called me Little Thunder. He said he heard rumblings inside me while I slept, a sound like thunder from far over the Nahal Zippori valley or even farther beyond the Jordan. I don't doubt he heard something. All my life, longings lived inside me, rising up like nocturnes to wail and sing through the night. That my husband bent his heart to mine on our thin straw mat and listened was the kindness I most loved in him. What he heard was my life begging to be born.

ii.

My testament begins in the fourteenth year of my life, the night my aunt led me to the flat roof of my father's grand house in Sepphoris, bearing a plump object wrapped in linen.

I followed her up the ladder, eyeing the mysterious bundle, which was tied on her back as if it were a newborn baby, unable to guess what she secreted. She was humming a Hebrew song about Jacob's ladder, doing so rather loudly, and I worried the sound would tumble through the slit windows of the house and awaken my mother. She had forbidden

us to go to the roof together, afraid Yaltha would fill my head with audacities.

Unlike my mother, unlike every woman I knew, my aunt was educated. Her mind was an immense feral country that spilled its borders.
She trespassed everywhere. She had come to us from Alexandria four
months ago for reasons of which no one would speak. I'd not known my
father *had* a sister until she'd appeared one day dressed in a plain, undyed tunic, her small body erect with pride, eyes glowering. My father
didn't embrace her, nor did my mother. They gave her a servant's room
that opened onto the upper courtyard, and they ignored my interroga-
tions. Yaltha, too, avoided my questions. "Your father made me swear
not to speak of my past. He would rather you think I dropped from the
sky in the manner of bird shit."

Mother said Yaltha had an impudent mouth. For once, we were in
agreement. My aunt's mouth was a wellspring of thrilling and unpredictable utterances. It was what I most loved about her.

Tonight was not the first time we'd sneaked to the roof after dark to
escape prying ears. Huddled beneath the stars, my aunt had told me of
Jewish girls in Alexandria who wrote on wooden tablets that contained
multiple wax slates, contraptions I could scarcely imagine. She'd recounted stories of Jewish women there who led synagogues, studied
with philosophers, wrote poetry, and owned houses. Egyptian queens.
Female pharaohs. Great Goddesses.

If Jacob's ladder reached all the way to heaven, so, too, did ours.

Yaltha had lived no more than four and a half decades, but already
her hands were becoming knotted and misshapen. Her skin lay in pleats
on her cheeks and her right eye drooped as if wilted. Despite that, she
moved nimbly up the rungs, a graceful climbing spider. I watched as she
hoisted herself over the top rung onto the roof, the pouch on her back
swinging to and fro.

We settled on grass mats, facing each other. It was the first day of the month of Tishri, but the cool fall rains had not yet come. The moon sat like a small fire on the hills. The sky, cloudless, black, full of embers. The smell of pita and smoke from cook fires drifted over the city. I burned with curiosity to know what she concealed in her bundle, but she gazed into the distance without speaking and I forced myself to wait.

MY OWN AUDACITIES lay hidden inside a carved cedar chest in a corner of my room: scrolled papyri, parchments, and scraps of silk, all of which bore my writings. There were reed pens, a sharpening knife, a cypress writing board, vials of ink, an ivory palette, and a few precious pigments my father had brought from the palace. The pigments were mostly gone now, but they'd been luminous the day I'd opened the lid for Yaltha.

My aunt and I had stood there gazing down at all that glory, neither of us speaking.

She reached into the chest and pulled out parchments and scrolls. Not long before she arrived, I'd begun writing down the stories of the matriarchs in the Scriptures. Listening to the rabbis, one would've thought the only figures worth mention in the whole of history were Abraham, Isaac, Jacob, and Joseph . . . David, Saul, Solomon . . . Moses, Moses, Moses. When I was finally able to read the Scriptures for myself, I discovered (behold!) there were women.

To be ignored, to be forgotten, this was the worst sadness of all. I swore an oath to set down their accomplishments and praise their flourishings, no matter how small. I would be a chronicler of lost stories. It was exactly the kind of boldness Mother despised.

On the day I opened the chest for Yaltha, I had completed the stories of Eve, Sarah, Rebekah, Rachel, Leah, Zilpah, Bilhah, and Esther. But there was so much remaining to be written—Judith, Dinah, Tamar, Miriam, Deborah, Ruth, Hannah, Bathsheba, Jezebel.

Tensed, almost breathless, I watched my aunt pore over my efforts.

"It's as I thought," she said, her face candescent. "You've been greatly blessed by God."

Such words.

Until that moment I'd thought I was merely peculiar—a disturbance of nature. A misfit. A curse. I'd long been able to read and write, and I possessed unusual abilities to compose words into stories, to decipher languages and texts, to grasp hidden meanings, to hold opposing ideas in my head without conflict.

My father, Matthias, who was head scribe and counselor to our tetrarch, Herod Antipas, said my talents were better suited for prophets and messiahs, for men who parted seas, built temples, and conferred with God on mountaintops, or for that matter, any common circumcised male in Galilee. Only after I taught myself Hebrew and cajoled and pleaded did he allow me to read the Torah. Since the age of eight, I'd begged him for tutors to educate me, scrolls to study, papyrus to write on, and dyes to mix my own inks, and he'd often complied—whether out of awe or weakness or love, I couldn't say. My aspirations embarrassed him. When he couldn't subdue them, he made light of them. He liked to say the only boy in the family was a girl.

A child as awkward as I required an explanation. My father suggested that while God was busy knitting me together in my mother's womb, he'd become distracted and mistakenly endowed me with gifts destined for some poor baby boy. I don't know if he realized how affronting this must have been to God, at whose feet he laid the blunder.

My mother believed the fault lay with Lilith, a demon with the talons of an owl and the wings of a carrion bird who searched for newborn babies to murder, or in my instance, to defile with unnatural tendencies. I'd arrived in the world during a savage winter rain. The old women who delivered the babies refused to venture out even though my high-ranking father had sent for them. My distraught mother sat on her birthing chair with no one to relieve her pain or protect us from Lilith with the proper prayers and amulets, so it was left to her servant Shipra to bathe me in wine, water, salt, and olive oil, wrap me in swaddling bands, and tuck me into a cradle for Lilith to find.

My parents' stories found their way into the flesh of my flesh and the bone of my bone. It had not occurred to me that my abilities had been intended, that God had *meant* to bestow these blessings on me. On Ana, a girl with turbulent black curls and eyes the color of rainclouds.

VOICES FLOATED FROM nearby rooftops. The wail of a child, a goat bleating. Finally, Yaltha reached behind her back for the bundle and unwrapped the linen cloth. She peeled away the layers slowly, her eyes alight, casting quick glances at me.

She lifted up the contents. A limestone bowl, glowing and round, a perfect full moon. "I brought it with me from Alexandria. I wish you to have it."

When she placed it in my hands, a quiver entered my body. I ran my palms over the smooth surface, the wide mouth, the milky whorls in the stone.

"Do you know what an incantation bowl is?" she asked.

I shook my head. I only knew it must be something of great magnitude, something too perilous or wondrous to unveil anywhere except on the roof in the dark.

"In Alexandria we women pray with them. We write our most secret prayer inside them. Like this." She placed a finger inside the bowl and moved it in a spiraling line around the sides. "Every day we sing the prayer. As we do, we turn the bowl in slow circles and the words wriggle to life and spin off toward heaven."

I gazed at it, unable to speak. A thing so resplendent, so fraught with hidden powers.

She said, "At the bottom of the bowl, we draw an image of ourselves to make certain God knows to whom the petition belongs."

My mouth parted. Surely she knew no devout Jew would look upon figures in human and animal form, much less create them. The second commandment forbade it. *Thou shalt not make a graven image of anything living in heaven, or on the earth, or in the sea.*

"You must write your prayer in the bowl," my aunt told me. "But take care what you ask, for you shall surely receive it."

I stared into the hollow of the vessel and for a moment it seemed like a firmament unto itself, the starry dome turned upside down.

When I looked up, Yaltha's eyes were settled on me. She said, "A man's holy of holies contains God's laws, but inside a woman's there are only longings." Then she tapped the flat bone over my heart and spoke the charge that caused something to flame up in my chest: "Write what's inside here, inside your holy of holies."

Lifting my hand, I touched the bone my aunt had just struck to life, blinking furiously to hold back a tumult of emotion.

Our one true God dwelled inside the Holy of Holies in the Temple at Jerusalem, and I was sure it was impious to speak of a similar place existing inside humans, and worse still to suggest that yearnings inside girls like me had intimations of divinity. It was the most beautiful, wicked blasphemy I'd ever heard. I could not sleep that night for the ecstasy of it.

My bedstead was lifted off the floor on bronze legs, swathed in pillows dyed crimson and yellow, stuffed with beaten straw, feathers, coriander, and mint, and I lay there in all that softness and those scents long past the midnight hour composing my prayer in my head, struggling to compress the vastness of what I felt into words.

Rousing before dawn, I crept along the balcony that overhung the main floor, moving in bare feet without a lamp, stealing past the rooms where my family slept. Down the stone steps. Through the portico of the reception hall. I crossed the upper courtyard, measuring my steps as if walking on a field of pebbles, fearful of waking the servants who slept nearby.

The mikvah where we bathed in keeping with the laws of purity was enclosed in a dank room beneath the house and was accessible only from the lower courtyard. I descended, feeling my way along the stair wall. As the trickle of water in the conduit rose and the gloom faded, I made out the contours of the pool. I was adept at performing my ritual ablutions in the dark—I'd been coming to the mikvah since my first bleeding, as our religion required, but doing so at night, in private, for I'd not yet confessed my womanhood to my mother. For several months now I'd been burying my rags in the herb garden.

This time, though, I'd not come to the mikvah for reasons of womanhood, but to make myself ready to inscribe my bowl. To write down a prayer—this was a grievous and holy thing. The act itself of writing evoked powers, often divine, but sometimes unstable, that entered the letters and sent a mysterious animating force rippling through the ink. Did not a blessing carved on a talisman safeguard a newborn and a curse inscription protect a tomb?

I slipped off my robe and stood unclothed on the top step, though it was customary to enter in one's undergarments. I wished to be laid bare. I wished nothing between me and the water. I called out for God to make me clean so I might write my prayer with rightness of mind and heart. Then I stepped into the mikvah. I wriggled beneath the water like a fish and came up gasping.

Back in my room I robed myself in a clean tunic. I gathered the incantation bowl and my writing implements and lit the oil lamps. Day was breaking. A blurred blue light filled the room. My heart was a goblet running over.

iii.

Sitting cross-legged on the floor, I drew tiny letters inside the bowl with a newly sharpened reed pen and black ink I'd mixed myself from oven ash, tree sap, and water. For a year I'd searched for the best combination of ingredients, for the precise amount of time to cook the firewood, for the right plant gum to keep the ink from clumping, and here it was, adhering to the limestone without run or smear, shining like onyx. The ink's acrid, smoky scent filled the room, causing my nostrils to burn and my eyes to water. I breathed it like incense.

There were many secret prayers I might have written. To journey to the place in Egypt my aunt had set loose in my imagination. For my brother to come home to us. For Yaltha to remain with me all the days of my life. To be wed one day to a man who would love me for who I was. Instead, I wrote the prayer that lay at the bottom of my heart.

I formed each letter in Greek with slow, reverential movements, as if my hands were building little ink temples for God to inhabit. Writing inside the bowl was more arduous than I'd imagined, but I persevered in adding flourishes that were mine alone—thin upstrokes, thick down-strokes, spirals and chevrons at the ends of my sentences, dots and cir-clets between the words.

Out in the courtyard, I could hear our servant, sixteen-year-old Lavi, pressing olives, his rhythmic grinding of the millstone echoing from the stone pavement, and when it ceased, a dove on the roof, offering its small sound to the world. The little bird encouraged me.

The sun kindled and the sky paled from pink gold to white gold. In-side the house nothing stirred. Yaltha rarely woke before the noon hour, but by this time Shipra would've brought fry bread and a plate of figs. Mother would've appeared in my room eager to order me about. She would've scowled at my inks, reproached me for accepting such a bold gift, and blamed Yaltha for giving it to me without her permission. I could not imagine what delayed her from inflicting her daily round of persecution.

Nearly finished with my prayer, I cocked one ear for my mother and the other for the return of my brother, Judas. He had not been seen for days. At twenty, his duty was to settle down and seek a wife, but he preferred to madden Father by consorting with the radicals who agitated against Rome. He'd gone off with the Zealots before, but never so long as this. Each morning I hoped to hear him clomping through the vestibule hungry and spent, contrite over the worry he'd put us through. Judas, though, was never contrite. And this time was different—we all knew it, but didn't say it. Mother feared, as I did, that he'd finally joined Simon ben Gioras, the most inflamed fanatic of them all, for good. It was said his men swooped down upon small bands of Herod Antipas's mercenaries and General Varus's Roman soldiers and slit their throats. They also preyed on rich travelers on the road to Cana, taking their money to give to the poor, but leaving their necks intact.

Judas was my adopted brother, the son of my mother's cousin, but he was closer to me in spirit than my parents. Sensing how separate and alone I'd felt growing up, he'd often taken me with him to wander the terraced hills outside the city, the two of us climbing the stone walls that separated the fields, surprising the girls who tended sheep, plucking grapes and olives as we went. The slopes were pocked with honeycombed caves, and we explored them, calling our names into their gaping mouths, listening for the voice that spoke them back to us.

Inevitably Judas and I would find our way to the Roman aqueduct that brought water into the city, and there we made a ritual of throwing stones at the columns between the arches. It was while we'd stood in the shadows of that massive Roman marvel—he, sixteen, and I, ten—that Judas first told me about the revolt in Sepphoris that had taken his parents from him. Roman soldiers had rounded up two thousand rebels including his father and crucified them, lining the roadsides with crosses.

His mother had been sold into slavery with the rest of the city's inhabitants. Judas, only two, was given shelter in Cana until my parents came for him.

They adopted him with a legal contract, but Judas never belonged to my father, only my mother. My brother despised Herod Antipas for his collusion with Rome, as did every God-loving Jew, and it incensed him that our father had become Antipas's closest adviser. Galileans were forever plotting sedition and looking for a messiah to deliver them from Rome, and it fell to Father to counsel Antipas on how to pacify them while at the same time maintaining his loyalty to their oppressor. It was a thankless task for anyone, but especially for our father, whose Jewishness came and went like the rains. He kept the Sabbath, but with laxity. He went to synagogue, but left before the rabbi read the Scripture. He made the long pilgrimages to Jerusalem for Passover and Sukkoth, but with dread. He adhered to the food laws, but entered the mikvah only if he encountered a corpse or a person with a skin outbreak, or sat on a chair my menstruating mother had just vacated.

I worried for his safety. This morning he left for the palace accompanied by two of Herod Antipas's soldiers, Idumaean mercenaries whose helmets and gladiuses glinted with flashes of sunlight. They'd been accompanying him since last week when he was spit upon in the street by one of Simon ben Gioras's Zealots. The insult provoked a vicious argument between Father and Judas, a tempest of shouts that swept from the vestibule into the upper rooms. My brother disappeared that same night.

Occupied with these anxious thoughts of Mother, Father, and Judas, I overloaded my pen, which dripped into the bowl, leaving a black dewdrop of ink on the bottom. I stared at it horror-struck.

Carefully, I dabbed the ink with a wiping rag, which left an ugly gray splotch. I'd only made it worse. I closed my eyes to calm myself. Finally, drawing my concentration back to my prayer, I wrote the last few words with the fullness of my mind.

I waved a sheaf of feathers over the ink to quicken the drying. Then, as Yaltha had instructed, I drew the figure of a girl in the bottom of the bowl. I made her tall with long legs, a slim torso, small breasts, an egg-shaped face, large eyes, hair like brambles, thick brows, a grape of a mouth. Her arms were lifted, begging *please, please.* Anyone would know the girl was me.

The stain from the dribbled ink hovered above the girl's head like a dark little cloud. I frowned at it, telling myself it meant nothing. It presaged nothing. A lapse of concentration, that's all, but I couldn't help feeling troubled. I sketched a dove over the girl's head just below the blemish. Its wings arched over her like a tabernacle.

Rising, I took my incantation bowl to the small high window, where skeins of light fell. I rotated the bowl in a full circle, watching the words move inside it, rippling toward the rim.

Lord our God, hear my prayer, the prayer of my heart. Bless the largeness inside me, no matter how I fear it. Bless my reed pens and my inks. Bless the words I write. May they be beautiful in your sight. May they be visible to eyes not yet born. When I am dust, sing these words over my bones: she was a voice.

I gazed upon the prayer and the girl and the dove, and a sensation billowed in my chest, a small exultation like a flock of birds lifting all at once from the trees.

I wished God might notice what I'd done and speak from the whirlwind. I wished him to say: *Ana, I see you. How pleasing you are in my sight.* There was only silence.

It was while I busied myself putting away my writing tools that the second commandment appeared in my mind as if God had spoken after all, but it was not what I wished to hear. *Thou shalt not make a graven image of anything living in heaven, or on the earth, or in the sea.* It was said God himself had written the words on a stone tablet and given them to Moses. I couldn't imagine he'd really intended us to go to such an extreme, but the commandment had taken on a strict interpretation as a way to keep Israel pure and separate from Rome. It had become a measuring rod of loyalty.

I grew still. A coldness passed through me. *People have been stoned to death for creating images cruder than the one I've drawn.* Sinking to the floor, I braced my back against the sturdiness of my cedar chest. Last evening when my aunt instructed me to place my likeness in the bowl, the admonition against graven images had tormented me for several moments, but I'd dismissed it, blinded by her self-assurance. Now my disregard for the consequences left me weak.

I wasn't concerned about being stoned—matters could never go so far as that. Stonings took place in Galilee, even in Sepphoris, but not here in my father's Greek-loving household, where what mattered was not keeping Judaic laws, but the *appearance* of keeping them. No, what I felt was fear that if my image were discovered, my bowl would be destroyed. I feared the precious contents of my chest would be taken away, that my father would finally heed my mother and forbid me to write. That he would unleash his wrath upon Yaltha, perhaps even send her away.

I pressed my hands against my breast as if to compel myself back to the person I'd been the night before. Where was the self who composed a prayer girls dare not pray? Where was the self who entered the mikvah? Who lit the lamps? Who believed?

I'd recorded the stories my aunt had told me of the girls and women in Alexandria, afraid those, too, would be lost, and I dug now through my scrolls until I found them. I smoothed them out and read. They emboldened me.

I searched for a piece of flax among my wiping rags. Draping it over my bowl, I disguised it as a waste pot, then slipped it beneath my bed. Mother would never come near it. It was her spy, Shipra, I must worry about.

iv.

My mother's name, Hadar, means splendor, a name she did her best to uphold. She stepped into the room wearing a robe the color of emeralds and her finest carnelian necklace, trailed by Shipra, who was laden with a stack of luxuriant clothes and an array of purses containing jewelry, combs, and eye paint. Balanced on top of her pile was a pair of honey-colored sandals with tiny bells sewn to the straps. Even Shipra, a servant, wore her best coat and a carved bone bracelet.

"We will leave soon for the market," Mother announced. "And you will accompany us."

If she hadn't arrived with such a pressing mission, she might have noticed me glancing at the bowl beneath the bed and wondered at the object of my fascination. But her curiosity wasn't aroused, and in my relief I didn't at first question the irrationality of attending the market in such finery.

Shipra removed my robe and replaced it with a white linen tunic heavily embroidered with silver thread. She wrapped an indigo girdle about my hips, slid the musical sandals onto my feet, and admonished me to stand still as she lightened my brown face with chalk and barley flour. Her breath smelled of lentils and leeks, and when I twisted away, she pinched the lobe of my ear. I stamped my foot, unleashing a gust of bell ringing.

"Stand still; we can't be late," Mother said, handing Shipra a stick of kohl and watching as she lined my eyes, then rubbed oil into my hands.

I could hold my tongue no longer. "Must we dress so lavishly to attend the market?"

The two women exchanged a look. A patch of red bloomed beneath Mother's chin and spread across her neck, as it often did when she was being devious. She ignored me.

I told myself there was no reason for unease. Mother's pageants were not uncommon, though they were typically confined to the banquets she orchestrated for Father's patrons in the reception hall—extravaganzas of roasted lamb, honeyed figs, olives, hummus, flatbread, wine, glittering oil lamps, musicians, acrobats, a fortune-telling magus. Her exhibitions never included ostentatious walks to the market.

Poor Mother. She seemed always in need of proving something, though I'd never known what, precisely, until Yaltha arrived. During one of our roof talks, my aunt had revealed that my mother's father had made his living as a poor merchant in Jerusalem selling cloths, and not especially fine ones. Father and Yaltha, however, descended from a noble line of Greek-speaking Jews in Alexandria with ties to the Roman authorities. Naturally, arranging a marriage between two families separated by a chasm like this would've been impossible unless the bride possessed extraordinary beauty or the groom bore some bodily defect. As it was, Mother's face was unsurpassed and the thigh bone of Father's left leg was shorter than his right, causing him to limp ever so slightly.

Realizing that my mother's displays of grandeur were motivated not by conceit alone, but by an attempt to offset her low bearing, had come as a relief. It made me pity her.

Shipra pinioned my hair with ribbons and fastened a headband of silver coins across my forehead. She draped me in a stifling woolen cloak dyed scarlet, and not from cheap madder root, but from the rich red of female insects. As a last torment, Mother dropped a yoke of lapis beads around my neck.

"Your father will be pleased," she said.

"Father? He's coming, too?"

She nodded, pulling a saffron coat about her shoulders and drawing the mantle over her headdress.

When has Father ever walked to the market?

I couldn't comprehend what was happening, only that I seemed to be at the center of it, and it felt ill-omened. If Judas were here, he would take my part; he always took my part. He insisted to Mother I be exempt from the spindle, loom, and lyre and left to my studies. He asked my questions of the rabbi when I wasn't allowed to speak at synagogue. I wished for him now with all my heart.

"What of Judas?" I asked. "Has he returned?"

Mother shook her head and looked away from me.

He had always been her favorite, the lone heritor of her adoration. I wanted to believe it was because he accorded her the status that came from having a son or because he'd been troubled and broken-hearted as a child and needed the extra portion. And Judas was, after all, handsome and affable, filled with equal measures of principle and kindness, the rarest of combinations, while I was willful, impulsive, composed of strange hopes and selfish rebellion. I must have been very hard for her to love.

"And Yaltha?" I asked, desperate for an ally.

"*Yaltha . . .* " She spit the word. "Yaltha will remain here."

v.

We moved along the main thoroughfare of Sepphoris like an imperial barge, gliding along the colonnaded street, over the gleaming crushed limestone, forcing people aside—Father leading the way, then Mother, Shipra, and I, flanked by two soldiers, who shouted to passersby to make way. I watched Father's stocky frame striding ahead, listing a little side to side. He wore a red coat, as I did, and a matching hat that rose from his head like a loaf of bread. His large ears protruded on either side of the hat like little shelves, while underneath, his great bald head, which he considered a reproach from God, was hidden from view.

Earlier, upon seeing me, he'd nodded at Mother in some tacit way and, studying me further, said, "You mustn't frown so, Ana."

"Tell me the purpose of our excursion, Father, and I'm sure I'll appear more agreeable."

He didn't answer, and I asked again. He ignored me, as Mother had. It was not unusual for my parents to disregard my queries—it was their daily habit—but their refusal to answer alarmed me. As we paraded along the street, my growing panic sent me wandering in wild and terrified imaginings. It occurred to me the market was inside the same vast Roman basilica that housed the court, as well as the public hall where our synagogue met, and I began to agonize that we weren't going to the market at all, but to a tribunal where Judas would be accused of banditry, and our show of wealth was meant to deter his punishment. That was certainly it, and my fear for my brother was no less than it'd been for myself.

Moments later, however, I pictured us at the synagogue, where my parents, weary of my constant pleas to study as boys did, would accuse me of dishonoring them with my ambition and self-importance. The rabbi, the supercilious one, would write a curse and force me to swallow an infusion of the ink with which it was written. If I were sinless, the curse would have no effect, and if I were guilty, my hands would waste away so I could no longer write, and my eyes would grow too dim to read, or perhaps they would fall out of my head altogether. Hadn't a test such as this been given to a woman accused of adultery? Wasn't it said that her thighs wasted and her belly swelled as warned in the Scriptures? Why, I could be handless and blind by this very night! And if the synagogue is not our destination, I told myself, perhaps we would go to the market after all, where I would be bartered to an Arabian prince or a spice dealer who would carry me across the desert on the back of a camel, ridding my parents of me once and for all.

I took a breath. Then another, calming my spinning, senseless thoughts.

Gazing at the sun, I judged it was almost noon, and I imagined Yaltha waking to find the house empty with only Lavi left to tell her we'd all traipsed off to the market in our most splendid dress. I willed her to come in search of us. She could scarcely miss us—there was nothing omitted from our procession except cymbals and trumpets. I glanced over my shoulder in hopes of seeing her, picturing how she would appear— winded, clothed in her simple flax tunic, somehow knowing I was in peril. She would fall in step with me, her shoulders drawn back in that proud way she had. She would take my hand, saying, *I'm here, your aunt is here.*

The city was clogged with the affluent citizenry of Sepphoris, as well as foreigners from across the empire—I caught snatches of Latin and Phrygian, as well as Aramaic, Hebrew, and Greek—and, as usual, there were throngs of day laborers from Nazareth: the stonemasons, carpenters, and quarry workers who made the hour-long walk across the Nahal Zippori valley each day to find work in one of Herod Antipas's building projects. They clattered carts through the streets in a din of bellowing donkeys and shouts, drowning out the jingle of coins on my forehead, the bells on my sandals, the pandemonium in my chest.

As we neared the city mint, someone in the crowd shouted, "Behold, Herod Antipas's dogs!" in the Aramaic dialect of the Nabataeans, and I saw Father flinch. When others took up the chant, our guard at the rear trudged into the mob, pounding his shield for effect, which caused the laughter to die.

Ashamed of our extravagance and only mildly startled by the hatred for us among the peasants, I lowered my head, not wanting to meet their stares, and it came back to me, what I most wished to forget about the day Judas disappeared.

. . .

ON THAT MORNING, he had accompanied me to the market where I'd hoped to find some papyri. Typically it was left to Lavi to be my chaperone, but Judas had offered and I'd been jubilant. Strolling along the same route we traveled now, we'd come upon an overturned barrow and beside it a laborer whose arm was partially pinned beneath a marble slab. Blood crept from beneath the stone on feathery spider legs.

I tried to restrain Judas from rushing to his side. "He's unclean!" I cried, grabbing his arm. "Leave him."

Judas jerked free and looked at me with disgust. "Ana! What do you know of his plight—*you*, a privileged girl who has never known a hard day of work or a pang of hunger! Are you your father's daughter after all?"

His words were no less crushing than the slab of stone. I remained immobile and shamed as he lifted it off the man and bound his wound with a strip of cloth torn from his own tunic.

Returning to me, he said, "Give me your bracelet."

"What?"

"*Give me your bracelet.*"

It was a band of pure gold carved with a twisting grapevine. I drew back my arm.

He leaned close to my face. "This man"—he broke off, gesturing at the entire ragged collection of sweat-slick laborers who had stopped to stare—"*all* of these men deserve your mercy. They know nothing but taxes and debt. If they cannot pay, Herod Antipas takes their land and they have no way to live other than this. If this man cannot work, he will end up a beggar."

I slid the band from my wrist, and watched as Judas placed it in the injured man's hand.

It was later that same night that Judas and Father had clashed while Mother, Yaltha, and I listened from the balcony above the reception hall, pressed into the shadows.

"I regret that a follower of Simon ben Gioras spit on you, Father," Judas said. "But you cannot condemn him. These men alone fight for the poor and dispossessed."

"I *do* condemn them!" Father shouted. "I condemn them for their banditry and rabble-rousing. As for the poor and dispossessed, they have reaped what they sowed."

His pronouncement on the poor, rendered with such ease, such malice, incensed Judas, who bellowed back, "The poor have reaped only the brutality of Antipas! How are they to pay his taxes on top of Rome's tributes, *and* their mandatory tithes to the Temple? They are being broken, and you and Antipas are the pestle."

For moments there was not a sound. Then Father's voice, barely a hiss: "Get out. Leave my house."

Mother sucked in her breath. As uncaring as Father had been to Judas over the years, he'd never gone so far as this. Would Judas have lashed out if I hadn't provoked his disgust earlier that day with my own words of malice? I felt sickened.

My brother's footsteps echoed in the flickering light below, then died away.

I turned to look at Mother. Her eyes were shining with abhorrence. For as long as I'd had memory, she'd despised my father. He'd refused to allow Judas into the narrow precincts of his heart, and Mother's revenge had been methodical and spectacular—she pretended to be barren. Meanwhile, she swallowed wormwood, wild rue, even chasteberries, known to be rare and of great price. I'd found the preventatives in the herb box Shipra kept hidden in the storeroom below the courtyard. With my own ears I'd heard the two of them discuss the wool Mother soaked in linseed oil and placed inside herself before Father visited her and of the resins with which she swabbed herself afterward.

It was said women were made for two things: beauty and procreation. Having granted Father beauty, Mother saw to it he was denied procreation, refusing him children besides me. All these years, and he'd never caught on to her deception.

At times it had crossed my thoughts that my mother might not be driven solely by vengeance, but also by her *own* female peculiarity—not an unbounded ambition like mine, but an aversion to children. Perhaps she feared the pain and risk of death that came with birthing them, or she abhorred the way they ravaged a woman's body, or she resented the exhausting efforts required to care for them. Perhaps she simply didn't like them. I couldn't blame her for any of that. But if she feigned an inability to give birth for such reasons, why, then, did she birth *me*? Why was I here at all? Had her chasteberries failed to work?

The question vexed me until I reached thirteen and heard the rabbi speak of a rule that allowed a man to divorce his wife if she had not given birth in ten years, and it was as if the heavens parted and the reason for my existence toppled from God's throne and landed at my feet. I was my mother's safeguard. I was born to protect her from being cast out.

Now Mother walked behind my father holding herself erect, her chin high, looking neither right nor left. In the sunlight, her golden coat seemed lit with a hundred flames. The air shone brighter around her than the rest of us, filled with haughtiness and beauty and the scent of sandalwood. Searching the crowded streets once more for Yaltha, then Judas, I began to repeat my secret prayer, moving my lips but making no sound. *Lord our God, hear my prayer, the prayer of my heart. Bless the largeness inside me, no matter how I fear it . . .*

The words calmed me as the city flowed past, magnificent structures that awed me each time I ventured out. Antipas had filled Sepphoris with imposing public buildings, a royal treasury, frescoed basilicas, a bathhouse, sewers, roofed sidewalks, and paved streets laid out in perfect Roman grids. Large villas like Father's were common throughout the city, and Antipas's palace was as rich as any kingly residence. He'd been reconstructing the city since Rome razed it all those years ago when Judas lost his parents, and what had risen from the ashes was a wealthy metropolis that rivaled any but Jerusalem.

Lately, Antipas had begun construction on a Roman amphitheater on the northern slope of the city that would seat four thousand people. Father himself had come up with the idea as a way for Antipas to impress the emperor Tiberius. Judas said it was just another way to shove Rome down our throats. Father, however, wasn't finished with his scheming. He advised Antipas to mint his own coins, but break from Roman custom by leaving off his image and replacing it with a menorah. The ingenious gesture gave Antipas the appearance of reverencing the same Mosaic law I'd broken earlier that morning. The people called Herod Antipas the Fox, but my father was the slyer one.

Was I like him, as Judas had implied?

As the market came into sight, the crowd thickened. We plowed past clusters of men—members of court, scribes, government officials, and priests. Children hauled sheaves of herbs, barley, and wheat, armloads of onions, doves in stick cages. Women bore wares on their heads with bewildering steadiness—jars of oil, baskets of late-harvest olives, bolts of cloth, stone pitchers, even three-legged tables, whatever they could sell, all the while greeting one another, "*Shelama, shelama.*" I never saw these women without envy for how they came and went freely without the bondage of a chaperone. Surely peasantry was not all bad.

Inside the basilica, the commotion intensified along with the airless heat. I began to sweat inside my elaborate coat. I swept my eyes over the cavernous room, over row after row of stalls and market carts. There was an odor of sweat, charcoal, skewered meat, and the putrid salted fish from Magdala. I pushed the back of my hand to my nostrils to lessen the stench and felt the soldier who'd tromped behind us nudge me forward.

Up ahead, my mother stopped midway along a row of stalls that sold goods from the silk route—Chinese paper, silks, and spices. She idly inspected an azure cloth while my father continued on to the row's end, where he lingered, his eyes roaming the multitudes.

From the moment we'd set out, I'd feared we were walking toward something calamitous, sensing it not only in the oddness of our expedition, but in the minute movements of my parents' faces, and yet here was my mother serenely shopping for silk and my father patiently watching the crowd. Had she come to trade after all? My breath left me in a rush of relief.

I didn't notice the small man who approached my father, not until the crowd parted a bit and I saw him stride forward and greet Father with a bow. He was clothed in an expensive coat of deep purple and a towering cone-shaped hat, perhaps the tallest hat my eyes had ever beheld, which drew attention to his exceptionally short stature.

My mother laid down the sheath of azure. Looking back, she waved me forward.

"Who is Father's companion?" I asked, reaching her side.

"He is Nathaniel ben Hananiah, your father's acquaintance."

He could have been a boy of twelve except for the voluminous beard that plunged to his chest like twisted hanks of flax fiber. He plucked at it, his ferret eyes darting toward me, then away.

"He owns not one, but two estates," she informed me. "One grows dates, the other olives."

Then one of those small, nameless moments occurred that would loom large only later—a sweep of color at the edge of my eye. Turning toward it, I spotted a young man, a peasant, with uplifted hands and long strands of spun thread looped about his outspread fingers—red, green, lilac, yellow, blue. The threads streamed to his knees like bright falls of water. In time, they would remind me of rainbows, and I would wonder if God had sent them as a sign of hope as he'd done for Noah, something for me to cling to amid the drowned ruins that awaited, but right then the sight was nothing more than a lovely distraction.

A girl not much older than I was attempting to coil the lengths of thread into neat whorls in order to sell them. I could tell they were tinted with cheap vegetable dyes. The young man laughed, a deep, booming laugh, and I noticed he was wiggling his fingers, making the threads flutter, rendering them impossible to capture. The girl laughed, too, though she was trying very hard not to.

There was so much unexpectedness in the scene, so much gladness, that I fixed on it. I'd seen women offering their fingers as sorting pegs, never men. *What manner of man assists a woman with the balling of her yarn?*

He appeared older than I by several years, as old as twenty. He had a short, dark beard and thick hair that fell to his chin, as was the custom. I watched him push a lock behind one ear, where it refused to stay, tumbling back onto his face. His nose was long, his cheekbones broad, and his skin the color of almonds. He wore a coarse, rough-weave tunic and an outer garment sewn with tzitzit—the blue tassels marking him as a follower of God's laws. I wondered if he could be a Pharisee of the fanatical sort, one of those unyielding followers of Shammai who were known to travel ten fathoms out of the way to avoid encountering one unrighteous soul.

I glanced back at Mother, worried she would observe me staring, but she was absorbed in her own enthrallment with Father's acquaintance. The haggling in the market faded and I heard Father's raised voice cut through the commotion: "One thousand denarii and a portion of your date groves." Their meeting, it seemed, had progressed to an impassioned exchange of business.

The girl in the yarn stall finished winding her threads and placed the last orb on a wooden plank that served as a shelf. I'd thought at first she was the young man's wife, but seeing now how closely she resembled him, I decided they must be siblings.

As if feeling the intensity of my stare, the man suddenly looked around, his gaze falling on me like a veil I could almost feel, the heat of it touching my shoulders, my neck, my cheeks. I should've looked away, but I could not. His eyes were the most remarkable thing about him, not for their beauty, though they *were* beautiful in their way—widely spaced and black as my blackest ink—but it wasn't that. There was a tiny fire in them, an expressiveness I could see even from where I stood. It was as if his thoughts floated in the wet, dark light of them, wanting to be read. I perceived amusement in them. Curiosity. An unguarded interest. There was no trace of disdain for my wealth. No judgment. No pious smugness. I saw generosity and kindness. And something else less accessible, a hurt of some kind.

While it's true I thought myself skilled at reading the language of the face, I didn't know whether I really saw all of these things or I *wanted* to see them. The moment stretched beyond propriety. He smiled slightly, a faint lifting of his lips, then turned back to the woman I thought to be his sister.

"Ana!" I heard Mother say, her eyes trailing from me to the peasants. "Your father has summoned you."

"What does he want of me?" I asked. But already it was breaking over me—the truth of why we were here, the diminutive man in purple, the business matter.

"Your Father wishes to present you to Nathaniel ben Hananiah," Mother was saying, "who wishes to see you more closely."

I looked at the man and felt something tear beneath the flat bone in my chest.

They mean to betroth me.

Panic started again, this time like a wave in my belly. My hands began to tremble, then my jaw. I whirled toward her. "You cannot betroth me," I cried. "I haven't yet come of age!"

She took my arm and whisked me farther away so Nathaniel ben Hananiah could not hear my objections or see the horror on my face. "You can stop perpetuating your lie. Shipra found your bleeding rags. Did you think you could keep it from me? I am not witless. I am only angered that you've carried out such a contemptible deceit."

I wanted to scream at her, to hurl words like stones: *Where do you think I learned such deceit? From you, Mother, who hides chasteberries and wild rue in the storage room.*

I scrutinized the man they'd chosen for me. His beard more gray than black. Curved ruts beneath his eyes. A weariness about his countenance, a kind of bitterness. They meant to give me to *him. God slay me.* I would be expected to obey his entreaties, oversee his household, suffer his stubby body upon mine, and bear his children, all the while stripped of my pens and scrolls. The thought sent a spasm of rage through me so fierce I clutched my waist to keep from clawing at her.

"He is old!" I finally managed to say, offering the most feeble recrimination of all.

"He's a widower, yes, with two daughters. He—"

"He wants a son," I said, finishing her sentence.

Standing in the middle of the market, I paid no heed to the people who stepped around us, to Father's soldier waving them along, to the utter spectacle we were. "You could've told me what awaited me here!" I cried.

"And did you not betray *me?* An eye for an eye—that would be reason enough to have kept this meeting from you." She smoothed the front of her coat and glanced nervously toward Father. "We didn't tell you because we had no wish to endure your fit of protest. It's bad enough that you raise a dispute now in public."

She sweetened her tongue, eager to bring an end to my revolt. "Gather yourself. Nathaniel is waiting. Do your duty; much is at stake."

I glimpsed the sour-looking little man observing us from a distance and jutted out my chin in the defiant way I'd seen Yaltha do when Father forbade her some small freedom. "I will not be inspected for blemishes like a Passover lamb."

Mother sighed. "One cannot expect a man to enter something as binding as a betrothal without judging his bride worthy. This is how it's done."

"And what about me? Shouldn't I be allowed to judge *him* worthy?"

"Oh, Ana," she said. She gazed at me with the tired old sorrow she felt from enduring such a fractious child. "Few girls find happiness in the beginning, but this is a marriage of honor. You will want for nothing."

I will want for everything.

She gestured for Shipra, who appeared beside us as if she might be called upon to drag me to my fate. The market closed in around me, the feeling of having nowhere to go, no escape. I was not like Judas, who could just leave. I was Ana—the entire world was a cage.

I squeezed my eyes shut. "Please," I said. "Do not ask this of me."

She nudged me forward. The howling in my head returned, but softer, like someone moaning.

I walked toward my father, my feet the carapaces of two turtles, my sandals tolling.

I was a head taller than Nathaniel ben Hananiah, and I could see he was repulsed by the need to look up at me. I rose on my toes even higher.

"Ask her to speak her name so I may hear her voice," he said to Father, not addressing me.

I did not wait for Father. "Ana, daughter of Matthias." I half shouted it as if he were old and deaf. Father would be livid, but I would give the man no cause to think me modest or easy to tame.

He glowered at me, and I felt a smidgen of hope that he would find a reason to reject me.

I thought of the prayer inside my bowl, of the girl beneath the cloud. Yaltha's words: *Take care what you ask, for you shall surely receive it.*

God, please. Do not desert me.

The moments sagged beneath a thick, implacable silence. Finally, Nathaniel ben Hananiah looked at my father and nodded his consent.

I stared into the dim, hazed light of the market, seeing nothing, feeling nothing, listening to them speak of the betrothal contract. They debated the months until the marriage ceremony, my father arguing for six, Nathaniel for three. Not until I turned away did grief close over me, a dark forsakenness.

My mother, her triumph secured, turned her attention back to the cloth in the silk stall. I walked toward her, fighting to hold myself erect, but midway there the floor tilted and the world slid sideways. Dizzied, I slowed, my red cloak cascading around me, the hem snatching at the bells on my sandals, my foot torquing. I fell onto my knees.

I tried to stand but slumped back, surprised by a sharp pain in my ankle. "She has taken ill," someone shouted, and people scattered as if to flee a leper. I remember their shoes like hooves, the little dust storm on the floor. I was the daughter of Matthias, head scribe to Herod Antipas— no one would dare touch me.

When I looked up, I saw the young man from the yarn stall coming toward me. A tuft of red thread dangled from the sleeve of his robe. It drifted to the floor as he bent in front of me. It occurred to me he'd witnessed everything that had transpired—the argument with my mother, the transaction for my betrothal, my suffering and humiliation. He had *seen*.

He reached out his hand, a laborer's hand. Thick knuckles, calluses, his palm a terrain of hardships. I paused before taking it, not from aversion, but fascination that he'd offered it. I leaned against him the slightest bit, testing the weight on my foot. When I turned my face to his, I found my eyes almost level with his own. His beard was so close I could, if I were bolder, nod my head and feel it graze my skin, and it surprised me that I wanted to. My heart bounded up, along with an odd smelting in my thighs, as if my legs might give way once again.

He parted his lips as if to speak. I remember the eagerness I felt for his voice, for what he would say to me.

What happened next would plague me through the strange months to come, raining down at odd moments and sometimes waking me in the night, and I would lie there and wonder how it might have been different. He might have led me to the yarn stall, where I would sit on the wood plank among the balls of thread, waiting for the throb in my ankle to subside. My parents would find me there. They would thank the kind man, give him a coin, buy all the yarn the girl had so carefully sorted and wound. My father would say to him: *For your kindness, you must dine with us.*

Those things did not happen. Instead, before my rescuer could utter the words on his lips, the soldier who'd traipsed behind us through the streets rushed at us, shoving the man violently from behind and catching my fall as I lost my balance. I watched him go down, unable to look away as his forehead struck the hard tile.

I heard the girl call out his name, "Jesus," as she ran to him, and I must have tried to go to him, too, for I felt the soldier restraining me.

The man got to his feet, the girl pulling his arm. She seemed terrified, frantic for them to escape before the soldier assailed him further, before the crowd was riled against them, but he took his time and I remember thinking what dignity he had, what calm. He lifted his fingers to a vicious red welt above his right brow, then straightened his cloak and walked away as prudence dictated, but not without looking back at me—a kind, burning look.

My whole being ached to call out to him, to ensure he was not severely harmed, tell him I was sorry, offer him the bracelet from my arm, offer him all the bracelets in my jewel box. But I said nothing, and he and the girl disappeared behind the wall of spectators, leaving their humble lumps of yarn behind.

My father and Nathaniel ben Hananiah arrived shouting their inane question—not "Are you well?" but "Did the peasant assault you?"

The soldier hurried to justify his actions. "The man rushed at your daughter. I acted to defend her."

"No!" I exclaimed. "The man came to my aid! My ankle—"

"Find him," my father shouted, and immediately the brute of a soldier dashed off in the direction the man called Jesus had disappeared.

"No!" I cried again, breaking into a frenzied explanation, but Father did not listen or hear.

"Quiet," he said, slashing his hand through the air. The pleasure Nathaniel took in witnessing me silenced was not lost on me. His smile was no smile. It was the wriggle of a viper.

I squeezed my eyes shut, hoping God was still able to see me, tiny shrinking sun that I was, and I prayed he would let Jesus find his way to safety.

When I opened my eyes, I looked at the tile where he had fallen. A slender red thread was curled there. I bent and picked it up.

vi.

Yaltha was waiting outside the main door of our house. She reminded me of a gray mouse, alert, sniffing the air, her hands fussing beneath her chin. I hobbled toward her, my lashes dripping kohl paint that splatted on my red coat.

She opened her arms so I could step inside their little circle. "My child, you're injured."

Bending, I lowered my head onto the small ledge of her shoulder and stood there, a broken stalk, wishing to tell her of the tragedy that had befallen. *My betrothal. The young man wrongly pursued because of me.* The words rose in me like a yeasted awfulness, then fell away. I doubted she could fix any of it. Where was dear Judas?

I had not spoken a word since the market. Before leaving, Mother had poked her finger into the soft, swollen skin around my ankle. "Are you able to walk?" she'd asked. It had been the first recognition of my injury. I nodded, but the trip home soon became torturous—a stab of pain with each step. I had no choice but to use the remaining soldier's thick, bushy arm as a crutch.

The red thread I'd scooped from the market floor was tied securely about my wrist, concealed beneath my sleeve. As I clung to Yaltha, I glimpsed a wisp of it peeking out and knew I'd kept it to remind me of the few vivid moments I'd leaned my body against the man with expressive eyes.

"This is not a day for sorrow and consolation," Father said.

"Ana is to be betrothed," Mother announced with forced cheer, as if to offset my display of bereavement. "It is an honorable match and we give thanks to the Lord, for he is good."

Yaltha's hands stiffened at my back and I thought now of a great bird lifting me with its claws, carrying me over the rooftops of Sepphoris out to the nest of hills with their cave mouths.

Shipra opened the heavy pinewood door into the vestibule and there was Lavi poised inside with a bowl of water and towels for cleansing our hands. Mother pried me from my aunt and thrust me inside. The reception hall floated in afternoon shadows. Steadying myself on one foot, I waited for the day blindness to leave before finally dragging my voice from its hovel.

"I refuse the betrothal," I said, barely above a whisper. I hadn't known I would say this—it shocked me, in fact—but I drew a breath and repeated it more forcefully. "I refuse the betrothal."

Father's hands, wet and dripping, went still over the ewer.

"Truly, Ana," Mother said. "Will you now flaunt your disobedience in front of your father, too? You have no choice in this matter."

Yaltha planted herself before my father. "Matthias, you know as I do that a daughter must give consent."

"*You* have no say in the matter either," Mother said, speaking to Yaltha's back.

Both Father and Yaltha ignored her. "If it were left up to Ana," he said, "she would never consent to a marriage with anyone."

"He's a widower; he has children already," I said. "He's repulsive to me. I would rather be a servant in his house than his wife. Please, Father, I beg you."

Lavi, who'd been staring grimly into the basin of water, lifted his gaze, and I saw that his eyes swam with sorrow. Mother had an ally in Shipra—scheming Shipra—but I had Lavi. Father had bought him a year ago from a Roman legate who was glad to rid himself of a North African boy better suited to housework than military life. Lavi's name meant lion, but I'd never heard the faintest roar in him, only a gentle need to please me. If I left to marry, he would lose his only friend.

Father assumed the air of a sovereign issuing a decree. "It is my duty to see that you marry well, Ana, and I will perform that duty with your consent or without it. It makes no difference. I would like your consent—things would go much smoother that way—but if you do not give it, it will not be difficult to convince a rabbi to preside over the betrothal contract without it."

The finality in his tone and the hard set of his face abolished my last hope. I'd not known Father to be this cruel in the face of my pleas. He strode toward the study where he conducted business, pausing to look back at Mother. "Had you performed your duty better, she would be more compliant."

I expected her to lash back, to remind him that he was the one who'd given in to my pleas for a tutor, who'd allowed me to make inks and purchase papyrus, who'd led me astray, and any other time she would have, but she restrained herself. Instead she turned her wrath on me.

Wrenching me by the arm, she summoned Shipra to grasp my other one and together they dragged me up the stairs.

Yaltha trailed us. "Hadar, release her!" A demand that did nothing but stir a mighty wind at Mother's back.

I do not think my feet touched the floor as they whisked me along the balcony past the array of doors that opened to our various quarters—my parents', then Judas's, and finally my own. I was pushed inside.

Mother followed, instructing Shipra to remain outside and prevent Yaltha from entering. As the door banged shut, I heard my aunt shout a curse at Shipra in Greek. A beautiful one having to do with donkey dung.

I'd rarely seen Mother so lit with fury. She stomped about as she castigated me, flame-cheeked, puffing clouds from her nostrils. "You've disgraced me before your father, your aunt, and the servants. Your shame falls on *me*. You will remain confined here until you offer your consent to the betrothal."

Beyond the door, Yaltha was now hurling slurs in Aramaic. "Bloated swine . . . putrid goat flesh . . . daughter of a jackal."

"You shall never have my consent!" I spewed the words at Mother.

Her teeth sharpened in her mouth. "Do not mistake my meaning. As your father explained, he will make sure the contract is sanctioned by a rabbi without your permission—your wishes are irrelevant. But for my sake, you will at least appear to be a compliant daughter whether you are or not."

As she started for the door, I felt the weight of her callousness, of being locked away in a future I didn't know how to bear, and I struck out at her without thinking. "And what would Father say if he knew the lie you've been perpetuating all these years?"

She halted. "What lie?" But she knew what I referred to.

"I know you take herbs to keep you from becoming with child. I know about the linseed and resins."

Mother said, "I see. And I suppose if I were to convince your father to abandon the betrothal, you would make sure this news did not reach his ears? Is that it?"

In all truth, such an ingenious thing had not occurred to me. I'd meant only to wound her as she'd wounded me. She'd come up with the threat herself and offered it to me as if on a platter, and I seized on it. I was fourteen, desperate. A betrothal to Nathaniel ben Hananiah was a form of death. It was life in a sepulchre. I would've done anything to be delivered.

"*Yes*," I said, stunned by my fortune. "If you convince him, I'll say nothing."

She laughed. "Tell your father what you wish. It's of no concern to me."

"How can you say that?"

"Why should I care if you tell him what he already guesses?"

When Mother's footsteps faded, I cracked the door to find her minion posted at the threshold, hunched on a low stool. There was no sign of Yaltha.

"Will you sleep here, too?" I asked Shipra, not disguising my anger.

She slammed the door shut.

Inside my room the silence became a searing aloneness. With a glance back at the door, I pulled my incantation bowl from beneath the bed and removed the cloth to expose the words of my prayer.

I heard wind scratching the sky, and the room dimmed as the clouds scattered. Sitting on the floor mat, I cradled the bowl against my belly for several moments, then turned it slowly, like stirring silt, and canted my prayer into the drab light. I sang it over and over until I was weary of begging God to return to me. The largeness in me (what a cruel jest that was!) would find no blessing, nor would my reed pens and inks. The words I wrote would not be read by unborn eyes. I would become the forgotten wife of a horrid little man lusting for a son.

I cursed the world God had created. Could he not have thought up anything better than *this*? I cursed my parents for bartering me off without a care for my feelings, and Nathaniel ben Hananiah for his dismissiveness, his sneer, his silly purple hat—what was he trying to offset by wearing that towering protuberance? I cursed the rabbi Ben Sira, whose words flapped through the synagogues of Galilee as if borne by angels: "The birth of a daughter is a loss. Better is the wickedness of a man than a woman who does good."

Offspring of serpents. Bags of rotten foreskins. Decayed pig flesh!

I leapt to my feet and kicked the damnable incantation bowl and its empty words, wincing at the pain that jarred through my injured ankle. Dropping back on the bed, I rolled side to side, my body possessed by a soundless keening.

I lay there until my rage and grief subsided. I caressed the red thread tied on my wrist, rubbing it between my thumb and forefinger, and his face flared in my mind. This deep, clear sense of him. We hadn't exchanged a word, Jesus and I, but I felt the ripple of intimacy when his hand had clasped mine. It caused a voracious pining at the center of me.

Not for him, I didn't think. For myself. Yet a thought pushed into my mind, a sense that he was as wondrous as inks and papyrus, that he was as vast as words. That he could set me free.

Dusk came, then nightfall. I did not light the lamps.

vii.

I dreamed. No, not a dream exactly, but a memory echoing in the coils of my sleep.

I AM TWELVE, studying with Titus, a Greek tutor my father has hired after giving in to my inconsolable begging. Mother has assured me I would have a tutor over her dead and buried body, and yet she did not succumb. She lived to rail at me, at Father, and at the tutor, who was no more than nineteen and terrified of her. On this day, Titus hands me a true wonder—not a scroll, but a stack of dried palm leaves evenly bound with a leather cord. On them are Hebrew words in black ink and embellishments along the margins in a lustrous golden color I could never have imagined, an ink prepared, he says, from yellow arsenic. I bend close and sniff it. It smells strange, like old coins. I rub my finger across the color and touch the residue to my lips, unleashing a tiny eruption on my tongue.

He compels me to read the words aloud, not in Hebrew but in Greek. "Such a thing is beyond me," I tell him.

"I doubt that's so. Now begin."

The exercise maddens me with the need to stop and dissect entire passages, then piece them back together in a different tongue, while all I really want is to tear through the story on the palm leaves, which is as great a wonder as the golden ink. It's the tale of Aseneth, an arrogant Egyptian girl forced to marry our patriarch Joseph, and the ferocious tantrum she throws as a result. I fight

*through the tortures of translation in order to discover her fate, which must
have been the strategy all along.*

*After Titus departs, I lift my copper mirror and gaze at my face as if to as-
sure myself it was really I who accomplished that impossible feat, and as I do, a
tiny pain pricks my right temple. I think it's nothing more than the strain of
thinking so hard, but then I'm engulfed by a curdling in my stomach and a
searing headache, which is followed by a flash of light behind my eyes, a ferocious
brightness that flares out and swallows the room. I stare, mesmerized, as it
contracts into a red disk that hovers before my eyes. Inside it floats the image of
my face, a precise reflection of what I've just seen in the mirror. It startles me
with a blinding sense of my own existence: Ana who shines. Gradually it crumbles, becoming ash in the wind.*

MY EYES SHOT OPEN. The darkness in the room was suffocating, like
being inside a ripe, black olive. Shipra's snores thudded against the door.
I got up and lit a single clay lamp and quenched my thirst from the stone
pitcher. It was said that if one slept with an amethyst, it would cause a
momentous dream. I'd had no such stone in my bed, yet what had unfolded in my sleep felt auspicious and God-sent. I'd dreamed the incident exactly as it'd happened two years ago. It had been the most peculiar
event of my childhood, yet I'd told no one. How could they understand?
I myself couldn't fathom what had happened, only that God had tried to
tell me something.

For weeks afterward I scavenged the Scriptures, discovering the
strange tales of Elijah, Daniel, Elisha, and Moses and their visions of
fire, beasts, and chariot thrones. Was it hubris to think God had sent
me an apparition, too? At the time I couldn't decide if my vision was a
blessing or a curse. I wanted to believe it was a promise that the light
in me would shine forth one day, that I would be seen in this world,
I would be heard, yet I feared it was a warning that such desires

would come to nothing. It was entirely possible the vision meant little more than that I was possessed of some demonic illness. With time I thought of the episode less and less, and finally not at all. Now here it was once more.

Across the room my incantation bowl lay on its side, a small abused creature. I went over and righted it, muttering my sorrow. Holding the bowl in my lap, I loosened the red thread from my wrist and laid it inside the bowl, circling it about the figure of the girl.

I breathed out and the sound swept over the room, and then the door creaked open and closed. "My child," Yaltha whispered.

I ran to her, oblivious of my sore ankle. "How did you get past— where's Shipra?"

She pressed a finger to her lips and cracked open the door to reveal my mother's servant slumped on her stool, her head drooped to her chest and a web of spittle woven at the corner of her mouth.

"I brewed a cup of hot wine steeped with myrrh and passionflower, which Lavi was happy to serve her," Yaltha said, closing the door and beaming a little. "I would've come sooner, but it took longer than I thought for the drink to overtake the old camel."

We sat on the edge of the bed and gripped each other's hands. Her bones were sycamore twigs. "They cannot betroth me to him," I said. "You cannot let them."

She reached for the lamp and held it between us. "Ana, look at me. I would do anything for you, but I cannot stop them."

When I closed my eyes, there were blurs of light like stars falling.

It couldn't be happenstance that the memory had resurfaced in my sleep the same night I was locked in my room, doomed to marriage. Surely the story I'd translated of the Egyptian girl forced into an abhorrent marriage was a message urging me to be resolute. Aseneth had been merciless in her resistance. I, too, would be merciless.

And my face inside that tiny sun! Even if my parents married me to the repugnant Nathaniel ben Hananiah, I would not be his; I would still be Ana. The vision was a promise, was it not, that the light in me would not be extinguished. The largeness in me would not shrink away. I would yet become visible in this world. My heart tumbled a little at the revelation.

"I think, though, I could persuade your parents of one thing," Yaltha was saying. "It would not be a remedy, but it would be a consolation. When you marry, I will go with you to your husband's house."

"Do you think Nathaniel ben Hananiah would permit it?"

"He won't like having a widow to feed and clothe and take up space, but I will convince my brother to write the arrangement into your betrothal contract. It won't be difficult. He and Hadar will dance on the roof at the mention of being rid of me."

In my fourteen years I'd never had a true and constant friend, only Judas, and I felt a momentary elation. "Oh, Aunt, we will be like Naomi and Ruth in the Scriptures. Where I go, you will go."

Yaltha had kept her pledge not to speak of her past, but now that she'd bound herself to me, I wondered if she might reveal her secret.

"I know Father has sworn you to silence," I said. "But we are joined now. Don't withhold yourself from me. Tell me why you came here to Sepphoris."

The bone-kindling inside her hand grew hot. "All right, Ana. I will tell you the story, and your parents will not hear of it."

"Never," I said.

"I was married to a man named Ruebel. He was a soldier in the Jewish militia charged with protecting Roman rule in Alexandria. I bore him two sons, both of whom died before a year of age. It embittered him. Since he could not punish God with his fists, he punished me. I spent my days bruised, swollen, and in dread. On the Sabbath he rested from his cruelties and thought himself virtuous."

I hadn't expected this. It rent something in me. I wanted to ask if

Ruebel had been responsible for the drooping of her eye, but remained quiet.

She said, "He fell ill one day and died. It was so abrupt and vile a death, it set loose the tongues of Alexandria. His friends claimed I poisoned him in revenge for his beatings."

"Did you?" I blurted. "I wouldn't blame you."

She took my chin in her hand. "Remember when I told you that in your heart there is a holy of holies, and in this room dwells your secret longing? Well, *my* longing was to be free of him. I begged God to grant me this, to take Ruebel's life if he must as the just price for his transgressions. I inscribed the prayer on my incantation bowl and sang it every day. If God were a wife, she would have acted sooner. It took a year for him to take mercy on me."

"You didn't kill your husband; God did," I said, relieved, but vaguely disappointed, too.

"Yes, but his death was brought about by my prayer. It's why I cautioned you to take care what you wrote in your bowl. When the longing of one's heart is inked into words and offered as a prayer, that's when it springs to life in God's mind."

Does it? "Earlier tonight, I sent my bowl across the room with my foot," I said.

She smiled. Her face looked ancient and somehow beautiful. "Ana, your betrothal has stolen your hope. Return to your longing. It will teach you everything."

Her words seemed to release a raw power in the air around us.

"Be patient, child," she continued. "Your moment will come, and when it does, you must seize it with all the bravery you can find."

She went on describing the rumors that had circulated about her in Alexandria, stories that grew so dire she was arrested by the Romans, whose punishments were well known for their brutality. "Our oldest brother, Haran, is on the Jewish council in Alexandria and he struck a deal with the Romans to allow the council to determine my fate. They sent me away to the Therapeutae."

"*Therapeutae?*" I repeated, feeling how thick the word was on my tongue. "What is it?"

"It's a community of Jews. Philosophers, mostly. Like me, like you, they come from educated and affluent families with servants to chew their food and haul their dung, yet they gave up their comforts to live in little stone houses on an isolated hillside near Alexandria."

"But why? What do they do there?"

"They contemplate God with a fervor you can scarcely imagine. They pray and fast and sing and dance. I found it to be too much fervor for me. They do practical work, too, like growing food, hauling water, sewing garments and such, but their real work is to study and write."

Study and write. The thought filled me with wonder and stirring. How could there be such a place? "And are there women among them?"

"I was there, wasn't I? As many women dwell there as men and they bear the same zeal and purpose. They're even led by a woman, Skepsis, and there's a great reverence for God's female spirit. We prayed to her by her Greek name, Sophia."

Sophia. The name shimmered in my head. Why had I never prayed to her?

Yaltha grew quiet, so quiet I feared she'd lost the desire to go on. Turning, I saw our shadows against the wall, the bent stick of Yaltha's spine, the waves and tangles of my hair spewing like a fountain. I could barely sit still. I wanted her to tell me everything about the women who lived in stone houses on the side of a hill, about the things they studied and wrote.

As I gazed at her now, she seemed different to me. *She'd lived among them.*

Finally she spoke. "I spent eight years with the Therapeutae, and tried to embrace their life—they were caring; they didn't judge me. They saved me, but in the end I was not suited to their life."

"And you wrote and studied?"

"My job was to tend the herbs and vegetables, but yes, I spent many hours in the library. Mind you, it's nothing like the great library in Alexandria—it's a donkey shed by comparison—but there are treasures in it."

"Like what?"

I was bouncing a little on the bed. She patted my leg. "All right, all right. There's a copy of Plato's *Symposium* there. In it he wrote that his old mentor Socrates was taught philosophy by a woman. Her name was Diotima."

Seeing my eyes grow wide, she said, "And, there's a badly stained copy of *Epitaphios* written by a female named Aspasia. She was the teacher of Pericles."

"I've heard of neither of them," I said, pierced to think of my ignorance and awed that such women existed.

"Oh, but the real treasure is a copy of a hymn, the 'Exaltation of Inanna.' It came to us from Sumeria."

This I'd heard of—not the hymn, but Inanna the Goddess, queen of heaven, and Yahweh's adversary. Some Jewish women secretly made sacrificial cakes for her. "Did you read the 'Exaltation'?" I asked.

"'Lady of all the divine powers, resplendent light, righteous woman clothed in radiance, mistress of heaven . . .'"

"You can recite it?"

"Only a small part. It, too, was written by a woman, a priestess. I know because two millennia ago she signed her name to it—Enheduanna. We women revered her for her boldness."

Why had I never signed my name to what I wrote? "I don't know why you would leave such a place as that," I said. "If I should be so fortunate as to be banished to the Therapeutae, you couldn't pry me from it."

"It has its goodness, but also its hardships. One's life is not entirely one's own, but is ruled by the community. Obedience is required. And there's a great deal of fasting."

"Did you run away? How did you come to be here?"

"Now, where would I have run to? I'm here with you because Skepsis did not cease in pleading my case to Haran. He's a cruel man and a belligerent ass, but eventually he petitioned the council to let me leave the Therapeutae on the condition I also left Alexandria. They sent me here to your father, who is the youngest of us and had no choice but to obey his brother."

"Does Father know of these things?"

"Yes, as does your mother, whose first thought upon rising each morning is that I am a thorn in her right side."

"And I am the thorn in her left," I said with some pride.

We were startled by a noise, a scrape of furniture beyond the door, and we drew up in silence and waited, rewarded at last by Shipra settling back into her voluminous snores.

"Listen to me," Yaltha said, and I knew she was about to divulge the true reason she'd dosed Shipra's drink and come to me in the middle of the night. I wanted to tell her about my vision, how it'd visited my dream—*Ana, who shines*—and hear her affirm the meaning I'd given to it, but that would have to wait.

"I've been meddling," Yaltha said. "I took it as my task to listen at your parents' door. Tomorrow morning they will come to your room and remove the scrolls and inks from your chest. Whatever it contains will be taken and—"

"Burned," I said.

"Yes."

I wasn't surprised, but I felt the crush of it. I forced myself to look over at the chest of cedar in the corner. Inside were my narratives of the matriarchs, of the women and girls of Alexandria, of Aseneth—this my small collection of lost stories. It also contained my commentaries on the Scriptures, treatises of philosophy, psalms, Greek lessons. The inks I'd mixed. My carefully honed pens. My palette and writing board. They would make ash of all of it.

"If we are to thwart this, we must make haste," said Yaltha. "You must remove the most cherished items from the chest and I will hide them in my room until we can find a better place for safekeeping."

I sprang up, Yaltha trailing behind me with the lamp. I knelt over the chest, the slick of light coming to rest above my head, and lifted out armfuls of scrolls. They clattered across the floor.

"Sadly, you cannot remove *all* of them," Yaltha said. "It would raise suspicion. Your parents expect to find the chest full. If it's not, they will turn the house over, searching." She produced two goatskin pouches from the girdle inside her robe. "Take only the number of scrolls that will fit inside these skins." Her gaze bore down.

"I suppose I must leave behind my palette and writing board and most of my inks?"

She kissed my forehead. "*Hurry.*"

I selected my corpus of lost stories, leaving the rest behind. I arranged them in the pouches, which still carried the faint stink of an animal pen, wedging the thirteen scrolls into tight honeycombs inside the bags. Into the last one, I managed to slip two vials of ink, two reed pens, and three sheets of clean papyrus. I wrapped the goatskins in a faded purple robe and tied it with a leather thong. I placed the bundle into Yaltha's arms.

"Wait," I said. "Take my incantation bowl, too. I fear they will find it here." Leaving the red thread in place, I quickly redraped the bowl in flax and added it to the bundle.

Yaltha said, "I'll hide it in my room, but it may not be safe there very long either."

As I'd stuffed my writings into the goatskins, an idea had formed in my mind, one designed to gain me freedom from my room. I tried now to put it into words. "Tomorrow when my parents come, I will behave like a repentant daughter. I will confess I've been disobedient and stubborn. I will plead for forgiveness. I will be like one of those professional mourners who pretend grief and wail at the graves of strangers."

She studied me a moment. "Take care you don't weep too much. A river of tears will make them wary. A trickle will be believed."

I opened the door to be sure Shipra was still asleep and watched Yaltha creep past her with my precious belongings. My aunt had made her freedom. I would make mine.

viii.

They came late in the morning. They came bearing smugness, stern faces, and a betrothal contract freshly inked. I met them with smudges of twilight beneath my eyes and acts of guile and obsequiousness. I kissed my father's hand. I embraced my mother. I begged them to pardon my defiance, pleading shock and immaturity. I cast down my eyes, willing tears—*please come*—but I was dry as the desert. Only Satan knows how hard I tried to squeeze them out. I pictured every grief I could think of. Yaltha beaten, battered, and sent away. Nathaniel spreading my legs. A life without inks and pens. The scrolls in the chest becoming a conflagration in the courtyard. And nothing, not a drop. What a failure I should be as a professional mourner.

My father lifted the contract and read it to me.

> I, Nathaniel ben Hananiah of Sepphoris, betroth Ana,
> daughter of Matthias ben Philip Levias of Alexandria, on
> the 3rd day of Tishri and cause us to enter an inchoate
> marriage according to Rabbinic law.

I shall pay to her father 2,000 denarii and 200 talents of split dates from the first fruits of my orchard. I pledge to feed, clothe, and shelter her along with her aunt. In exchange, her guardianship shall pass into my hand on the day she is transferred to my house, where she will perform all the duties of wifehood.

This contract cannot be broken except by death or by divorce for Ana's blindness, lameness, afflictions of skin, infertility, lack of modesty, disobedience, or other repulsions or displeasures so deemed by myself.

She shall enter my house four months hence on the 3rd of Shebat.

He held the contract out before me so I could witness the words myself. They were followed by Nathaniel's signature in large brutish letters, as if slashed onto the parchment. Then my father's name in bold imperial slants. Last, Rabbi Shimon ben Yohai, my father's instrument, his signature so small and cramped I could glimpse the shame of his collusion.

"We are waiting to hear you acknowledge your consent," Mother said, cocking her eyebrow, the crook of a warning.

I lowered my eyes. Clasped my hands to my breast. A small tremble of my chin. There. I was the compliant and docile daughter. "I give it," I said. Then, wondering if they might be inclined to change their minds about the contents of my writing chest, added, "With all my heart."

They did not change their minds. Shipra arrived with one of the soldiers who'd escorted us to the market. Mother went to my writing chest and threw back the lid. Her head vacillated back and forth as she took in the contents. "For all the time you spent writing, I should think you would have more to show for it."

I felt a twinge of trepidation on the back of my neck.

"You will not partake in any more of this nonsense," Mother said. "You are betrothed now. We expect you to put all of *this* out of your mind." She dropped the lid. A resounding thud.

Father ordered the soldier to remove the chest to the courtyard. I watched as he hefted it onto his shoulder. Once again I tried to summon tears from the dust clefts in my eyelids, but my relief at having salvaged my most ardent work was too great. Mother watched me, lifting her brow once more, this time in curiosity. She was not easily fooled, my mother.

After Yaltha had left me the night before, I'd spent the wan hours thinking of where to hide the purple bundle—my scrolls were at risk here in the house under Mother's nose. I'd pictured the caves on the hillsides that surrounded the valley, the places I'd explored with Judas as a girl. For centuries, those caves had been burying places not just for people, but for family valuables and forbidden texts. In order to hide my scrolls in one, though, I would have to secure Father's permission to walk among the hills. It was an unusual request.

Beyond the window, the smell of fire and cinder erupted in the courtyard. They came then, tears gurgling up like a springhead. I went and stood before my father. "I am but a girl, but I've wanted to be like you, a great scribe. I wanted you to look on me with pride. I know now I must accept my lot. I've disappointed you and that is worse to me than a marriage I do not want. I will go willingly to Nathaniel. I beg for only one thing." The tears flowed and I didn't wipe them away. "Allow me to walk outside in the hills. I will take my comfort there and pray to be delivered from my old ways. Lavi can accompany me to keep me safe."

I waited. Mother tried to speak, but he waved his hand for silence.

"You're a good daughter, Ana. Walk in the hills with my blessing. But only in the mornings, never on the Sabbath, and always in the company of Lavi."

"Thank you, Father. Thank you."

I couldn't hide my relief and exuberance. As they left, I refused to meet my mother's gaze.

ix.

The following morning I waited for Lavi in my room. I'd instructed him to pack goat cheese, almonds, and diluted wine so we could take our breakfast along the way, impressing upon him the importance of leaving early. One hour past sunrise, I'd told him. One hour.

He was late.

Since Father had confined my excursions to the mornings, I meant to make the most of them. I'd risen in the dark and dressed hurriedly, a plain coat. No ribbon in my braid or anklet at my foot.

I paced. What kept him? Finally, I went in search of him. His room was empty. No sign of him in the upper courtyard. I'd come halfway down the steps into the lower courtyard when I saw him on his knees scraping soot and cinder from the oven, his dark face white with ash. "What are you doing?" I cried, unable to keep the exasperation from my voice. "I've been waiting for you—we should have left already!"

He didn't answer, but tensed his eyes and looked toward the doorway beneath the stairs that led to the storeroom. I descended the remaining steps slowly, knowing whom I would find there. Mother smiled with satisfaction. "Your plans will have to be postponed, I'm afraid. I discovered the oven was hazardous with grime."

"And it couldn't wait until the afternoon?"

"Certainly not," she said. "Besides, I've arranged for you to have a visitor this morning."

Not Nathaniel. Please, God. Not Nathaniel.

"You remember Tabitha?"

Not her either.

"Why would you invite her? I've not laid eyes on her in two years."

"She has only recently been betrothed. You have much in common."

The daughter of one of my father's underling scribes, Tabitha had made a handful of visits to our house when we were both twelve, those, too, at my mother's instigation. She was female and Jewish, and that was the extent of our similarities. She didn't read or write or care to learn. She liked to steal into my mother's room and rummage among her powders and perfumes. She performed playful dances, pretending to be Eve, sometimes Adam, and once, the serpent. She oiled and braided my hair while singing songs. Occasionally she speculated aloud on the mysteries of the marriage bed. I found all of these things profoundly boring except her musings on the marriage bed, which were not boring in the least.

I'd understood even then that bringing Tabitha into my life was Mother's attempt to distract me from my studies and lure me from things unbefitting girls. Clearly she did not know Tabitha had rouged her nipples with henna and proudly displayed them for me.

I glared at my mother. This time she would use Tabitha to divert me from my morning walks in the hills. While she didn't know my true motive for these excursions, her suspicion seemed aroused. *Be careful*, I told myself.

TABITHA CAST HER GAZE about my room. "When I was here last, your bed was covered with scrolls. I remember you read one of them while I wove your hair."

"I did?"

"Even when I sang, you read. You are very serious!" She laughed, not unkindly, and I absorbed her amusement without comment. I resisted telling her that my seriousness had only worsened.

We sat on a floor mat in an awkward silence, eating the goat cheese and almonds Lavi had packed for breakfast. I glanced toward the window. The morning was seeping away.

"So, we are both betrothed now," she said and chattered on about her betrothed, a man of twenty-one named Ephraim. I learned more about him than I cared to know. He'd been apprenticed to her father as a palace scribe and now worked penning documents for a member of Antipas's high council. He had little wealth. He was "firm in his demeanor," which didn't sound encouraging, but overall he was infinitely better than who Father had come up with for me.

I listened with one ear. I did not ask questions about her wedding date or her dowry price.

"Tell me of *your* betrothed," she said.

"I would rather not speak of him. I find him vile."

"I don't find Ephraim vile, but I do find him ugly. My wish is that he had the face and stature of the soldier who accompanies my father to and from the palace." She giggled.

I sighed, too heavily.

She said, "I think you don't like me very much."

Her directness caused me to choke on a piece of almond. I coughed so fitfully, she leaned forward and pounded my back. "I'm sorry," she said. "I'm often accused of blurting my thoughts. My father says my mind is weak, and my tongue, weaker." She looked at me with stricken eyes that began to fill.

I placed my hand on her arm. "I'm the one who's sorry. I've been rude. I'd planned to walk in the hills this morning, and when you came, I felt . . . diverted." I'd almost said disappointed. She wiped her cheeks with her sleeve, trying to smile.

"I'm glad you're here," I added, and it was almost true. My remorse had softened me toward her. "Sing for me and I promise not to read." There were no scrolls left in my room to tempt me, but even so, I wanted to hear her.

She beamed and her sweet, high-pitched voice poured through the room as she intoned the song the women sang when they went out to meet the bridegroom before the wedding.

> *Sing, the groom comes soon.*
> *Lift your timbrel. Raise your voice.*
> *Dance with the rising moon.*
> *Let all of creation rejoice.*

I'd thought Tabitha shallow, but perhaps she wasn't superficial so much as lighthearted. She was a girl, that's all. A playful girl who lifted her timbrel. At that moment she seemed everything I was not, and this came as a small revelation. I had hated in her what I lacked in myself.

You are very serious, she'd told me.

Despite the soreness that lingered in my ankle, I pulled her to her feet, joining my voice with hers, and we twirled in circles to the point of dizziness and collapsed onto the floor, laughing.

Mother's plot to bring Tabitha back into my life had indeed affected me, though not in the way she'd hoped—I could never be dissuaded from my studies or my walks, but I was far more pleased to sing.

x.

Tabitha came often to our house in the mornings, hindering my quest in the hills. I worried constantly that Shipra or Mother would discover my scrolls and my bowl in Yaltha's room, and yet I was happy for my friend's presence. Her visits were bright splotches amid the grimness of anticipating a marriage to Nathaniel. She knew untold songs, most of which she'd composed herself in hexameters and trimeters. There was one about a madwoman who starts laughing and can't stop; another about a peasant who bakes a worm into a loaf of bread and serves it to the tetrarch; and my favorite, about a girl who escapes a harem by pretending to be a boy.

Even Yaltha would rise earlier than usual from her bed to hear what Tabitha had concocted, bringing an Egyptian rattling musical instrument called a sistrum and shaking it in rhythm with the songs. Tabitha would free her straight black hair from its constraints and, without a trace of shyness, dance out the story as she sang. She had a small, lithe body and a lovely face with high arching brows. Watching her move was like gazing at mesmeric curls of smoke.

One morning when Tabitha arrived, she had an amused, conspiratorial look about her. She said, "Today we shall perform a dance *together*." When I protested, she snorted. "You have no choice—I've written a song that requires both of us."

I had never danced, not ever. "What's the song about?" I asked.

"We shall be two blind girls who pretend we can see in order to keep our betrotheds."

I didn't know if I cared for her song's proposition. "Could we be blind and pretend to see in order to keep our tutors?"

"No girl would enact such an elaborate pretense for a *tutor*."

"*I* would."

She rolled her eyes upward, but I saw she was more amused than exasperated. "Then you shall pretend that your betrothed *is* your tutor."

There was something strangely beautiful about this, the coming together of two ways of life that I'd thought irreconcilable: duty and longing.

We slipped into Mother's room while she was occupied in the courtyard and lifted the lid on her storage chest, the oak one carved on top with braided circles and fastened with a brass clasp. Tabitha dug out dyed scarves the color of rubies and tied them about our hips. She rummaged among the pouches for a kohl stick and drew a pair of staring eyes atop my closed lids, and when it was my turn to draw the same upon hers, I giggled so uncontrollably the stick of kohl made a streak across her temple. She said, "We will dance with our eyes closed, completely blind, but we will look as if we can see."

At the bottom of the chest, Tabitha found Mother's wooden jewel box. Would we now plunder her jewelry, too? I glanced back at the door while Tabitha draped the carnelian necklace about her neck and tied lapis beads about mine. She adorned us with gold and amethyst headbands and pushed gold rings on our fingers. She said, "Just because we're blind doesn't mean we can't look beautiful."

Coming upon a vial of perfume, she opened it and the sharp smell of a thousand lilies cut the air. Spikenard, the costliest of all the scents.

"Not that one," I said. "It's too expensive."

"Surely we poor blind girls deserve spikenard." She blinked and the eyes I'd painted on her lids flashed me an imploring look.

I gave in easily, and she placed a drop of the oil on her finger and touched it to my forehead as mothers did when anointing and naming their babies. "I anoint you Ana, friend of Tabitha," she said and let out a quiet laugh, making it hard to know whether she was being serious or playful, but then she held my eyes and repeated the words *friend of Tabitha*, and I realized she was being both.

"Now me," she said.

I dipped my finger into the vial and touched her forehead. "I anoint you Tabitha, friend of Ana." And this time she didn't laugh.

We repacked the chest as we'd found it and hurried from the room, exhilarated and reeking, leaving behind a great deal of olfactory evidence of our plundering.

Yaltha waited for us in my room. She shook the sistrum, setting loose a shimmering sound. Tabitha began to sing, and with a nod at me to follow her lead, sank her eyelids closed and danced. I closed my eyes, too, but stood there, motionless and inhibited. *You are very serious*, I told myself, and then let my arms and legs do as they pleased. I swayed. I was a willow reed. A floating cloud. A raven. I was a blind girl pretending to see.

Once I careened into Tabitha, and she found my hand and didn't let go. I didn't think once of Nathaniel. I thought of the young man in the market who'd lifted me to my feet. I thought of scrolls and ink. In the darkness behind my eyes, I was free.

xi.

On the days Tabitha didn't visit, Lavi and I departed the house early and ventured across Sepphoris to the southern gate of the city, where I would pause to take in the valley, making a ceremony of it, gazing down on clouds and birds, then up at the sharp blue edges, and the wind would blow wild around me. Then I would descend onto the footpath that led across the hills, determined to find·a cave to hide my scrolls and incantation bowl. Time pressed on me. Thus far, Mother had failed to search my aunt's room. Perhaps it hadn't yet occurred to her that the two of us were in collusion, but it might, and soon. Each day upon waking, I tore from my room, frantic to find Yaltha and inquire if the bundle was safe.

I asked myself why the prospect of losing thirteen scrolls, two vials of ink, two reed pens, three clean sheets of papyrus, and a bowl set off such desperation in me. Only now do I see the immensity I assigned to these objects. They not only represented those fragile stories I wanted to preserve. They also held the full weight of my craving to express myself, to lift out of my small self, out of the enclosure of my life, and find what lay beyond. I wanted for so much.

The urgency of finding a cave possessed me. Lavi threw himself into the mission, too, though he fretted when I veered from the path. The isolated thickets were populated with badgers, boars, wild goats, hyenas, and jackals. Each time we went out, I wandered farther and farther afield. We came upon men laboring in a limestone quarry, women washing garments in a stream, shepherd boys pretending their crooks were swords, Nazarene girls gathering the late olive harvest. Now and then we passed a pious man praying in a nook of rock or beneath an acacia tree. We found dozens of caves, but none were well suited. They were too accessible, or showed signs of habitation, or had been claimed as a tomb and were sealed with a stone.

We walked the hills to no avail.

xii.

It was rare that Father, Mother, Yaltha, and I shared a meal together other than on the Sabbath, so when Mother insisted we all sit down together, I knew there must be news. Father, however, had taken up the better part of our supper with a tirade about bowls made of gold that were missing from the palace.

"But why should you be concerned with it?" Mother asked.

"They're the bowls used to serve scribes and subordinates in the library. First, one went missing, then two. Now four. Antipas is angered. He has charged me to find the thief. I cannot see what I'm to do about it—I'm not a palace guard!"

This could hardly be the reason for our family convocation. "We've had enough of stolen bowls, Matthias," Mother said and stood, ebullient, full of leaven. Ah, here it was.

"I have important news, Ana. Your betrothal ceremony will take place at the palace!"

I stared at a sprinkle of pomegranate seeds strewn on the serving platter.

"Did you hear me? Herod Antipas himself will host the betrothal meal. He will act as one of the two witnesses. The *tetrarch*! The *tetrarch*, Ana. Can you imagine?"

No. I could not. A betrothal had to be publicly formalized, but did it have to be a spectacle? This bore signs of my mother's scheming.

I'd never been inside the palace where my father went each day to give the tetrarch advice and record his letters and edicts, but Mother had once attended a banquet there with Father, albeit confined to a separate women's meal. It had been followed by weeks of obsessive talk about what she'd seen. Roman baths, monkeys chained in the courtyard, fire dancers, platters of roasted ostrich, and most alluring of all, Herod Antipas's young wife, Phasaelis, a Nabataean princess with a crown of shining black hair that reached the floor. Sitting on her banquet couch, the princess had wrapped locks of her hair about her arms like snakes and entertained the women by undulating her arms. So Mother said.

"When will this take place?" I asked.

"The nineteenth of Marcheshvan."

"But that is . . . that is only a month away."

"I know," she said. "I cannot think how I'll manage it." She returned to her place beside Father. "It falls on me, of course, to purchase gifts for the tetrarch and Nathaniel's family and to accumulate your bridal goods. You will need new tunics, coats, and sandals. I'll need to purchase hair ornaments, powders, glassware, pottery—I cannot have you arriving at Nathaniel's house with tattered belongings . . ." On she yattered.

I felt myself swept like a twig into a coursing river. I cast a drowning look at Yaltha.

xiii.

One morning, while Tabitha and I nibbled honey cakes, Yaltha entranced us with an Egyptian story, a tale about Osiris, who was murdered and dismembered, then reassembled and resurrected by the Goddess Isis. She left out no grisly detail. Tabitha was so awed by the telling, she began to wheeze a little. I nodded at her as if to say, *My aunt knows everything*.

"Did this really happen?" Tabitha asked.

"No, dear," Yaltha said. "It's not meant to be a factual story, but it's still true."

"I don't see how," Tabitha said. I wasn't sure I did either.

"I mean that the story can happen inside us," Yaltha said. "Think of it—the life you're living can be torn apart like Osiris's and a new one pieced together. Some part of you might die and a new self will rise up to take its place."

Tabitha scrunched her face.

Yaltha said, "Right now you are a girl in your father's house, but soon that life will die and a new one will be born—that of a wife." She turned her gaze on me. "Do not leave it to fate. You must be the one who does the resurrecting. You must be Isis re-creating Osiris."

My aunt nodded at me, and I understood. If my life must be torn apart by this betrothal, then I must try to reassemble it according to my own design.

That night I lay on my bed determined to become free of my be-trothal by a divorce before the marriage ritual ever occurred. It would be difficult, nearly impossible. A woman couldn't appeal for a divorce unless her husband refused his conjugal duties after marriage—and if he refused those, I would consider myself the most blessed woman in Gali-lee, perhaps in the entire Roman Empire. Oh, but a man . . . he could divorce a woman before or after the marriage for practically anything. Nathaniel could divorce me if I went blind or lame or exhibited afflic-tions of the skin. He could do so for infertility, lack of modesty, disobe-dience, or other so-called repulsions. Well, I would not go blind or lame for the man, but I would gladly offer up any of the other reasons. If they failed, I would reverse Tabitha's song and be a seeing girl who pretended to be blind. Even such small and ridiculous plots comforted me.

It was while slipping over the edge of sleep that a worrisome thought came to me. If I should be so fortunate as to goad Nathaniel to divorce me before the marriage, a second betrothal would be improbable—a divorced woman was more or less unmarriageable. I'd thought this would be a blissful state, but since seeing the young man in the market, I was no longer sure.

xiv.

As Lavi and I traversed the city, sunrise was loitering about the streets, pink light everywhere like little doused flames. I hadn't lost hope of finding a cave to bury my writings, but I was growing impatient. It was our seventh trip into the hills.

Catching sight of the palace's glinting white walls and arched red roofs, I came to a stop. A ceremony in the presence of the tetrarch would bring attention to our betrothal from every corner of Galilee and give it the appearance of a royal sanction. Prodding Nathaniel into a divorce would be even more difficult. I feared I would never rid myself of him.

We arrived at the eastern gate of the city; it was called Livia, named for the Roman emperor's wife. Girded with cedar pillars, the gate had recently been slashed with swords and axes. I presumed the Zealots had passed through and left evidence of their contempt, and I wondered if Judas had been among them. Tales of Simon ben Gioras and his men had become rampant in the city. Lavi brought stories back from the metalsmith, the grain mill, the wine press, and each time they grew in violence. Two nights previous, I heard Father shout at Mother that if Judas were among the bandits, Antipas would have him executed and he would be unable to stop it.

Before descending into the valley, I stood at the Livia Gate for a while watching people below on the road from Nazareth. From this height the village with its white houses was visible in the distance, no larger than a flock of sheep.

The first cave we found showed the unmistakable signs of an animal lair and we abandoned it quickly. Then, wandering from the path, we strolled into a balsam grove. We walked toward a bright opening where the trees stopped and an outcrop of limestone began. I heard him first, his low, impenetrable chant. Then I saw him, and behind him the dark opening of a cave. The man stood framed in stone, his back to me, hands lifted, droning words. A prayer of some kind.

I crept as close as I dared without being seen. On a rock nearby was a leather belt that held an awl, a hammer, a chisel, and some other bowed instrument. His tools.

Sunlight sparked on the rock—an auspice. He turned his head slightly, confirming what I knew already. It was the man from the market. Jesus. I lowered myself to the ground, motioning Lavi to do the same.

The dirge of his song went on and on. It was the Aramaic Kaddish, the one for mourners. Someone had died.

His voice cast a spell of beauty over me. My breath shortened. Heat rose along my face and neck. A ripple in my thighs. I wanted to go to him. I wanted to tell him my name and thank him for coming to my aid in the market. I wished to inquire about the injury to his head and if he'd avoided the soldier who'd pursued him. What had he meant to say to me before he was assaulted? Was the woman who used his fingers as sorting pegs his sister? Who had died? I had so many questions, but I dared not disturb his grief or his prayers. Even if he'd been engaged in nothing more than collecting plants for his sister's or wife's dyes, it would've been an indecency to approach him.

I glanced past him to the cave. Had God not brought me here?

From behind my shoulder Lavi whispered, "We must leave now." I'd forgotten his presence.

I collected my thoughts. *This man, Jesus, is a stonemason who walks to Sepphoris from Nazareth. He's devout, coming here to pray before his labors.*

I looked skyward for the sun, noting the time, then slipped back into the trees, parting the blue shadows.

XV.

I found Yaltha in her room. She was my ally, my place of mooring, but when I attempted to tell her about Jesus and the longing I'd felt to speak to him, I was seized by an inexplicable diffidence. How could I explain, even to her, the pull I felt toward a complete stranger?

Sensing my reserve, she said, "What is it, child?"

"I found a cave in which to hide my bowl and my writings."

"I'm relieved to hear it. It's none too soon. Earlier today I found Shipra rummaging among my things."

She looked at the cypress chest she'd brought from Alexandria. Soon after arriving she'd opened it for me, just as I'd opened my chest for her. Inside had been the sistrum, a beaded head scarf, a pouch of amulets and charms, and a wondrous pair of Egyptian scissors composed of two long bronze blades connected by a metal strip. Had she placed my treasures in the chest? Had Shipra discovered them? I felt a prick of panic, but she quickly retrieved the bundle of my scrolls from beneath a stack of clothing on a tripod stool—hidden in plain view—then withdrew my incantation bowl from beneath her sleeping mat.

Taking the bowl from her, I peeled away the flax cloth, spying the red thread still coiled at the bottom, and my limbs went loose. It came to me then—I *did* know what to say to her about Jesus, but I was too frightened to confess it.

The one text Father had forbidden me was the Song of Solomon, a poem of a woman and her lover. Naturally, therefore, I'd sought it out and read it four times. I'd read it with the same heat in my face and rippling in my thighs that I'd felt watching Jesus in the clearing. Fragments of the text lodged in me still and came back to me easily.

Under the apple tree I awakened you . . .

My beloved put his hand to the latch, and my heart was
   thrilled within me . . .

Many waters cannot quench love, neither can floods
   drown it . . .

I ISOLATED MYSELF in my room, tucking my scrolls and my bowl beneath my bed. I would have to hold my breath and pray they would
be protected until I could return to the cave and bury them. They did
at least seem safer here than in Yaltha's room, where Shipra felt free
to pry.

Lavi brought me a bowl of grilled fish, lentils, and bread, but I
couldn't eat. While I'd been out, Mother had hung my betrothal robe on
a peg in my room, a white tunic of fine linen with purple bands in the
style of Roman women. Judas would've been enraged to see me in such
traitorous garb. And what of Nathaniel—did my dress mean that he, like
Antipas, was a Roman sympathizer? The thought of him precipitated a
seizure of despair.

Under the apple tree I awakened you.

Remembering that I'd tucked three sheets of clean papyrus into the
goatskin pouch, I pulled the bundle from beneath the bed and removed
a vial of ink, a pen, and one of the empty papyri. Having no lock on
my door, I sat with my back braced against it to bar anyone entering and
spread the sheet before me on the tiles. My writing board was ash now.

I didn't know what I would write. Words engulfed me. Torrents and
floodwaters. I couldn't contain them, nor could I release them. But it
wasn't words that surged through me, it was longing. It was love of him.

I dipped my pen. When you love, you remember everything. The
way his eyes rested on me for the first time. The yarns he held in the
market, fluttering now in hidden places in my body. The sound of his

voice on my skin. The thought of him like a diving bird in my belly. I loved others—Yaltha, Judas, my parents, God, Lavi, Tabitha—but not in this way, not with ache and sweetness and flame. Not more than I loved words. Jesus had put his hand to the latch and I was flung open.

I set it all down. I filled the papyrus.

When the ink was dry, I rolled it up and slid it into the bundle beneath the bed. The air in the room felt dangerous. My writings could not remain in the house much longer.

xvi.

At midafternoon Mother strode into my room. She glanced toward my bed, where my bowl and writings were concealed, then away. She clicked her teeth at the sight of my betrothal dress in a crumpled pile on the floor. That she didn't chastise me should have forewarned me something awful was coming.

"*Dearest* Ana," she said. Her voice dripped nectar. That, too, was an ominous sign. "Nathaniel's sister, Zopher, is here to see you."

"No one told me of a visit."

"I thought it better to surprise you. You will treat her with deference, won't you?"

The hairs on my neck debated whether to stand up. "Why would I not?"

"She has come to inspect you for afflictions of the skin and other blemishes. You shouldn't worry, she'll be quick about it."

I didn't know such an indignity was possible.

"It's only to satisfy the contract," Mother went on. "Nathaniel must be given a guarantee by one of his own relatives that your body meets the terms he set forth."

Blindness, lameness, afflictions of skin, infertility, lack of modesty, disobedience, or other repulsions.

She eyed me with circumspection, waiting for my reaction. Insults caught in my throat. Obscenities I couldn't have dreamed of until Yaltha. I swallowed them. I could not risk losing my freedom to walk in the hills.

"As you wish," I said.

She didn't look entirely convinced. "You will submit gracefully?"

I nodded.

To inspect me as if I were donkey teeth! If I'd known of this, I could've given myself a brilliant red rash using gopher pitch. I could've washed my hair with garlic and onion juice. I could've presented her with any number of repulsions.

The woman greeted me kindly, but without smiling. She was small like her brother, with the same pouched eyes and vinegary face. I'd hoped Mother might leave us, but she posted herself beside my bed.

"Remove your clothing," Zopher said.

I hesitated, then drew my tunic over my head and stood before them in my undergarment. Zopher lifted my arms, bending close to study my skin as if it was some inscrutable piece of writing. She examined my face and neck, my knees and ankles, behind my ears and between my toes.

"Now your undergarment," she said.

I looked at her, then at Mother. "Please, I cannot."

"Remove it," Mother said. The nectar had been sucked from her voice.

I stood naked before them, sick with humiliation while Zopher walked a circle around me, scrutinizing my backside, my breasts, the patch between my legs. Mother looked away; she at least did me that small courtesy.

I bore my stare into the woman. *I wish you dead. I wish your brother dead.*

"What is this?" Zopher inquired, pointing at the black dot of a mole on my nipple. It had been all but forgotten to me, but I wanted to bend and kiss it, this magnificent imperfection. "I believe it to be leprosy," I told her.

Her hand snapped back.

"It's no such thing," Mother cried. "It's nothing at all." She looked at me. A dagger flew out of her eyes.

I hurried to ameliorate her. "Forgive me. I was trying to soothe my unease over my nakedness, that's all."

"Dress yourself," Zopher said. "I will report to my brother that your body is acceptable."

Mother's sigh was like a squall of wind.

DARK CAME AND THE MOON did not appear. I lay down, but without sleep. I revisited all the things Yaltha had said about her marriage, how she'd rid herself of Ruebel, and I felt hope leak back into me. Making certain to hear the plow of Father's snores behind his door, I slipped down the stairs to his study, where I pilfered a pen, a vial of ink, and one of the small clay tablets he used for mundane correspondence. Tucking them into my sleeve, I hurried back to my room and closed the door.

Yaltha had asked God to take Ruebel's life if he must as the just price for his cruelty, and he'd deserved his fate, but I wouldn't go so far as that. Death curses were common in Galilee, so prevalent it was a miracle the population had not died off entirely, but I didn't really wish Nathaniel dead. I only wanted him removed from my life.

The tablet was no bigger than the palm of my hand. Its smallness forced me to shrink my letters, which caused the fervency inside them to strain at the ink.

> Let the powers above look with disfavor upon my
> betrothal. Visit a pestilence upon it. Let it be broken
> by whatever means God chooses. Unbind me from
> Nathaniel ben Hananiah. May it be so.

I tell you, there are times when words are so glad to be set free they laugh out loud and prance across their tablets and inside their scrolls. So it was with the words I wrote. They reveled till dawn.

xvii.

I went in search of Lavi, hoping we might slip away quietly and return to the cave, but Mother had taken him off to the market. Posting myself on the balcony, I waited for their return.

When I was a child, I sometimes woke from sleep knowing things before they occurred: Judas will take me to the aqueduct; Shipra will roast a lamb; Mother will suffer a headache; Father will bring me ink dyes from the palace; my tutor will be late. Shortly before Yaltha arrived, I woke certain that a stranger would come into our lives. These glimmers would manifest as I clambered up from the dregs of sleep. Before I opened my eyes, they were there, silent and pure and clear, like pieces of blown glass, and I would wait to see if they would happen. They always happened.

Sometimes my pre-sights were not about events, but snatches of an image that floated behind my eyes. Once, a shofar appeared and that same day we heard it being blown to announce the Festival of Weeks.

I wasn't granted these mysteries often, and with the exception of Yaltha's arrival and the appearance of the ink dyes, they were revelations of the most mundane and useless kind. Why would I need to be informed of the meal Shipra cooked, or the delay of my tutor, or that a ram horn would be blown? There had been no presentiment of my incantation bowl or my betrothal. I'd had no hint of Jesus, the burning of my writings, or the cave.

For nearly a year I'd been free of these premonitions, and happily so, but as I waited there on the balcony, an image appeared in my mind with vividness: a tongue, pink and grotesque. I shook my head to clear it away. Another inane visage, I told myself, but the strangeness of it disturbed me.

When finally Mother returned, she looked flushed and excited. She sent Lavi to the storeroom lugging a basket of vegetables, then swept past me into her quarters.

I caught up with Lavi in the courtyard. "Mother is out of sorts."

He studied the ground, his hands, the crescents of dirt beneath his nails.

"Lavi?"

"We came upon the girl who visits you."

"Tabitha? What about her?"

"Please do not make me speak of it. Not to you. Please." He took several steps backward, gauging my response, then fled.

I hurried to Mother's room, fearing she would turn me away, but she allowed me in. She was white-faced.

"Lavi said you saw Tabitha. Has something happened?"

She strode to her storage chest, the one into which Tabitha and I had pried, and for one irrational moment I wondered if Mother had simply discovered our interloping.

She said, "I can't see how to avoid telling you. You will learn of it anyway. The city is already brimming with talk. Her poor father—"

"*Please.* Just tell me."

"I came upon Tabitha on the street near the synagogue. She was making a terrible commotion, wailing and tearing at her hair, crying out that one of Herod's soldiers had forced her to lie with him."

I tried to comprehend. *Forced her to lie . . .*

"Tabitha was raped?" came a voice from behind us, and I turned to see Yaltha standing in the open doorway.

"Must you use the vulgar term?" Mother said. She looked implacable standing there, arms crossed, morning shadows blossoming around her shoulders. Was this what mattered to her? The indelicacy of the word?

A pressure started in my chest. I opened my mouth and heard a strange howl fill the room. My aunt came and placed her arms about me and no one uttered a sound. Even Mother thought better than to reprimand me.

"I don't understand why—"

Mother interrupted. "Who can say why she stood on the street like that and cried out news of her defilement to every passerby? And she did so using the same crude word as your aunt. She bellowed the soldier's name and spit and swore curses in the vilest language."

She'd misunderstood me—I wasn't wondering why Tabitha shouted her outrage on the street. I was glad she accused her rapist. What I didn't understand was why such horrors happened at all. Why did men inflict these atrocities? I wiped my face with my sleeve. Through my shock, I pictured Tabitha on the first day of her renewed visits when I'd been rude to her. *My father says my mind is weak, and my tongue, weaker,* she'd told me then. It seemed now her tongue was not weak, but the fiercest part of her.

Mother, however, was not done rebuking her. "It wasn't enough that she made a show of cursing the soldier; she cursed her father for trying to seal her lips. She cursed those who passed by and closed their ears to her. She was distraught, and I'm sorry for her, but she shamed herself. She brought dishonor to her father and to her betrothed, who will surely divorce her now."

The air crackled around Yaltha's head. "You are blind and stupid, Hadar."

Mother, unused to being spoken to in that manner, narrowed her eyes and jutted out her chin.

"The shame is not Tabitha's!" Yaltha practically roared. "It belongs to the one who raped her."

Mother hissed back, "A man is what he is. His lust can be greater than himself."

"Then he should cut off his seed sacs and become a eunuch!" Yaltha said.

"Leave my quarters," Mother ordered, but Yaltha didn't budge.

"Where is Tabitha now?" I asked. "I'll go to her."

"You most certainly will not," Mother said. "Her father came and dragged her home. I forbid you to see her."

THE REST OF THE DAY unfolded with unbearable ordinariness. Mother kept me sequestered in her room while she and Shipra paraded out bolts of cloth, threads, and a ridiculous array of baubles for my dowry and talked with endless banality about preparations for the betrothal ceremony. I could scarcely hear them for the screaming in my head.

That night in my room, I lay atop the coverings on my bed and drew my knees up, fashioning myself into a little ball.

Everything I knew about rape I'd learned from the Scriptures. There was an unnamed concubine raped and murdered and her body cut into pieces. There was Dinah, the daughter of Jacob, who was raped by Shechem. Tamar, the daughter of King David, raped by her half brother. These women were among the ones I meant to write about one day, and now there was Tabitha, not a forgotten figure in a text, but a girl who sang while she plaited my hair. Who would avenge her?

No one had avenged the unnamed concubine. Jacob did not seek vengeance on Shechem. King David did not punish his son.

Fury welled in me until I could no longer keep myself small.

I left my bed and crept to Yaltha's room. I lay down on the floor next to her sleeping mat. I didn't know if she was awake. I whispered, "Aunt?"

She rolled on her side to face me. In the dark her eyes gleamed bluish white. I said, "When morning comes, we must go and find Tabitha."

xviii.

A servant, an old man with a deformed arm, met Yaltha, Lavi, and me at the gate. "My aunt and I have come to pay respects to Tabitha," I told him.

He studied us. "Her mother has ordered that no one should see her."

Yaltha spoke in a commanding voice. "Go and tell her mother this is the daughter of Matthias, head scribe to Herod Antipas and the overseer of her husband. Tell her he would be offended if his daughter were refused."

The servant shuffled back to the house and returned minutes later to open the gate. "Only the girl," he said.

Yaltha nodded at me. "Lavi and I will wait for you here."

Their house wasn't as splendid as ours, but like those of most palace officials, it had at least one upper room and two courtyards. Tabitha's mother, a large woman with a bulbous face, led me to a closed door at the back of the house. "My daughter is not well. You may visit her for only a few minutes," she said, and, thankfully, left me to enter alone. Turning the latch, I felt the drumbeat start in my chest.

Tabitha huddled on a mat in the corner. At the sight of me, she turned her face to the wall. I stood there a moment adjusting to the thick, dim light and the uncertainty of what to do.

I went and sat beside her, hesitating before resting my hand on her arm. She faced me then, covering my hand with hers, and I saw that her right eye had disappeared into the swollen fold of her lid. Her lips were bruised purple and blue, and her jaw was puffed out as if stuffed with food. A bowl, a very fine gold one, sat beside her on the floor glinting in the shadowy light, brimming with what looked like blood and spittle. A sob rose in my throat. "Oh, Tabitha."

I pulled her head to my shoulder and smoothed her hair. I had nothing to offer her but my willingness to sit there while she endured her pain. "I'm here," I murmured. When she didn't speak, I sang her a familiar lullaby, for it was all I could think to do. "Sleep, little one, night has come. Morning is far, but I am near." I sang it over and over, rocking her body with mine.

When I ceased singing, she offered me a faint smile, and it was then I saw a ragged bit of cloth protruding oddly from the side of her mouth. Keeping her eyes fastened on mine, she reached up and pulled it slowly through her lips, a long bloody strip of linen. There seemed no end to it. When it was fully disgorged, she lifted the bowl and spit into it.

I felt a wave of revulsion, but I didn't flinch. "What has happened to your mouth?"

She opened it so I could see inside. Her tongue, what was left of it, was a morass of raw, mutilated flesh. It writhed helpless in her mouth as she tried to form words, utterances that flailed about and made no sense. I stared at her, uncomprehending, before the truth hit me. *Her tongue has been cut out.* The tongue from my premonition.

"Tabitha!" I cried. "Who did this?"

"Faah-er. Faaaah-er." A dribble of red ran down her chin.

"Are you trying to say Father?"

She grabbed my hand, nodding.

I only remember getting to my feet, stunned and desperate. I don't remember screaming, but the door flew open and her mother was there, shaking me, telling me to stop. I tore away from her. "Don't lay your hands on me!"

Rage shredded my breath. It clawed straight through my chest. "What crime did your daughter commit to cause her father to cut her tongue from her mouth? Is it a sin to stand on the street and cry out one's anguish and beg for justice?"

"She brought shame on her father and this house!" her mother viciously exclaimed. "Her punishment is spoken of in Scripture—'the perverse tongue shall be cut out.'"

"You have raped her all over again!" I ground the words slowly through my teeth.

Once, after Father had upbraided Yaltha for her lack of meekness, she'd said to me, "*Meekness*. It isn't meekness I need, it's anger." I'd not forgotten this. I knelt beside my friend.

The shine of the bowl caught my eye once again, and I knew what, until that moment, had been obscured. Getting to my feet, I picked up the bowl, careful not to spill the contents. I thundered at Tabitha's mother, "Where is your husband's study?" She frowned and did not answer. "Show me, or I will find it myself."

When she didn't move, Tabitha rose from her mat and led me to a small room, while her mother followed behind shrieking at me to leave her house. His sanctum was furnished with a table, a bench, and two wooden shelves that were laden with his scribal possessions, shawls and hats, and as I suspected, the three other golden bowls stolen from Antipas's palace.

I looked at Tabitha. I would give her more than lullabies; I would give her my anger. I flung her blood across the walls, the table, the shawls and hats, Antipas's bowls, the scrolls, vials of ink, and clean parchments. I went about it with calm and measure. I could not punish her rapist or give back her voice, but I could do this one act of defiance, this small revenge, and because of it her father would know his brutality had not gone unwitnessed. He would at least suffer the rebuke of my anger.

Tabitha's mother charged at me, but she was too late—the bowl was empty. "My husband will see you punished," she cried. "Do you think he won't go to your father?"

"Tell him my father has been charged with finding the one who stole Herod Antipas's bowls. I would be pleased to inform Father of the thief's identity."

Her face slackened and the fight left her. She understood my threat. My father, I knew, would hear nothing of this.

. . .

BECAUSE TABITHA HAD tried so hard to reveal what happened to her and been silenced for it, I removed the last two sheets of papyrus from the goatskin pouch beneath my bed and inscribed the story of her rape and the maiming of her tongue. Once again, I sat with my back against the door, knowing if Mother were to come seeking me, I could not prevent her from entering for long. She would push her way in and find me writing, ransack my room and find my hidden scrolls. I pictured her reading them—the words of love and want that I'd written about Jesus, the blood I'd splashed on the walls in Tabitha's house.

I risked everything, but I couldn't stop myself from writing her story. I filled both papyri. Grief and anger streamed from my fingers. The anger made me brave and the grief made me sure.

xix.

The clearing where I'd seen Jesus praying was empty, the air spiky with shadows. I'd come early enough to perform my burial task before he appeared, stealing from the house before the sun hefted its red belly over the summit of the hills. Lavi carried the bundle of my scrolls, the clay tablet on which I'd written my curse, and a digging tool. I bore the incantation bowl beneath my coat. The thought that Jesus might return sent a shock of joy and fright through me. I couldn't say what I would do—whether I would speak to him or slip away as I'd done before.

I waited at the cave opening while Lavi inspected it for bandits, snakes, and other menacing creatures. Finding none, he beckoned me inside, where it was cool and gloomy, speckled with bat droppings and pieces of stoneware, a few of which I gathered. Holding my head scarf over my nose to lessen the smell of animal dung and moldering earth, I found a spot near the back of the cave, beside a column of stone that I could easily recognize when it was time to reclaim my belongings. Lavi jabbed at the ground with the digging tool, opening a gash in the dirt. Dust flew. Cobwebs floated down to make nets on my shoulders. He grunted as he worked—he was slight, unused to heavy toil, but eventually he fashioned a cavity two cubits deep and two cubits wide.

Lifting up the flax that draped the incantation bowl, I gazed inside it at my prayer, at the sketch I'd made of myself, the gray smudge, the red thread, then placed the bowl into the hole. Beside it, I laid the bundle of scrolls, and last, the clay tablet. I wondered if I would see any of this ever again. I raked the dirt over them and spread the pebbles and bits of pottery I'd collected over the site to conceal that it'd been disturbed.

When we emerged into the sunlight, Lavi spread his cloak on the ground and I sat looking toward the balsam grove. I drank from the wineskin in my pouch and nibbled a piece of bread. I waited past the second hour. I waited past the third.

He did not come.

xx.

On the day Mother announced my betrothal ceremony would take place in thirty days, I'd sewn thirty ivory chips onto a swath of pale blue linen. Each day since, I'd cut one off. Now, alone on the roof of the house, I stared at the cloth, sobered by the meagerness of chips that remained. *Eight.*

It was the twilit hour. Moroseness didn't come easily to me—anger did, yes; passion and stubbornness, always—but sitting here, I felt bereft. I'd returned twice to Tabitha's house but had been denied entry. Earlier today Mother had informed me that my friend had been sent to live with relatives in the village of Japha, south of Nazareth. I was certain I would never see her again.

I was afraid I would never see Jesus again either. I saw nothing but God's backside.

Had it always been so? When I was five, visiting the Temple in Jerusalem for the first time, I'd attempted to follow Father and Judas up the circular steps through the Nicanor Gate, when Mother yanked me back. Her hand clamped tight on my arm as I tried to twist free, my eyes straining after my brother, who moved toward the gleaming marble and gold gilt of the sanctuary where God lived. The Holy of Holies. She shook my shoulders to get my attention. "Under penalty of death, you can go no further."

I stared at the smoke plumes rising from the altar beyond the gate. "But why can't I go, too?"

For years, whenever I recalled her answer, it would bestow on me the same jolt of surprise I'd felt the day she'd uttered it. "Because, Ana, you are female. This is the Court of Women. We can go no further." In this manner I discovered that God had relegated my sex to the outskirts of practically everything.

Taking up the snipping knife, I sliced away another ivory chip from the cloth. *Seven.*

Eventually I told Yaltha about Jesus. About the colorful threads draped over his fingers in the market stall, and how, but for them, I wouldn't know of him at all. I described the rough feel of his palm when he'd come to my aid, the sickening thud of his head on the tile when the soldier had shoved him. When I revealed how I came upon him again at the cave as he prayed the Kaddish and the exigency I felt to speak to him but stifled, she smiled. "And now he inhabits your thoughts and inflames your heart."

"Yes." I didn't add that he caused heat and light to move about in my body as well, but I felt she knew that, too.

I could not have borne Yaltha telling me that my longing for him only came from my despair over Nathaniel. It was true that Jesus had stepped into my path at the same moment the rest of my world collapsed. I suppose he was, in part, a consolation. She must've known it, but she refrained from saying it. Instead she told me that I had traveled to a secret sky, the one beyond this one where the queen of heaven reigns, for Yahweh knew nothing of female matters of the heart.

FOOTSTEPS JARRED THE LADDER, and I turned to see Yaltha's head pop up like a fishing bob. She was agile enough, but I feared one evening she would topple off into the courtyard. I hurried to offer her my hand, but instead of taking it, she said in a low voice, "Hurry. You must come down. Judas is here."

"*Judas!*"

She hushed me and peered into the shadows below. Earlier, one of Antipas's soldiers, the vicious one, had been positioned close by at the back entrance to the house. "Your brother waits for you at the mikvah," she whispered. "Take care no one sees you."

I waited for her to descend, then followed, remembering Father shouting that if Judas were caught, Antipas would execute him.

A thin blue darkness filled the courtyard. I didn't see the soldier, but he could be anywhere about. I heard Shipra somewhere nearby cleaning the brazier. Overhead, the windows in the upper rooms of the house stared down, narrow and flickering. Yaltha thrust a clay lamp and towel at me. "May the Lord cleanse you and make you pure," she said loudly for Shipra's benefit, then disappeared into the house.

I wanted to fly across the courtyard and down the steps to my brother, but I clipped the wings in my feet and walked slowly. I sang aloud the song of purification. As I descended to the mikvah, I heard the heartbeat in the cistern—*drip, drip . . . drip, drip.* The air in the small underground room felt thick in my throat. Lifting the lamp, I watched a skin of light form on the surface of the pool.

I called in a quiet voice, "Judas."

"I'm here."

Turning, I saw him leaning against the wall behind me. The dark, handsome features, his quick smile. I set down the lamp and threw my arms about him. His woolen tunic smelled of sweat and horses. He was different. Thinner, browned, a new smoldering in his eyes.

Unexpectedly, my joy was overtaken by an upwell of anger. "How could you leave me here to fend for myself? Without even saying good-bye."

"*Little sister*, you had Yaltha with you. If she'd not been here, I wouldn't have left you. What I'm doing is larger than either of us. I'm doing this for God. For our people."

"Father said Antipas will put you to death! His soldiers are looking for you."

"What can I do, Ana? It's the fullness of time. The Romans have occupied our land for seventy-seven years. Can't you see how auspicious that is? *Seventy-seven*. That's God's holiest number, a sign to us the time has come."

Next he would tell me he was one of the two Messiahs God had promised. Judas had suffered from messianic fever since he was a boy, a condition that rose and fell according to Rome's brutalities. It afflicted almost everyone in Galilee, though I couldn't say I was much affected by it. The Messiahs *were* prophesied—I couldn't dispute it—but did I really believe a priest Messiah of Aaron and a king Messiah of David would suddenly appear arm in arm and lead an army of angels that would save us from our oppressors and restore the throne to Israel? God could not be swayed to break a mere betrothal, and Judas would have me believe the Lord meant to defeat the might of Rome.

There would be no dissuading my brother, though; I wouldn't try. I walked to the edge of the pool, where his shadow floated on the water. I stood there, staring at it. Finally I said, "Much has happened since you left. They've betrothed me."

"I know. It's why I've come."

I couldn't think how he might've learned of my betrothal or why it would bring him here. Whatever the reason, it was important enough for him to risk being caught.

"I came to warn you. Nathaniel ben Hananiah is a devil."

"You imperiled your life to tell me *that*? Do you think I don't know what a devil he is?"

"I don't think you do. The steward who manages Nathaniel's date grove is a sympathizer to our cause. He overheard certain things."

"The steward spies on Nathaniel for you?"

"Listen—I must speak quickly. There's more to your betrothal than what's written in the contract. There is one thing Father doesn't have, and we know it well."

"He owns no land," I said.

Most everyone has a private torment, some voracious badger that gnaws at them without ceasing, and this was Father's. His own father had owned sizable papyrus fields in Egypt, and by law, his brother, Haran, the firstborn, should have received a double portion and he a single, but Haran, the same tormenter who had banished Yaltha to the Therapeutae, had secured a position for Father far away, here in the court of Antipas's father, King Herod. My father was only eighteen then, too young and trusting to perceive the deceit. In his absence, Haran manipulated the law to take possession of Father's portion, too. Just as it was with Jacob and Esau, a stolen birthright was the golden badger.

Judas said, "Nathaniel went to him, offering a quarter measure of his estates."

"In exchange for me?"

He looked down. "No, little sister; marriage to you wasn't a thought in either of their minds then. Nathaniel wanted a seat of power within the palace and he was willing to give up large portions of his land for it. Already Father has promised him a place on the high council, where he can leverage his power for the rich and keep his tax low. If that isn't enough, Father has pledged to rent Nathaniel's storehouses to hold Herod Antipas's taxes and the Roman tributes collected throughout Galilee. This will make Nathaniel the richest man in Galilee other than Antipas. And in exchange Father gets what he craves—the title that was stolen from him: landowner."

"What of me?"

"It was Father who made you part of their pact. I don't doubt our mother had been nagging him to find you a worthy betrothal, and suddenly here was Nathaniel. It must've seemed propitious to Father—Nathaniel had wealth and because of their arrangement, he would soon possess all the clout of the governing class."

Father!

"I am sorry," he said.

"There's no escape from my betrothal. The contract has been signed. The bride price is paid. It can't be ended except by divorce and I've tried to affront him every way I could. . . ." I stopped, realizing it would never matter how repugnantly I behaved. Because of his agreement with Father, Nathaniel would never divorce me.

I said, "Help me, Judas. Please do something. I cannot bear this marriage."

He straightened. "I will give Nathaniel a reason to end the betrothal. I'll do what I can—I swear it," he said. "I must go. You should leave first and be sure the soldier I saw earlier is not in sight. I will leave by the gate at the back of the lower courtyard. If the way is clear, sing the song that was on your lips when you arrived."

"I must appear as if I've bathed," I said. "Turn your back so I can disrobe and immerse myself."

"Quickly," he said.

Peeling away my tunic, I stepped into the coolness of the water, then dipped under, splintering his reflection into a thousand black drops. Hurriedly, I dabbed myself half-dry.

"God keep you, Judas," I said as I mounted the steps.

I went to the house, brokenhearted and singing.

xxi.

One morning three days after Judas's visit, I woke with the image of a date palm branch. Had I dreamed of it? I sat up, pillows tumbling. The frond was a twisted contortion of deformed green-black fingers.

I couldn't get it out of my thoughts.

The wind began to thrash about, and I knew the rains would come soon. The ladder thumped against the roof. The cooking griddles clattered in the courtyard.

It was early still when an urgent and relentless pounding began on the front door. Slipping from my room onto the balcony, I peered over the railing and saw Father hurrying across the reception hall. Mother stepped onto the loggia beside me. The heavy bolt on the door lifted. The cedar door groaned, and Father said, "Nathaniel, what's all this commotion about?"

Mother reeled toward me, as if I were the reason he'd come. "Go and finish grooming your hair."

I ignored her. If my betrothed wished to see me, I preferred to look my worst.

Tromping into the atrium, Nathaniel looked defeated. He was hatless, his fine clothes soot-stained and bedraggled. His eyes darted about, irate. His whole countenance was such an astonishment that Mother gasped. Father traipsed after him.

Nathaniel beckoned to someone behind him, and I had the feeling of something terrible looming. I felt like a bird waiting for the stone to fly from the slingshot. A man in worker's garb stepped into view. In his hands was the branch of a date palm. It was partially torched, dropping char onto the tiles. He tossed it at my father's feet. It landed in a clatter, a shower of black cinders. The smell of smoke wafted over the room.

Whatever this is, it is the workings of Judas.

"My date palms have been maliciously burned," Nathaniel said. "Half of my grove set on fire. My olive trees survived only because I took care to put a man in the watchtower who raised the alarm in time."

Father looked from the branch to Nathaniel. He said, "And you think it prudent to beat on my door and toss the evidence on my floor?" He seemed genuinely confounded by Nathaniel's anger.

Nathaniel, this little man. His head didn't reach Father's jaw, but he stepped toward him, puffed up and righteous. He would tell Father now who was to blame, for I could see he knew. I pictured Judas's earnest face at the mikvah.

"It was your son who set the torch," Nathaniel bellowed. "Judas and Simon ben Gioras and their brigands."

"It cannot be Judas," Mother cried, and the men looked up, Nathaniel noticing me for the first time, and in that unguarded moment, even from this high distance, I saw his loathing for me.

"Leave us," Father ordered, but of course we did not. We backed from the rail, listening. "Did you see him yourself? Are you certain it was Judas?"

"I saw him with my own eyes as he laid waste to my trees. And if there was doubt of it, he cried out, 'Death to the rich and unscrupulous. Death to Herod Antipas. Death to Rome.' Then, raising his voice even louder, he shouted, 'I am Judas ben Matthias.'"

I dared to creep to the edge of the balcony. Father had turned his back to Nathaniel and was attempting to gather himself. For women, the cruelest state is to be denied; for men it's to be stricken with shame, and Father was awash in it. I felt a prick of sorrow for him.

When he turned to Nathaniel, his face was a mask. He questioned Nathaniel about every detail. How many men did you see? What hour did they come? Were they on horseback? Which way did they retreat? As they spoke, Father's disgrace was set aside by rage.

"There's a reason Judas went out of his way to declare himself your son," Nathaniel said. "He meant to put you in disfavor with Herod Antipas. If that happens, Matthias . . . if you lose your power with Antipas, you will be in no position to carry out our arrangement and there will be no reason for me to go through with it."

Had Nathaniel just put forth a threat to end the betrothal? *Oh, Judas, how clever you are.* Of course, Antipas would not tolerate Father's son waging these attacks. It would drive a wedge between them, making it impossible for Father to hold up his end of the bargain!

"Judas is no son to me," Father said. "He's not of my flesh, but adopted from my wife's family. From this day, he is anathema to me. He is a stranger. If I must, I will declare it before Antipas himself."

I couldn't bring myself to look at Mother.

"I will see him punished," he went on. "There are rumors that Simon and his men hide in Arbel Gorge. I will dispatch soldiers to scavenge every cleft and turn over every rock."

Standing beside Nathaniel, the worker who'd brought in the branch shifted nervously. *Let him be the spy Judas spoke of. Let him warn my brother.*

Father had done a good job of pacifying Nathaniel. Too good, I feared.

After he departed, Father withdrew to his study and Mother dragged me into her room and closed the door. "Why would Judas commit this atrocious act?" she cried. "Why would he call out his name? Didn't he know doing so would antagonize Antipas against your father? Did he mean to punish Matthias at the risk of his own life?"

I said nothing, hoping she would spew her shock and alarm and be done with it.

"Have you spoken to Judas? Did you put him up to this?"

"No," I said, too quickly. I had an outstanding talent for committing deceit, but none for hiding it.

She slapped me hard across my cheek. "Matthias should never have let you leave the house. There will be no more walking the hillsides with Lavi. You will remain at home until the betrothal ceremony."

"*If* there's a ceremony," I said. And she lifted her hand and struck my other cheek.

xxii.

That evening, as the day spilled the last of its pale lights over the valley, Yaltha and I took once more to the roof. On my cheeks were the rouged imprints of my mother's hand. Yaltha brushed her fingertip over them. She said, "Did Judas tell you he intended to burn Nathaniel's grove? Did you know?"

"He swore to do his part to end my betrothal, but I didn't think he would go so far as this." I lowered my voice. "I'm glad he did."

The first chill of the season had arrived. Her shoulders were hunched up like bird wings. She drew her scarf around them. "Tell me, how does destroying Nathaniel's dates help your cause?"

When I described the bargain between Father and Nathaniel, she said, "I see. By causing your father to lose favor with Antipas, Judas wagers Nathaniel will end the agreement. Yes, it's cunning."

For the first time, I tasted hope on the back of my tongue. Then I swallowed and it was gone. I thought of the prayer in my bowl, of my face inside the tiny sun. I'd cleaved to them as things that might somehow save me and yet doubts repeatedly consumed them.

Frantic for reassurance, I told her about the vision I'd had of my face. "Do you believe it's a sign I'll avoid this marriage and realize my hopes?" I waited. The moon shone bright. The rooftop, the sky, and the houses nestled tightly across the city seemed made of glass.

"How can we know the ways of God?" she answered. Her skepticism showed not only in the evasiveness of her words, but in the way her mouth twitched with words she didn't say.

I persisted. "But a vision such as this can't mean I'm fated to disappear into Nathaniel's house to live out my days in misery. It must be a promise of some kind."

She turned the force of her eyes on me. I watched them gather into small brown cruxes. "Your vision means what you want it to mean. It will mean what you *make* it to mean."

I stared at her, baffled, perturbed. "Why would God send me a vision if it has no meaning other than what I give to it?"

"What if the point of his sending it is to make you search yourself for the answer?"

Such uncertainty, such unpredictability. "But . . . Aunt." It was all my lips could manage.

Could we know the ways of God or not? Did he possess an intention for us, his people, as our religion believed, or was it up to us to invent meaning for ourselves? Perhaps nothing was as I'd thought.

Overhead, the black magnitude, the shining, breakable world. Yaltha had made a crack in my certainty about God and his workings. I felt it give way and a crevasse open.

xxiii.

When there were two ivory chips remaining on my reckoning cloth, Lavi and I slipped from the house, despite Mother's decree, and made our way to the cave where I'd buried my possessions. The sky was in a sunken mood—grayed and heavy and wind-struck. Lavi had pled with me not to venture out. But knowing he put large measure in dreams and omens, I'd told him I'd dreamed a hyena dug up my belongings and I was compelled to go to the cave and reassure myself they were still safely concealed. It was a shameless fabrication. It was true I worried about my writings and my bowl, but that was not the reason for my lie. I hoped to find Jesus.

Arriving at the same hour that I'd found him praying before, I wandered about the little clearing, peering over the outcrops of rock, then searching the cave. There was no trace of him.

After making a display of inspecting my burial spot, I stood with Lavi just inside the cave, studying the heavens. The sun had tunneled so far into the clouds, the world had blackened.

"We should go back," Lavi said. "Now." He'd brought a small rolled canopy of thatched palm to protect us if the rains began. I watched as he unfurled it. I had an awful feeling inside, something sad and sodden like the sky.

He was right, we should leave—once the rains began, they would not let up, perhaps for hours. I pulled my mantle over my head, then lifted my eyes toward the balsam grove, and there he was, moving through the trees. He stepped quickly, glancing upward, his tunic a smear of white in the murky light. Drops of rain began to fall. They splatted on the limestone, the treetops, the hard-shell earth, sending up the smell of fertility. As he broke into a run, I stepped back into the shadows. Lavi, seeing him, tensed, setting his jaw.

I said, "He's of no danger to us. He's known to me."

"And did you have a dream of his coming, too?"

Within seconds, the rain became a swarm of locusts, thick and deafening. Jesus bolted into the cave as if coming up out of the sea, his clothes dripping, his hair hanging in dark wet tendrils on his cheeks. His leather belt jangled with tools.

Seeing us, he started. "May I share your refuge or would you have me seek shelter elsewhere?"

"The hillsides belong to everyone," I answered, pulling the mantle back from my head. "Even if that were not true, I wouldn't be so cruel as to send you back into the rainstorm."

Recognition broke across his face. His eyes drifted to my feet. "You are no longer lame?"

I smiled at him. "No. And you, I trust, were not arrested by Herod Antipas's soldier."

His smile was a broad, crooked arrangement on his face. "No, I was faster than he was."

Thunder cracked over our heads. Whenever the sky quaked, women uttered a blessing: *Lord preserve me from the wrath of Lilith.* But I could never bring myself to say it. I would whisper instead, *Lord, bless the roaring*, and that was what rose now to my lips.

He greeted Lavi. "*Shelama.*"

Lavi muttered the greeting back, then moved some distance away to the cave wall, where he sank onto his haunches. His surliness surprised me. He was piqued that I'd lied about the hyena, that I'd spoken to a strange man, that I'd dragged him here at all.

"He's my servant," I said, then immediately regretted drawing attention to the difference in our stations. "His name is Lavi," I added, hoping to sound less supercilious. "I am Ana."

"I'm Jesus ben Joseph," he replied, and a disturbance of some kind passed over his face. I didn't know if it was because I'd appeared arrogant, or due to the oddity that we should meet again, or something in the utterance of his name.

"I'm glad our paths crossed," I said. "I've wished to thank you for your kindness in the market. You weren't rewarded very well for it. I hope your head wasn't hurt badly."

"It was little more than a scratch." He smiled and rubbed his forehead. Tiny droplets sheened his brow. He dried them with his cloak, then rubbed the wool over his hair, leaving the locks askew, sprigs everywhere. He looked boyish, and I felt the same hot whirring in my breast as before.

He stepped deeper into the cave, away from the mist and nearer to where I stood.

"You're a stonemason?" I asked.

He touched the awl that dangled from his belt. "My father was a carpenter and a stonemason. I took up his trade." Grief flared in his face, and I guessed that speaking the name Joseph moments ago had caused the shadow to enter his eyes. It was for his father he'd prayed the Kaddish that day.

"Did you think me to be a yarn sorter?" he asked, quick to cover his sadness with wit.

"You did seem adept at it." My tone was teasing, and I saw a ripple of the smile I'd observed earlier.

"I go with my sister Salome to the market when there's no work of my own to be had. I've become an expert with yarn from too much practice. My brothers even more so—they're the ones who usually accompany her. We don't let her cross the valley alone."

"You come from Nazareth, then?"

"Yes, I make door lintels, roof beams, and furniture, but my work doesn't rival my father's—there have been few commissions for me there since he died. I'm compelled to come to Sepphoris now to be hired as one of Herod Antipas's laborers."

How was it he spoke so freely? I was female, a stranger, the daughter of a wealthy Roman sympathizer, yet he didn't hold himself apart.

His eyes swept over the cave. "I sometimes stop to pray here on my way. It's a lonely place . . . except *today*." He laughed, the soaring sound I'd heard in the market, and it caused me to laugh as well.

"Do you labor on Herod Antipas's amphitheater?" I asked.

"I cut stone for it in the quarry. When quotas are reached and hiring ceases, I travel to Capernaum and join a band of fishermen on the Sea of Galilee and sell my portion of the catch."

"You are many things, then. A carpenter, a stonemason, a yarn sorter, *and* a fisherman."

"I'm all of those," he said. "But I belong to none of them."

I wondered if, like me, he possessed a longing for something forbidden to him, but I didn't ask, for fear of probing too far. Instead I thought of Judas and said, "You don't mind working for Antipas?"

"I mind my family's hunger more."

"It falls on you to feed your sister and brothers?"

"And mother," he added.

He did not say wife.

He spread his damp cloak on the ground and gestured for me to sit. As I did so, I looked at Lavi, who appeared to sleep. Jesus sat down at a discreet distance, cross-legged, facing the cave opening. For a long interval we watched the rain and the wild, untethered sky without speaking. The nearness of him, his breathing, the way everything I felt inhabited me—I found rapture in these things, in this being together in the lonely place, and all around the thundering world.

He broke the silence by asking about my family. I told him my father had come from Alexandria to serve Herod Antipas as head scribe and counselor, that my mother was the daughter of a cloth merchant in Jerusalem. I confessed I would be beset with loneliness if not for my aunt. I didn't mention that my brother was a fugitive or that the disagreeable man he'd seen with me in the market was now my betrothed. I wanted so badly to tell him my writings were buried not far from where he sat, that I was a student, an ink maker, a composer of words, a collector of forgotten stories, but I kept these things inside, too.

"What brought you outside of the city on the day the rains begin?" he wanted to know.

I could not say *You, the reason is you.* "I walk often in the hills," I told him. "This morning I was impetuous, believing the rains would not arrive so soon." It was at least a partial truth. "And you? Did you come here to pray? If so, I fear I've kept you from it."

"I don't mind. I doubt God does either. Lately, I've been poor company for him. I bring him nothing but questions and doubts."

I thought of my conversation with Yaltha on the roof and the doubts about God that had assailed me ever since. "I don't think doubts are wrong if they are honest," I said quietly.

He turned his face to mine and his eyes felt different on me. Was it a revelation to him that a girl would presume to instruct a devout Jewish man on the vagaries of devotion? Had he caught a glimpse of me, Ana, the girl at the bottom of the incantation bowl?

His belly groaned. He pulled a pouch from the pocket in his sleeve and removed a flatbread. He broke it into three even pieces and offered a portion to me and the other to Lavi, who had woken.

"You would break bread with a woman and a Gentile?" I said.

"With friends," he answered, offering me his uneven grin. I allowed myself to smile back and felt something tacit pass between us. The first tiny sprout of our belonging.

We ate our bread. I remember the taste of barley and peasantry in my mouth. The sadness that came to me as the rain lessened.

He walked to the opening and looked at the sky. "The foreman at the quarry will be hiring laborers soon. I must go."

"May this meeting not be our last," I said.

"May God will it yet again."

I watched him hurry away through the balsam grove.

I would never tell him that our meeting in the cave that day was not by chance. I would not reveal I'd seen him there once before as he'd prayed. To the very end I would let him believe God's hand was in our meeting. Who's to say? Yaltha's words remain with me—how can we know the ways of God?

xxiv.

I entered the palace bedecked and perfumed, henna vines on my arms, kohl beneath my eyes, ivory bracelets on my wrists, and silver anklets at my feet. On my head, I wore a gold leaf coronet that was woven intricately into the braids of my hair. My betrothal dress was adorned with twenty-four ornaments, every precious stone commanded by Scripture. Mother had hired the finest seamstress in Sepphoris to sew the gems along the purple bands on my neck and sleeves. I was laden down and sweating like a donkey.

We mounted the steps to Herod Antipas's great hall beneath a wind-ravaged canopy held aloft by four servants who strained to keep it from flying away. My betrothal ceremony had arrived on a day full of rain and drear. I followed behind my parents, stumbling up the wide stone stairs, holding on to Yaltha's arm. My aunt had seen to it that I drank a full cup of undiluted wine before setting out, which had caused the edges of things to grow furred and my distress to shrink into something small and mewling.

Two days ago, when Lavi and I had returned from the cave, Mother had met us at the gate with typical fury. Poor Lavi was sent straight to the rooftop to scour away the plenitude of bird droppings. She restricted me again to my room, warning my aunt to keep her distance.

Undeterred, Yaltha came to me late in the nights with cups of wine and dates and listened to my tale of meeting Jesus. I'd found no rest since seeing him, and whenever I fell asleep, I dreamed of him coming through the rain.

In the great hall, torches were mounted on the columns, and the walls were lavishly frescoed with fruits and flowers and twisting ropes. A mosaic covered a vast portion of the floor—tiny bits of white marble, black pumice, and blue glass arranged into magnificent creatures. Fishes, dolphins, whales, and sea dragons. Looking down, I saw that I stood upon a large fish swallowing a small one. I could almost feel its tail swish. I tried hard not to be awed, but it was impossible. Wined and dazed, I moved across the mosaics as if walking upon water. Only later would it occur to me that Herod Antipas, a Jew, had broken God's second commandment with a flamboyance that drew my breath. He'd made a sea of graven images. Father had once said our tetrarch was schooled in Rome and spent years gorging on the city. Now he imitated that world within his palace, a hidden shrine to Rome that the devout, common Jew would never see.

Mother appeared at my elbow. "You will wait for the ceremony in the royal apartments. You must not be seen by Nathaniel until it's time. It will not be long." She made a motion with her hand and a silver-haired woman led me along a portico, past the wing of Roman baths, then up a second flight of stairs into a bedchamber without fresco or mosaic, but paneled with the golden wood of the terebinth tree.

"So, you are the lamb to be sacrificed," a voice said in Greek.

Turning, I saw a dark-skinned, wraithlike woman standing beside a grand bed that was swathed in jewel-colored silks. Her black hair cascaded down her back like a spill of ink. It had to be Phasaelis, Antipas's wife. All of Galilee and Peraea knew that her father, Aretas, King of the Nabataeans, had conspired with Herod Antipas's father to arrange their marriage as a way to stop skirmishes along their common border. It was said that upon learning her fate, Phasaelis, only thirteen at the time, cut her arms and wrists and cried for three days and three nights.

The shock of her presence in the room left me momentarily mute. She was dazzling standing there in her scarlet dress and golden mantle, but pitiable, too, her life turned into a ploy by two men.

"Are you capable of speaking Greek or are you simply too docile to answer me?" Her tone was scoffing, as if I were an object of amusement to her.

Phasaelis's rebuke was a slap, and it was like waking. A feeling of loss and wrath rose in me. I wanted to shout at her—*I am betrothed to someone I despise and who despises me in return. I have little hope I will see the man I love ever again. I don't know what has become of my brother. Words are life to me, yet my writings are buried in the ground. My heart is sickled like wheat tares and you speak to me as if I am weak and imbecilic.*

I did not care if she possessed the stature of a queen. I thundered at her, "I AM NO LAMB."

A flash in her eyes. "No, I see you're not."

"You heap condescension on me, but we are no different, you and I."

A sneer slid into her voice. "Inform me. Please. How are we no different?"

"You were forced to marry as I am now forced. Were not each of us used by our fathers for their own selfish purposes? We are both wares to be traded."

She walked toward me and her scent floated out—nard and cinnamon. Her hair swayed. Her hips oscillated. I thought of the lurid dance my mother had seen her perform. How I would have loved to see it. I feared she was coming to slap me for my insolence, but I saw her eyes had softened. She said, "When I last saw my father seventeen years ago, he wept bitterly and begged forgiveness for sending me to this wasteland. He told me it was for a noble reason, but I spit on the floor before him.

I cannot forget he loved his kingdom more than me. He married me to a jackal."

I saw the difference then—her father had traded her for peace. My father had traded me for greed.

She smiled, and I saw this time there was no guile in it. "We shall be friends," she said, taking my hand. "Not because of our fathers or our shared misfortune. We shall be friends because you are no lamb, and I, too, am no lamb." Phasaelis leaned her head to my ear. "When your betrothed repeats the blessings, do not look at him. Do not look at your father. Look to yourself."

WE STOOD in the torch-dark light atop the watery mosaic—my parents, Yaltha, Herod Antipas, Phasaelis, Rabbi Shimon ben Yohai, Nathaniel and his sister, Zopher, and at least two dozen other extravagantly coiffed people I could not name and did not care to. I planted my toes upon the scaly back of a fierce-eyed sea dragon.

I'd never seen Antipas up close. He seemed the age of my father, but heavier, with a belly that protruded. His hair was oiled and fell about his ears from beneath a strange crown that resembled an upside-down, gold-plated stew pot. He wore bracelets and silver circlets in his ears, and his eyes were too small for his face, as small as date pits. I thought him repulsive.

The old rabbi recited the Torah—"It is not good for man to be alone"—and then spoke the rabbinic teachings.

"A man without a wife is not a man.

"A man without a wife establishes no household.

"A man without a wife has no progeny.

"A man without a wife, household, and children does not live as God ordained.

"Man's duty is to marry."

His voice was perfunctory and tired. I did not look at him.

My father read the betrothal contract, which was followed by a token payment of the bride price, passed ceremoniously from Nathaniel's hand to his. I did not look at them.

"Do you attest to your daughter's virginity?" the rabbi asked.

My head jerked up. Would they now make the pink-brown folds between my legs their business? Nathaniel leered, a reminder of the miseries that lay in store for me in the bedchamber. Father anointed the rabbi with oil as a sign of my purity. All of this I watched. I wanted them to witness the contempt shining on my face.

I cannot record how Nathaniel looked as he read the groom's blessings, for I refused to offer him even a glance. I stared at the mosaic, imagining myself far away beneath the sea.

I am no lamb. I am no lamb. . . .

IN THE BANQUETING HALL Herod Antipas reclined on a luxurious couch, propped on his left elbow. He sat behind the center table of the triclinium while everyone waited to see who would be seated to his right and left, and who would be escorted to the sad little couches at the far ends of the tables. The only true and precise measure of the tetrarch's favor was how near to him one was seated. We women—Phasaelis among us—were gathered at a separate table altogether, farther away than the hapless and wretched persons who would soon find themselves consigned to the distant seats. Here we would be served the less fine dishes and the poorer wines, just as they would.

Father typically received the seat of honor at Herod's right—he boasted of it often, though not as much as Mother, who seemed to think Father's power and glory extended to her. I glanced at Father, standing with Nathaniel, full of pompous expectation. How could he be so confident? His son had joined Antipas's enemies and committed public acts of treason. The entire city knew of his actions—I could not believe they would go completely unnoticed by the tetrarch. Surely not. The sins of the son were visited on the father just as the father's sins were visited on the son. Hadn't Antipas once ordered his soldier to cut off the hand of a man whose son was a thief? Did Father truly think there would be no repercussion for him?

It had perplexed me that Judas's rebellion had thus far yielded no apparent consequence to Father. It occurred to me now, however, that the tetrarch would strike at Father unexpectedly, in a moment when he could inflict the most humiliation. Mother's face was strained with worry, and I could see she had the same thoughts as I.

We watched the men being escorted to their places one by one until only four places remained: the two seats of gloat beside Antipas and the two seats of shame at the end. Left waiting were Father and Nathaniel and two men unknown to me. Shiny diadems of sweat had formed on the brows of the two strangers. Father, however, showed no sign of concern.

With a nod to his palace steward, Chuza, Antipas had Father and Nathaniel escorted to the seats of honor. Nathaniel clasped Father's arm, a gesture that seemed to celebrate the alliance the two of them had made. Father's power was intact. Their treaty was safe. I turned to Yaltha and saw her frown.

The women dipped their bread and ate. They prattled and tossed back their heads and laughed, but I had no stomach for food or gaiety. Three musicians played the flute, cymbal, and Roman lyre, and a barefoot dancer, no older than I, leapt about with her brown breasts protruding like mushroom tops.

Visit a pestilence upon my betrothal. Let it be broken by whatever means God chooses. Unbind me from Nathaniel ben Hananiah. The curse I'd written formed lips of its own and repeated inside me. I no longer had faith God would hear it.

Antipas lifted himself from the couch with some labor. The music ceased. The voices hushed. I saw Father smile to himself.

Chuza struck a little brass bell and the tetrarch spoke. "Let it be known that my counselor and chief scribe Matthias has not rested in his search for my enemies. Today, he delivered unto me two Zealots, the most vicious of rebels, who have waged transgressions against my government and the government of Rome."

He looked toward the doorway, raising his arm in dramatic fashion, pointing, and every guest turned in unison. There, bare chested, his skin a bewilderment of whip marks and blood crust, stood Judas. His hands were bound and he was cinched about his waist with a rope that was tied to that of a wild-eyed man I guessed to be Simon ben Gioras.

I leapt to my feet, and my brother turned and found me. *Little sister*, he mouthed.

Yaltha caught my arm as I bolted toward him, forcing me back onto the stool. "There's nothing you can do but draw trouble on your own self," she whispered.

"Behold the traitors of Herod Antipas," called Chuza, and a soldier led them stumbling into the room. It seemed they would be made into a sport for our entertainment. They were dragged a full circuit about the banquet hall to the sound of my mother's crying. The men spewed abuses on them as they passed. I stared at my hands in my lap.

The bell was rung again. The parade halted, and Antipas read from a scroll that I imagined my father had penned. "On this day, the nineteenth of Marcheshvan, I, Herod Antipas, Tetrarch of Galilee and Peraea, decree that Simon ben Gioras will be executed by sword for traitorous acts and that Judas ben Matthias will be imprisoned at the fortress of Machaerus in Peraea for the same offense, his life spared as a dispensation to his father, Matthias."

It passed through my mind that my father had not acted as monstrously as I'd thought, that he'd delivered Judas into the hands of Antipas in order to save him from certain death, but I knew that was more wishful than true.

Mother was slumped onto the table like a discarded cloak, her hair braid falling into a bowl of honeyed almonds. Just before Judas was led away, I looked at him, wondering if it would be my last glimpse.

xxv.

A fever sickness descended on Sepphoris. It came like an unseen smoke, blown down from heaven to afflict the unrighteous. God had always chastised his people with plagues, fevers, leprosy, paralysis, and boils. So people said. But how could this be when the sickness bypassed Father and took hold of Yaltha?

Lavi and I bathed her face with cool water, anointed her arms with oil, and sponged her lips with balm of Gilead. One night when delirium took hold of her, she sat up in bed and clasped me to her saying the name *Chaya, Chaya.*

"It's me, Ana," I told her, but she smoothed her palm along my cheek and spoke the name again. *Chaya.* The name means life, and I thought maybe in her feverish state she was calling out for her life not to leave her, or perhaps she'd simply mistaken me for someone else. I dismissed the incident, but I didn't forget it.

The entire city was closed up tight as a fist. Father did not venture to the palace. Mother withdrew to her quarters. Shipra went around with a garland of hyssop around her neck and Lavi kept a talisman of lion's hair in a pouch at his waist. Day and night I climbed onto the roof in quest of stars and rain and birdsong. There, I witnessed the dead carried along the street to be laid in cave tombs beyond the city, where they would remain sealed until their flesh rotted and their bones were gathered into ossuaries.

"Keep out of God's sight," Mother cautioned me. As if in getting a glimpse of me on the roof, God would be reminded of my wrongdoings and strike me down with sickness, too. Part of me wished for it. My guilt and sorrow over Judas was so grave, I wondered if my going to the roof wasn't really an attempt to contract the fever and die in order to escape my distress. The day after my disastrous betrothal ceremony, Judas left for the palace-fortress in Machaerus. Father announced his departure at the evening meal, then forbade Judas's name to be spoken again in his house.

The war between my parents inhabited the house like a silent, prowling creature. Whenever Father left the room, my mother would walk to the threshold and spit on the place his foot had last fallen. She believed the fever would be God's retribution upon Antipas and Father. She waited for the Lord to smite them dead. She waited to no avail.

Then one afternoon, a messenger arrived. We were seated on the couches in the reception hall, taking our midday meal, nothing more than dried fish and bread since Mother forbade Shipra and Lavi to venture out to the market. Nor would she allow the messenger into the house, ordering Lavi to receive his message at the door. When he returned, he cast a look at me I couldn't quite read.

"Well, what is it?" Mother said.

"It is news from the house of Nathaniel ben Hananiah. He has fallen victim to the fever."

My heart fluttered strangely. Then came an upwelling of relief and hope and gladness. I stared into my lap, afraid my feelings would blossom into my face.

Glancing sideways at Mother, I watched her plunge her elbows onto the tripod table and drop her head into her hands. Father's face looked pale and grim. With a colluding glance at Yaltha, I rose from my couch and climbed the stairs to my room, closing the door behind me. I would have danced, except for the guilt I felt over my happiness.

When the same messenger arrived two weeks later with news that Nathaniel had survived, I wept into my pillow.

Ever since the conversation with my aunt that had provoked my doubts, my old understanding of God had begun to fray. Now questions roiled inside me. Had God intervened to spare Nathaniel, ensuring my marriage to him, or was his recovery merely a matter of luck and resilience? Had God caused my aunt's fever in order to chastise her, as my mother said? And when she, too, was restored, did it mean she'd repented? And Judas—had God willed him to be imprisoned by Herod Antipas? Why had he failed to save Tabitha?

I could no longer believe in the God of punishments and rescues.

When I was nine, I discovered God's secret name: I Am Who I Am. I thought it was the truest, most wondrous name I'd ever heard. When my father overheard me speak it aloud, he shook my shoulders and forbade me to say the name ever again, for it was too holy to be uttered. I did not stop thinking of it, though, and during those days when I questioned God's nature, I repeated the name over and over. I Am Who I Am.

xxvi.

Phasaelis summoned me to the palace on the fourth of Tebet, unaware it was the fifteenth anniversary of my birth. A soldier had arrived at our gate well before noon bearing her message written in Greek on a sheet of ivory hammered so thin it was like a peel of milk. I'd never seen a missive written on ivory. I took it in my hands. Light quivered on the black script, every word taut and perfect—and my old longing was ripped open. *Oh, to write again . . . and on such a tablet!*

> 4th of Tebet
>
> Ana, I hope you have survived the fever and the
> confinement of these long and woeful weeks. I bid
> your presence at the palace. If you deem it safe,
> leave your cage this day and come to mine. We shall
> take the Roman baths and resume our friendship.
>
> Phasaelis

A shiver ran through me. *Leave your cage.* It had been a month and a half since the sickness had first appeared in the city. Only yesterday we'd heard of a child who'd become newly infected, but the disease seemed to be taking its leave. The funerary processions had nearly ceased, the market had reopened, Father had resumed his business, and Yaltha, though still delicate, had left her bed.

It was Friday—Sabbath would begin that evening. Nevertheless, Mother, her eyes full of jealousy, gave me permission to visit the palace.

THE MOSAIC OF SEA CREATURES on the floor in the great hall was even more glorious in daylight. Phasaelis's silver-haired attendant, Joanna, left me staring at it while she went to seek her mistress. I had the feeling once again of standing on fishes, of waves moving beneath my feet, of the world reeling toward something I couldn't see.

"My husband's enthrallment with Roman mosaics has no beginning and no end," Phasaelis said. I'd not seen her enter. I smoothed the folds of my pale yellow tunic and touched the amber bead at my neck, struck, as I'd been before, by the sight of her. She wore a brilliant blue robe and a string of pearls across her forehead. Her toenails were painted with camphire.

"It's beautiful," I said, letting my eyes sweep once more across the sea floor.

"Soon we will not have a tile left that hasn't been turned into an animal, a bird, or a fish."

"Does it concern the tetrarch that he's violating the Jewish law against graven images?" I don't know what made me ask such a thing. Maybe it came from my own brush with fear when I'd drawn the image of myself inside my incantation bowl. Whatever prompted it, my question was ill-thought.

She released a high, chirruping laugh. "It would concern him only if he were caught. Though a Jew himself, he cares little for Jewish customs. It is Rome he lusts for."

"And you? You have no fears for him?"

"Should a host of Zealots drag my husband through the streets for breaking this law, it would not arouse the slightest care in me as long as they left the mosaics undamaged. I, too, find them beautiful. I would miss them more than I would miss Antipas."

Her eyes snapped brightly. I tried to read her face. Beneath her easy indifference and her lighthearted dismissal of her husband lay something blistering.

She said, "Even as the fever scourged the city and his subjects were dying, he commissioned a *new* mosaic. It will be even more flagrant than the rest of them. The artisan himself is afraid to create it."

I could think of only one reason for such trepidation. "It will depict a human form?"

She smiled. "A face, yes. A woman's face."

WE DESCENDED THE STEPS onto the portico, then another set to the baths. A frail cloud of dampness floated up to us, the smell of wet stone and perfumed oils. "Have you taken the Roman baths before?" Phasaelis asked.

I shook my head.

"I take them weekly. It's an elaborate and time-consuming ritual. They say the Romans indulge in them daily. If that's the case, one wonders when they found time to conquer the earth."

In the changing room, we stripped naked except for towels, and I followed Phasaelis to the tepidarium, where the air flickered with lamps in high niches. We dipped in a pool of tepid water, then lay on stone-top tables while two female attendants thrashed our arms and legs with olive branches and rubbed oil into our backs, kneading us like balls of dough. This odd ministration caused me to leave my body and sit on a little ledge just above my head, free of fret and fear.

In the next room, however, I came hurtling back into myself. The hot vapors of the caldarium were so profuse, I struggled to breathe. We had entered the torments of Gehenna. I sat on the hard, slick floor, gripping my towel and rocking to and fro to keep myself from fleeing. Phasaelis, meanwhile, walked placidly through the mist unclothed, her hair falling around her knees, her breasts full as muskmelons. My own body, though fifteen, was still thin and boyish, my breasts like two brown figs. My forehead throbbed and my belly pitched. I don't know how long I waited through that small enduring, only that it made what came next a paradise.

The most spacious of the bathing rooms, the frigidarium had curved bright walls with wide arches and bays bordered with vine-painted columns. Entering, I threw off my towel and plunged into the cold pool, then reclined on the bench that wrapped about the walls, sipping water and eating pomegranate seeds.

"It's here that Antipas intends to place his new mosaic," Phasaelis said. She pointed to the tiles in the center of the room.

"Here? In the frigidarium?"

"It's a room hidden from prying eyes, and it's his favorite room in the palace. When he entertains Annius, the Roman prefect, they spend all of their time in here conducting business. Among *other* things."

The suggestive tone of her last sentence was somehow lost on me. "I don't see why he wishes to install a woman's face here. Wouldn't fishes be more fitting?"

She smiled. "Oh, Ana, you are still young and naive about the ways of men. They conduct their business here, it's true, but they also give way to other . . . interests. Why do they wish a woman's face here? Because they are men."

I thought of Tabitha. I wasn't as naive about men as Phasaelis thought.

A scraping sound came from the alcove behind us. The click of bracelets. Then a low, guttering laugh.

"So, you've been spying on us," Phasaelis called out. She looked past me, over my shoulder, and I spun around, grabbing for my towel.

Herod Antipas stepped from behind the arch. He fastened his gaze on me, his eyes moving from my face to my bare shoulders, then along the edges of the towel that barely covered my thighs. I swallowed, trying to force down my fear and disgust.

Phasaelis made no attempt to cover herself. She addressed me. "He sometimes watches me bathe. I should've warned you."

Lascivious old man. Had he observed me step naked and dripping from the pool?

Recognition flickered in his face. "You're the daughter of Matthias, the one we betrothed to Nathaniel ben Hananiah. I didn't recognize you without your clothes."

He stepped toward me. "Look at this face," he said to Phasaelis, as if I were a sculpted object to be examined and discussed.

"Leave her be," she said.

"It's perfect. Large, well-spaced eyes. The high plump cheeks. Look at her mouth—I've never seen a more beautiful one." Coming closer, he slid his thumb along my lower lip.

I glared at him. *May you become crippled, blind, deaf, mute, and impotent.*

His finger wound to my cheek, down to my neck. If I fled, what then?

Would he send his soldiers after me? Would he do worse than rub his thumb across my face? I sat unmoving. I would endure this, and then he would leave.

He said, "You will sit for my artisan so he can sketch your face."

Draping herself, Phasaelis said, "You want her face for your mosaic?"

"Yes," he said. "It's young and pure—it suits me."

I sought his rodent eyes. "I will not allow my face to be in your mosaic."

"You will not *allow*? I'm your tetrarch. One day I will be called King, as my father was. I can force you, if I wish."

Phasaelis stepped between us. "If you force her, you'll offend her father and her betrothed. But that's for you to decide. You are the tetrarch." I saw she was practiced at managing his caprices.

He pressed his fingers together, seeming to consider what she'd said. In that brief interim, I wondered if I was to become visible in the world not through my writings, but through pieces of broken glass and marble. Could the vision I'd had of my face inside the tiny sun refer to a mosaic in Antipas's palace?

As I gripped the edge of the bench, an idea came to me. I didn't stop to consider how it might turn into something unforeseen, even dangerous. I took a measured breath. "You may have my face for your mosaic, but on one condition. You must release my brother, Judas."

He let loose a laugh that bounded off the walls. I glimpsed Phasaelis tuck her chin and grin.

"You think I should release a criminal who plots against me only for the pleasure of seeing your face on the floor of my baths?"

I smiled. "Yes, I do. My brother will be grateful and cease his rebellions. My parents will bless you, and the people themselves will call you blessed."

It was those last words that snared him. He was a man despised by his people. He craved to be named King of the Jews, a title that had belonged to his father, who'd ruled Galilee, Peraea, and all of Judea. Antipas had been bitterly disappointed when his father carved up his kingdom into three portions for his sons and gave him a lesser part. Failing to get his father's blessing, he spent his days seeking the approval of Rome and the adoration of his people. He'd found neither.

Phasaelis said, "She could be right, Antipas. Think of it. You could say that your clemency is a gesture of mercy for your people. It could turn their hearts. They will heap praise upon you."

From my mother I'd learned the skills of deception. I'd secreted my womanhood, hidden my incantation bowl, buried my writings, and feigned reasons to meet Jesus in the cave, but it was Father who'd shown me how to strike a despicable bargain.

Antipas was nodding. "Setting him free would be a magnanimous act on my part. It would be unexpected, a shock perhaps, and that would draw even more attention to it." He turned to me. "I'll make the proclamation on the first day of the week, and the next day you will commence to sit for my artisan."

"I will sit for him when I've seen Judas with my own eyes, and only then."

xxvii.

Judas was delivered to our door twelve days after my visit to the palace. He arrived gaunt and dirty with a sunken stomach, grime-matted hair, and pus-infested lash marks. His left eye was swollen into a slit, but his right eye contained a flame that hadn't been there before. Mother fell upon him, sniveling. Father stood apart, arms crossed over his chest. I waited for Mother's frantic attentions to cease and then took his hand. "Brother," I said.

"You have your sister to thank for your release," Mother said.

I'd had no choice but to tell my parents about the scheme I'd devised with the tetrarch—I knew Antipas would speak of it to Father—but Judas had no need to be informed. I'd begged my parents to keep it from him.

Father had shown little reaction to my arrangement with Antipas—he desired only to keep the tetrarch happy—but Mother had been predictably jubilant. It was Yaltha, dear Yaltha, who'd kissed my cheeks and thought to worry about me. "I fear for you, child," she'd said. "Take care around Antipas. He's dangerous. Tell no one about the mosaic. It could be used against you."

Judas stared at me with his one blinking eye while Mother expounded on the whole perverse story.

"You would have your face mounted on the floor of a Roman bath for Herod Antipas and his cohorts to leer at?" he said. "I would rather you'd let me rot in Machaerus."

The next day, Herod Antipas sent for me.

I WAS MADE TO SIT on a low tripod stool in the frigidarium. The artisan used a string and a Phoenician measure to mark off a large circle at least three paces across, then set to work sketching my face on the floor with a finely sharpened stick of charcoal. He worked on his knees, his back hunched, painstakingly creating his pattern, sometimes wiping away the lines and starting again. He admonished me when I moved or sighed or shifted my eyes. Behind him, his workers hammered disks of glass into even-edged tesserae—red, brown, gold, and white, each one the size of a baby's thumbnail.

The artisan was young, but I saw his talent. He filled the borders with braided leaves and here and there a pomegranate. He would sit back and tilt his head to study his work so that his cheek lay nearly on his shoulder, and when he drew my head, it tilted, too, but slightly. He sketched a garland of leaves in my hair and drop pearl earrings at my ears, none of which I was wearing. A chimera of a smile played on my lips. My eyes bore the faint suggestion of something sensual.

For three days he worked while I sat, hours and hours, while all around us the endless tap, tap, tapping of mallets. On the fourth day, he sent a servant to inform Herod Antipas the sketch was completed. When the tetrarch arrived to inspect it, the hammering ceased and the workers shrank against the wall. The artisan, racked with nerves, sweating and fidgety, awaited judgment. Antipas circled the sketch with his fingers laced behind his back, looking from the sketch to me as if judging the likeness.

"You've captured her with precision," he told the artisan.

He walked to where I sat on the stool and stood over me. There was a raw and frightening light in his face. He cupped his hand around my breast and squeezed hard. He said, "The beauty of your face makes me forget your lack of breasts."

I looked up at him, at the girth of him, at the lust in his eyes, and I could barely see for the rage I felt, for the way it turned everything white and blinding. I sprang up, my hands lashing out. I shoved him once. Twice. My reaction was spontaneous, but not unconsidered. Even as he'd reached out to hurt me, even as the pain twisted in the little mound of flesh around my nipple, I told myself I would not sit there willing myself to be small and imperceptible as I had that day he'd smeared his thumb across my lips.

I shoved him a third time. He was like a stone, unmoved. I thought he would strike me. Instead he smiled, showing his pointy teeth. He leaned toward me. "So you're a fighter. I'm fond of women who fight," he whispered. "Especially in my bed."

He strode away. No one spoke, and then all at once the workers let out small gasps and murmurs. With relief, the artisan acknowledged he had no more need of me.

Now they would mix the plaster and lay the bright tesserae, immortalizing me in a mosaic on which I hoped never to lay eyes. Phasaelis had been kind to me and I would miss her, but I vowed when I left the palace this day, I would never return.

As I departed, Joanna waylaid me in the great hall. "Phasaelis wishes to see you."

I went to her room, glad for the chance to tell my friend goodbye. She reclined at a low table, engaged in a game of knucklebones. Seeing me, she said, "I've had a meal prepared for us in the garden."

I hesitated. I wished to be far away from Herod Antipas. "Just us, alone?"

She read my thought. "Don't fear, Antipas would think it beneath him to dine with women."

I was not so sure of it, not if it provided him an opportunity to grasp a breast, but I accepted her hospitality, not wanting to offend her.

The garden was a portico surrounded by Teashur trees, Babylon willows, and juniper bushes bowed over with pink flowers. Reclining on couches, we dipped our bread in common bowls, and I drank in the bright light. After so many hours in the dark frigidarium, the shock of it raised my spirits.

Phasaelis said, "Herod Antipas's proclamation freeing Judas has made him faintly popular among the people. He even spared the life of Simon ben Gioras, though he kept him imprisoned. At least now his subjects don't spit quite as far when they hear his name." She laughed, and I thought how much I loved to see her snicker at her own wicked humor.

She went on. "The Romans, however, were unamused. Annius sent a legate from Caesarea to express his disapproval. I overheard Antipas trying to explain that such gestures were needed from time to time to keep the rabble in check. He sent Annius assurances that Judas would no longer be a threat."

I didn't want to think of Antipas, nor of Judas. Since returning, my brother had spent his time tending his wounds and gathering his strength. He'd spoken not a word to me since learning of the mosaic.

Phasaelis added, "But we both know, don't we, that Judas is more of a threat now than before."

"Yes," I said. "Far more."

I watched a white ibis pick at the ground, and I thought of the white sheet of ivory she'd sent to me, of its bold, exquisite script. "Do you remember the invitation you sent inviting me to leave my cage and come to yours? I've never seen a more beautiful tablet."

"Ah, the ivory leaves. They're the only ones of their kind in all of Galilee."

"Where did you come upon them?"

"Tiberius sent a parcel of them to Antipas some months ago. I took one of them for myself."

"And did you write the invitation yourself?"

"Are you surprised that I write?"

"Only at the power of your script. Where did you learn it?"

"When I first arrived in Galilee, I spoke only Arabic, but I couldn't read or write it. I missed my father terribly despite him sending me away—it was always in my mind to return to him. I set out to learn Greek so I could write to him. It was your father who taught me."

My father. The revelation cut through me.

"Did he teach you, also?" she asked.

"No. But he brought me inks and papyrus from time to time." That sounded self-pitying and meager. I wanted to believe that teaching her Greek was what had softened Father to my own desire to read and write, why he'd given in to my pleadings despite Mother's disapproval, why he'd hired Titus as my tutor, but it didn't change the envy that had surfaced from some old, deep place.

Then, as if we'd conjured him, my father was limping toward us on the portico. His feet dragged as if shackled. His eyes were cast down. Phasaelis, too, studied him. Something was wrong. I sat up and waited for what would come.

"May I speak freely?" he asked Phasaelis. When she nodded, he eased onto the couch beside me, grunting like an old man, and up close, I saw that it was not only sadness on his face, but a quiet infuriation. He looked plundered, as if he'd lost the thing dearest to him.

He said, "Nathaniel recovered from the fever sickness, but it left him weakened. It is my burden to tell you, Ana, he died this day while walking in his date grove."

I said nothing.

"I know the betrothal was a yoke for you," he continued. "But now your condition is worse. You will be treated as a widow." He shook his head. "Yours is a stigma we will all bear."

In the curve of my ear I heard the rush of wings. I saw the ibis lift away.

xxviii.

In the aftermath of Nathaniel's death I was required to wear a robe the color of ash and go about with bare feet. Mother put dust on my head and fed me the bread of affliction and complained that I did not cry with loud and bitter wails or rend my clothes.

I was a fifteen-year-old widow. I was free. *Free, free, free!* I would not enter the chuppah with despair and dread over what my husband would do to me. The cloth of virginity would not be placed beneath my hips and paraded around afterward for witnesses to inspect. Instead, when the seven days of mourning ended, I would beg Father to let me resume my writing. I would go to the cave and dig up the incantation bowl and the goatskins stuffed with my scrolls.

At night when I lay still in my bed, the knowledge of these things would break over me and I would laugh deep into my pillow. I assured myself the curse I'd written played no part in Nathaniel's dying, but still, my jubilation often brought on bouts of guilt. I rebuked myself for rejoicing in his death, I truly did, but I would not have wished him back.

O blessed widowhood.

At his burial, I walked with his sister, Zophar, and his two daughters at the forefront of a throng of mourners, as we accompanied Nathaniel's body to the family's cave. His linen shroud had been poorly wrapped and when he was carried to the cave entrance, the hem of it snagged on a thornbush. It necessitated a laborious effort to extricate him. It gave the impression of Nathaniel fighting his interment, and it struck me as comical. I pressed my lips together, but the smile broke through, and I saw Nathaniel's daughter, Marta, not much younger than I, glare at me with hatred.

Afterward at the funeral banquet, remorseful that she'd observed my amusement, I said, "I'm sorry you've lost your father."

"But you are not sorry you lost your betrothed," she snapped and turned away. I ate the roasted lamb and drank the wine, unconcerned that I'd made an enemy.

xxix.

On the first day of mourning, Mother found a tablet at her door inscribed in Judas's hand. Not able to read it herself, she sought me out and thrust the message at me. "What does it say?"

My eyes flowed over his terse script.

I can remain no longer in my father's house. He has no wish for me here, and while Simon ben Gioras is imprisoned, the Zealots have need of a leader. I will do what I can to rally their spirits. I pray you will not blame me for departing. I do what I must. I bid you well, your son, Judas

Then, set apart at the bottom . . .

> Ana, you did your best for me. Be wary of Herod
> Antipas. With Nathaniel gone, may you be free.

I read it aloud to her.

She walked away, leaving the tablet in my hands.

THAT SAME DAY MOTHER dismissed the spinners and weavers who'd spent the past two weeks creating garments for my dowry. I watched as she folded the tunics, robes, shifts, girdles, and head scarves and stacked them in the chest of cedar that had once held my writings. Atop the clothes she placed the bridal dress, smoothing her hands over it before closing the lid. Her eyes were wellsprings. Her lower lip trembled. I couldn't determine whether her sorrow was over Nathaniel's death or Judas's departure.

I regretted my brother leaving, but I felt no anguish over it. I'd expected it, and he'd made peace with me in his note. I stood there trying to look impassive, but Mother sensed my gladness over Nathaniel, how it made a small brightness on my skin. "You think you've escaped a great misfortune," she said. "But your tribulation has only begun. Few men, if any, will want you now."

This she thought to be a tribulation?

Her misery had been so great since learning of Nathaniel's death, it was a miracle she hadn't shaved her head and dressed in sackcloth. Father, too, had gone about withdrawn and glum, not over the loss of his friend, but over the forfeiture of their bargain and the land he would never own.

Feeling pity for Mother, I said, "I know men are reluctant to marry a

widow, but I can only be counted as one by the strictest of interpreta-
tions. I'm a girl whose betrothed has died, that's all."

She was on her knees beside the chest. She got to her feet and lifted
one brow, always a poor sign. "Even of *those* girls, men say, 'Do not cook
in a pot in which your neighbor has cooked.'"

I flushed. "Nathaniel did not cook in my pot!"

"Last evening at the banquet Nathaniel's own daughter, Marta, was
heard to say you'd lain with her father in his house."

"But that's a falsehood."

I minded little if betrothed couples lay together. It happened often
enough; some men even claimed it was their right to lay with the woman
to whom they were already legally bound. What I minded was the lie.

Mother laughed, a throat rattle of condescension. "If you had not
despised Nathaniel so thoroughly, I might believe the girl's words to be
true. But it doesn't matter what I think, only what others believe. The
gossipmongers saw you roaming all over the city, even beyond the walls.
Your father was stupid to permit it. Even after I confined you again to
the house, you slipped out. I myself heard people talk of your roving.
The men and women of Sepphoris have spent weeks speculating over
your virginity, and now this girl, Marta, has thrown a log on their fire."

I waved my hand at her. "Let them think what they will."

Anger seared across her face, then fell away bit by bit in little crumbles. In the sullen gray light of my room, her shoulders sagged, her eyes
closed; she seemed very tired. "Don't be unwitting, Ana. Being a widow
is deterrent enough, but if you're also thought to be defiled . . ." Her
voice trailed off into the doom and gloom of having a husbandless
daughter.

I thought of Jesus then, that day in the cave, rain-soaked hair, the
crook of his grin, the ragged portion of bread he offered, the things he
said while the storm raged. It caused a tipping over in my stomach. But
perhaps he would not have me now either.

"Husbands may be loathsome creatures," she was saying, "but they're necessary. Without their protection, women are easily mistreated. Widows can even be cast out. The young ones resort to harlotry; the old ones, to beggary."

Like Sophocles, my mother was capable of tragic sweeps of imagination.

"Father will not cast me out," I told her. "He takes care of Yaltha, who's a widow—do you think he would not take care of me, his daughter?"

"He won't always be here. He, too, will die and what will happen to you then? You cannot inherit."

"If Father dies, you will be a widow as well. Who will care for *you*? You cannot inherit either."

She sighed. "My care will fall to Judas."

"And you think he would not provide for me? Or for Yaltha?"

"I don't think he will be able to provide for *any* of us," she answered. "He does nothing but seek trouble. Who can say what means Judas will have? Your fool of a father has disclaimed him. He went so far as to write his disownment into a contract. Now on his death, this house and everything in it will go to his brother, Haran."

It took a moment to grasp the magnitude of what she was saying. Haran had cast out Yaltha once. He wouldn't hesitate to cast her out again, along with me and Mother. A wave of fear passed through me. Our lives and fates left to men. This world, this God-forsaken world.

From the corner of my eye, I saw Yaltha standing in the doorway. Had she heard? Mother spied her as well and left us. As my aunt stepped inside, I took a mocking tone; I didn't wish her to see how Mother's words had disturbed me. "It seems the entire populace has picked over the state of my virginity like a flock of scavengers and has determined it's missing. I've become a mamzer."

Mamzers were of all varieties—bastards, harlots, adulterers, fornicators, thieves, necromancers, beggars, lepers, divorced women, cast-out widows, the unclean, the destitute, those possessed of devils, Gentiles—all of them shunned accordingly.

Yaltha wove her fingers through mine. "I've been without a husband for many years. I will not mislead you, child—you will live even further on the outskirts now. I've spent my life there. I know the uncertainty Hadar spoke about. And now that Haran will inherit the house, our fates are threatened even more. But we shall be all right, you and I."

"Will we, Aunt?"

She tightened the hitch of her fingers. "The day you met Nathaniel in the market you returned home bereft, and that night I came to your room. I told you your moment would come."

I'd thought Nathaniel's death would be that moment, a portal I could step through and find some measure of freedom, but now it seemed his dying would only leave me scorned and my future would leave me destitute.

Seeing my dejection, Yaltha added, "Your moment will come because you'll *make* it come."

Even though my window was boarded over until the spring, I went and stood before it. Cold air seeped around the wood panel. I felt incapable of making any moment come that would change my circumstance for the better. The longing of my heart was for a man I scarcely knew. It was buried with my bowl and my writings. God, too, was hidden from me now.

Behind me, Yaltha spoke: "I told you how I came to be rid of my husband, Ruebel, but not how I came to marry him."

We went to sit among the bed pillows, which only a short time ago had been plump with my laughter. Settling herself, she said, "On the fifteenth of Ab, the Jewish girls in Alexandria, the ones who were not yet betrothed, the ones with little appeal, went into the vineyards during the grape harvest and danced for the men in need of brides. We went late in the day before the sun set, all of us wearing white dresses and bells sewn on our sandals, and the men would be there, waiting. You should've seen us—we were scared, clinging to one another's hands. We carried drums and danced in a single line that moved like a serpent through the vines."

She paused in the telling and I could see it clearly—the sky singed red, the girls twittering with apprehension, the sway of white dresses, the long, serpentine dance.

As she resumed her story, her eyes seemed to darken at the edges. "I danced each year for three years until finally someone chose me. Ruebel."

I wanted to cry, not for myself, but for her. "How would a girl know she was chosen?"

"The man would come and ask her name. Sometimes he would go to her father that very night and the contract would be drawn."

"Could she refuse?"

"Yes, but it was rare. She would not risk displeasing her father."

"You didn't refuse," I said. This both captivated and dismayed me. How different her life might have been.

"No, I didn't refuse. I didn't have the courage." She smiled at me. "We make our moments, Ana, or we do not."

Later, alone in my room, the house deep in slumber, I removed the white marriage dress from the chest and with the snipping knife, I cut the hem and the sleeves into long tatters. I slipped it on and crept from the house. The air caused cold scintillas of flesh to rise on my arms. I mounted the ladder to the roof and climbed like a night vine, the shreds of my dress fluttering. A small wind stirred the dark, and I thought of Sophia, the very breath of God in the world, and I whispered to her, "Come, lodge in me, and I will love you with all my heart and mind and soul."

Then, on the roof, as close to the sky as I could get, I danced. My body was a reed pen. It spoke the words I couldn't write: *I dance not for men to choose me. Nor for God. I dance for Sophia. I dance for myself.*

XXX.

When the seven days of mourning ended, I walked through the center of Sepphoris with my parents and aunt to synagogue. Father had been reluctant for us to appear in public so soon—rumors about my missing virginity blanketed the city like rotted manna, but Mother believed a demonstration of my devoutness would soften the vitriol toward me. "We must show the entire population we bear no shame," she said. "Otherwise they'll believe the worst."

I can't imagine why Father went along with such stupid reasoning.

It was a clear, cool day, the air oiled with the smell of olives, everyone in their woolen cloaks. It didn't seem like the kind of day trouble would find us; nevertheless Father had ordered Antipas's soldier to traipse behind us. Yaltha didn't usually come with us to synagogue, which was a relief to my parents as well as my aunt, but here she was today, adhered to my side.

We walked without speaking, as if holding our breath. We wore no splendor; even Mother was clad in her simplest dress. "Keep your head bowed low," she'd told me when we first set out, but I found now I couldn't do it. I walked with my chin lifted and my shoulders back, the tiny sun perched over me trying very hard to shine.

As we neared the synagogue, the street grew crowded. Spotting our subdued little entourage and then me in particular, the people halted their progress, clumped together, and stared. A swell of muttering rose up. Yaltha leaned close to me. "Fear nothing," she said.

"She's the one who laughed at the death of her betrothed, Nathaniel ben Hananiah," someone shouted.

Then another voice that sounded vaguely familiar cried, "Harlot!"

We kept walking. I kept my eyes straight ahead as if not hearing. *Fear nothing.*

"She's possessed by devils."

"She's a fornicator!"

The soldier waded into the crowd, scattering it, but like some dark slippery creature, it re-formed on the other side of the street. People spit as I passed. I smelled the shame streaming off my parents. Yaltha took my hand as the familiar voice came again, "The girl is a harlot!" This time I turned and found the accuser, the round, bulbous face. Tabitha's mother.

xxxi.

I waited three weeks before approaching Father. I was patient and, yes, sly. I continued to wear my grim, gray dress, though it was no longer required, and when Father was about, I made myself downcast and dutiful. I rubbed my eyes with bitter herbs, a speck of horseradish or tansy, turning them red rimmed and watery. I poured oil on his feet while swearing my purity and bemoaning the stigma brought upon my family. I served him honeyed fruit. I called him blessed.

Finally, on a day Father appeared amiable, at an hour Mother was nowhere near, I knelt before him. "I will understand if you refuse me, Father, but I beg you to let me return to my writing and my studies while I wait and hope for another betrothal. I only wish to keep occupied so I'm not consumed with dismay at the sad state I'm in."

He smiled, pleased with my humility. "I'll grant you two hours each morning to read and write, but no more. The rest of the day, you will do as your mother wishes."

As I bent to kiss his foot, I drew back and wrinkled my nose at the smell of his freshly made sandal. It caused him to laugh. He placed his hand on my head, and I saw that he felt at least something for me, something between pity and affection. He said, "I will bring you some clean papyri from the palace."

. . .

I REMOVED MY MOURNING DRESS, immersed myself in the mikvah, and donned a tunic without pattern or dye and an old tanned coat. I wove a single white ribbon into my braid and covered my head with a scarf that was once as blue as the sky, but now washed of its color.

It was shortly past daybreak when I set out to the cave, slipping through the back gate with a small digging tool and a large pouch strapped to my back containing bread, cheese, and dates. I'd determined not to be without my writings and my bowl any longer. I would hide them in Lavi's quarters if I must, but I would have them near me, and surely soon I could blend them among the new scrolls I would write and my parents would not suspect I'd saved them from being burned. My mind overflowed with new narratives I would compose, beginning with those of Tamar, Dinah, and the unnamed concubine.

I had ventured out without Lavi or concern for what vicious tongues would say. Everything had already been said. Shipra returned each day from the market eager to impart the tales she'd heard of my depravity, and when Mother or I went out, people of our own standing hurled imaginative insults. The kinder ones merely turned away from us on the street.

When I reached the city gate, I looked toward Nazareth. The valley floors ran wild with coriander, dill, and mustard, and already workers were making their way to building sites in the city. I wondered if I might find Jesus praying at the cave. I'd timed my trip well for seeing him. The sun's pink fingers were still wrapped around the clouds.

It was close to the end of Shebat, when the almond trees blossomed. The wakeful tree, we called it. Midway down the hill, I smelled its rich brown scent, and winding farther, I came upon the tree itself, its canopy lush with white flowers. I stepped beneath it, thinking of the marriage canopy I'd escaped, of my dance on the rooftop, that choosing of myself. I plucked one of the small white flowers and tucked it over my ear.

Jesus stood at the cave entrance with his fringed cloak pulled over his head and his arms lifted in prayer. Drawing near, I placed my tool and pouch on a rock and waited. My heart pounded. For a moment it was as if everything that had come before did not matter.

His prayer was whispered, but over and over again I heard him address God as *Abba*, Father. When he finished, he pulled his cloak back around his shoulders. I walked toward him with my chin set, with no falter in my step. I didn't recognize myself, the young woman with the almond blossom in her hair.

I called out, "*Shelama*. I fear I've intruded upon you."

He paused, taking me in. Then came the smile. "We are on level pegging then. When we met before, I was the one who intruded on you."

I feared he might leave—there was no rain to detain him this time. A little intoxicated by my audacity, I said, "Please be kind enough to share my meal. I don't wish to eat alone."

Last time he'd proved to be a man who interpreted the law liberally, open-minded about interacting with women and Gentiles, but an unbetrothed man and woman alone on a hillside without a chaperone was a forbidding matter. The Pharisees, those who prayed loudly only to be heard and wore phylacteries twice as large as normal, would think it a reason to throw stones at us. Even those less pious might say such a meeting bound the man to ask the girl's father for a betrothal contract. I watched him waver for several moments before he accepted.

We sat in a puddle of sunlight near the cave mouth and broke bread, wrapping it about small hunks of cheese. We nibbled the dates and spit the pits and talked haltingly of small, heedless things. Throughout, he lifted his hand to shield his face from the glare and glanced toward the path through the balsam grove. When a long and awful silence fell over us, I made up my mind. I would speak as I wished to speak. Say what I wanted to say.

"You call God Father?" I asked. Referring to God in that way was not unheard-of, but it was unusual.

After pausing, perhaps out of surprise, he said, "The practice is new to me. When my father died, I felt his absence like a wound. One night in my grief, I heard God say to me, 'I will be your father now.'"

"God speaks to you?"

He stifled a grin. "Only in my thoughts."

"I've just observed my own time of mourning," I said. "My betrothed died five weeks ago." I refused to lower my eyes, but I kept the gladness from reaching them.

"I'm sorry," he said. "Am I right to think he was the rich man in the market?"

"Yes, Nathaniel ben Hananiah. I was made to go to the market that day by my parents. It was the first time I'd ever seen Nathaniel. You must have witnessed my revulsion for him. I regret I showed no subtlety, but a betrothal to him felt like dying. I was given no choice."

Silence, but this time it lit upon us like something winged. He watched my face. The earth hummed. I saw his body sigh and the last of his inhibitions fall away.

"You've suffered much," he said, and it seemed he spoke of more than my betrothal.

I got to my feet and stepped into the shadow that edged the cave opening. I'd been deceitful with him before and I didn't wish to be so again. I would have him know the worst. "I cannot be unfair to you," I said. "You should know with whom you speak. Since Nathaniel's death, I've become a scourge to my family. In Sepphoris, I'm a pariah. It's falsely rumored that I'm a fornicator. And because I'm the daughter of Herod Antipas's chief scribe and counselor, it has become a grand and notorious scandal. When I leave our house, people cross the road to avoid me. They spit at my feet. They shout 'harlot.'"

I wanted to protest my innocence further, but couldn't bring myself to do so. I waited to see if he would withdraw, but he rose, coming to stand with me in the thin shade, his expression unchanged.

"The ways of people can be cruel," he said. Then, quieter, "You're not alone in this suffering."

Not alone. I met his eyes, trying to understand his meaning, and I saw again how everything floated there.

He said, "You should know with whom you speak as well. I am also a mamzer. In Nazareth some say I'm Mary's son, not Joseph's. They say I was born from my mother's fornication. Others say my father is Joseph, but that I was illicitly conceived before my parents married. I've lived all twenty years of my life with this stigma."

My lips parted, not in surprise at what he'd said, but that he'd chosen to divulge it to me.

"You're shunned still?" I asked.

"As a boy I wasn't allowed in synagogue school until my father went and pleaded with the rabbi. When he was alive, he shielded me from gossip and slights. Now that he's gone, it's made worse. I believe it's why I can find no work in Nazareth." He'd been rubbing the hem of his sleeve between his fingers as he talked, and he let go now, straightening. "But that is as it is. I only mean to say I know the pain you speak of."

He appeared uncomfortable that he'd turned the conversation to himself, but I couldn't cease my questions. "How have you endured their scorn for so long?"

"I tell myself their hearts are boulders and their heads are straw." He laughed. "Lashing out at them did no good. As a boy, I was always coming home scraped and bloodied from some fight. You'll think me soft compared to other men, but now when I'm reviled, I try to look the other way. It does the world no good to return evil for evil. I try now to return good to them instead."

What manner of person is this? Men would think him weak, yes. Women, too. But I knew the strength it took to forgo striking back.

He began to pace. I could sense some stirring inside him. "So many suffer this kind of contempt," he said. "I cannot separate myself from them. They are cast down because they're destitute or diseased or blind or widowed. Because they carry firewood on the Sabbath. Because they're not born a Jew but a Samaritan or they're born outside of marriage." He spoke like someone whose heart had overflowed its banks. "They are condemned as impure, but God is love. He would not be so cruel as to condemn them."

I didn't answer. I think he was struggling to understand why God, his new father, did not plead more insistently with his people to take these outcasts in, just as Jesus's father, Joseph, had pled with the rabbi to let him into synagogue school.

"Sometimes I can't bear what I see around me. Rome occupies our land; Jews sympathize with them. Jerusalem is filled with corrupt Temple priests. When I come to pray here, I ask God to bring his kingdom to earth. It cannot come soon enough."

He went on speaking of God's kingdom much like Judas did—as a government free of Rome with a Jewish king and righteous rule, but also as a great feast of compassion and justice. At our last meeting I'd called him a stonemason, a carpenter, a yarn sorter, and a fisherman. I saw now he was, in truth, a sage, and perhaps like Judas, an agitator.

But even that didn't fully explain him. I knew of no one who put compassion above holiness. Our religion might preach love, but it was based on purity. God was holy and pure; therefore we must be holy and pure. But here was a poor mamzer saying God is love; therefore we must be love.

I said, "You speak as if God's kingdom is not just a place on earth, but a place inside us."

"So I believe."

"Then does God live in the Temple in Jerusalem or in this kingdom inside us?"

"Can he not live in both?" he asked.

I felt a sudden blazing up inside and threw my arms open. "Can he not live *everywhere*?"

His laughter resounded off the cave walls, but his smile lingered on me. "I think for you, too, God cannot be contained."

Having grown chilled in the shade, I went to sit on a rock in the sun, thinking of the endless debates I'd held in my head about God. I'd been taught God was a figure similar to humans, only vastly more powerful, which failed to comfort me because people could be so utterly disappointing. It reassured me suddenly to think of God not as a person like ourselves, but as an essence that lived everywhere. God could be love, as Jesus believed. For me, he would be I Am Who I Am, the beingness in our midst.

Jesus gazed toward the sky as if to judge the hour, and in the hush of that moment, in my exhilaration of being near him, of conversing with him about divine immensities, I said, "Why should we contain God any longer in our poor and narrow conceptions, which are so often no more than grandiose reflections of ourselves? Let us set him free."

His laugh rose and fell and rose again, and I told myself I could love him for that alone.

"I would like to hear further how we might set God free," he said. "But I must be on my way. I work now at the amphitheater."

"No longer in the quarry?"

"No; I'm glad to be in the open air. I hew stones into blocks that will serve as seats. Perhaps one day you'll attend the theater and sit on a stone I myself have chiseled and fitted."

We'd found our alikeness, our bond, but his words, though meant kindly, reminded me of how we were divided—he was the one who hewed the stone; I was the one who sat on it.

I watched him fasten his tool belt. He hadn't asked me why I'd come here—perhaps he thought it would be prying, or he assumed I was simply walking in the hills as I'd claimed before—but I wished now to tell him. Nothing hidden.

"I'm a scribe," I said. The audacity of the claim momentarily stalled my breath. "Since I was eight, my father has allowed me to study and write, but when I was betrothed, the privilege was taken from me and my scrolls were burned. I salvaged what I could of them, and buried them in this cave. I came this morning to dig them up."

"I could tell you were different from other women. It wasn't very difficult." He looked back at my digging tool balanced on the rock. "I'll help you."

"No," I said quickly. I wanted to do it alone. I wasn't ready for him to see my writings, my bowl, or the curse I'd written. "You mustn't tarry. I'll dig them up myself. I spoke of them because I wish you to know and understand me."

He offered me a parting smile and strode off toward the balsams.

Finding the spot where my treasure was buried, I drove the tool into the hard-packed dirt.

xxxii.

Eight days later, Herod Antipas summoned me to the palace to view the completed mosaic. I'd sworn never to return and begged to be excused, but Father refused my pleas. I feared defying him too strongly—I couldn't risk ruining my newfound freedom. Already I'd made a fine new ink and, working through the mornings and sometimes at night, I'd completed my narratives of the women in the Scriptures who'd been raped. I'd bound them together with Tabitha's story. I named them "The Tales of Terror."

At midafternoon, my father accompanied me to the palace, making an uncommon effort at appeasement. Did I find the papyri he'd brought me to my liking? Was I pleased to have Phasaelis as a friend in the palace? Was I aware that while Herod Antipas was thought to be ruthless, he was kindly to those loyal to him?

I began to hear a noise in my head, a voice of warning. Something was not quite right.

ANTIPAS, PHASAELIS, AND MY FATHER gazed at the mosaic as if it had been dropped from heaven. I could barely bring myself to look at it. The tiny tiles replicated my face with near perfection. They shimmered in the dimness of the frigidarium, the lips seeming to part, the eyes blinking, a deception, a trick of light. I watched them watching it—Herod Antipas leering, his eyes hungry and salivating, and Phasaelis, too crafty not to see his lust. My father had placed himself between me and Antipas as if forming a barrier. Now and then, he patted the place between my shoulders, but rather than comforting me, his unctuous behavior added to my wariness.

"Your face is beautiful," Phasaelis said. "I see that my husband thinks so, too." Antipas's philandering was well known, and so, too, was Phasaelis's intolerance of it. In the Nabataean kingdom of her father, infidelity was regarded as a heinous disrespect to a wife.

"Leave us!" he bellowed at her.

She turned and addressed me so all could hear. "Be cautious. I know my husband well. But whatever happens, don't fear, we shall still be friends."

He shouted again, "*Leave us!*"

She walked out slowly, as if departing was her idea. I wanted to rush after her. *Take me with you.* Something treacherous had slipped into the room. I felt it on the back of my neck.

Antipas took my hand, resisting my tug to pull it away. He said, "I would have you for my concubine."

I jerked my hand from him and stepped backward until the back of my knees collided with the stone bench that encircled the wall. I sank onto it. *Concubine.* The word slithered before me on the floor.

Father came and sat beside me, leaving Antipas to stand alone beside the mosaic, arms crossed over his belly. Father spoke in a low, groveling tone that was foreign to my ears. "Ana, daughter of mine, for you to be the concubine of the tetrarch is the best we can hope. You would be like a second wife."

I turned narrowed eyes on him. "I would be what they whisper I am, a harlot."

"A concubine is not a harlot. She is faithful to one man. She differs from a wife only in the status of her children."

I realized he had agreed to this despicable notion already, yet he seemed to want my consent. He couldn't risk me inflaming Antipas with my disgust and rejection. His status in the tetrarch's court would surely be affected.

"Our fathers Abraham and Jacob had concubines that bore them children. King Saul and King Solomon kept concubines, as did Herod Antipas's own father, King Herod. There is no shame in it."

"There's shame in it for *me.*"

Across the room, Antipas watched us. His eyes glowed yellow. A fat hawk judging his prey.

"I will not consent."

"You must be reasonable," he said, angering. "You are no longer marriageable. I can find no husband for you now that you are widowed and besmirched, but the tetrarch of all Galilee and Peraea will have you. You'll live in the palace and be well cared for. Phasaelis has promised to befriend you, and Antipas has granted my request that you be allowed to read, write, and study to your content."

I stared straight ahead.

"A concubine does not receive a bride price," he went on. "Yet Antipas has agreed to pay the sum of two manehs. It shows your great worth. There will be a contract drawn to protect your rights."

His patience exhausted, Antipas strode across the room and stood before me. "I've prepared a gift for you." He motioned to his steward, Chuza, who brought a tray laden with a stack of ivory sheets like the one on which Phasaelis had sent her invitation. There were reed pens and vials of dyed inks—two green, one blue, three red. He was followed by a servant who carried a sloped lap desk made from red wood and carved with two dragons.

The sight of these things created both longing and nausea in me. I pressed the back of my hand to my mouth. "My answer is no."

Antipas shouted at my father, "Why doesn't she obey as women should?"

I leapt to my feet. "I will never submit," I said. I looked at the lap desk and the tray bearing his gifts—all that beauty and bounty, and on impulse I picked up a single sheet of the ivory and slid it into the pocket inside my sleeve. "I take this as your parting gift to me," I said, and turning, I fled the room.

Behind me, I heard Antipas shout, "Chuza! Bring her back."

I broke into a run.

xxxiii.

On the street I pulled my mantle over my head and walked briskly, staying beneath the roofed sidewalks along the cardo, looking behind me for Chuza and now and then entering a small shop in hopes of avoiding him. It was the day before the Sabbath and the city was thronged with people. I tried my best to disappear among them.

I thought of hiding myself in the cave, a shelter no one but Jesus and Lavi knew about, but I could not sleep or eat there, nor would Jesus come at this hour. He would be at the building site for the theater on the northern slope. The realization halted me, as if a hand had been laid on my shoulder. I heard Yaltha's voice float up: *Your moment will come, and when it does, you must seize it with all the bravery you can find. . . . Your moment will come because you'll make it come.*

I turned toward the northern slope.

The building site was a commotion of pounding mallets and pluming limestone dust. I stood on the street and stared at two-wheeled carts lurching through the bustle, wooden cranes and hoists lifting unhewn stones, men stirring mortar with long staves. I hadn't expected so many workers. I spotted him finally near the top of the ridge, bent over a stone, smoothing it with a trowel.

The sun was dipping toward the valley and the shadow from a nearby scaffold fell across his back, forming a tiny ladder. The poet's words began to sing in me of their own accord. *Under the apple tree I awakened you . . . Many waters cannot quench love, neither can floods drown it . . .*

Around me, the street was busy with vendors peddling tools, bolts of cheap flax, butchered animals, and stews for the workers, a second-rate bazaar compared to the market in the basilica. I found a spot beside a vegetable stall where I could wait for the day's labor to end.

The sun slid deeper into the valley and my spirits thinned with the slippage of light. Lost in my brooding, I jumped at the sound of a ram's horn being blown. Abruptly, the hammering ceased and the men began to put away their tools. They streamed up the hill onto the street, Jesus among them, his cheeks and forehead dusted with stone powder.

A man shouted, "Seize her!"

Jesus turned toward the cry, and then I, too, reeled about. Chuza stood on the sidewalk a short distance from me, pointing. "Seize her!" he cried again. "She has stolen from my master."

Workers, vendors, shoppers, passersby stopped. The street muted.

I drew back into the market stall. Yet he followed me into the baskets of onions and chickpeas. He was an old man, but he was strong. Grabbing my wrist, he dragged me into the crowd, into their stares and spit and invective.

Hemmed in by a host of angered people, I was struck with fear like a slash of lightning moving from the crown of my head, down my back, along my legs, to the nubs of my toes. I looked at the sky, the breath gone from me.

Chuza lifted his voice. "I charge her with thievery and blasphemy. She stole a precious sheet of ivory from my master, and she sat for an artisan while he made a graven image of her face."

I closed my eyes and felt the heaviness of my lashes. "I have stolen nothing."

Ignoring me, he spoke to the crowd. "If there's no ivory in the pocket of her sleeve, I will be satisfied she's not a thief. Either way, she cannot deny the graven image made of her face."

A woman pushed her way through the swarm of people. "She's the daughter of Matthias, head scribe to Herod Antipas, and known to be a fornicator."

I called out again in protest, but my denial was swallowed by the black odium that boiled out of their hearts.

"Show us your pocket!" a man yelled. One by one, they took up the petition.

Gripping my forearm, Chuza let their shouts grow fevered before he reached for my sleeve. I writhed and kicked. I was a fluttering moth, a hapless girl. My skirmish yielded nothing but jeers and laughter. He snatched the sheet of ivory from my coat and lifted it over his head. A roar erupted.

"She is a thief, a blasphemer, and a fornicator!" Chuza cried. "What would you do with her?"

"Stone her!" someone cried.

The chant began, the dark prayer. *Stone her. Stone her.*

I shut my eyes against the dazzling blur of anger. *Their hearts are boulders and their heads are straw.* They seemed to be not a multitude of persons, but a single creature, a behemoth feeding off their combined fury. They would stone me for all the wrongs ever done to them. They would stone me for God.

Most often victims were dragged to a cliff outside the city and thrown off before being pelted, which lessened the laborious effort of having to throw so many stones—it was in some way more merciful, at least quicker—but I saw I would not be accorded that lenience. Men and women and children plucked stones from the ground. These stones, God's most bountiful gift to Galilee. Some rushed into the building site, where the stones were larger and more deadly. I heard the sizzle of a rock fly over my head and fall behind me.

Then the commotion and noise slowed, elongating, receding to some distant pinnacle, and in that strange slackening of time, I no longer cared to fight. I felt myself bending to my fate. I ached for the life I would never live, but I yearned even more to escape it.

I sank onto the ground, making myself as small as I could, my arms and legs tucked beneath my chest and belly, my forehead pressed to the ground. I fashioned myself into a walnut shell. I would be broken apart and God could have the meat.

A stone struck my hip in a sunburst of pain. Another fell beside my ear. I heard the stomp of sandals running toward me, then a voice glittering with indignation. "Cease your violence! Would you stone her on the word of this man?"

The mob quieted, and I dared to raise my head. Jesus stood before them, his back to me. I stared at the bones in his shoulders. The way his hands were drawn into fists. How he'd planted himself between me and the stones.

Chuza, though, was more fox than Father, more jackal than Antipas. He diverted the rabble from Jesus's question. "She had the ivory. You saw it for yourself."

I felt life returning to me. "I did not steal it. It was a gift!" I exclaimed, getting to my feet.

Jesus's voice boomed. "I ask you again, who is this accuser whose word you take so easily?" When no one spoke, Jesus shouted even louder, "*Answer me!*"

Knowing that anyone associated with Herod Antipas would be suspect to them, I called out, "He is Chuza, the steward of Herod Antipas," which brought an eruption of mutterings.

Someone shouted at Chuza, "Are you Herod Antipas's sycophant?"

"Do not ask who I am," Chuza cried. "Ask who *this* man is. Who is he to speak for her? He has no standing here. Only her father, husband, or brother can speak for her. Is he one of these?"

Jesus turned and looked at me, and I saw his anger in the set of his jaw. "I am Jesus ben Joseph," he said, turning back to them. "I am neither father, brother, nor husband to her, but I will soon be her betrothed. I can testify she is no thief, or blasphemer, or fornicator."

My heart caught. I looked at him in confusion and strained to understand if what he'd just declared was his true intention or a shrewd means to save me. I could not tell. I remembered him in the cave, how he'd shared my breakfast, how he'd come to stand beside me when I'd poured out my shame, all that we'd made known to each other.

There was a lull as the crowd deliberated whether to believe Jesus's witness over Chuza's. Jesus was one of them, and he'd pledged himself to be my upholder. Chuza was the minion of their despised tetrarch.

The crowd's ferocity was draining away—I could feel it leaving—yet they went on standing there, glaring, clutching stones in their fists.

Jesus lifted out his palms to them. "Let the one who is without sin cast the next stone."

A moment passed, a tiny lifetime. I listened to the sound of dropping stones. They were like mountains moving.

xxxiv.

Jesus remained beside me until Chuza slunk away and the mob disbanded. I was shaken by the savagery of the crowd and my bare escape from death, and he seemed reluctant to leave me to myself.

He gazed at the diminishing light. "I will walk with you as far as your house."

"Were you injured?" he asked as we set out. Though my hip throbbed from the single stone that had struck me, I shook my head.

His declaration that I would soon be his betrothed was like a fire in my head. I wanted to ask what he'd meant, whether his admission had been sincere or was calculated to win over the crowd, but I was afraid of his answer.

Quiet fell. The city floated in a soupy twilight, his face half in shadow. The silence lasted only moments, but I thought I might choke on it. In an effort to breathe, I recounted the unexpurgated story of the mosaic, how I'd agreed to sit for it in order to save my brother, Judas. When I told him of Antipas's lust, of his intent to make me his concubine, and described my panicked escape to the building site, I saw the anger flare again at his jaw. I confessed that the sheet of ivory, which was back again in my sleeve, had perhaps been more taken than given. I wanted him to know the truth, but I had the sense that my chatter was making matters worse, entirely worse. He listened. He asked no questions.

Upon reaching the gate of our palatial house, I stared at my feet. It was excruciating to look at him. Finally, lifting my face, I said, "I doubt I'll see you again, but please know I will always be grateful for what you did. I would be dead if not for you."

His forehead wrinkled and I saw disappointment in his eyes. "When

I told the crowd we would soon be betrothed, I didn't mean to assume your answer," he said. "I overstepped in an effort to assert my authority with them. I accept your refusal. We shall part well, as friends."

"But I didn't think . . . I didn't think you meant the betrothal seriously," I said. "We walked all this way and you said nothing."

He smiled. "We walked all this way with you talking."

I laughed, but my face burned, and I was glad for the gathering darkness.

"I'm required to marry," he said. "All Jewish men are. The Talmud does not sanction a man without a wife."

"Are you saying you're required to marry, therefore you'll settle on me?"

"No, I'm trying to say men are required to marry, but I often see things differently than others. It may be that for some men it's better not to marry. I thought that was true of me. Before my father died, he wanted to arrange a betrothal for me, but I couldn't agree to it."

I stared at him, bewildered. "Are you saying you're not meant for marriage, but it's a duty you must endure?"

"No, only listen."

I would not. "Why would it be required for some not to marry? Why would you be among a group such as that?"

"Ana, hear me. There are men who are summoned to something even more pressing than marriage. They're called to go about the country as prophets or preachers, and they must be willing to give up everything. They must leave their families behind for the sake of bringing God's kingdom—they cannot give themselves to both. Wouldn't it be better to never marry than to abandon their wives and children?"

"You believe you're one of these? A prophet or a preacher?"

He turned his face from me. "I don't know." I watched him press the tips of his thumb and forefinger between his brows and squeeze. "Since I was a boy of twelve I've felt I might have some purpose in God's mind, but that seems less likely to me now. I've had no sign. God has not spoken to me. Since my father died, it has been pressed on me anew that I'm the eldest son. My mother, sister, and brothers depend on me. It would be difficult to leave them with little provision." He faced me again. "I've wrestled with it, and more and more I think the calling I sensed was more in my own mind than in God's."

"You are sure?" I said. Because I was not.

"I cannot know for certain, but for now God is silent on the matter, and I've come to believe I can't forsake my family and leave them to fend for themselves. The truth of these things has set me free to think of marriage."

"You think of me like the fulfillment of a duty, then?"

"I'm compelled by duty, yes; I won't deny it. But I would not speak of a betrothal to you if I weren't also compelled by what's in my heart."

And what's in your heart, I wanted to ask, but the question was brash and dangerous and I sensed that what lay there was a difficult puzzle—a jumble of God, destiny, duty, and love that couldn't be solved, much less explained.

If we married, I would always look over my shoulder for God.

"I'm unsuited for you," I said. "Certainly you know this." I couldn't think why I would try to discourage him, except to test his resolve. "I don't just refer to my family's wealth and ties to Herod Antipas, but to myself. You said you're not like other men. Well, I'm not like other women—you've said so yourself. I have ambitions as men do. I'm racked with longings. I'm selfish and willful and sometimes deceitful. I rebel. I'm easy to anger. I doubt the ways of God. I'm an outsider everywhere I go. People look on me with derision."

"I know all of this," he said.

"And you would still have me?"

"The question is whether you will have me."

I heard Sophia sigh into the wind—*Here, Ana, here it is.* And despite all that Jesus had just said, all his prevarication and provisos, the most curious feeling came over me, that I was always meant to arrive at this moment.

I said, "I will have you."

XXXV.

Having no father or elder brother, Jesus bore the responsibility of arranging his own betrothal. He promised to return in the morning to speak with my father, a pledge that rendered me almost impervious to the anger I encountered when I entered the house. In retaliation for my refusal to be his concubine, the tetrarch had demoted Father from head scribe and counselor to a mere scribe among many other mere scribes. It was a dazzling fall from favor. Father was livid with me.

I couldn't feel bad for him. His willingness to hand me over, first to Nathaniel, then to Herod Antipas, had severed the last tie that bound me to him. I knew somehow he would find a way to ingratiate himself to Antipas once again and recover his position. I would be proven right about that.

As Father berated me that night, Mother paced back and forth, interrupting him with outbursts of fury. They didn't even know yet that the good citizens of Sepphoris had nearly stoned me to death for reasons of thievery, fornication, and blasphemy. I decided to let them discover this on their own.

"Do you think of no one but yourself?" Mother shrieked. "Why do you persist in these shameful acts of disobedience?"

"Would you rather I'd become Herod Antipas's concubine?" I asked, genuinely shocked. "Would that not be an act even more shameful?"

"I would rather you had—" She cut herself off, leaving the rest unspoken but hanging conspicuously in the air. *I would rather you had never been born.*

. . .

A PALACE COURIER arrived the following morning before Father broke his fast. I was perched on the balcony awaiting Jesus's arrival when Lavi ushered the messenger into Father's study. Had Father struck some deal with Herod Antipas during the night? Would I be dragged off to become his concubine after all? Where was Jesus?

Their meeting was short. I stepped away from the rail as Father emerged. When the courier departed, his voice drifted up to me. "I know you're there, Ana."

I peered down. He looked defeated, his posture slumping toward the floor.

He said, "Last evening, I sent a message imploring Herod to set aside your refusal and take you for his concubine anyway, hoping the humiliation you'd caused him might have subsided. His response has just arrived. He ridiculed me for thinking he would condescend to have you in his palace after you were nearly stoned on the street. You might have told me of this and saved me from further disgrace." He shook his head in disbelief. "A stoning? The city will be set against us even more. You have ruined us."

Had I dared, I would've asked if he cared at all that I'd endured a harrowing escape from death. I would've told him it was Chuza he should blame for the stoning, not me. But I held my tongue.

He walked back toward his study, a man utterly vanquished, then stopped midway. Without turning, he spoke. "I do give thanks you were unharmed. I'm told it was a builder who prevented your death."

"Yes, his name is Jesus."

"And he spoke to the crowd of becoming your betrothed?"

"Yes."

"Would you welcome that, Ana?"

"I would, Father. With all my heart."

When Jesus arrived soon afterward, Father wrote and signed a contract of betrothal without consulting Mother. Jesus would pay the humble bride price of thirty shekels and would feed, clothe, and shelter my aunt, who would accompany me. There would be no betrothal ceremony. The wedding would be a simple transfer from my father's house to my husband's in thirty days, on the third of Nisan, the shortest time allowed.

NAZARETH

17–27 CE

i.

The day I entered Jesus's house, his family stood in a silent clump in the courtyard, watching as Lavi led the cart containing me, my aunt, and our belongings through the gate. There were four of them—two men besides Jesus, and two women, one of whom rested her hand across her nearly imperceptible pregnant belly.

"Do they think we have the spaciousness of a palace?" I heard the pregnant one say.

To my mind, we'd brought a bare handful of possessions. I'd packed the plainest of my clothes, one ordinary silver headband, my copper mirror, an ornamental brass comb, two red woolen rugs, undyed bed coverings, my incantation bowl, and most precious of all, my cedar chest. Inside it were my scrolls, reed pens, a sharpening knife, two vials of ink, and the ivory sheet that had nearly gotten me stoned. The clean papyri my father had obtained for me were gone—I'd exhausted them during the brief writing frenzy that had commenced soon after retrieving my possessions from the cave. Yaltha had brought even less than I: three tunics, her bed mat, the sistrum, and the Egyptian scissors.

Still, we were a spectacle. Over my protests Father had sent us off in a cart drawn by a royally bedecked horse from Herod Antipas's stable. I'm sure he wanted to impress the Nazarenes, to remind them that Jesus was wedding far above his standing. I offered my new family a smile, hoping to endear myself, but a cart lined with fine woolen rugs, pulled by an imperial horse led by a servant, did nothing to help my cause. Jesus had met us on the village outskirts and even he'd frowned before greeting us.

To worsen matters, Father had also forbidden the wedding under his roof. It was customary for the chuppah to be in the bride's house, but he feared annoying Antipas by hosting a marriage the tetrarch was certain to resent. Nor did Father want village peasants in his house. His refusal to host Jesus and his family must have been a terrible insult to them. And who knew what tales might have reached them of my fornicating, thieving, and blasphemy?

I let my eyes drift about the little compound. Three small dwellings were cobbled together within the enclosure, built from stacked stones and held together with mud. I counted five or six rooms opening onto the courtyard. A ladder led to the rooftops, which were covered with reed bundles and packed mud, and I wondered if Yaltha and I would be able to sit up there and share our secrets.

I quickly scanned the courtyard. An oven strewn with pots and utensils, firewood, dung pile, mortar and pestle, loom. There was a sun-cooked vegetable garden and a little stable with four chickens, two sheep, and a goat. A single olive tree. I took it all in. *This is where I'll live.* I tried not to feel the shock that undulated through me.

His family huddled in the shade of the lone tree. I wondered where Jesus's sister was, the one from the market—the yarn spinner. His mother wore a colorless tunic and a pale yellow head scarf with wisps of dark hair escaping the edges. I guessed her to be near the age of my mother, but she was far more frayed by her years. Her face, so like her son's, was well worn from chores and childbearing. She had a slight rounding in her shoulders, and the corners of her mouth had begun to droop slightly, but I thought how lovely she looked standing there with

the sun filtering through the leaves, coins of light on her shoulders. Jesus's confession to me in the cave slipped into my thoughts. *In Nazareth*
some say I'm Mary's son, not Joseph's. They say I was born from my mother's
fornication. Others say my father is Joseph, but that I was illicitly conceived
before my parents married.

"Welcome, Ana," she said, coming to embrace me. "My daughter Salome was married only a few weeks ago and lives now in Besara. One
daughter has gone and another has come." There was a plaintive note
beneath her smile, and it occurred to me that not only had her daughter
left, but her husband had died only six months before.

The two men were Jesus's brothers, James, nineteen, and Simon, seventeen, both dark skinned and thick haired like Jesus, with the same
short beards and posture—the wide stance, arms crossed—but their eyes
had none of the passion and depth Jesus's did. The pregnant woman
with the prickly tongue was Judith, married to James, whose age, I would
discover, was fifteen, the same as mine. They looked at me with mute
stares.

Yaltha removed her bridle. "One would think a two-headed sheep
had arrived in your midst!"

I winced. "Greet my aunt Yaltha."

Jesus grinned.

"She's impertinent," James said to Jesus, as if she wasn't standing
there.

Rankled, I said, "It's what makes her so dear to me."

Jesus, I would discover, was a peacemaker and a provocateur in equal
measures, but one could never say which he would be at any given
moment. In this moment he became the peacemaker. "You're welcome
here. Both of you. You are our family now."

"You are indeed," Mary said.

Judith remained silent, as did Jesus's brothers. My aunt's honesty had
laid the friction bare.

. . .

WHEN THE CART WAS UNPACKED, I bid Lavi goodbye. "I will miss you, friend," I told him.

"Be well," he said, and his eyes watered, causing mine to do the same. I watched him lead the horse through the gate, listening to the clatter of the empty wagon.

When I turned back, the family had dispersed. Only Yaltha and Jesus stood there. He took my hand and the world righted herself.

We were to marry that same day when the sun set, but without ceremony. There would be no procession. No virgins raising their oil lamps and calling out for the groom. No singing, no feasting. By law, a marriage was the act of sexual union, nothing more and nothing less. We would become husband and wife in the solitude of each other's arms.

Not allowed to enter the chuppah beforehand, I spent the afternoon in the storeroom, where Yaltha had spread her bed mat. Mary had offered to share her room with Yaltha, but she'd declined, preferring to be on her own amid storage jars, food provisions, wool shares, and tools.

"Do they think we have the spaciousness of a palace?" I said when we were alone, mimicking my soon-to-be sister-in-law.

Yaltha said, "She's impertinent!" mocking James's assessment of her.

We fell upon each other laughing. I put my finger to my lips. "Shhhh, we'll be heard."

"Am I required to be well behaved *and* quiet?"

"Never," I replied.

I began to meander about the little room, touching the tools, running my thumb across a stained dye vat. "Are you worried about entering the chuppah?" Yaltha asked.

I supposed I was—what girl wasn't nervous her first time?—but I shook my head. "As long as I don't conceive, I will welcome it."

"Welcome it then, for you will have no worries there."

Yaltha had procured blackseed oil for me from a midwife in Sepphoris, a foul liquid more potent than anything my mother had used. I'd been swallowing it for a week. We'd agreed she would conceal it here among her things. Most men knew nothing of the ways in which women avoided pregnancy. When it came to children, they didn't much consider the agony of birth and the possibility of death; they thought instead of God's mandate to be fruitful and multiply. It seemed to be a command God had devised with men in mind, and it was the only one they were universally good at obeying. I didn't think Jesus was like other men, but I'd determined for now to keep the blackseed oil to myself.

When it was time, I dressed in a dark blue tunic that my aunt pronounced bluer than the Nile. She smoothed out the wrinkles with her hands and placed the silver headband on my forehead. I draped a white linen shawl over my head.

At exactly sunset, I entered the chuppah, where Jesus waited. Stepping inside the mud-walled room, I was greeted by the smell of clay and cinnamon and a dim miasma pierced with a beam of orange light falling from a high window.

"This will be our abode," Jesus said, stepping back with a sweep of his arm. He wore his blue-tasseled cloak. His hair was damp from washing.

The room had been arranged with care—whether by Jesus or by the women, I didn't know. My red rugs had been spread across the dirt floor. Two bed mats lay side by side, sprinkled with ground cinnamon—one freshly woven. My mirror, comb, and a neat stack of my clothes had been placed on a bench, with my chest of cedar set into a corner. My incantation bowl sat on a small oak table beneath the window for all the world to see, so exposed I had an irrational urge to hide it somewhere, but I forced myself to remain still. I said, "If you inspected my bowl, I'm sure you saw the graven image inside it. I drew it myself."

"Yes, I saw," he answered.

I watched for traces of condemnation on his face. "It doesn't offend you?"

"I'm more concerned with what's in your heart than what's in your bowl."

"To look into the bowl is to see into my heart."

He walked over and peered into it. Could he read Greek? Taking the bowl in his hands, he turned it as he read aloud, "Lord our God, hear my prayer, the prayer of my heart." Looking up, he held my gaze a moment before continuing. "Bless the largeness inside me, no matter how I fear it. Bless my reed pens and my inks. Bless the words I write. May they be beautiful in your sight. May they be visible to eyes not yet born. When I am dust, sing these words over my bones: she was a voice."

He set the bowl back on the table and smiled at me, and I felt the unbearable ache of loving him. I went to him, and there on the thin straw mats in the crumbles of light, I knew my husband and he knew me.

ii.

The morning after I became his wife, I woke to hear him repeating the Shema and then a woman's voice in the courtyard calling, "Ana, it's time to milk the goat."

"Hear, O Israel: The Lord our God is one Lord," Jesus intoned.

"Can you hear me?" the voice called. "The goat is in need of milking."

"And you shall love the Lord your God with all your heart, and with all your soul, and with all your might."

"Ana, the *goat*."

I lay still, eyeing Jesus across the room, ignoring the urgent need for goat milk, listening to his voice rise and fall, the quiet song of it. Somehow in my privileged ignorance it hadn't occurred to me that I would be given an equal share of the chores. The thought was faintly alarming— I'd arrived here unskilled at every conceivable task assigned to women.

Jesus faced the window, his back to me. When he lifted his palms, I glimpsed his arms ripple beneath his tunic. The sight summoned forth the memory of last night, moments so innermost and beautiful, they caused an exquisite ache inside me. I let out an involuntary moan, and he finished his prayer and came to sit on the mat beside me.

He said, "Do you always sleep so late?"

I propped on my elbow, tilting my face to his, and tried to look both coy and innocent. "It's not my fault. I was kept awake last night."

His laughter rebounded from the walls to the ceiling, then out through the little window. Pushing the mass and tangle of hair from my face, he drew me against his chest. "Ana, Ana, you have awakened me and made me alive."

"And you have done the same to me," I said. "I have only one fear in being here."

He cocked his head. "And what is that?"

"I have no idea how to milk a goat."

He laughed his uproarious laugh once more and pulled me to my feet. "Get dressed and I will show you. The first thing you must learn is that this is a very particular goat. She only eats winter figs, almond blossoms, and barley cakes, and insists on being fed by hand and having her ears scratched . . ."

He carried on like this while I slipped a tunic over my undergarment and tied a scarf around my head, giggling at him under my breath. He was still traveling to Sepphoris to work on the theater and it seemed he should've been on his way by now, but he appeared to be in no hurry.

"Wait," I said as he started toward the door. Opening my chest, I retrieved a small pouch, from which I pulled the red thread. "Can you guess where I acquired this?"

His brow wrinkled.

"It fell from your sleeve the day we met in the market," I said.

"And you kept it?"

"I did, and I shall wear it every day while you're away." I held out my arm. "Tie it on for me."

As he wrapped it about my wrist, he returned to his teasing. "Am I so faint in your thoughts that when I'm away you need this reminder?"

"Without this thread, I would forget I had a husband altogether."

"Then keep it close," he said and kissed my cheeks.

We found Judith in the stable. The goat was standing defiantly in the water trough, daring the sheep to drink. She was a dainty creature with a white body, a black face, a white beard, and wide-spaced eyes, one of which rotated in and the other out. I thought her outrageously funny-looking.

"She is a menace!" Judith said.

"I find her endearing," I replied.

My sister-in-law made a derisive noise. "Then you won't mind inheriting her care."

"I don't mind," I said. "But I need instruction."

Sighing, she looked at Jesus as if they might commiserate together over my stupidity.

He took my hand, letting his thumb rub against the thread. "I should go. As it is, I'll have to walk at a quick pace so as not to be late."

"Your mother has packed your meal," Judith told him, glancing accusingly at me, and I realized that task, too, belonged to me. I'd never cooked anything but ink.

When he left us, Judith lifted the goat from the water trough, provoking kicks, bleats, and a splatter of water, and dropped her roughly onto the ground. I watched as the animal lowered her head and butted Judith's thigh.

Already I felt an affinity with the creature.

DURING THOSE FIRST MONTHS it was plain to everyone, including me, that I'd spent my life as a pampered rich girl. Yaltha was of little help— she'd read Socrates, but knew nothing about pounding grain into flour or drying flax. Jesus's mother gathered me under her wing, trying to teach me, and protected me as best she could from Judith's reproaches, which gurgled like an unceasing spring: I didn't light the dung fire correctly. I left chaff in the wheat. I left wool on the sheep. I could not cook pottage without scorching the lentils. My goat cheese tasted like hooves.

Judith complained of me even more vociferously when others were about, notably my husband, telling him once that I was less useful than a lame camel. She not only disparaged my domestic skills, but I half suspected her of efforts to disrupt them. When it was my turn to pound the wheat, the pestle went missing. When I laid the fire, oddly, the dung was wet. Once when Mary instructed me to latch the gate, it miraculously unlatched itself and the chickens escaped.

The only task I excelled at was caring for the goat, whom I named Delilah. I fed her fruit and cucumbers and brought her a little basket that she liked to toss about with her head. I talked to her—Hello, girl, do you have milk for me today? . . . Are you hungry? . . . Do you want your ears scratched? . . . Do you find Judith as annoying as I do?—and she occasionally responded with a string of bleats. Some days, I tied a piece of rope about her neck and fastened it to my girdle and she accompanied me as I went about my chores and waited for the sun to slope toward the hills and Jesus to return. At the sight of him, Delilah and I would rush to the gate, where I embraced him, oblivious to the stares of his family.

James and Simon took fun in mocking our devotion, which Jesus took in stride, laughing with them. There was truth in their teasing, but I didn't find it as good-natured as my husband. They taunted him out of jealousy. Simon, two years from having a wife, was eager for the intimacies of marriage, and James and Judith's union was like that of two yoked oxen.

iii.

One hot day in the month of Elul, while the courtyard baked, I milked Delilah in the stable, then placed the ewer of frothy milk outside the gate, where the sheep couldn't capsize it. When I turned back, Delilah was in the water trough again. She'd taken to standing and sometimes sitting in it for long periods. I made no effort to deter her. I thought of climbing in myself. As Mary approached us with a basket of grain, however, I tried to lure her out.

"Leave her," she said, chuckling. She looked tired and flush with heat. Now that Judith's time was near, we'd taken over her portion of the chores, the bulk of which fell to Mary, since I was still an apprentice.

I took the basket from her. Even I could toss grain to chickens.

She leaned against the gate. "Do you know what we should do, Ana? Just the two of us? We should go to the village mikvah and immerse ourselves. Yaltha can remain here with Judith in case the baby decides to come."

I gestured at Delilah. "I know, I envy her, too."

She laughed. "Let's shirk our work and go." A lovely impish light had come into her eyes.

A LINE OF WOMEN had formed outside the stone enclosure that housed the pool, not because they'd suddenly grown devout, but because, like us, they craved a respite from the heat. We joined it, clutching our drying rags and clean tunics. Mary called out a greeting to the toothless old midwife who would soon attend Judith, and was greeted in return, but without enthusiasm. The women ahead of us stole glances at me, whispering and holding themselves stiffly, and I realized that my ill repute had followed me from Sepphoris. I couldn't tell if Mary noticed or if, for my sake, she pretended not to.

When we stepped inside the cool dwelling and descended into the mikvah, the women's undertones grew louder. *Yes, it's the chief scribe's daughter, the one sent away for promiscuity. . . . They say she was nearly stoned for thievery. . . . What reason could Mary's son have for marrying her?* Overhearing their gossip, the women behind us, including the midwife, refused to enter the water after me, preferring to wait until I'd vacated.

My cheeks stung with humiliation. Not because I cared what this puerile gaggle of women thought but because Mary had witnessed the indignities. "Pay them no mind," she told me. "Turn the other cheek." But the lovely light had gone from her eyes.

As we walked home, she said, "Jesus and I have also been the recipients of this kind of malice. They called me promiscuous, too. They said Jesus was conceived before my marriage and some said he didn't belong to Joseph."

I didn't tell her Jesus had spoken to me of these things. I waited for her to refute their accusations, but she said nothing, refusing to defend herself.

She took my hand as we walked and I felt how difficult, how bold, how loving it was for her to bare herself to me like this. "Jesus suffered more than I," she said. "He was branded as a child who was born outside of marriage. Some in the village shun him to this day. As a boy, he would come home from synagogue school with bruises and scrapes, always getting into a fight with his tormentors. I told him what I told you, 'Pay them no mind and turn the other cheek. Their hearts are boulders and their heads are straw.'"

"I've heard Jesus use those same words."

"He learned well, and his suffering didn't harden him. It's always a marvel when one's pain doesn't settle into bitterness, but brings forth kindness instead."

"I think the marvel has a lot to do with his mother," I told her.

She patted my arm and turned her concern back to me. "I know you suffer, too, Ana, not just from gossip and scandal, but daily at the hands of Judith. I'm sorry she makes it difficult for you."

"I can do nothing right in her eyes."

"She envies your happiness." Abruptly, she guided us off the path to a fig tree and motioned for me to sit in the green shade. "There's a story I must tell you," she said. "Last year, when Jesus was close to twenty, well before you came along, Joseph attempted to betroth him. My husband was ailing then—weak and short of breath with a blue hue about his mouth." She paused, closing her eyes, and I saw the freshness of her grief. "I think he knew he would die soon, and it spurred him to fulfill his duty and find his first son a wife."

A memory stirred. That evening Jesus had asked me to become his betrothed, he'd said his father had tried to arrange a marriage for him, but he hadn't agreed to it.

"Judith's father, Uriah, owns a small parcel of land and keeps sheep, even hiring two shepherds," Mary said. "He was a friend to Joseph, one who paid no attention to lingering stories of Jesus's birth. Joseph intended to seek a betrothal for Jesus with Judith."

The revelation dazed me.

"Of course, it never happened," she continued. "Our son had some notion he wouldn't marry at all. That was a great shock to us. Not to marry would've made him even more of a pariah. We pleaded with him, but his reason had to do with God's wishes, and he asked his father not to approach Uriah. Joseph complied."

The sunlight broke through the limbs and I frowned, more from confusion than the glare. "Why should Judith be envious of me if she knows nothing about this?"

"But she does know. Joseph had been so assured of the betrothal, he had already hinted his intention to Uriah. Judith's mother came to me, saying her daughter was pleased at the notion. Joseph, poor man. He felt to blame and was relieved when James offered to betroth Judith instead. James was barely nineteen, so young. Naturally, the story spread throughout Nazareth."

How embarrassed Judith must've been—getting the second-born because the firstborn declined. How hard it must have been for her to see me ride through the gate only months later.

"Jesus believed his decision was right," Mary was saying. "Still, he felt sorry for the shame it caused Judith's family and he went to Uriah and humbled himself, saying he meant no disrespect, that he was uncertain if he would marry at all, that he still wrestled with God over it. He praised Judith as worthy, her price far above rubies. This satisfied Uriah."

It didn't, apparently, satisfy Judith. I was squeezing a handful of my tunic so tightly that when I let go, my knuckles throbbed. Jesus had told me nothing of this.

Mary read my thought. "My son didn't want you burdened with this. He believed it would make it more difficult for you, but I thought it would help you understand Judith better, and perhaps make it easier."

I said, "I'm sure you are right," but all I could think was that my husband had a separate place inside himself where he kept certain privacies that I would never know. But did I not also have such a place?

Mary got to her feet, and when I stood, too, she faced me. "I'm glad my son changed his mind about marriage. I don't know if it was God who changed it or if it was you." She cradled my cheeks in her hands. "I've never seen him so glad of heart as he is now."

As we walked on, I told myself I would let Jesus have his hidden place that was his alone. We had our togetherness—why should we not have our separateness?

iv.

I began to slip away from the straw mat while Jesus slept, light a lamp, and creak open my chest. Sitting cross-legged on the floor, trying to make no sound, I would stretch out one of my papyri and read.

I often wondered if Jesus had ever opened my cedar chest and peered inside it. We'd never spoken of the contents, and though he'd read the prayer in my bowl and knew the depth of my desire, he hadn't broached the topic again.

One night he woke to find me huddled in the small spout of light, poring over my half-finished story of Yaltha's travails in Alexandria, which I'd embarked upon during those last insufferable days before leaving Sepphoris.

Coming to stand over me, he gazed into the open chest. "These are the scrolls you buried in the cave?"

The question stopped my breath. "Yes. There were thirteen of them buried there, but shortly after digging them up, I added several more." My mind traveled to the three scrolls that contained my tales of terror.

I held out the scroll I'd been reading and felt my hand shake. "This one is an account of my aunt's life in Alexandria. I regret I wasn't able to finish it before running out of papyrus."

As he took it, I realized this text, too, was replete with brutality. In it, I'd progressed no further than describing the mistreatment my aunt had endured at the hands of her husband, Ruebel, and I'd spared no detail of his cruelty. I suppressed an urge to take the scroll back—no one had ever read my words but Yaltha, and I suddenly felt bared, as if I'd been lifted out of my skin.

Jesus sat beside me, and leaned into the lamplight. Upon finishing, he said, "Your story caused your aunt's suffering to lift off the papyrus and enter inside me. I felt her suffering as my own and she was made new to me."

Heat started in my chest, a kind of radiance that spread through my arms. "When I write, that's what I most hope for," I told him, struggling to remain composed.

"Do the other scrolls contain stories such as this one?" he asked.

I described my collection of narratives, even my tales of terror.

"You will write again, Ana. One day you will."

He was saying what had never been acknowledged out loud, that the privilege was not possible now. Even he, the eldest son, could not make a way for me to write and study, not in this poor compound in Nazareth where there were no coins for papyri, where men scrabbled for work and women toiled from daybreak to day's end. Women's duties and customs were inviolable here, more so even than in Sepphoris. The leisure and affront of making inks and writing words were as unthinkable as spinning gold from flax, but doing so would not be lost to me forever— that's what he was telling me.

He blew out the lamp and we returned to our mats. His words had flooded me with an odd mixture of hope and disappointment. I told myself I would put aside my desire, that it would wait. The thought saddened me, but from that night I did not doubt he understood my longing.

v.

On the day that Jesus and I had been married a full year, Mary patted my belly and teased, "Have you got a baby in there yet?" Overhearing this, Jesus cast his mother an amused look that cut through me. Was he, too, waiting and hoping for a child?

We were in the courtyard huddled over an inventive new oven Jesus had made out of clay and straw, the three of us staring inside at balls of dough clinging to its smooth, curved walls. Mary and I had taken turns throwing the fistfuls of dough against the sides while Jesus praised our efforts. Unsurprisingly, two of my dough balls had refused to stick and landed in the hot coals at the bottom. The smell of burned bread was everywhere.

Across the compound, Judith stepped from her doorway and wrinkled her nose. "Have you burned the bread again, Ana?" She glanced sideways at Jesus.

"How do you know it was I who did so and not my mother-in-law?" I asked.

"I know the same way I know it was your goat who ate my cloth and not the chickens." Of course, she would bring *that* up. I'd let Delilah roam free in the compound and she'd eaten Judith's precious cloth. You would think I'd put the cloth on a plate and fed it to her.

In a perfectly timed moment, Delilah emitted a forlorn bleat, and Jesus broke into laughter. "She overheard you, Judith, and wishes to be forgiven."

Judith huffed away, her baby, Sarah, tied onto her back. The child had been born seven months ago and already Judith was pregnant again. I felt a wave of pity for her.

Mary was removing the small loaves from the oven, tossing them into a basket. "I'll pack these for your journey," she said to Jesus.

He would leave tomorrow as a journeyman, traveling from village to village as a stonemason and woodworker. The theater in Sepphoris was finished and jobs there had disappeared as Herod Antipas erected a new capital to the north, named Tiberias for the Roman emperor. Jesus could've found employment there, of course, but Antipas had stupidly, wantonly built the city atop a cemetery, and only those who cared little for the purity laws would work there. My husband was an outspoken critic of the purity laws, probably too outspoken for his own good, but I think he'd been relieved to have a reason not to be part of the tetrarch's ambitions.

I slid my arm about Jesus's waist as if to tether him. "Not only will Delilah and I remain unforgiven, but my husband is leaving with all our bread," I said, making an effort to disguise my sadness. "I wish you didn't have to go."

"If I had my way, I would stay, but there's little work for me in Naza-reth, you know that."

"Don't people in Nazareth need plows and yokes and roof beams?"

"Jobs here will go more readily to James and Simon than to me. I'll try not to remain away too long. I'll go first to Japha and if I find no work there, I'll go on to Exaloth and Dabira."

Japha. It was the village Tabitha had been banished to. A year and a half had passed since I'd seen her, but she was not gone from my thoughts. I'd told Jesus about her, holding nothing back. I'd even sung some of her songs for him.

"When you're in Japha, would you seek word of Tabitha for me?" I asked.

He hesitated only slightly. "I'll inquire about her, Ana, but the news, if there is any, may not be what you hope to hear."

I scarcely heard him. Her song about the blind girls was playing un-bidden in my head.

IN THE AFTERNOON I found Jesus mixing mud-brick mortar to repair the crumbling stone in the compound wall, mud to his elbows, and I couldn't bear to keep my secret from him any longer. I handed him a cup of water. I said, "Do you remember when you told me some men possessed an inner knowledge that caused them to leave their families and go out as prophets and preachers?"

He looked at me bemused, squinting through the sunlight.

"You thought that you yourself might even be among them," I con-tinued. "Well, I, too, have my own knowing inside . . . that I'm not meant for motherhood, but for something else."

Such an impossible thing to explain.

"You're talking about the prayer in your bowl. The stories you've written."

"Yes." I took his hands in mine, even though they were caked. "What if my words could, like men's, prophesy or preach? Would that not be worth the sacrifice?"

I was so young, sixteen then, and exorbitantly hopeful. I still believed I would not have long to wait. Some miracle would intervene. The sky would part. God would rain down papyri.

I studied his face. I saw regret, uncertainty. Not to have children was considered a great misfortune, a thing worse than death. I thought suddenly of the law that permitted a man to divorce his childless wife after ten years, but unlike my mother, I didn't fear that possibility. Jesus would never countenance such a law. My fear lay in disappointing him.

"But do you need to make this sacrifice now?" he said. "There's time. Your writing will be there for you one day."

I understood more clearly—when he said one day, he meant one far-away day.

"I do not want children," I whispered.

This was my deeper secret, but I'd never spoken it aloud. Good women had babies. Good women *wanted* babies. It was pressed upon every girl precisely what good women did and did not do. We lugged those dictates around like temple stones. A good woman was modest. She was quiet. She covered her head when she went out. She didn't speak with men. She tended her domestic tasks. She obeyed and served her husband. She was faithful to him. Above all, she gave him children. Better yet, sons.

I waited for Jesus to respond, but he dipped his trowel in the mortar and smoothed it over the stones. Had he ever prodded me to be a *good* woman? Not once.

I waited several moments and when he didn't speak, I turned to leave.

"Do you wish, then, to bed apart?" he asked.

"No, oh no. But I do wish to use the midwife's herbs. I . . . already take them."

His eyes held mine for so long, I fought not to look away. They were tinged with disappointment that slowly softened, then ebbed. He said, "Little Thunder, I won't judge the knowing in your heart or what choice you make."

It was the first time he spoke the pet name he would call me until the end. I accepted it as an endearment. He heard the quake that lived at my center, and he didn't seek to silence it.

vi.

The days he was away crept on tiny, unhurried feet. Sometimes in the evening my feeling of aloneness was so great, I snuck Delilah into our room and fed her citrus peels. Other times I carried my mat to the storeroom and slept beside Yaltha. I marked Jesus's absence with pebbles, adding one each day atop his sleeping mat, watching the little pile grow. Nine . . . ten . . . eleven.

On the twelfth day I woke knowing Jesus would return before dark, bearing some sort of propitious news. I couldn't concentrate on my tasks. In the afternoon, Mary came upon me staring idly at a spider that dangled from the lip of a water jug. "Are you well?" she asked.

"Jesus will come today. I know it."

She didn't question my certainty. She said, "I'll ready his meal."

I bathed myself and dabbed clove oil behind my ears. I let my hair loose and dressed in the dark blue tunic he loved. I poured wine and set out bread. Over and over I went to the doorway and looked toward the gate. A blaze of yellow on the hill . . . the first grains of darkness floating in the air . . . dusk skulking across the compound.

He arrived with the last trace of light, bearing his tools and enough wages to replenish our wheat stores and add a lamb to the stable. In the privacy of our room, he gathered me into an embrace. I could smell the weariness on him.

Filling his cup, I said, "What tidings do you bring?"

He described his days, the work he'd been hired to do.

"And Tabitha? Do have any word of her?"

He touched the bench beside him. "Sit."

Was the news so grave I must sit to receive it? I sank down close to him.

"I was hired by a man in Japha to fashion a new door for his house. Everyone in the village knew of Tabitha, including the man's wife, who said that few had ever seen her and most feared her. When I asked why this was, she said Tabitha was possessed by demons and kept locked inside."

This was not the favorable news I'd expected. "Would you take me to her?"

"She's no longer there, Ana. The woman said she was sold to a man from Jericho, a landowner."

"Sold? She's a slave in his house?"

"It seems so. I asked others in Japha about her and they told me the same story."

I laid my head in his lap and felt his hand stroke my back.

vii.

Throughout the year that followed, I grew accustomed to Jesus's absences. The temporary loss of him became less like a spear in my side and more of a splinter in my foot. I went about my chores, relieved when I'd completed them and could sit with Mary or Yaltha and beg for stories of Jesus's boyhood or tales of Alexandria. I thought sometimes of my parents, an hour's walk away, and of Judas, who was I knew not where, and a gnawing forlornness would rise in me. There'd been no word from any of them. I tried not to think of Tabitha, enslaved to a stranger.

Whenever Jesus was away, I wore the red thread on my wrist, as was my custom, but early in the spring, on a day when my mind could settle on nothing, I noticed how frayed the thread had become over the past year, so wizened I feared it would soon wear apart. Touching it with my fingertip, I assured myself that if such a thing happened, it would signify nothing ominous, but then I thought of the ink splotch in my incantation bowl, the gray cloud over my head. It was hard to imagine *that* meant nothing. No, I would not risk a broken thread. I undid the knot and slid my tattered bracelet into its goatskin pouch.

I was tightening the cord when I heard Mary shout from the courtyard, "Come quickly, Jesus has returned."

For the past two weeks he'd been in Besara making cabinets for a winemaker and staying with his sister, Salome. I knew Mary was anxious for news of her daughter.

"Salome is well," he reported when the flurry of greetings had subsided. "But I have bitter news. Her husband has a weakness in his leg and arm and a slur in his voice. He no longer leaves the house."

I looked at Mary, how she gathered herself, her arms wrapping about her sides, her body saying what her mouth did not: *Salome will be a widow soon.*

That night all of us except Judith and the children huddled about the cook fire speculating about Salome's husband and sharing stories. When the heat had nearly gone from the embers, James turned to Jesus. "Will you make the Passover pilgrimage for us this year?"

James, Simon, and Mary had traveled to the Temple in Jerusalem the year before while the rest of us stayed home to work and tend the animals. It was Jesus's turn to go, but he vacillated.

"I don't yet know," he said.

"But *someone* must go from our family," James responded, sounding annoyed. "Why do you hesitate? Can't you leave work behind for those few days?"

"It isn't that. I'm struggling to understand if God wishes me to go at all. The Temple has become a den of thieves, James."

James rolled his eyes skyward. "Must you always concern yourself with such things? We have a duty to sacrifice an animal at Passover."

"Yes, and the poor bring their animals and the priests refuse to accept them, claiming they're blemished, and then they charge exorbitant prices for another one."

"What he says is true," Simon offered.

"Shall we speak of something else?" Mary said.

But Jesus pressed on. "The priests insist on having their own currency and when the poor try to exchange their coins, the money changers charge them excessive rates!"

James stood. "Would you force me to make the trip again this year? Do you care more for the poor than your brother?"

Jesus answered, "Aren't the poor also my brothers and sisters?"

THE NEXT MORNING as the sun stirred awake, Jesus trekked into the hills to pray. It was his daily habit. At other times I would find him sitting cross-legged on the floor with his prayer shawl drawn over his head, unmoving, eyes closed. It had been so since we married, this devotion, this feasting on God, and I'd never minded it, but today, seeing him walk away in the half-light, I understood what until now I'd only glimpsed. God was the ground beneath him, the sky over him, the air he breathed, the water he drank. It made me uneasy.

I prepared his breakfast, trimming corn from the husk and parching it over the fire, the sweet aroma drifting over the compound. I glanced repeatedly toward the gate, as if God lurked out there, ready to pluck my husband from me.

When he returned, we sat together beneath the olive tree. I watched him wrap bread around a hunk of goat cheese and eat hungrily, saving the corn, his favorite, for last. He was quiet.

Finally, he said, "When I saw my brother-in-law's infirmity, I was moved with pity. Everywhere I look, there's suffering, Ana, and I spend my days making cabinets for a rich man."

"You spend your days caring for your family," I said, perhaps too sharply.

He smiled. "Don't worry, Little Thunder. I'll do what I must." He wrapped an arm about me. "Passover is soon. Let us go to Jerusalem."

viii.

We took the pilgrim road, leaving the green hills of Galilee and descending into the dense thickets of the Jordan River valley, traveling through stretches of wilderness filled with jackals. At night we put out the fire early and, clutching our staffs, slept beneath little lean-tos we fashioned from brush. We were on our way to Bethany, just outside Jerusalem, where we would lodge with Jesus's friends Lazarus, Martha, and Mary.

The Jericho road was the last, most treacherous part of our journey, not because of jackals, but because of the robbers who hid in the barren cliffs that lined the valley. At least the road was well traveled; for miles now we'd trodden behind a man with two sons and a priest wearing an elaborate robe, but I couldn't help feeling uneasy. Sensing my nervousness, Jesus began telling me stories of his family's Passover visits with his friends in Bethany when he was a boy.

"When I was eight," Jesus said, "Lazarus and I came upon a dove merchant who was treating his birds cruelly, poking them with sticks and feeding them pebbles. We waited until he left his stall, opened the cages, and set them free before he returned. He accused us of stealing and our fathers were compelled to pay him a full price. My family was forced to remain in Bethany two extra weeks while Father and I worked to pay the debt. At the time I thought it was worth it. The sight of the birds flying away . . ."

Imagining them flapping off to freedom, I didn't notice the way his steps slowed and his story ceased midsentence. "*Ana.*" He pointed toward a bend in the distance, at a heap of white robe spattered with red lying on the side of the road. I thought, *Someone has cast off his garment.* Then I saw the shape of a person beneath it.

Ahead of us, the father and his sons and then the priest came to a halt, judging, it seemed, whether the person was dead or alive.

"He's been set upon by robbers," Jesus said, scanning the rocky terrain as if they might still be nearby. "Come." He walked quickly, while I scampered to keep up. Already the others had passed by the wounded man, giving him a wide berth.

Jesus knelt beside the figure as I stood behind him dredging up the courage to look. A soft moan drifted up. "It's a woman," Jesus said.

I gazed down then, seeing her but not seeing her, my mind unwilling to yield to what was before me. "My Lord and my God, it's *Tabitha*!"

Her face was smeared with blood, but I saw no wound. "The gash is on her scalp," Jesus said, pointing to a mass of sticky, dark blood in her hair.

I stooped and wiped her face with my robe. Her eyes fluttered. She stared at me, blinking, and I was certain she knew me. The stub of her tongue thrashed about in her mouth, looking for a way to speak my name.

"Is she dead?" a voice called. A tall young man approached. I could tell from his dialect and dress he was a Samaritan and I tensed reflexively. Jews had nothing to do with Samaritans, regarding them as worse than Gentiles.

"She's wounded," Jesus said.

The man pulled out his waterskin, bent, and tipped it to Tabitha's lips. Her mouth opened, her neck arched upward. She looked like a featherless baby bird craning for food. Jesus dropped his hand onto the man's shoulder. "You're Samaritan, yet you give a Galilean your water."

The man made no reply and Jesus unwound his girdle and set about binding Tabitha's wound. The Samaritan hoisted her onto Jesus's back, and we walked the rest of the way with excruciating slowness.

ix.

I heard the slap of sandals in the courtyard, then women's voices, high-pitched and eager. "Coming . . . We're coming."

Tabitha groaned. I said, "You're safe now."

Throughout the long, torturous day, Tabitha had appeared inert, as if sleeping, rousing a little only when the men transferred her from one to the other, and each time I'd patted her face and offered her water. The Samaritan had parted with us a short while before we'd reached Bethany, pressing a copper coin into my hands, a sesterce. "See that she has lodging and food," he'd said.

I began to protest, but Jesus spoke up. "Let him give his coin." I dropped it into my pouch.

Now the creak of a latch and two women appeared, short, thick-waisted with round, plump faces that were nearly identical. Their exuberance faded as they glimpsed Tabitha, but they asked no questions and hurried us to a room, where we laid her on a pillowed bed mat.

"I'll tend her," the one called Mary said to us. "Go, take the evening meal with Martha and Lazarus. You must be hungry and tired."

When I tarried, reluctant to leave Tabitha, Jesus gave me a little tug.

Lazarus was not as I'd expected. He was slight of build with a sallow face and weak, watery eyes. So unlike his sisters. He and Jesus greeted each other like brothers, kissing cheeks and embracing. We gathered about a round slat table that rested on the floor, an arrangement new to me. In Sepphoris we'd reclined on plush couches around a long table. In Nazareth we had no table at all, but held bowls in our lap and sat on the ground.

"Who's the injured girl?" Lazarus asked.

"Her name is Tabitha," I answered. "I knew her as a girl in Sepphoris. She was my friend, my only friend. She was sent away to live with relatives, who sold her to a man in Jericho. I don't know how she came to be beaten and left on the side of the road."

Lazarus replied, "She may stay with us as long as she wishes."

THE HOUSE WAS clay-baked with tiled floors, dyed woolen mats, and its own mikvah, an abode far better than our house in Nazareth, but there was only one room for guests and that night Jesus slept on the roof, while I made my bed beside Tabitha.

While she slept, I lay in the dark and listened to her breath, a croaking sound that erupted at times into puffs and moans. Her small, lissome body, the one that had danced with such grace and abandon, was bony and clenched as if in a perpetual state of recoil. I could see the protuberances of her cheekbones like sharp little hills on her face. Mary had bathed her and dressed her in a clean tunic and covered her wound with a plaster of olive oil and onion to draw the pus. The sour smell of it hung over the room. I longed to speak to her. She'd wakened earlier, but only long enough to drink a full cup of lemon water.

I thought of Lazarus's words. Until he'd spoken them, I'd not considered where Tabitha would go. What would become of her? If I had my way, I'd take her to live with us in Nazareth, but even if the entire family welcomed her, which was unlikely given that Judith was Judith and James was James, there was little room left in our cramped compound. Already Yaltha slept in the storeroom. Simon was betrothed to a girl named Berenice, who would soon join the household, and it seemed likely Salome might return any day as a widow.

When Tabitha stirred on the mat, I lit the lamp and stroked her cheek. "I'm here. It's Ana."

"I 'ough I 'ream you."

What is she saying? What was left of her tongue could provide only the bare rudiments of a word—I would have to guess at the rest. As she repeated herself, I concentrated. "You thought you dreamed me?"

She nodded, smiling a little, not taking her eyes from me. *How long,* I thought, *has it been since she was listened to, much less understood?*

"My husband and I found you on the Jericho road."

She touched her bandage, then gazed about the room.

"You're in Bethany, in the house of my husband's closest friends," I told her, and realized suddenly she would think my husband was Nathaniel. "I was wed two years ago, not to Nathaniel, but to a stonemason and carpenter from Nazareth." Her eyes brightened with curiosity—the twitch of her old self still inside there—but her lids were weighted with fatigue and the chamomile Mary had put in her lemon water. "Sleep now," I told her. "I'll tell you more later."

I dipped my finger in the bowl of olive oil Mary had left and touched it to her forehead. "I anoint you, Tabitha, friend of Ana," I whispered, and watched the memory float into her face.

x.

In the days leading up to Passover, the wound on Tabitha's head formed a healing scab. Strength seeped into her limbs. She left her bed and ventured into the courtyard to take meals with the rest of us, eating ravenously, at times laboring to swallow. Her face started to lose its hills and valleys.

I scarcely left my friend's side. When we were alone, I filled the silence with stories of what had transpired since we'd parted . . . burying my scrolls, meeting Jesus at the cave, Nathaniel's death, befriending Phasaelis, Herod Antipas and the mosaic. She listened with parted lips, offering up little grunts, and when I described the scheme to make me

Antipas's concubine and how close I came to being stoned, she let out a cry, took my hand, and kissed each knuckle in turn. "I'm scorned in Sepphoris and Nazareth both," I said. I wanted her to know she was not alone—I was a mamzer, too.

She prodded me to speak of Jesus, and I related the strange way I had come to marry him and the sort of man he was. I told her about the compound in Nazareth, about Yaltha, Judith, my mother-in-law. I talked and talked, but always pausing to say, "Now, tell me, what has your life been like these last years?" and each time she waved away my query.

Then one afternoon, as Tabitha, Mary, and I stood together in the courtyard gazing out at the olive trees in the Kidron Valley, she abruptly began to speak. We'd just finished preparing the bitter herbs for the Passover meal—horseradish, tansy, and horehound, symbols of the bitterness our people experienced during their slavery in Egypt—and I couldn't help but think that was what provoked her to blurt out her own tribulation.

She spoke a garbled sentence I couldn't interpret.

"You ran away?" Mary responded. The two of them had grown close during the hours Mary had spoon-fed her stew.

Tabitha's head bobbed furiously. Through broken words and gesticulation, she told us she'd run away from the man in Jericho who'd purchased her. She mimicked slaps to her face and arms that had been delivered by the man's wife.

"But where were you running to?" I asked.

She labored to pronounce Jerusalem. Then she cupped her hands into a bowl and lifted them up as if begging.

"You meant to become a beggar in Jerusalem? Oh, Tabitha."

Mary said, "You will not have to beg on the streets. We'll make certain of that."

Tabitha smiled at us. She never spoke of it again.

. . .

THE NEXT DAY I heard a high-pitched pinging inside the house. I was in the courtyard helping Martha bake the unleavened bread for Passover, while Jesus had gone off with Lazarus to purchase a lamb from a Pharisee merchant on the outskirts of Bethany. Tomorrow Jesus and I would take the poor creature to Jerusalem to be sacrificed on the Temple altar as required, then bring it home for Martha to roast.

Ping-ping. I set down the dough bowl and followed the sound to Tabitha's room. My friend sat on the floor, holding a lyre, plucking each string one by one. Mary took her hand and brushed it across all the strings at once, setting loose a rippling sound—wind and water and bells. Tabitha laughed, eyes shining, wonder moving through her face.

Looking up at me, she lifted the lyre and pointed to Mary.

"Mary gave you the lyre?"

"I haven't played it since I was a girl," Mary said. "I thought Tabitha would like to have it."

I stood there a long while and watched her experiment with the strings. *Mary, you have given her a voice.*

xi.

We crossed the valley with the little lamb on Jesus's shoulders and entered Jerusalem through the Fountain Gate near the Pool of Siloam. We planned to cleanse ourselves there before entering the Temple, but we found the pool glutted with people. A score of cripples lay on the terraces waiting for some sympathetic soul to lower them into the water.

"We can purify ourselves at one of the mikvahs near the Temple," I said, feeling repulsed by all the infirmities and foul bodies.

Ignoring me, Jesus thrust the lamb into my arms. He lifted a paralytic boy from his litter; his legs were twisted like tree roots.

"What are you *doing*?" I said, trailing after him.

"Only what I'd want if I were the boy," he replied, carrying him down into the water. I clutched the squirming lamb and watched as Jesus kept the child afloat while he splashed and bathed.

Naturally, his deed set off shouts and pleas from the other cripples, and I knew we would be here awhile. My husband bore every one of them into the pool.

Afterward, dripping, invigorated, Jesus delighted in chasing after me, shaking his head, imparting a spray of water that made me squeal.

WE WOUND THROUGH the tight alleys of the lower city with peddlers, beggars, and fortune-tellers tugging at our robes, finally moving into the upper echelons, where the wealthy citizens and priests lived in houses grander than the finest ones in Sepphoris. When we neared the Temple, the crowds swelled, along with the smell of blood and animal flesh. I wrapped my scarf over my nose, but it didn't help much. Roman soldiers were everywhere; revolts and riots were a danger at Passover. It seemed each year some messiah or revolutionist was crucified.

I'd not laid eyes on the Temple in years, and the sight of it sprawled across the mount ahead brought me to a halt. I'd forgotten the vastness of it, the sheer splendor. Its white stones and gold filigree blazed in the sun, a spectacle of such grandiosity, it was easy to believe God dwelled there. *Does he?* I thought. *Perhaps like Sophia, he prefers a quiet stream somewhere in the valley.*

As if our thoughts were conjoined, Jesus said, "The first time we met in the cave, we spoke of the Temple. Do you remember? You asked me if God lived there or if he lived inside people."

"You answered, 'Can he not live in both?'"

"And you said, 'Can he not live *everywhere*? Let us set him free.' That's when I knew I would love you, Ana. That's when I knew."

. . .

AS WE CLIMBED the grand staircase into the Temple, the cacophony of bleating lambs in the Court of Gentiles was deafening. Hundreds of them were crowded into a makeshift enclosure, waiting to be purchased. The stench of dung burned my nostrils. The crowds pushed and shoved and I felt Jesus's hand tighten on mine.

Approaching the tables where the merchants and money changers sat, Jesus paused a moment to stare. "There is the den of thieves," he said to me.

We pushed our way through the Gate Beautiful into the Court of Women, then wound through the masses to the circular steps where my mother had once restrained me from going any farther. *Only men . . . only men.*

"Wait for me here," Jesus said. I watched him climb the steps and meld into the crush of men beyond the gate. The lamb was a white blur bouncing above the fray.

Jesus returned with the animal hanging lifeless about his shoulders, dribbles of blood on his tunic. I tried not to look at the animal's eyes, two round black stones.

Passing back by the money changers' tables, we saw an old woman weeping. She wore a widow's robe and blew her nose on the folds of it. "I have only two sesterce," she cried, and hearing this, Jesus stopped abruptly and turned around.

"Three are required!" the money changer snapped. "Two to purchase the lamb, one to change your money into Temple coins."

"But I have only two," she said, holding the coins out to him. "Please. How am I to observe Passover?"

The money changer pushed her hand away. "Go, leave me!"

Jesus's jaw tightened, his face dark red, the color of ocher. I thought for a moment he would seize the man and give him a shake, or perhaps give the widow our own lamb, but surely he wouldn't deprive *us* of Passover. "Do you have the sesterce from the Samaritan?" he asked.

I pulled it from my pouch and watched as he strode over and slammed the coin onto the table before the money changer. The din was too frenetic for me to hear what Jesus was saying, but I could tell he was expounding on the shortcomings of the Temple, gesturing indignantly, the slaughtered lamb on his back, jostling about.

Can God not live everywhere? Let us set him free. That's when I knew I would love you, Ana.

Those words welled up in me, and I remembered the story he'd told me just before we found Tabitha on the road, the one in which he'd freed the doves from their cages. I didn't pause to think. I walked to the crowded paddock that held the lambs, undid the latch, and yanked open the gate. Out they poured, a white flood.

Frantic merchants rushed to herd them back into the pen. A man pointed at me. "There. She's the one who opened the gate. Stop her!"

"You rob poor widows," I shouted back and fled into the small pandemonium—lambs and people merging like two rivers, bleating and shouting.

"Stop her!"

"We must go," I said, finding Jesus at the money changer's table. "*Now!*"

Scooping up a passing lamb, he placed it into the widow's arms. We hurried from the court, down the staircase, and into the street.

"Was it you who set them loose?" he asked.

"It was."

"What possessed you?"

"*You* did," I said.

xii.

The day we departed Bethany, I found Tabitha in her room strumming her lyre. Already she could make it sing. I paused unnoticed in the doorway as she sang a new song she seemed in the midst of composing. The best I could tell, it was about a lost pearl. When she looked up and saw me, her eyes were glittering.

She would remain and I would go. I hated to part, but I knew she would be better off here with Lazarus, Mary, and Martha. They'd made her into a little sister.

"She'll be safer here, too," Jesus had pointed out. "In Nazareth she would be too close to Japha." I hadn't considered this. If she came to Nazareth, her relatives would surely hear of her presence and come for her. They would send her back to the man in Jericho or sell her all over again.

"Before I go, I want to tell you something," I said to her.

She set down the lyre.

"Years ago, after that day I came to your house, I wrote down your story on papyrus. I wrote about your ferocious spirit, how you stood in the street and cried out what happened to you and were silenced for it. I think every pain in this world wants to be witnessed, Tabitha. That's why you shouted about your rape on the street and it's why I wrote it down."

She stared at me unblinking, then pulled me to her and clung there.

WHEN WE CAME through the compound gate in Nazareth, Yaltha, Mary, Judith, James, and Simon hurried to greet us. Even Judith kissed my cheek. Mary linked her arm through her son's and led us to the large stone basin across the courtyard. It was the custom in our household that those who remained behind would wash the feet of those who'd made the Passover pilgrimage. Mary motioned for Judith to remove my sandals, but my sister-in-law, misunderstanding, perhaps deliberately, perhaps not, bent and untied Jesus's sandal strap instead. Mary shrugged, then did me the honor of bathing my feet herself, water splashing cold on my toes, her thumbs circling my ankles.

"How was your time in the Temple?" James asked.

"A most remarkable thing occurred," Jesus said. "There was a stampede of lambs in the Court of Gentiles. Somehow they escaped their pen." He grinned at me.

"It was . . ." I searched for the right word.

"Unforgettable," he said. Beneath the water, his foot nudged mine.

xiii.

One fall morning, I vomited my breakfast. Even after my stomach emptied, I remained bent over the waste pot retching plain air. When the heaving subsided, I washed my face, cleaned the spatter from my tunic, then went on slow, solemn feet to find my aunt. The blackseed oil had finally failed me.

Over the past few years, the compound had begun to spill over with people. Salome's husband had died, and we'd all traveled to Besara for the funeral banquet, then brought her home, childless and bereft, her husband's meager properties having gone to his brother. The following year, Simon's wife, Berenice, had arrived, and then came a baby, to which Judith had responded by producing her third. Now there would be one more.

It wasn't long past daybreak, and Jesus was off in the hills with his prayer shawl. I was glad he was absent—I didn't want him to see my stricken face.

Yaltha was sitting on the floor of the storeroom eating chickpeas and garlic. The smell convulsed my stomach and nearly sent me back to the waste pot. After she set aside the bowl and its vile-smelling contents, I lay down beside her, resting my head in her lap. I said, "I'm with child."

She rubbed my back and neither of us spoke for a while. Then she asked, "And you are certain?"

"My bleeding is late, but I gave it little thought—it has been late many times. It wasn't until I retched my breakfast that I knew. I'm pregnant, I know it." I sat up, suddenly a little frantic. "Jesus will be back from his prayers soon, and I can't tell him, not yet, not when I'm like *this*." I felt possessed by a strange, almost debilitating numbness. Beneath it, though, disappointment, fear, and anger rattled against some lid inside me.

"Give yourself the time you need. If he questions your demeanor, say your belly is unsettled. There's truth in that."

I got to my feet. "For six years I've swallowed that hellish oil," I said, the anger leaking out. "Why would it fail me now?"

"No preventative is perfect." She gave me a mischievous look. "And you have certainly tested the limits of it."

JESUS TRAVELED TO TABOR the following day to find work, returning four days later. I met him at the gate, kissed his cheeks and hands, then his lips. "You are in need of a haircut," I said.

The sun was going down, a tiny rampage of color in the sky—red, orange, indigo. He squinted at it and the smile formed, the one I loved. "Am I?" he said. His locks hung about his shoulders. He combed through them with his fingers. "I thought my hair was just right."

"Then I'm sorry to tell you that tomorrow morning I will accompany you into the hills and wait while you pray, and then I shall cut your hair."

"I've always cut my own hair," he said, giving me a curious look.

"Which explains why it's so unkempt," I teased.

I wanted a way to steal him away from the compound, that was all—away from all the people and the busyness so we could be alone and uninterrupted. I felt like he guessed this, that he sensed I had some other intention besides his hair.

"I'm happy you're home," I added.

He lifted me up then and swung me about, which precipitated a wave of nausea. My unsettled stomach, as Yaltha had called it, didn't confine itself to the mornings. I closed my eyes and pressed my hand to my mouth, letting the other one float instinctively to the new little mound of my belly.

He watched me in that deep, probing way of his.

"Are you well?" he asked.

"Yes, only a little tired."

"Then we'll go and rest." But he lingered, gazing at the bloodshot sky. "Look," he said and pointed to the east, where a slivered moon rose, so pale it seemed like nothing more than a winter breath. "The sun is setting while the moon rises."

He said the words in a deliberate way, and I felt like I knew what he was saying, that this was a sign to us. My mind flashed to the story of Isis that Yaltha had told Tabitha and me so long ago. *Think of it*, she'd said. *Some part of you might die and a new self will rise up to take its place.*

It seemed I was seeing my old life die before me in a splurge of color and a faint new life rising up. It was a thing of wonder, and the anguish I'd felt over having the child left me.

"DON'T TRIM TOO MUCH," he said.

"Like Samson, do you believe your strength lies in your hair?" I asked.

"Like Delilah, are you bent on shearing me?"

Our banter was trifling and playful, but there was a thin layer of tension beneath it, as if we were both waiting to let out our breaths.

Earlier, we'd found a grassy hillock on which to sit and he'd left me

while he went apart to pray, but he'd come back sooner than I'd expected—
I doubt he could've repeated the Shema more than a dozen times. I'd
brought Yaltha's Egyptian scissors. I held up the long bronze blades.

"I trust you know how to work this thing," he said. "I'm at your mercy."

Kneeling behind him, I squeezed the blades, snipping off the ends of
his hair. They drifted down like dark, curled wood shavings. I could
smell his skin, brown and earthen.

When it grew quiet, I set down the scissors. "There's something I
must tell you." I waited for him to turn and lift his eyes to mine. "I am
with child."

"It is true, then," he said.

"You're not surprised?"

"Last evening, when you placed your hand to your belly, I thought it
might be so." He closed his eyes for a moment and when he opened
them, they were bright with worry. "Ana, tell me truly—are you glad to
have this child?"

"I am content," I said.

And I was. By now, after such a long drought of ink, I could barely
remember why I had taken the blackseed oil at all.

WHEN WE ENTERED THE COURTYARD, Jesus summoned everyone to
the olive tree, which is where the family gathered to announce betroth-
als, pregnancies, and births, and to discuss matters of household business.
Mary and Salome came smelling of mulberries, followed by Judith and
Berenice and their small flock of children. James and Simon wandered
over from the workshop. Yaltha needed no summons—she'd been waiting there when we arrived. Everyone but my aunt appeared curious, but
unsuspecting—it wouldn't have occurred to them I carried a child. I was
Jesus's barren wife.

I clung to Jesus's arm.

"We have good news," he said, turning his eyes to his mother. "Ana is with child!" Several strange moments passed while no one moved, and then Mary and Salome rushed to me, Mary bending to kiss my belly and Salome smiling at me, so much longing in her face that I almost looked away. I thought how incongruous it was that I, who hadn't wanted a child, should conceive one, while Salome, who yearned for one, could not.

Simon and James slapped Jesus's back and dragged him to the center of the courtyard, where the three of them folded their arms about one another's shoulders and danced. His brothers let out whoops and shouts—*Praise God, who has poured his blessing on you. May God grant you a son.*

How happy my husband looked out there, his uneven hair swirling about his cheeks.

xiv.

The months that followed our announcement passed quickly and without incident. Even when I couldn't hold down my meals, when my back throbbed from my ever-protruding belly, I rose each day to carry out my chores. In my fifth month, I began to feel a little foot or an elbow ripple inside me, the strangest of sensations, and I would experience a burst of love for the child that shocked me in its intensity. When my seventh month arrived, I grew ridiculously cumbersome. Once, observing my struggling efforts to sit up on my sleeping mat, Jesus playfully likened me to an overturned beetle, then placed his arms beneath mine and hoisted me up. How we laughed at my awkwardness. Yet at odd hours in the night when he was away and I couldn't sleep, I sometimes felt like pieces of me were sloughing away—Ana, the scribe of lost stories, Ana and the tiny sun.

. . .

BIRTHING PAINS WOKE ME before dawn. Lying on my mat on the earthen floor, muddled with sleep and confusion and a goring pain in my back, I reached for Jesus in the darkness and found his mat empty. It took a moment to remember he'd departed for Capernaum three days ago.

He's not here. Our baby would come too soon, and he was not here.

A spasm encircled my belly, tightening. Pressing my fist against my mouth, I listened to a moan escape between my fingers, a quashed, eerie sound. Tighter, tighter, the pain bit down, and I saw how it would be, bearing a child. The fangs would chomp and let go, chomp and let go, and there would be nothing to do but give myself to the slow devouring. I placed my arms around my swollen belly and rocked side to side. Fear sloshed in my chest. I'd only been with child seven months.

For the past few months, Jesus had helped to keep us fed by traveling to Capernaum to fish on the Sea of Galilee. He relied on his comradery with the local fishermen, who took him out on their boats to cast nets and let him barter his portion of the catch for whatever we most needed.

I couldn't be angry with him for his absence. He may not have detested our separations as much as I did, but neither did he relish them. This time he'd promised to return in less than a month, well before my time came. He couldn't have known the child would come in this precipitous way. He would be distraught he wasn't here.

Rolling onto my side, I pushed to my knees, then my feet, reaching for the wall to brace myself as the birth waters broke onto my legs. I began to shake, first my hands, then my shoulders and thighs, the uncontrollable palsy of fear.

I lit the lamp and made my way to the storeroom. "Aunt, wake up," I cried. "Aunt! The baby is coming." She didn't pause for her sandals, but hurried to me in the flickering dark, slinging the midwife bag over her arm. She was fifty-two now, stooped, her face a drawn pouch. She took my face in her hands and measured my apprehension. "Don't fear; the baby will live or it will not. We must let life be life."

No assurance, no platitude, no promise of God's mercy. Just a stark reminder that death was part of life. She offered me nothing but a way to accept whatever came—*Let life be life*. There was a quiet relinquishment in the words.

As Yaltha led me back to my room, she paused to rap on Mary's door.

Jesus's mother shared her room with Salome, and I heard them behind the door, lighting lamps and speaking in low tones. I'd been careful to specify who I wished to attend me. Not Judith, not Berenice. Not the horrid, toothless midwife. Salome, Mary, and Yaltha—this trinity alone would be at my side.

When I was born, my mother had sat on a resplendent chair with an opening in the seat, but I would squat over a crude hole dug in the dirt floor of a mud-walled room. Yaltha had scooped it out the day Jesus left, as if she knew it would be needed early. As I sat before it now on a low stool, pain coiling about my torso, I wished for my mother to be here. I'd seen or heard nothing of her since my marriage and I'd hardly cared, but now . . .

Mary and Salome entered bearing vessels of water, wine, and oil, while Yaltha laid out the contents of the midwife pouch on a piece of flax. Salt, swaddling strips, a snipping knife, a sea sponge, a bowl for the afterbirth, herbs to stop the bleeding, a biting stick, and finally a pillow covered with undyed gray wool on which to lay the newborn.

Mary made an altar, laying an old plank of oak within my view. She stacked three stones on it, one on top of the other. No one acknowledged it—it was simply done whenever women labored to bring forth a life. An offering to Mother God. I watched as she drizzled a libation of Delilah's goat milk over the stones.

As the hours passed, the early summer heat rose and the moon in my belly waxed and waned. The women hovered—Mary, a ballast at my back; Salome, the angel at my side; and Yaltha, the sentinel between my legs. It came to me then that my mother wouldn't want to be here, and even if she did, she would never set foot in such a lowly abode. Yaltha, Mary, Salome—here were my mothers.

No one spoke of the cloud that hung everywhere in the room, the knowledge that the baby was arriving too soon. I heard them droning prayers but the words were far away. There were violent seizures of pain and the short, winded respites between them, and that was all there was.

Nearing the ninth hour, squatting over the hole, I pushed the baby from my body. She slipped soundlessly into my aunt's hands. I watched Yaltha turn her upside down and gently thump her back. She repeated the action once, twice, three times, four times. The baby didn't move or cry or draw a breath. My aunt slid her finger into the tiny mouth to clear it of mucus. She blew air into her face. She held her by the feet and thumped her harder, harder.

Finally, she laid the child on the pillow. She was tiny as a kitten. Her lips lapis blue. Her stillness terrible.

A sob broke from Salome's lips.

Yaltha said, "The child doesn't live, Ana."

As my aunt tied and severed the birth cord, Mary wept.

"Life will be life and death will be death," I whispered, and with those words, grief filled the empty place in me where the baby had lain. I would carry it there like a secret all the days of my life.

"Do you wish to bestow a name on her?" Yaltha asked.

I looked at my daughter lying wilted on the pillow. "Susanna," I said. The name meant lily.

LATE IN THE AFTERNOON on the same day I gave birth, I wrapped my daughter in the dark blue dress I'd worn when I married, for it was the best cloth I had, and walked with Yaltha and Jesus's family to the cave where his father was buried. I insisted on carrying the baby in my arms, though the custom was for an infant to be placed in a basket or upon a small bier. I was weak from giving birth only hours before, and Mary walked with her hand beneath my elbow as if I might crumple. She, Salome, Judith, and Berenice wept and wailed. I made no sound.

At the cave, as we repeated the Kaddish, Judith and James's six-year-old daughter, Sarah, tugged on my tunic. "May I hold her?" she asked.

I didn't want to relinquish my baby, but I knelt beside her and placed Susanna in her arms. Judith immediately plucked the blue bundle from her daughter and returned it to me. "I will have to take Sarah to the mikvah now to cleanse her," she whispered. She didn't say it unkindly, but it stung. I smiled at Sarah and felt her little arms wind around my waist.

As they intoned the Shema, I thought of Jesus. When he returned, I would tell him how our daughter looked lying on the pillow, the smear of dark hair, the trellis of blue on her eyelids, her nails like pearl shavings. I would tell him that as we walked to the cave through the barley harvest, the workers ceased their labor and stood silent as we passed. I would describe how I laid her in a cleft inside the cave and when I bent to kiss her, she smelled of myrrh and coriander leaves. I would say, I loved her the way you love God, with all my heart and soul and might.

As James and Simon pushed the stone slab across the cave opening to seal it, I cried out for the first time.

Salome rushed to my side. "Oh, sister, you will have another child."

IN THE DAYS THAT FOLLOWED, I remained in my room, separated from the others. Childbirth rendered a woman ceremonially unclean for forty days if she'd delivered a male child and twice as long if the baby was female. My confinement would last until the month of Elul, when the blister of summer was well formed. We would, according to the custom, then go to Jerusalem to offer a sacrifice and be pronounced clean by a priest, after which I would reenter the cycle of endless chores.

I was grateful for my solitude. It gave me time to mourn. I slept with grief and woke to it. It was always there, a black strap around my heart. I didn't ask God why my daughter had died. I knew he couldn't help it. Life was life, death was death. It was the fault of no one. I asked only for someone to find my husband and bring him home.

Days passed and no one sent for him. Salome told me James and Simon argued against it. The day after the burial, the publicans had come to Nazareth and taken a half portion of our wheat, barley, oil, olives, and wine, along with two of the chickens, and Jesus's brothers were deeply troubled over the loss. According to Salome, they had scoured the village for carpentry work, but in the wake of the tax collectors no one had the resources to pay for a repaired ceiling beam or new door lintel.

I asked Salome to summon James. He appeared hours later, standing beyond the doorway so as not to become fouled. Seated on the bench across the room, I said, "I beg you, James, send for my husband. He must come and mourn his daughter."

He spoke not to me but to a scrim of sunlight on the window. "We all wish for him to be here, but it's better he should remain in Capernaum for the entire month as he planned. We are desperate to resupply our food stores."

"We don't live by bread alone," I said, repeating words I'd heard Jesus speak.

"But still, we must *eat*," he said.

"Jesus would want to be here to grieve his child."

He would not be moved. "You would have me force him to choose between feeding his family and grieving his child?" he said. "I would think he'd be glad to have the burden removed from him."

"But James, it's *his* decision. His child has died, not yours. If you take the choice from him, he will be angered."

My words struck.

He sighed. "I'll send Simon to him. We'll let Jesus decide."

Capernaum was a day and half walk. I couldn't expect to see my husband for four days, three at best. I knew Simon would press him with news of the tax collectors and describe our food stores with direness. He would urge Jesus to delay his return.

Surely, though, he would come.

XV.

The following day, Yaltha came to my room carrying the broken pieces of a large clay pot in the folds of her robe.

"I broke it with a mallet," she said.

As she spread the fragments across the rug, I gaped at her in astonishment. "You did this on purpose? Why, Aunt?"

"A broken pot is almost as good as a stack of papyrus. When I lived among the Therapeutae, we often wrote on the shards—inventories, letters, contracts, psalms, missals of all kinds."

"Pots are precious here. They're not easily replaced."

"It's only the pot for watering the animals. There are other pots that can replace it."

"All the rest are stone pots, and they are pure—you can't use them for the animals. Oh, Aunt, you know this." I gave her a stern, baffled look. "For you to shatter a pot just for me to write upon . . . they'll think you're possessed."

"Then let them take me to a healer and have the demon cast out. You just make certain I didn't break the pot for no reason."

For the past two days, my chest had been bound with tight rags, but now I felt milk engorge my breasts, followed by a thick clot of pain. Dark, wet circles appeared on my robe.

"Child," Yaltha said, for even though I was a woman, she still sometimes called me by her pet name. "There's no worse feeling than one's breasts filled with milk and no one to suckle."

The words opened a raw, furious place in me. She wanted me to write? My daughter was dead. My writing was dead, too. *One day* had never come. *I* was the shattered pieces on the floor. Life had taken a mallet to me.

I lashed out. "How would you know how I feel?"

She reached for me, but I wrenched away and dropped onto my bed mat.

Yaltha knelt down and cradled me with her body as I wept for the first time since Susanna had died. When I was spent, she re-bound my breasts with clean rags and wiped my face. She brought a wineskin and filled my cup and we sat awhile in silence.

Out in the courtyard the women were in the heat and throes of work. Curls of smoke from the dung fire drifted in through the window. Berenice was shouting at Salome to return to the village well for more water, blaming her for the parched plot of vegetables. Salome yelled back that she was not a pack donkey. Mary complained that the pot used to water the animals had gone missing.

Yaltha said, "I do know what it's like to have full breasts and no baby."

I remembered then the story she'd told me many years ago of birthing two sons, neither of whom had lived, and of her husband, Ruebel, who'd punished her for it with his fists. Remorse scorched my cheeks. "Forgive me. I forgot your dead sons. My words were cruel."

"Your words were understandable. I remind you of my loss only because I wish to tell you something. Something I left out of my story." She drew a deep breath. Outside the sun dipped and the room guttered.

"There were two sons who died in infancy, yes. But there was also a daughter who lived."

"*A daughter.*"

Her eyes brimmed—a rare sight. "When I was sent to the Therapeutae, she was two years old. Her name is Chaya."

All at once a memory unwound. "Back in Sepphoris when you contracted the fever sickness, there was one night when you were lost in delirium and you called me by her name. You called me Chaya."

"Did I? I can't say I'm surprised. If Chaya is alive, she would be twenty-one years, almost as old as you. She had unruly hair like yours. I often think of her when I look at you. I've dreaded telling you about her. I feared what you would think of me. I left her behind."

"Why do you tell me about her now?" I didn't mean it cruelly. I truly wished to know.

"I should have told you long ago. I do so now because the death of your daughter has made my loss fresh again. I thought it might be a small solace for you to know I've suffered in a similar way, that I comprehend what it is to lose a daughter. Oh, child, I want no secrets between us."

I couldn't be angered by her deceit—it didn't come from treachery. We women harbor our intimacies in locked places in our bodies. They are ours to relinquish when we choose.

"You may ask me the question," she said. "Go ahead."

I knew which one she meant. I said, "Why did you leave her?"

"I could tell you that I had no choice, and I think that's mostly true; at least I believed it true at the time. It's hard now to look back and know for certain. I told you once it was widely believed in Alexandria that I killed my husband with sorcery and poison, and for that I was sent away to the Therapeutae. They didn't take in children, and I went to them anyway. Who can say now whether I might have found a way to keep my daughter? I did what I did." Her face shone with pain as if her loss had only just happened.

"What became of her? Where did she go?"

She shook her head. "My brother Haran assured me he would care for her. I believed him. During all those years I was with the Therapeutae, I sent him many messages asking about her, without any response. After eight years, when Haran finally agreed I could leave the Therapeutae if I left Egypt, I begged to take her with me."

"And he refused? How could he keep her from you?"

"He said he'd given her out for adoption. He would not tell me to whom or where she lived. For days I pleaded with him, until he threatened to revive the old charges against me. In the end I left. I left her behind."

I pictured the girl, Chaya, with hair like mine. It was impossible to imagine what I might have done had I been in my aunt's place.

"I made my peace with what happened," she said. "I reasoned that Chaya was wanted and cared for. She had a family. Perhaps she didn't even remember me. She was only two when I last saw her."

She stood abruptly, stepping around the arrangement of broken pottery. She rubbed her fingers as if trying to unpeel them.

"You don't look at peace," I told her.

"You're right, the peace has left me. Since Susanna died, Chaya has come every night in my dreams. She stands on a summit and begs me to come to her. Her voice is like the song of a flute. When I wake, it goes on singing in me."

I rose and walked past her toward the window, seized by a sudden foreboding that my aunt would leave and return to Alexandria in search of her daughter. I told myself it wasn't a premonition like the others I'd had, but fear. Only fear. Anyway, by what means could Yaltha possibly leave Nazareth? She no longer had access to my father's wealth and power, and even if she did, how could a woman travel alone? How could she set about locating a daughter who'd been lost for nineteen years? No matter how haunting the flute's call, she could not leave.

She tossed back her shoulders as if casting off a heavy cloak and looked down at the potsherds. "That's enough of my story. Tell me that you will make use of these shards."

I knelt and picked up one of the larger pieces, hoping to mask my ambivalence. It had been more than seven years since I'd held a reed pen. Seven years since Jesus had wakened and assured me I would write again one day. Without realizing it, I'd given up on one day. I'd even given up on faraway day. I no longer opened the chest of cedar and read my scrolls. The last vial of ink had turned into a thick gum years ago. My incantation bowl was buried at the bottom of my chest.

"I've watched you over the years since we arrived here," Yaltha said. "I see you're happy with your husband—but in every other way you seem lost to yourself."

"I have no ink," I told her.

"Then we shall make some," she said.

xvi.

When Jesus returned, he found me sitting on the floor of our room, writing on a piece of potsherd. My breasts were dry now, but the ink Yaltha and I had made from red ocher and oven soot flowed each day from my reed pen. I looked up to see him standing in the doorway still clasping his staff. He was covered in dust from the road. I could smell the faint stench of fish on him from across the room.

Ignoring the purity laws, he strode into the room and put his arms about me, burying his face at my shoulder. I felt his body quiver, then a small heaving in his chest. Smoothing my hand across the back of his head, I whispered, "She was beautiful. I named her Susanna."

When he lifted his face, his eyes were filled with tears. "I should've been with you," he said.

"You are here now."

"I would've arrived sooner, but I was out on the boat when Simon arrived in Capernaum. He waited two days for me to come ashore with our catch."

"I knew you would come as soon as you could. I had to beg your brothers to send for you. They seem to think your earnings are more important than your mourning."

I saw his jaw tighten and guessed they'd had words over it.

"You shouldn't be in here," I told him. "I'm still considered unclean."

He pulled me closer. "I'll go to the mikvah later, and I'll sleep on the roof, but right now I won't be denied your nearness."

I filled a bowl with water and led him to the bench, where I removed his sandals and washed his feet. He leaned his head against the wall. "Oh, Ana."

I rubbed his hair with a damp towel and brought him a clean robe. As he donned it, his eyes drifted to the potsherds and the inkpot on the floor. One day I hoped to continue writing the lost stories, but the only words that I had now were for Susanna, bits and pieces of grief that fit onto the small jagged shards.

"You're writing," Jesus said. "I'm glad."

"Then you, Yaltha, and I are alone in this particular gladness."

I tried to keep my resentment contained but found it flaring up uncontrollably. "It's as if your family believes God has decided to destroy the world again, not by flood this time, but by Ana writing. Your mother and Salome have said nothing, but I think even they disapprove. According to Judith and Berenice, the only women who write are sinners and necromancers. I ask you, how do they know this? And James . . . he means to speak to you about me, I'm sure."

"He has done so already. He met me at the gate."

"And what did he say?"

"That you broke a water pot in order to write on the shards and then stripped the oven of its kindling to make ink. I believe he fears you'll smash all the pots and deprive us of cooked food." He smiled.

"Your brother stood right there in the doorway and said I should give up my perverse craving to write and give myself to prayer and grief for my daughter. Does he think my writing is not a prayer? Does he think because I hold a pen I don't grieve?"

I took a breath and continued, calmer. "I'm afraid I spoke sharply to James. I told him, 'If by craving you mean I have a longing, a need, then yes, you're right, but don't call it perverse. I dare to call it godly.' He left me then."

"Yes, he mentioned this, too."

"I'm confined here for sixty-eight more days. Salome brought me flax to spin and threads to sort and Mary gave me herbs to grind—but mostly I have a reprieve from daily tasks. At last there's time for me to write. Don't take it from me."

"I won't take it from you, Ana. Whether you'll be able to write in the same manner after your confinement—I don't know, but for now write all you wish."

He looked so weary all of a sudden. Because of me, he'd returned to find a small war had broken out. I laid my cheek against his and felt his breath skim my ear. I said, "I'm sorry. I tried for so long to belong, to be as they needed me to be. Now I wish to be myself."

"I'm sorry, Little Thunder. I, too, have kept you from being yourself."

"No—" He placed his finger at my lips, and I let my protest fall silent.

He picked up the shard on which I'd been writing. There in Greek, in tiny brokenhearted letters: *I loved her with all my heart, and with all my soul, and with all my might.*

"You write of our daughter," he said, and his voice broke.

xvii.

After Jesus observed his seven days of mourning, he found work in Magdala hewing stone for an elaborate synagogue. The city wasn't as far away as Capernaum, only a day's walk, and every week he came home for Sabbath with tales of a resplendent building that would hold two hundred people. He told me of a small stone altar on which he'd carved a chariot of fire and a seven-branched menorah.

"Those are the same images on the altar in the Holy of Holies in Jerusalem," I said, a little aghast.

"Yes," he said. "So they are." He didn't have to elaborate—I knew what he was doing, and it struck me as more radical than anything he'd done before. He was declaring in the most prominent and irrevocable way that God could not be confined any longer to the Temple alone, that his Holy of Holies, his presence had broken out and lodged everywhere.

When I look back on it, I see that act as a kind of turning point, a heralding of what was to come. It was around this time he became more outspoken, openly critical of the Romans and Temple priests. Neighbors began to show up at our house to complain to Mary and James that Jesus had been at the well or the olive press or the synagogue deriding the false piety of the Nazareth elders.

One day a rich Pharisee named Menachem came while Jesus was away. Mary and I met him at the gate and listened as he fulminated. "Your son goes about condemning rich men, saying they build their wealth off the backs of the poor. It's slanderous! You must appeal to him to cease or there will be little work for your family in Nazareth."

"We would rather be hungry than silent," I told him.

When he'd gone, Mary turned to me. "Would we?"

Every week, Jesus came home from Magdala telling me about the blind and sick he saw on the road with no one to help them, stories of widows turned out of their homes, of families so heavily taxed they were forced to sell their lands and beg in the streets. "Why does God not act to bring his kingdom?" he would say.

A fire had been lit in him and I blessed it, but I questioned, too, where the spark had come from. Had Susanna's death caused him to step from the periphery? Had it stunned him with the brevity of life and the need to seize what we had of it? Or was it all just the fullness of time, the coming of something that was coming anyway? Sometimes when I looked at him I saw an eagle on its branch and the world beckoning. I feared what would happen. I had no branch of my own.

Daily, I penned words behind the walls of my room on potsherds no one would ever read.

I stacked the used pieces of clay into wobbly towers along the walls of the room. Little pillars of grief. They didn't take away my sorrow, but they gave me a way to make what meaning I could from it. To write again felt like a return to myself.

On the day I inscribed the last of the potsherds, Yaltha was sitting with me, rattling her sistrum. The writing would end now; even my aunt understood this. She'd endured a chastisement from Mary for shattering the pot and couldn't risk breaking another. She watched me set down my pen and cover the inkpot. She did not cease playing, the percussion of her sistrum darting like a dragonfly about the room.

THE NEXT WEEK, Jesus didn't arrive home from Magdala before sunset as he always did. Dusk came, then dark, and he didn't appear. I stood in the doorway and watched the gate, glad for the fullness of the moon. Mary and Salome delayed the Sabbath meal and sat with James and Simon in a little clump beneath the olive tree.

When he appeared, I disregarded my confinement and ran to him.

He bore a heavy sack on his back. "I'm sorry to be delayed," he said. "I detoured to Einot Amitai to the vessel workshop at the chalkstone cave."

The road there was known to be populated with lepers and brigands, but when his mother admonished him about the danger, he lifted his hand to stop her, and without further comment he strode toward our room, where he poured the contents of his sack into a magical heap outside the door.

Potsherds! *Stone* potsherds.

I laughed at the sight. I kissed his hands and cheeks, then chastised him. "Your mother is right. You shouldn't have traveled such dangerous country for me."

"Little Thunder, it wasn't for you," he teased. "I brought the shards for you to write on in order to save my mother's pots."

xviii.

As the end of my confinement neared, I began to dream of going back to Jerusalem.

A woman was required to present a sacrificial offering at the Temple. If she had the means, she purchased a lamb. If she was needy, she offered two turtledoves. The poor, pilloried dove mothers. They bore a certain stigma, but I didn't mind becoming one of them. I had no interest in the size of my sacrifice or whether the priest pronounced me clean, unclean, or hopelessly squalid. What I wished for was a respite from the compound—the walls that shrank like figs in the sun, the quiet hostilities, the unchanging daily-ness. Traveling to Jerusalem during the dull month of Elul would be more placid than Passover and a welcome reprieve before returning to my chores. I imagined it daily. Jesus and I would stay again with Mary, Martha, and Lazarus. I would revel in seeing Tabitha. We would go to the Pool of Siloam, where I would bid Jesus to lift the paralytics into the water. At the Temple, we would purchase two turtledoves. I would try to leave the lambs alone.

The thought of these things filled me with elation, but they were not my true intent. I meant to trade my silver headband, copper mirror, brass comb, even my precious ivory sheet for papyri and inks.

"ONLY A WEEK REMAINS before my captivity ends," I whispered to Jesus. "Yet you haven't spoken of going to the Temple. I will need to make my sacrifice."

We were reclined on the roof, where I, too, had begun to sleep in order to escape the heat, spreading my bed mat an acceptable distance from his. The entire family, except Yaltha, had taken to sleeping up here. Gazing across the mud thatch, I could see their bodies lined up under the stars.

I waited. Had Jesus heard my question? Voices traveled easily up here—even now I heard Judith at the far end of the roof murmuring to her children, trying to settle them.

"Jesus?" I whispered, louder.

He edged closer so we could keep our voices low. "We cannot go to Jerusalem, Ana. The journey is five days at a quick pace, and five days back. I'm unable to leave my labors for so long. I've become one of the head builders of the synagogue."

I didn't want him to hear my disappointment. I lay back without responding and looked up into the night, where the moon was just brandishing her forehead.

He said, "You can make your offering to the rabbi here instead. It's sometimes done that way."

"It's just that . . . I hoped—" Hearing the quiver in my throat, I stopped.

"Tell me. What do you hope?"

"I hope for *everything*."

After a pause, I heard him say, "Yes, I hope for everything, too."

I didn't ask what he meant, nor did he ask me. He knew what my everything was. And I knew his.

Soon I heard his breath deepen into sleep.

An image swam into my mind and floated there: *Jesus is at the gate. He's wearing his travel cloak, a bag strapped over his shoulder. I am there, too, my face full of sorrow.*

My eyes broke open. I turned and looked at him with sudden sadness. The rooftop was quiet, the night showering down its heat. I heard a creature of some kind—a wolf, perhaps a jackal—howl in the distance, then the animals restless in the stable. I didn't sleep, but lay there remembering the admission Jesus had made the night he asked me to become his betrothed. *Since I was a boy of twelve I've felt I might have some purpose in God's mind, but that seems less likely to me now. I've had no sign.*

The sign would come.

His *everything*.

EIGHTY DAYS AFTER the birth and death of Susanna, I purchased two turtledoves from a farmer and carried them to the closest thing we had to a rabbi in Nazareth, a learned man who owned the village oil press and who stood there trying to look practiced at pronouncing women clean. He'd been feeding the donkey that turned the grinding stone when I arrived. I was accompanied by Simon and Yaltha; Jesus was not expected home from Magdala for four days.

The rabbi clutched a handful of straw in one hand as he received the doves, which flapped wildly in the little cage. He seemed uncertain whether he was required to quote the Torah in his pronouncement, which occasioned a fascinating blend of Scripture and invention.

"Go, be fruitful again," the rabbi said as we turned to leave, and I saw Yaltha look at me and lift her eyes.

I pulled my scarf low on my forehead, thinking of Susanna, of the beauty and sweetness of her. My confinement was over. I would take my place once more among the women. When Jesus returned I would be wife to him again. There would be no ink and potsherds. No papyri from Jerusalem.

Walking home from the rabbi's oil press, Yaltha and I trailed far behind Simon. "What will you do?" she asked, and I knew she referred to the rabbi's parting words about being fruitful again.

"I don't know."

She studied me. "But you *do* know."

I doubted this was true. All those years I'd used herbs to prevent becoming pregnant, believing I belonged not to motherhood but to some other amorphous life, pursuing dreams I would likely never realize—these things embarrassed me suddenly, this endless reaching for what couldn't be reached. It seemed foolish.

I thought again of Susanna and my hands slid to my belly. The weight of emptiness there seemed impossibly heavy. "I think I will choose to be fruitful again," I said.

Yaltha smiled. "You think with your head. You *know* with your heart."

She doubted me. I stopped and stood my ground. "Why should I not give birth to another child? It would bring my husband joy, and perhaps to me, as well. Jesus's family would embrace me again."

"I've heard you say more than once you don't wish to have children."

"But in the end, I wanted Susanna."

"Yes. That you did."

"I must give myself to something. Why shouldn't it be motherhood?"

"Ana, I don't doubt you should give yourself to motherhood. I only question what it is you're meant to mother."

For two days and nights I pondered her words, so vast and inscrutable. For a woman to birth something other than children and then mother it with the same sense of purpose, attention, and care came as an astonishment, even to me.

The evening before Jesus was due to arrive, I gathered up the potsherds, all of them covered now with words, placed them in a wool sack, and set them in the corner. I swept our room, filled the clay lamps, then beat our bed mats.

When darkness fell, I heard the others climb to the roof, but I didn't join them. I slept in the fragrance of the mat and dreamed.

I am giving birth, squatting over the hole in the corner. Susanna slips from me into Yaltha's hands, and I reach for her, surprised that this time she cries out, that her tiny fists wave in the air. When Yaltha places her in my arms, though, I'm startled to see the baby is not Susanna. She is myself. Yaltha says, "Why look, you are the mother and the baby both."

I woke in the dark. When first light arrived, I stole to Yaltha's bedside and gently shook her awake.

"What is it? Are you well?"

"I'm well, Aunt. I've had a dream."

She pulled a shawl about her. I thought of her own dream of Chaya on the summit calling for her, and wondered if she thought of it, too.

I told her what I'd dreamed, and then placing my silver headband in her hands, I said, "Go to the old woman and trade my headdress for blackseed oil. And for extra measure, wild rue and fennel root."

I SET OUT THE HERBS on the oak table in our room. When Jesus arrived late in the day, I greeted him with a kiss, and watched his eyes pass over my collection of preventatives. It was important to me that he understood. He acknowledged the herbs with a nod—there would be no more children. I sensed relief in him, a sad, wordless relief, and it came to me that if the time ever came for him to truly leave, it would be much simpler for him without children.

As we lay together, I clutched him to me, feeling my heart would break open and pour itself out. His fingers touched my cheek. "Little Thunder," he whispered.

"Beloved," I answered.

I rested my head on his chest and watched the night slipping past the high window. Pale-fringed clouds, floating stars, wedges of sky. I thought how alike we were, both of us mutinous, venturesome, shunned. Both seized by passions that needed to be set loose.

When he woke, even before he prayed the Shema, I described the dream to him that had caused me to trade my silver headband for the herbs. How could I keep it from him? "The newborn was myself!" I exclaimed.

A tiny shadow passed over his face—concern, it seemed, for what the dream augured for the future—then it passed.

He said, "It seems you will be born again."

xix.

Haul water.
Card flax.
Spin thread.
Weave clothes.
Mend sandals.
Make soap.
Pummel wheat.
Bake bread.
Collect dung.
Prepare food.
Milk goats.

Feed men.

Feed babies.

Feed animals.

Tend children.

Sweep dirt floors.

Empty waste pots . . .

Like God's, women's toil had no beginning and no end.

As the burnt summer gave way and the months passed, weariness hung along my bones like loom weights. It was hard then to imagine how my life could ever be different than it was now. Rising in the early hours to take up my chores, my fingers raw from the pestle and the loom. Jesus crisscrossing the towns and villages around the Sea of Galilee, home two days of seven. Judith's and Berenice's sharp judgments.

In the hidden forest in my chest, the trees slowly lost their leaves.

xx.

On the one-year anniversary of Susanna's death, Jesus and I walked to the cave where she was buried and collected her bones into a small limestone ossuary, which he had carved himself. I watched as he placed the stone box on the cave ledge, then left his hand resting upon it for several moments.

The grief in me could be unbearable at times, and I felt it now . . . pain so cutting, I wondered if I could go on standing. I reached for Jesus in the gray light and saw his lips moving in silence. If I bore my grief by writing words, Jesus bore his by praying them. How often had he said to me, "God is like a mother hen, Ana. She will gather us beneath her wing"? But I never felt gathered into that place where he seemed to dwell so effortlessly.

Coming out of the cave into the brightness, I drank in the summer air, green and tart. We were walking down into the valley back toward Nazareth, when Jesus stopped on a plateau where the lilies grew wild.

"Let's rest awhile," he said, and we sat among the grasses and the thick, sweet scent. I could feel Susanna everywhere, and perhaps he did as well, because he turned to me and said, "Do you ever picture how she would be if she'd lived?"

The question pierced me, but I seized it, for I ached to talk about her. "She would have your eyes," I said. "And your *very* long nose."

"Is my nose that long?" he asked, smiling.

"Yes, very. And she would have your boisterous laugh. She would be kindhearted like you. But she wouldn't be nearly so devout. She would take her religion from me."

When I paused, he said, "I imagine her with your hair. And she would be spirited, just as you are. I would call her Littlest Thunder."

This brought me a deep and sudden consolation, as if I'd been gathered, if only for a moment, into that most inscrutable place beneath Sophia's wing.

xxi.

Standing at the village well, I had the peculiar feeling of being watched. During my first years in Nazareth the feeling came often; indeed, every time I left the compound. *Look! There's the rich girl from Sepphoris, now nothing more than a peasant.* Eventually, though, I became too familiar for them to notice and the glowering stopped, but once again the hairs on my arms were lifting to attention, that sense of eyes watching me.

It was the first week of Tishri, just past the late-summer fig harvest. I wiped my brow and set the water pot on the stone wall built around the wellspring and looked about. The well was crowded—women milled about with jugs on their shoulders, children clinging to their robes.

Journeymen were lined up to fill waterskins. A clump of boys tugged on an obstinate camel. No one seemed interested in me. But I'd come to trust the odd ways I knew things—the images, the dreams, the nudges in my body. Alert, I waited my turn to draw water.

It was when I looped the rope about the handle of my pot and lowered it into the well that I heard footsteps behind me. "*Shelama*, little sister," a voice said.

My spirit leapt. "Judas!" He caught the rope as my hands let go of it in surprise. "So it's you who has been watching me."

"Yes, all the way from your house." I reached to embrace him, but he stepped back. "Not here. We shouldn't bring notice to ourselves."

His face had turned thin, leather brown, tough as a goat hide. A white scar in the shape of a scorpion tail hooked under his right eye. He looked as if the world had bitten into him and, finding him too gristly, spit him back. As he pulled up my pot from the well, I glimpsed the dagger tucked in his girdle, the way he cut his eyes left and right and over his shoulder.

"Come with me," he said, and strode off with the pot.

I pulled up the hood on my cloak and hurried behind him. "Where are we going?"

He turned toward the most crowded section of Nazareth, where the houses were pressed together amid a maze of narrow alleys, and stepped into a passageway between two courtyards, empty except for three men. There, amid the fragrance of donkeys, piss, and fermenting figs, he lifted me up and spun me around. "You look well."

I eyed the men.

"They are with me," he said.

"Your Zealot friends?"

He nodded. "There are forty of us living in the hills. We do our part to rid Israel of Roman pigs and sympathizers." He grinned and gave a little bow.

"That sounds . . ." I hesitated.

"Dangerous?"

"I was going to say impractical."

He laughed. "I see you still speak your mind."

"I'm sure you and your Zealots are an enormous thorn in Rome's side. But it's a *thorn*, Judas. It's no match for their might."

"You'd be surprised how much they fear us. We're good at inciting revolt, and there's nothing Rome dreads more than an uprising. Best of all, it's the surest way to get rid of Herod Antipas. If he cannot keep the peace, Rome will replace him." He paused, fidgety, looking back toward the alley entrance. "There's a century of eighty soldiers assigned to capture us, and yet in all these years not one of us has been caught. Some have been killed, but never caught."

"So, my brother is infamous." I gave him a good-natured shove. "Of course, here in Nazareth I've heard *nothing* of you."

He smiled. "Regrettably, my glory seems confined to the cities. Sepphoris, Tiberias, Caesarea."

"But Judas, look at you," I said, turning serious. "You're hunted, sleeping in caves, committing acts of defiance that could get you killed. Have you never wanted to give it up for a wife and children?"

"But I have a wife—Esther. She lives with four other Zealot wives in a house in Nain. It's overfilled with children, three of whom are mine." He beamed. "Two boys, Joshua and Jonathan, and a girl, Ana."

Hearing of his children, I thought of my Susanna and felt the knife cut that came every time her memory appeared. I decided not to speak of her. Feigning brightness, I said, "Three children—I hope to meet them one day."

He let out a sigh, and I heard the pining in it. "I haven't seen Esther in many months."

"Nor has she seen you." I wished to remind him *she* was the one left behind.

There was a clattering of horse hooves and men's voices, and Judas's hand went instinctively to the hilt of his dagger. He drew us deeper into the alley.

"How did you know where to find me?" I asked.

"Lavi. He keeps me informed of many things."

So, my faithful friend had become his spy. I said, "You disappeared from my life, and now you appear—there must be a reason."

He frowned into the slanted light and the scorpion tail lifted on the ridge of his cheek as if poised to sting. "I have grim news, sister. I've come to tell you our mother is dead."

I didn't make a sound. I became a piece of cloud, looking down, seeing things as birds see them, aloof and small. My mother's face was faint and far away.

"Ana, did you hear me?"

"I heard you, Judas."

I gazed at him impassively and thought of the night she locked me in my room, shouting, "Your shame falls on *me*. You will remain confined here until you offer your consent to the betrothal."

Why was I remembering these terrible things now?

"Do you know the last thing she said to me?" I asked. "She told me I would live out my days as a peasant in a wretched backwater village, that it was what I deserved. She said this a month before I left Sepphoris and wed Jesus, and she never uttered another thing to me. On the day I climbed into the cart and Lavi led the horse away, she didn't leave her room to see me off."

"She could be cruel to you," Judas said. "But she was our mother. Who will mourn her if not us?"

"Let Shipra mourn her," I said.

Judas gave me a reproachful look. "Your grief will come. Let it be sooner, than later."

I didn't think he was right about this, but I said, "I'll try, brother." Then, unable to help myself, I asked, "Why did you never come back to see me? You left me with Mother and Father and never returned. I married and you were not there. You were married and you didn't think to tell me. I didn't know if you were dead or alive. All these years, Judas."

He sighed. "I'm sorry, little sister. I couldn't return to Sepphoris for fear of being caught, and it would've been dangerous for you to have me about. After you married, I didn't know your whereabouts—I only began obtaining information from Lavi not long ago. But you're right— I could've tried sooner to find you. I've been too wrapped up in my war on the Romans." He gave me a repentant smile. "But I'm here now."

"Come home and stay the night with us. Jesus is there. You must meet him. He, too, is a radical. Not in the same way as you, but in his own way. You will find him worth meeting. You'll see."

"I'll gladly come and meet him, but I can't stay the night. My men and I must leave Nazareth well before dawn."

We walked side by side, the jar on my shoulder and the men trailing at a distance. I'd not returned to Sepphoris once in all these years, not even to attend the market, and I was eager for news. I said, "Jesus says Father is once again Antipas's chief scribe and counselor. It's hard to imagine him in Tiberias now. Harder still to imagine Mother buried there."

"You don't know, do you? When Antipas moved his government to Tiberias, your father went with him, but our mother refused. These past five years, she has lived in Sepphoris with no one but Shipra."

The revelation startled me, but only for a moment. It would've elated Mother to finally be rid of Father. I doubted he minded leaving her behind either.

"What of Lavi?" I asked.

"Your father took him to Tiberias to be his personal servant. It has worked out well for me."

"*My* father. Twice you've called him that. Do you no longer claim him?"

"Do you forget? He disowned me—it was written in a contract and signed by a rabbi."

I *had* forgotten. "I'm sorry," I said. "Father could be as cruel to you as Mother was to me."

"I'm glad to have no association to him. My only regret is that I won't inherit the house in Sepphoris. With Mother gone, it lies empty now. When your father dies, it will go to his brother, Haran. They've exchanged letters about it. Lavi slipped them to me. Haran wrote that when the time came, he would send an emissary from Alexandria to sell the house and its contents." It would happen as Mother had predicted: the house would belong to Haran, Yaltha's old adversary.

I said, "If Father is writing to his brother about such things as this . . . is he unwell?"

"According to Lavi, he suffers with a cough and sometimes sleeps sitting up in order to breathe. He no longer travels, but otherwise carries out his duties."

Father's face, too, was nearly lost to me.

JESUS MET US, holding the tool for rolling the roof thatch. He'd been fortifying the surface before the fall rains. I wiped a splotch of mud from his chin.

"Meet my brother, Judas," I said. "He came to tell me my mother has died."

Jesus placed his arm about my shoulders and gave me a tender look. "I'm sorry, Ana."

"I can find no tears," I told him.

The three of us sat on mats in the courtyard and spoke not of Judas's zealotry, but of common things—Jesus's work on the synagogue in Magdala, the childhood Judas and I had shared—and finally of Mother. She'd cut her hand on a powder box, leaving a wound that filled with poison. It was left to Shipra to see her buried. Even then, I sat dry-eyed.

When the light began to leach away, Jesus led Judas to the ladder that went to the roof. I followed, but Jesus said quietly, "Would you leave us to talk awhile?"

"Why shouldn't I come up, too?"

"Don't be offended, Little Thunder. We only want to speak as one man to another."

His stomach rumbled, and he laughed. "Perhaps you could hurry my mother and Salome to prepare some food."

He'd meant no slight, but I felt slighted nonetheless. He'd banished me. I couldn't recall it ever happening before.

Not long before this, four strangers smelling of fish had accompanied Jesus home and we women had had to serve them supper, too. I'd not asked to join in the men's conversation, but I'd watched as they huddled beneath the olive tree and spoke intently until dark. When they departed, I asked Jesus, "Who were those men?"

"Friends," he said. "Fishermen from Capernaum. It was their boat I was on when you gave birth to Susanna. They're on their way to barter in Sepphoris."

"What were you talking about for so long? Surely not fish."

"We spoke of God and his kingdom," he replied.

That same night, Mary, who must have overheard them while serving their supper, muttered to me and Salome, "These days my son speaks of nothing but God's kingdom."

"They talk about him in the village," Salome added. "They say he speaks with tax collectors and lepers." She looked at me and lowered her eyes. "And harlots."

I said, "He believes they have a place in God's kingdom, that's all."

"It's said he confronted Menachem," she said. "The one who came to our gate. Jesus admonished him for condemning the poor who carry wood on the Sabbath. He proclaimed his heart to be a sepulchre!"

Mary set down a bowl of wine-soaked bread with a thwack on the oven stone. "You must speak to him, Ana. I fear he will find trouble."

I feared he would not just find trouble, but *make* trouble. Associating with harlots, lepers, and tax collectors would stir up more rejection, but so what? I wasn't bothered that he befriended them. No, it was this new habit he had of speaking out against the authorities that worried me.

Now, as I watched Jesus and Judas climb the rungs, the same ominous feeling I'd had that night returned to me. I slipped to the side of the house, where I was unlikely to be seen, and there beneath the stick canopy over the workshop, I waited for their conversation to dribble down to me. His stomach would have to rumble awhile longer.

Judas was speaking of his Zealot exploits. "Two weeks ago in Caesarea we tore down the Roman emblems and defaced a statue of the emperor that stands outside their temple to Apollo. We could find no way to desecrate the temple itself—it was heavily guarded—but we stirred up a mob that cast stones at the soldiers. We're usually not so brazen. More often we look for small contingents of soldiers on the road, where they're easily attacked. Or we rob the rich as they travel in the countryside. What we don't need of their coins, we give to villagers to pay their taxes."

Jesus's back must've been turned to me, for his voice was faint. "I, too, believe the time has arrived to be rid of Rome, but God's kingdom won't come by the sword."

"Until the Messiah comes, the sword is all we've got," Judas argued. "My men and I will use our swords tomorrow to make off with a portion of grain and wine en route to Antipas's warehouse in Tiberias. I have a worthy source at the palace there who has informed me . . ." The rest of his words faded.

Hoping to hear them better, I edged around the house and pressed myself into the shadows, where I listened to Judas recount the splendors of Tiberias—a vast palace on a hill decorated with graven images, a Roman stadium, a shining colonnade that ran from the Sea of Galilee all the way to the hillside. Then Judas said my name, causing me to stiffen to attention. "I've told Ana her father isn't well. He will die soon, but he's as treacherous as ever. I asked to speak to you without her presence because I've learned news that will disturb her. She might be compelled to . . . well, who knows how she'll respond? My sister is impetuous and too fearless for her own good." Judas chuckled. "But perhaps you've learned that for yourself."

Impetuous and fearless. Once I'd been those things. But that part of me seemed like one of the forgotten women in the stories I'd written, diminished by years of chores, Susanna's death, and those long famines of spirit when I couldn't write.

My brother said, "Ana's father has concocted one last plot to convince the emperor Tiberius to make Antipas King of the Jews."

How predictably disappointing Father was. But this was hardly news that would alarm me in the manner Judas predicted.

There was an uneasy silence before Jesus's voice resounded. "It's prophesized the *Messiah* will bear the title King of the Jews—it would be a mockery for Antipas to steal the title for himself!"

"I tell you, his plot is cunning—I fear it could work."

Across the compound, Mary, Salome, and Judith walked toward the little courtyard kitchen to prepare the evening meal, leaving Berenice to tend the children. I worried that any moment they would call me and when I didn't answer, they would seek me out.

"Matthias wrote out the plot in meticulous detail," Judas said. "His servant, Lavi, is unable to read, so he passes me as many of Matthias's documents as he can. I was shocked to come upon the one that lays out his plan. Antipas will travel to Rome next month to make an official appeal to the emperor to be named king."

"It doesn't seem likely Tiberius will grant such a thing," Jesus said. "It's widely said the emperor opposes giving Antipas the title. He refused to do so even after Antipas named his new city Tiberias."

Across the way, the chatter of the women made it difficult to hear. I crept back around to the ladder and climbed halfway up.

Judas was saying, "Antipas is hated. The emperor has denied him being king in the past because he fears the people will rise up. But what if there was a way to lessen that possibility? That's the question Matthias put forth in his plot. He wrote that we Jews oppose Antipas as king because he has no royal bloodline, because he's not from the line of King David." He snorted. "That's hardly the only reason, but it's a paramount one, and Matthias has conspired a way around it. On Antipas's way to Rome, he will stop in Caesarea Philippi to visit his brother Philip, but what he's really after is his brother's wife, Herodias. She descends from the royal Hasmonaean line of Jewish kings."

Antipas would take a new wife? Had something tragic befallen Phasaelis, my old friend? Confused, fighting a sickening feeling in my stomach, I climbed two rungs higher.

Judas said, "Herodias is ambitious. Antipas will have an easy time convincing her to divorce Philip and marry him. He will promise her a throne. When Antipas arrives in Rome, it will be with the assurance of a royal marriage. If this doesn't win him the kingship, nothing will."

Jesus asked the question that burned a hole on my tongue. "But doesn't Antipas have a wife already?"

"Yes, the princess, Phasaelis. Antipas will divorce her and incarcerate her in secret somewhere. Most likely he'll quietly do away with her and claim the cause of her death to be a fever."

"You think Antipas would go so far?" Jesus asked.

"Matthias claims if she lives, she'll incite her father to take revenge. As you know, Antipas's own father executed his wife, Mariamme, and I doubt Antipas would hesitate to follow in his footsteps. You see, don't you, why I wished to keep this news from Ana? Phasaelis was once Ana's friend."

Dazed, I laid my forehead against the rung. While I'd been holding on to the ladder, night had closed over us. A voluptuous moon dripped light everywhere. The smell of bread curled through the darkness. They went on conversing, their voices like bees whirring far off in a broom tree.

As I started down the ladder, my hands, slick with sweat, slipped momentarily from the wood, causing the ladder to jar against the house. Before I could descend farther, I heard Jesus say, "Ana, what are you doing there?" His shadowed face peered over the edge of the roof.

Then Judas's face appeared beside his. "So you heard."

"Your supper is ready," I told them.

KNEELING BEFORE THE CHEST of cedar in my room, I removed the contents item by item—bowl, scrolls, pens, ink, the red thread in its tiny pouch. The hammered sheet of ivory that had gotten me in such grave trouble lay at the bottom, pearl white and shining. I didn't know then, nor do I fully know now, why I'd never written on it or bartered it away. It had seemed like a relic that should be preserved—without it my marriage to Jesus would never have happened. Now it seemed I'd kept it for this moment. Besides, there was nothing else on which to write.

I lifted the last vial of ink to the flame on the clay lamp and shook the sluggish black liquid awake. The fearless girl had not left me entirely. I wrote quickly in Greek, not bothering to perfect my letters.

> *Phasaelis,*
>
> *Be forewarned! Antipas and my father plot against you. Your husband conspires to marry Herodias, whose royal line may convince the emperor to crown the tetrarch king. With confidence I tell you that after Antipas departs for Rome, he will divorce you and make you his prisoner. Your life may be endangered as well. I'm reliably told Antipas will leave within the month. Flee, if you can. My heart yearns to see you safe.*
>
> *Ana*

I raised the hem of my tunic and fanned the ink dry, then tied the letter in a piece of undyed flax. When I entered the courtyard, Judas was already at the gate. "Brother, wait!" I ran toward him. "Would you sneak away without saying goodbye?"

He offered me a guilty look. "I couldn't risk you doing what I believe you're about to do this moment. What's inside the cloth?"

"Did you think I would do nothing? It's a letter of warning to Phasaelis." I thrust it at him. "You must deliver it for me."

He put up his hands, refusing to take it. "You heard me say I'm traveling to Tiberias, but I won't venture into the city itself and certainly nowhere near the palace. We plan to intercept the caravan of grain and wine outside the city."

"Her life is at stake. How can you not care?"

"I care about the lives of my men more." He turned toward the gate. "I'm sorry."

I grabbed his arm and shoved the package toward him once again. "I know you can find a way to avoid the soldiers in Tiberias. You bragged yourself that none of you have ever been caught."

He was taller than either Jesus or I, and he gazed over the top of my head toward the olive tree, where Yaltha, Jesus, and the others sat eating, as if hoping one of them would come and rescue him. Glancing back, I saw Jesus gazing at us, letting me have this moment alone with my brother.

"You're right," Judas said. "We can avoid the soldiers, but you haven't thought this through. If your letter is found and you are identified as the sender, you would be in danger. Did you sign your name to the letter?"

I nodded. I didn't bother to inform him that even without my signature, Antipas and my father would likely guess the sender. Had I not stolen the ivory sheet while they looked on?

"I need you to do this for me, Judas. I sat for Antipas's mosaic in order to gain your freedom. Surely you can do this much for me."

He threw back his head and let out a groan of resignation. "Give me the letter. I'll put it in Lavi's hands and ask him to see that it's smuggled to her."

Jesus waited for me in our room. He'd lit not one but two lamps. Light and shadow flitted about his shoulders. "Am I right that Judas is carrying your warning to Phasaelis?"

I nodded.

"It's dangerous, Ana."

"Judas said so as well, but don't admonish me. I couldn't abandon her."

"I won't reproach you for trying to help a friend. But I fear you've acted impulsively. There might have been another way."

Overcome with exhaustion, I stared at him, feeling hurt by his reproach. I could feel something mounting in me, too, that had nothing to do with Phasaelis, some excruciating need I couldn't comprehend. I swayed a little on my feet.

"It has been a day of suffering for you," he said, and the words opened a ravine of sadness in me. My eyes glazed, a sob creeping up the back of my throat.

He opened his arms. "Come here, Ana."

I laid my head against the rough weave of his tunic. "Mother is dead," I said, and I wept for her. For all that could have been.

xxii.

That fall, before the feast of Succoth, Jesus came home with news that a man from Ein Karem was baptizing people in the Jordan River. They called him John the Immerser.

Throughout the evening meal, Jesus did not cease speaking about this man who was wandering around in the Judean desert wearing a loincloth and eating roasted locusts and honey. To my mind, this didn't suggest a particularly alluring figure.

The entire family was sitting beside the cook fire in the courtyard as Jesus described the sensation the prophet was causing: great hosts of people flocking into the desert east of Jerusalem, so impassioned they waded into the river shouting and singing and afterward gave away their cloaks and sandals. "I met two men near Cana who heard him preach firsthand," Jesus said. "He urges people to repent and turn to God before it's too late. They say he condemns Antipas for his disregard of the Torah."

He was met with silent stares.

I asked, "When John immerses people in the river, does it mean the same as entering the mikvah?"

Jesus let his gaze rest on me. He smiled at my effort. "According to them, it represents a far more radical cleansing than the mikvah. John's immersion is an act of repentance, a turning away from one's sins."

The hush returned, even more smothering. Jesus squatted before the fire. I watched the reflection of the embers flick in his eyes and felt how incendiary our lives seemed right then. He looked very alone, almost lonely. I tried again. "This John the Immerser—does he believe that the apocalypse is upon us?"

There wasn't one of us who didn't know what the apocalypse meant. It would be a great catastrophe and a great ecstasy. The men spoke of it at synagogue, parsing the prophecies of Isaiah, Daniel, and Malachi. When it came, God would establish his kingdom on earth. Governments would crumble. Rome would be overthrown. Herod removed. Corrupt religious leaders driven out. The two Messiahs would appear, the kingly one from the line of David and the priestly one from the line of Aaron, who together would oversee the coming of God's kingdom.

It would be perfect.

I didn't know what to think of such things or of the frenzy of longing that surrounded them. Long ago, trying to explain it to me, Yaltha said our people were desolated by so much suffering, that it created in them a deep hope for an ideal future. She thought this alone lay behind the end-time prophecies. But was she right? Jesus seemed to believe fervently in them.

He answered me, "John preaches that the day of judgment is close when God will intervene to repair the world. Already people are saying John is the Messiah priest. If that's so, the Messiah king will appear soon."

A tremulous feeling swept over me. Whoever this Messiah king was, he was somewhere in Judea or Galilee, going about his life. I wondered if he knew who he was, or if God had yet to break the terrible news to him.

Mary rose and began to collect our bowls and spoons. When she spoke, her voice betrayed her fears. "Son, this man you describe could be a prophet or a madman—who's to say?"

James hurried to join in his mother's dissuasion. "We cannot know what manner of man he is or whether the things he says are truly from God."

Jesus stood and placed his hand on his mother's arm. "Mother, you are right to ask these questions. James, you are right, too. Sitting here, we cannot know."

I sensed what he was about to say. My heart quickened.

"I've decided to travel to Judea and discover for myself," he said. "I will leave tomorrow at dawn."

FOLLOWING HIM TO OUR ROOM, I was shaking with anger, furious that he would leave—no, furious that he *could* leave, while I had no such glorious freedom. I would remain here forever tending to yarn, animal dung, and wheat kernels. I wanted to scream at the sky. Did he not see how it wounded me to be left behind, to have no freedom to go and do, to always long for *one day*?

When I stomped through the doorway, he was already preparing his travel pouch. He said, "Fetch salt-fish, bread, dried figs, cheese, olives, whatever can be spared from the storeroom. Enough for both of us."

Both? "You wish to take me with you?"

"I want you to come, but if you'd rather stay here and milk the goat . . ."

I flung myself at him, covering his face with kisses.

"I would always take you with me if I could," he said. "Besides, I wish to hear what you think of John the Immerser."

I packed our pouches with food and waterskins, tying them with leather thongs. Remembering the ornamental brass comb I'd brought from Sepphoris more than ten years before, I pried one pouch back open and slid it inside. That and my copper mirror were the last possessions I had left of any value. The comb could be traded for food. Jesus liked to say we shouldn't worry about what we'd eat or drink, that God fed the birds, would he not also feed us?

He would trust God. I would carry a comb.

Later, I lay awake listening to him sleep, the soft clouds of his breath filling the room. I couldn't close my eyes for happiness. It sprouted in me like a bright green shoot. In those moments, I lost my fear that I would be left behind. If he should give up everything and follow John the Immerser—why, even if he went off to be a prophet himself—he would take me with him.

xxiii.

At daybreak, I sought out Yaltha to say goodbye. She slept on her mat in the storeroom, her wool cloak pulled to her chin, her head uncovered and her hair unfurled across the pillow.

On the wall behind her was a crude depiction of the Egyptian calendar she'd sketched with a piece of charred wood. Ever since I'd known her, she'd charted the twelve lunar months, marking births, deaths, and auspicious events. When we'd lived in Sepphoris, she'd drawn the calendar on papyrus using the inks I made. Here, she could only trace the wheel on a mud wall with soot. Stepping closer to examine it, I saw she'd recorded my mother's death in the month of Ab without attaching it to a specific day. On the fourth of Tebet, the day of my birth, she'd written my name and beside it my age, twenty-four. Then I noticed something I'd not seen before. Today was the twelfth of Tishri and next to it she'd recorded the name of her lost daughter, Chaya. Today was the anniversary of Chaya's birth. She, too, was twenty-four.

I gazed down at my aunt, watching her eyes move behind her closed lids—was she dreaming? At that moment a ray of light broke through a crack in the roof thatch, falling on her shoulder and spilling across the earthen floor to my feet.

My eyes beheld it with curiosity. A cord of light, connecting us. I saw it as a sign of the promise we'd made to each other when I was fourteen, that we would always be joined like Naomi and Ruth—where I would go, she would go; my people would be her people. But as I stood there watching, the beam of light faded, then vanished in the morning brightness.

I knelt down and kissed my aunt's forehead. Her eyes opened.

"I'm going with Jesus."

She lifted her hand in blessing. "May Sophia watch over you and keep you," she said, her voice groggy with sleep.

"And you as well. Now return to your dream." I left her quickly.

In the courtyard, Jesus was bidding Mary and Salome goodbye. "When will you return?" his mother asked.

"I cannot say for certain—two weeks, perhaps three."

I looked back toward the storeroom and I was filled with dread. I told myself Yaltha was well for her age and free of sickness. I told myself that if Jesus decided to follow John the Immerser and took me with him, he would take her, too; he would not separate us. I told myself the beam of light that connected us could not be broken.

xxiv.

It took several days to reach the village of Aenon, where we traded my brass comb for chickpeas, apricots, flatbread, and wine, restoring our empty pouches. There, we crossed into Peraea and traveled along the left bank of the Jordan. Each morning Jesus woke early and went off a short distance to pray alone, and I would lie in the green smells with day breaking over me and mutter praises to Sophia. Then I would rise, my legs snarled with cramps, my stomach panged with hunger, blisters on my heels—oh, but the world was large and mysterious and I was far from home, journeying with my beloved.

On the sixth day, we came upon John the Immerser on the pebbly banks of the river, not far from the Dead Sea. The multitude was so great, he had climbed onto a crop of stone and was shouting as he preached. Behind him, apart from the crowd, stood a band of men, twelve or fourteen of them, whom I guessed to be his disciples. Two of them seemed oddly familiar to me.

Though Jesus had prepared me for John's appearance, I was nonetheless startled at the sight. He was barefoot and thin as thread, his black beard bouncing around on his chest and his hair swinging at his shoulders in matted coils. Strangest of all, he wore a camel-hair sackcloth, a thick, wooly garb tied at his waist that barely reached the middle of his thigh. The spectacle made me laugh, not with ridicule but with appreciation for the outlandishness of him, at the realization one could dress like this and still be adulated as one of God's chosen.

We picked our way along the edge of the assembly, drawing as close to him as we could. It was late in the day and clouds had piled up over the limestone hills, cooling the air. Little fires burned here and there along the shore and we drew near one of them, warming our hands as we listened.

John was urging the throng to turn away from money and greed. "What good will your coins do now? The ax of judgment is ready to strike the root of the tree. The kingdom of God is at hand."

I watched Jesus. How he feasted on the prophet's words—his eyes gleaming, furrows of concentration on his face, the quick breath in his chest.

I thought John's talk about the apocalypse would never end—it unnerved me—but eventually he turned his fiery tongue to Herod Antipas, assailing him for his greed, for turning his back on God's laws, for decorating his palace in Tiberias with a menagerie of graven images. Nor did he spare the Temple priests, accusing them of growing rich off the animal sacrifices they performed in the Temple.

I knew Jesus would ask me what I thought of this peculiar man. What would I say? *He's eccentric and strange and I'm leery of all his talk about the end-time, but there's something charismatic and powerful about him, and while he hasn't captured my imagination, he has captured the people's.*

A man wearing the black-and-white robes of the Sadducees, the elite of Jerusalem, interrupted John's scorching criticisms, shouting, "Who are you? Some say you are Elijah resurrected—who do *you* say you are? The priests have sent me here to find out."

One of John's disciples, one who seemed familiar to me, shouted back, "Are you a spy?"

I whirled toward Jesus. "That disciple—he's one of the fishermen from Capernaum who sat with you in the courtyard, the one on whose boat you fished!"

Jesus had recognized him, too. "My friend, Simon." He scanned the other disciples. "And his brother, Andrew."

Simon continued to bellow at the Sadducee, demanding to know who he was. "Hypocrite! Leave us and go back to your lucre in Jerusalem!"

"Your friend is easily heated," I said to Jesus.

He grinned. "I once saw him threaten to toss a man over the side of his boat for accusing his brother of miscounting the fish."

John raised his hands to quiet the uproar. "You ask who I am—I will tell you who I am. I am a voice crying in the wilderness."

These words, this proclamation, fairly stunned me. I thought of the words inscribed in my incantation bowl: *When I am dust, sing these words over my bones: she was a voice.* I closed my eyes and imagined the words rising from their ink beds and escaping over the side of the bowl. The figure I'd drawn of myself at the bottom leapt up and danced along the rim.

Turning, Jesus laid his hand on my shoulder. "What is it, Ana? Why are you crying?"

I reached up and felt the wetness on my lids. "John is a voice," I managed to say. "What it must be to say such a thing of oneself! I'm trying to imagine it."

WHEN JOHN CALLED UPON the multitude to repent and be cleansed of their sins, we streamed into the river with the rest of them. I didn't go in hungry to turn back to God's law—I went desiring to cleanse myself of fear and deadness of spirit. I went repenting of my silence and of the meagerness of my hope. I went thinking of the newborn self I'd dreamed of birthing.

I gulped the air as John pushed me gently beneath the water. Coldness closed over me. The silence of water, the weight of darkness, the belly of a whale. I opened my eyes and saw small striations of light on the river bottom and the faint glint of pebbles. A moment only, a heartbeat, and I came up splashing.

My tunic clung around me in heavy folds as I trudged to shore. Where was Jesus? He'd been near me when we entered the water—now he was lost in the morass of penitents. I began to shiver with cold. I moved along the bank, teeth chattering, calling his name. "Je-Je-Jesus."

I spotted him out in the river, standing before John with his back to me, descending into the water. I watched the place where he disappeared, how the circles of water spread slowly outward and the surface grew quiet and still.

He bounded up, shaking his head, creating a swirling spray. He lifted his face to the sky. The sun was sinking toward the hills, pouring itself onto the river. A bird, a dove, flew out of the glare.

XXV.

We bedded that night alongside the road to Jericho beneath a gnarled sycamore tree, our robes still damp with baptism. I lay beside him, drawing warmth from his body. We stared up at the branches, at clusters of yellow fruit, at the black sky smeared with stars. How awake we were, how alive. I pressed my ear to his chest and listened to the slow drumming. I thought us inseparable. A single timbre.

My mind turned to Tabitha, as it often had throughout our trip, but until now, I'd made no mention of her. I said, "We aren't far from Bethany. Let's go and see Tabitha and Mary, Martha, and Lazarus."

I thought he'd be pleased at the notion, but he hesitated a long while before answering. "It's a full day's walk," he said. "And in the opposite direction of Nazareth."

"But we're not in a hurry to return. It would be worth the detour."

He said nothing. *Something troubles him.* He eased his arm from beneath me and sat up. "Will you wait here while I go and pray?"

"Pray? It's the middle of the night."

He stood and his tone grew sharp. "Don't deter me, Ana. Please."

"Where will you go?"

"A short distance where I can be alone."

"You would leave me here?" I asked.

He walked away, stepping through some portal of darkness, and disappeared.

I sat there angered by my aloneness. For a moment I considered wandering off somewhere myself. I pictured his confusion and fear when he came back and discovered I was gone. He would search for me, thrashing through the mulberry brush. When he found me, I would say, *I, too, went into the night to pray. Did you think you were the only one whose spirit was restless?*

Instead, I waited, sitting with my back to the tree.

He returned in the hour before daybreak with sweat on his brow. "Ana, I must speak gravely with you." He sat down on the hard bed of leaves. "I've decided to become John the Immerser's disciple. I will leave Nazareth and follow him."

The pronouncement startled me, yet there was little surprise in it. If Jesus could hear thunder inside me, I could hear the thud of God's pursuit inside him. For all the years I'd known him, it had been there, waiting.

"I can't do otherwise. Today in the river—"

I took his hand. "What happened in the river?"

"I told you once that when my father died, God became father to me, and today in the Jordan I heard him call me son. Beloved son."

I could see he'd made peace with the boy who'd been rejected by his village, the one, it was whispered, who had no real father, the one in search of who he was. He stood, the ecstasy of his experience seeming to lift him off his feet. "There will be a great revolution, Ana. The kingdom of God is coming—think of it! When I came up from the water, I felt as if God was asking me to help bring it in. You see why I can't go to Bethany—now that I've set my course, I want to avoid delay."

He became quiet, searching my face. A feeling of loss coursed through me. I would go with him to God's revolution, of course, but things between us wouldn't be the same. My husband belonged to God now . . . all of him.

I rose and with great effort said, "You have my blessing."

The tautness about his lips slackened. He held me to him. I waited for him to say, *You'll come with me. We'll follow John together.* Already I was thinking how I would persuade Yaltha to join us.

The silence hardened. "And myself?" I said.

"I will take you home."

Confused, I shook my head. "But—" I wanted to object, but nothing came from my mouth. *He means to leave me behind.*

"I'm sorry, Ana," he said. "I must take up this mission without you."

"You can't leave me in Nazareth," I whispered. The hurt of saying these words was so great, I felt my legs sinking back toward the ground.

"Before I join John, I must go into the wilderness for a time to ready myself for what's to come. I can only do that alone."

"After that . . . then I'll accompany you." I heard the desperation in my voice—how I hated the sound of it.

"There are no women among John's disciples—you saw this, as I did."

"But you of all people . . . you would not exclude me."

"No, I would take you if I could." He raked his fingers through his beard. "But this is John's movement. The reasons that prophets have no female disciples—"

Incensed, I cut him off. "I've heard these reasons tenfold. Traipsing about the countryside exposes us to dangers and hardships. We cause dissension among the men. We are temptations. We are distractions." My anger swelled, and I was glad for it. It drove away my hurt. "It's thought we're too weak to face danger and hardship. But do we not give birth? Do we not work day and night? Are we not ordered about and silenced? What are robbers and rainstorms compared to these things?"

He said, "Little Thunder, I'm on your side. I was going to say, the reasons that prophets have no female disciples are flawed reasons."

"Yet you will follow John anyway."

"How else can we hope to alter this wrong? I will do what I can to convince him. Give me time. I'll come back for you in the winter, or early spring before Passover."

I looked at him. I'd held the world too close and it had slipped from my arms.

xxvi.

Jesus returned me to Nazareth as he had said he would, and there, with unnecessary haste, he bid us farewell. Those first terrible weeks of his absence, I remained in my room. I didn't care to witness his mother crying with bitterness or hear the exclamations and questions his brothers and their wives hurled at me. *Was Jesus struck on the head? Is he possessed? Does he mean to follow a madman and leave us to ourselves?*

I imagined my husband alone in some dust pit in the Judean wilderness fending off wild boars and lions. Did he have food and water? Did he wrestle with angels like Jacob? Would he come back for me? Was he even alive?

I had no strength for chores. What did it matter if the olives weren't pressed or the lamp wicks went untrimmed? I took meals in my room, abetted by Yaltha.

I came out of my seclusion only at night and prowled about the courtyard like one of the mice. Worried for me, Yaltha moved her sleeping mat to my room and brought me hot wine spiked with bits of myrrh and passionflower to help me sleep, the same brew she'd given Shipra long ago when Mother had locked me in my room. The draft had sent Shipra into an unshakable sleep, but it did little more than dull my senses.

One morning I found I could not force myself from my pallet, nor swallow my fruit and cheese. Yaltha felt my brow for fever, and finding nothing, bent to my ear and whispered, "Enough, child. You've grieved enough. I understand he has abandoned you, but must you abandon yourself?"

Soon after, Salome appeared in my doorway with news that she would be wed in the spring. James had signed a betrothal contract with a man in Cana, someone who was an utter stranger to her.

"Oh, sister, I'm sorry," I said.

"It isn't a sorrow to me," she replied. "The bride price will help keep our family fed, especially with Jesus . . ."

"Gone," I said for her.

"James says my new husband will be kind to me. The man does not mind that I'm a widow. He's a widower himself, having lost two wives to childbirth." She made an effort to smile. "I must weave some bridal clothes. Will you help me?"

It was the thinnest of ploys, obviously meant to lure me back to my duties and to life itself, for who in her right mind would ask *me* to help with spinning and weaving—even ten-year-old Sarah could do it better. Somehow, though, her tactic worked. I heard myself say, "I'll help you, of course I will."

I went to my chest of cedar and dug out the copper mirror, the last possession of value I owned. "Here," I said, placing the mirror in her hands. It caught the sun that slanted through the window, a flash of ginger light. "I've looked upon myself in this mirror since I was a child. I want you to have it as a betrothal gift."

She lifted the mirror to her face. "Why, I am . . ."

"Lovely," I said, realizing she may not have glimpsed her image this clearly before.

"I cannot accept something so treasured."

"Please. Take it." I didn't tell her I wished to be rid of the self I saw reflected there.

After that, I returned to life within the compound. Salome and I spun threads from flax and dyed them in a rare solution of alizarin red, which came from the roots of a tincture tree. Yaltha had procured it through means I wished not to know. It was possible she'd traded for it with Judith's carved spindle, which mysteriously went missing around this time. We wove sitting in the courtyard, sending our shuttles back and forth, creating bright scarlet cloths that Judith and Berenice found immodest.

"There's not a woman in Nazareth who would wear such a color," Judith said. "Certainly, Salome, you won't get married wearing it." She complained to Mary, who must've had misgivings of her own, but she ignored Judith's grievances.

I sewed a red head scarf and wore it every day as I went about my duties. The first time I paraded into the village in it, James said, "Jesus would not want you to go about in such a scarf."

"Well, he isn't here, is he?" I said.

xxvii.

Winter came slowly. I marked the months of Jesus's absence on Yaltha's calendar. *Two full moons. Three. Five.*

I wondered if by now he'd convinced John the Immerser to let me join the disciples. I kept thinking about the image that had come into my mind near the end of my confinement. Jesus and I had been on the rooftop trying to sleep when I'd envisioned him at the gate wearing his travel cloak and pouch, and I was there, too, crying. It had seemed such a gloomy omen then—Jesus leaving, while I wept—but my visions could be unpredictable and cunning. Wasn't it entirely reasonable that I'd pictured myself at the gate because I was leaving *with* Jesus, not saying goodbye to him? Perhaps I was sorrowful over my separation from Yaltha. The explanation gave me hope that Jesus would sway John to accept me. *Yes*, I thought. *He'll appear soon, saying, "Ana, John bids you to come and join us."*

I asked Yaltha to move her sleeping mat back to the storeroom and I laid Jesus's mat beside my own. As the days passed, my eyes drifted to the gate. I jumped at slight sounds. Whenever I could slip away from my tasks, I climbed to the roof and scanned the horizon.

Then, with winter nearly past, on a cold day full of windy light, I stood in the courtyard boiling soapwort root and olive oil to make soap, and looking up, I saw a hooded figure at the gate. I dropped the spoon, and oil splashed across the hearthstone. I was wearing the red head scarf, which had faded in the sun. I heard it snap at my ears as I ran.

"Jesus," I cried, though I could see how different the figure was from my husband. Shorter, thinner, darker.

He drew back his hood. *Lavi.*

MY DISAPPOINTMENT THAT Lavi was not who I'd thought left quickly after I recognized my loyal old friend. I led him to the storeroom, where Yaltha brought him a cup of cool water. He bowed his head, slow to accept it, for he was still a slave and unaccustomed to being waited upon. "Drink," she ordered.

Though it was midday, she lit a lamp to break apart the shadows, and we sat, the three of us, on the packed dirt and stared at one another in wordless wonder. We'd not seen him since the day of my wedding when he'd led the horse-drawn wagon through the gate.

His face had ripened, his cheeks fleshier, his brow more jutting. He was clean-shaven in the Greek manner, his hair cut short. Hardship had tilled furrows at the corners of his eyes. He was no longer a boy.

He waited for me to speak. I said, "You're a welcome sight, Lavi. Are you well?"

"Well enough. But I bring . . ." He stared into his empty cup.

"You bring news of my father?"

"He has been dead for almost two months."

I felt the cold from the doorway. I could see my father standing in the luxurious reception hall of our house in Sepphoris in his fine red coat and matching hat. He was gone. Mother, too. For a moment I felt strangely abandoned. I looked at Yaltha, remembering that my father was also her brother. She stared back at me, that look that said, *Let life be life and death be death.*

I said to Lavi, my voice quivering a little, "When Judas came to report my mother was dead, he told me Father was ill, so I'm not surprised at this news, only that it's you who delivers it. Did Judas send you?"

"No one sent me. I've not seen Judas since last fall when he brought your message for the tetrarch's wife."

I didn't move or speak. *Did Phasaelis receive my warning, then? Is she safe? Is she dead?*

Lavi went on with his story. It poured, unstoppered. "I was with my master when he died. Antipas had been back from Rome for only a few weeks and he was angry the plot to make him King of the Jews had yielded nothing. As your father lay dying, he muttered his sorrow that he'd failed Antipas. It was the last thing I heard him say."

Father. He'd groveled before Antipas until the end.

"When he was gone, I was sent to work in the kitchen, where I was beaten for spilling a vat of grape syrup," Lavi said. "I determined then I would leave. I stole away from the palace six nights ago. I've come to be your servant."

He meant to live with us in this impoverished compound? There was no room to spare, the food stores were stretched as it was, and it was doubtful I would even be here much longer. No one kept servants in Nazareth—the thought was preposterous.

I cut my eyes to Yaltha. *What can we say to him?*

She was plainspoken, but kind. "You cannot stay here, Lavi. It would be better for you to serve Judas."

"Judas is never in one place. I would not know how to find him," Lavi said. "When I last saw him, he spoke of joining the prophet who baptizes in the Jordan. He believed him to be a Messiah."

I pushed to my feet. Father was dead. Lavi had run away and proclaimed himself my servant. And apparently, Judas had become a follower of John the Immerser. Standing in the doorway, I saw the weather had turned, the clouds boiling and blackening, the spring rains arriving early. For months, we'd gone with no tidings at all, and suddenly news fell on us in the manner of a hailstorm.

"You can remain here until you decide where to go," I said. With Jesus away, perhaps James wouldn't mind Lavi being here for a while; maybe he would welcome the help Lavi could provide. Lavi was a Gentile, though. James wouldn't take well to that.

"You have always been kind to me," Lavi said, which caused me to wince. Mostly I'd paid little attention to him.

I could be patient no longer. I returned to sit beside him. "You must tell me—did you give my message to Phasaelis?"

He looked down, as was his habit, but it gave me the sense there was news he dreaded to impart. "I befriended the kitchen steward who carried food to her room and asked him to place the ivory sheet on her tray. He was reluctant to do so; there are spies even within the palace. But Antipas was away in Rome then, and with the help of a small bribe, the steward slid the ivory beneath a silver flagon."

"You're sure she read it?"

"I'm certain of it. Three days later, she left Tiberias for Machaerus, saying she wished to spend time there taking the waters at Antipas's palace. Once there, she snuck away with two servants and slipped across the border into Nabataea."

I let out a breath. Phasaelis was safe with her father.

"I should like to have seen Antipas when he returned from Rome with his new wife and found his old one gone," Yaltha said.

"They say he raged and tore his robe and overturned furniture in

Phasaelis's quarters." I hadn't known Lavi to talk so freely. I'd thought him quiet, cautious, diffident, but then we'd never sat and spoken as equals. How little I really knew him.

"The soldiers who escorted Phasaelis to Machaerus have been imprisoned. Her servants were tortured, including the steward who delivered your message."

A huge cresting wave began in my chest—a rush of sorrow over the fate of the steward and the soldiers, followed by a stab of remorse for my part in their suffering, but mostly fear, crushing fear. "Did the steward tell his tormentors about my message?" I asked. "My name was signed to it."

"I cannot say what he confessed. I was unable to speak with him."

"Does he read Greek?" Yaltha asked. She was sitting very rigid, her face as grave as I'd ever seen it. When Lavi didn't answer immediately, she snapped, "Does he or doesn't he?"

"He reads a little . . . perhaps more than a little. When I first asked him to deliver the message, he studied it, complaining it was too dangerous."

The room receded before rushing back at me. He would have been able to tell Antipas everything, and with the aid of torture, perhaps he did. "The poor man was right, wasn't he?" I said. "It was too dangerous. I'm sorry for him."

"Some say it was Antipas's new wife, Herodias, who demanded the punishments to the soldiers and servants," Lavi said. "Now she constantly goads her husband to arrest John the Immerser."

"She wants John put in prison?" I said.

"The Immerser continues to attack both Antipas and Herodias," Lavi said. "He preaches that her marriage is incestuous because she's Antipas's niece and the wife of his brother. He goes about saying it's not a marriage at all, because as a woman, she had no standing to divorce her husband, Philip."

Rain pattered, then crashed on the roof. This ruinous disaster had started with my father's plot to make Herod Antipas king. He'd persuaded Antipas to divorce Phasaelis and marry Herodias, and in doing so, he'd set a perilous chain of events in motion: my warning message to Phasaelis, the prophet's condemnations, and now Antipas and Herodias's retribution. It was like a stone that strikes against another stone that causes the entire mountain to fall.

JAMES GAVE PERMISSION for Lavi to sleep on the roof. By then, the sky had dried, but the rains started again before dawn with torrents that dissolved the moon into thin, pale streaks. Awakened by the din, I hurried to the doorway and glimpsed Lavi's blurred figure skittering down the ladder and taking shelter beneath the workshop roof. It brought back the memory of him holding the canopy of thatched palm over my head on the day I'd met Jesus at the cave.

When the downpour turned into a dribble, I warmed a cup of milk for Lavi on the oven fire. Approaching the workshop with it, I heard voices—Yaltha was there.

"When Judas was last here," she said, "he brought news that upon Matthias's death, my brother in Alexandria would send an envoy to Sepphoris to sell his house and its possessions. What do you know about this?"

I halted abruptly to listen and the milk spilled over the side of the cup. Why had she sought out Lavi privately to ask this? Worry welled in me, some old, augured feeling.

Lavi said, "Before I fled Tiberias, I learned that a man named Apion had been dispatched from Alexandria to conclude the sale of the house. It is likely he is in Sepphoris already."

She is not being idly curious. She means to return to Alexandria with Haran's envoy. She will go in search of Chaya.

So. It was not I who would leave her, as I'd thought, but she who would leave me.

When I stepped into view, she didn't meet my gaze, but I'd read her face already. I handed Lavi the milk. The sky slunk low, grayness sticking to everything.

I said, "When were you going to tell me about your plans to return to Egypt?"

Her sigh floated through the wet cold. "I would've told you, but it was too soon to speak of it. It was not yet time."

"And now? Is it time now?" Sensing tension, Lavi skulked against the door of the workshop, his face retreating into the dark oval of his hood.

"Time is passing, Ana. Chaya still calls to me in my dreams. She wants to be found—I feel it in my bones. If I don't seize this chance to return, I won't have another."

"You meant to leave, and yet you kept it from me."

"Why should I burden you with my desire to leave when I saw no way to act upon it? Early last fall, when you learned Haran would send an emissary, it came to me that I might travel back to Alexandria with him, but I didn't know it might truly be possible until now." Her eyes filled with anguish. "Child, aren't you planning to leave Nazareth yourself? Each day you watch for Jesus, hoping he'll come for you. I cannot remain here without you. I've lost one daughter; now it will be two."

Remorseful, I held her face with my hands. The soft, drooping wrinkles. The candlewax skin. "I don't blame you for seeking your daughter. I'm upset we'll be separated, that's all. If Chaya calls to you, of course you must go."

Overhead, the sun was a tiny larva wriggling from the clouds. We watched it emerge, neither of us speaking. I turned to my aunt. "Lavi and I will go at once to Sepphoris and seek this emissary, Apion. I'll announce myself as Haran's niece and strike a bargain for your passage."

"And if Jesus returns while you're gone?"

"Tell him that he may wait. I have waited plenty for him."

She cackled.

xxviii.

James and Simon, thinking it was their duty to impose husbandly re-
strictions on me in their brother's absence, forbade me to leave Nazareth and travel to Sepphoris. How mistaken they were. I packed my
travel pouch and tied on my red scarf.

While Lavi waited for me at the gate, I kissed Mary and Salome, trying to ignore their petrified looks. "I will be fine; Lavi will be with me."
Then, smiling at Salome, I added, "You yourself used to cross the valley
with Jesus to sell your yarns in Sepphoris."

"James will be unhappy," she said, and I realized it was not my safety
they were concerned about, but my disobedience.

I left without their blessing. But as I walked away, the wind lifted its
arms and the olive tree sent a shimmer of leaves onto my head.

WHEN LAVI POUNDED at the door of my old house in Sepphoris, no one
answered. Moments later he shinnied over the back wall and unlatched
the gate. Stepping into the courtyard, I came to a standstill. Weeds, hip
high, grew between the stones. The ladder to the roof lay on the ground,
the rungs like a row of broken teeth. I smelled a stew of fetidness coming
from the stairs that led down to the mikvah and knew the conduit had
clogged. Bird excrement and flaking mortar. The house had sat empty for
little more than six months and already ruin had set in.

Lavi motioned me inside the vaulted storeroom, where we found the
door to the servant passage unlocked. Parting the cobwebs, we climbed
the steps into the reception hall. The room was the same—the pillowed
couches where we'd eaten, the four tripod tables with spiral legs.

We wandered up the stairway onto the loggia, past the sleeping quarters. Peering into my room, I thought of the girl who'd studied and read
and begged for tutors, who'd made inks and word altars and dreamed of

her face in a tiny sun. In my youth, I'd heard old Rabbi Shimon ben Yohai say that each soul possessed a garden with a serpent that whispered temptations. That girl I remembered would always be the serpent in my garden bidding me to eat forbidden things.

"Come," Lavi said urgently from the doorway.

I followed him to Judas's room, where he pointed to a half-full waterskin, mussed bedcovers, partially burned candles, and a fine linen coat tossed on a bench. On a table near the bed, two scrolls had been opened and marked in place with reading spools.

Haran's emissary had arrived and made himself welcome in our house. No, not *our* house, I reminded myself. It and everything in it belonged to Haran now.

I walked to the table and glanced over the unfurled scrolls. One contained a list of names—officials and landowners—and next to them, recorded sums of money. On the other, a recording of the house's contents, room by room.

"He could return at any moment. We should leave and return later when he's here," Lavi said. Careful, prudent Lavi.

He was right, yet as we swept past my parents' room, I stopped. An idea suddenly sat in my head, sunning itself. The flick of a scaly tail. I said, "Wait on the balcony and alert me if you hear anyone."

A protest formed on Lavi's face, but he did as I asked.

I stepped into my parents' room, where the sight of Mother's bed halted me with a sharp intake of loss. Her oak chest was coated with a glaze of dust. I creaked it open and my mind swept back to my girlhood—Tabitha and I pillaging through the contents, preparing for our dance.

The wooden jewel box was midway down, beneath neatly folded tunics and coats. Its heft in my hands reassured me it was still full. I opened it. Four gold bracelets, two ivory, six silver. Eight necklaces—amber, amethyst, lapis, carnelian, emerald, and gold leaf. Seven pairs of pearl earrings. A dozen jeweled and silver headbands. Gold rings. So much. Too much.

I would have Lavi trade the jewelry in the market for coins.

Thou shalt not steal. Guilt made me pause. Would I now become a thief? I strode across the room and back, shamed to think what Jesus would say. The Torah also said love your neighbor, I reasoned, and wasn't I taking the jewelry out of love for Yaltha? I doubted I could get her to Alexandria without a substantial bribe. Besides, I'd stolen the ivory sheet from Antipas—I was already a thief.

I said, "This is your parting gift to me, Mother."

On the balcony, I hurried past Lavi toward the stairs. "Let's take our leave."

As we reached the floor below, we heard someone at the door stomping mud from his sandals. We broke for the passageway, but we'd taken only a few strides when a man entered. He reached for the knife at his waist. "Who are you?"

Lavi stepped in front of me. It was as if I had a sparrow caged inside my ribs, flailing about. I edged around Lavi, hoping the man didn't notice my apprehension. "I'm Ana, niece to Haran of Alexandria and the daughter of Matthias, who was head counselor to Herod Antipas before his death. And this is my servant, Lavi. This was my home before I married. May I ask, sir, who are you?"

He dropped his hand to his side. "Your uncle in Alexandria sent me to dispose of this property, which is now rightfully his. I am Apion, his treasurer."

He was a young man of brutish strength and size, but he bore delicate, almost womanly features—lined eyes, full lips, well-shaped brows, and black, curling hair.

The travel pouch strapped across my chest bulged with odd contours. I nudged it toward my back, smiled, and bowed my head. "Then our Lord has blessed me, for you are the one I've come to see. Haran sent word to me through the palace that you were in Galilee, and I came immediately with my husband's blessing to beg a favor of you."

The lies rolled from my lips, water over river rocks.

Apion's eyes darted uncertainly from me to Lavi. "How did you come to enter the house?"

"We found the passage from the courtyard unbolted. I didn't think you would mind if I found shelter." My hand went to my belly, which I protruded as far as I could. "I am with child and felt weary." The audacious turn my lies were taking surprised even me.

He swept his hand toward one of the couches. "Please rest."

I plopped onto the cushion, wrinkling my nose at the fusty air that came wafting up.

"Speak your favor," he said.

I quickly gathered my thoughts. He'd accepted my lies easily enough, and he possessed a kind way—would I need the bribe? Should I forestall until I'd traded the jewelry? I studied the man. His curls were oiled with expensive spikenard. A gold scarab ring encircled his finger, the one he no doubt used to imprint Haran's seal onto documents.

"May I return tomorrow?" I said. "I find myself too tired."

What could he say? A woman with child was a mysterious creature.

He nodded. "Come at the sixth hour, and present yourself at the main door. You will find the passageway from the courtyard locked."

xxix.

The next day we returned at the designated hour. I felt confident. Lavi had traded my mother's jewelry for six thousand drachmae, the equivalent of one talent. It was an unexpected measure of riches. Minted in silver, the coins were so voluminous, Lavi had purchased a sizable leather bag to hold them. He'd paid out more drachmae for a room at an inn, choosing himself to pass the night in the alley. I slept only a little, dreaming that Jesus returned to Nazareth on a spitting camel.

If Lavi was shocked I'd taken the jewelry, he'd hidden it well. Nor had he appeared surprised when I explained I had no child in my womb, only a false tongue in my mouth. Indeed, he smiled a little. His spying and subterfuge in the palace for Judas seemed to have given him a certain appreciation for cunning.

"I would offer you food and wine, but I have neither," Apion said, opening the door. "Nor do I have much time."

I sat once again on the musty couch. "I will be quick. Haran's sister, Yaltha, has lived with me for many years. She knew your father and remembers you as a boy. She helped you with your Greek alphabet."

He gazed at me with a hint of wariness, and it occurred to me he probably knew a great deal about my aunt, none of it favorable. He would've heard the rumors in Alexandria that she'd murdered her husband. If so, he would know Haran had banished her first to the Therapeutae and then to Galilee. Some of that fine, bright confidence I'd felt earlier paled.

"She's old, but in good health," I continued. "And it's her wish to return to the land of her birth. She wishes to go home to serve her brother, Haran. I've come to arrange for you to take her with you to Alexandria when you return."

Still, nothing.

"Yaltha would be a pleasant and docile traveling companion," I said. "She's never trouble." This was an unnecessary falsehood, but I uttered it anyway.

He looked impatiently at the door. "What you're asking is impossible without Haran's permission."

"Oh, but he has given it," I said. "I sent a letter of request to him, but it reached him after you'd departed. In his return message, he expressed his wish for you to see my aunt safely back to Alexandria."

He hesitated, uncertain. There had hardly been time for such an exchange. "Show me the letter and I will be satisfied."

I turned to Lavi, who stood a few paces behind me. "Give me Haran's letter."

He looked at me, confused.

"You brought it as I instructed, did you not?"

It took a moment. "The letter, oh, yes. Forgive me, I fear I left it behind."

I made a show of anger. "My servant has failed me," I said to Apion. "But it's not a reason to ignore my uncle's consent. I will pay you, certainly. Would five hundred drachmae suffice?"

Now we would see if he loved money the way I loved words.

The arches of his brows swept up. I saw it the moment it came into his eyes: greed. "I would require at least one thousand drachmae. And I would expect no mention of the transaction to Haran."

I pretended to debate the matter in my head. "All right, it will be as you say. But you must treat my aunt with respect and kindness or I shall hear of it and report the arrangement to Haran."

"I will treat her as I would my own aunt," he pledged.

"When do you anticipate concluding your business and returning to Alexandria?"

"I had thought it would require weeks, but after only a few days I'm ready to finalize the sale of the house. I will leave for Caesarea in five days in order to take passage on the next merchant ship." He fixed his eyes on the bag strapped across Lavi's chest. "Shall we complete our business?"

"I will return in five days with my aunt, arriving early in the morning. You will be paid then, not before."

His lips curled. "Five days, then."

XXX.

As Lavi and I drew close to the compound, the aroma of roasting lamb filled my nostrils. "Jesus is home," I said.

"How can you know this?"

"Smell the air, Lavi. A fatted lamb!"

It would require a considerable event, such as the homecoming of her son, for Mary to trade for something as expensive as a lamb.

"How do you know the scent is not from some other courtyard?" Lavi said.

I quickened my pace. "I *know*. I just know."

I reached the gate winded and flushed. Yaltha was sitting near the courtyard oven, where Mary, Salome, Judith, and Berenice were busy turning the lamb on a spit. I went to my aunt, kneeling down to embrace her. "Your husband is home," she said. "He arrived last evening. I didn't tell him about your father, but I explained your absence before James had a chance to give his account of it."

"I will go to him," I said. "Where is he?"

"He has been in the workshop all morning. But first, did you persuade Apion?"

"He was persuaded not by me, but by one thousand drachmae."

"A *thousand* . . . How did you come by such riches?"

"It's a long story, and not one I wish overheard. It will keep."

The women had scarcely greeted me, but as I ran toward the workshop, Judith called out, "If you'd heeded James's commandment not to leave, you would've been here to greet your husband."

Her tongue was a pestilence. "His commandment? Did James receive it on a stone tablet? Did God speak to him from a burning bush?"

Judith huffed, and I caught sight of Salome swallowing her laugh.

JESUS SET DOWN the cross-saw he was sharpening. I'd not seen him for more than five months and he looked like a stranger. His hair hung long about his shoulders. His skin was darker and razed by desert winds, all the edges of his face severe. He seemed so much older than his thirty years.

"You've been gone too long," I said, letting my hands rest on his chest. I wanted to feel him, the flesh of him. "And you're too thin. Is that why Mary has a banquet in the making?"

He kissed my forehead. He said nothing about my red scarf. His only words: "I've missed you, Little Thunder."

We sat down on the workbench. "Yaltha said you were in Sepphoris," he said. "Tell me all that has happened since I've been gone."

I described Lavi's unexpected appearance. "He brought me news," I said. "My father is dead."

"I'm sorry, Ana. I know what it's like to lose a father."

"Mine was nothing like your father," I said. "When Nazareth treated you as a mamzer, your father protected you. Mine tried to make me the tetrarch's concubine."

"Is there nothing good you can say of him?"

Jesus's capacity for mercy baffled me. I didn't know if I could give up the wrongs my father had done, the way I hauled them around like an ossuary of precious old bones. Jesus made it seem as if one could just lay them down.

"I can say one thing for him," I said. "*One* thing. My father sometimes provided me with tutors, papyri, and ink. He begrudgingly indulged my writing. This, more than anything, made me who I am."

I'd known this simple truth, but putting it into words gave it an unexpected potency. I felt tears start. Finally, tears for my father. Jesus pressed me to him, burying my nose in his tunic, and I smelled the Jordan River flowing beneath his skin.

I removed my scarf and dried my face with it, unloosing my hair, and then went on, wanting to get through the rest of my telling. I spoke of my visit to Sepphoris, what it was like to be inside the house again, of Apion and his agreement to take Yaltha to Alexandria. There were things I didn't mention—the jewelry, the coins, the lies. When I relayed the news Lavi had brought from the palace, I held back any mention of my ivory sheet and the kitchen steward.

There was, though, information I couldn't withhold. I hesitated a moment before telling him. "Herodias seeks to have John arrested."

"John has already been arrested," he said. "Herod Antipas's soldiers came for him two weeks ago while he was baptizing at Aenon near Salim. He was taken to the fortress at Machaerus and imprisoned. I don't think Antipas will set him free."

My hand went to my mouth. "Will they arrest his disciples?"

He was forever telling me to consider the lilies in the fields, which were never anxious and yet God took care of them. I didn't wish to hear it. "Don't tell me not to worry. I'm alarmed for you."

"John's disciples have scattered, Ana. I don't believe they're looking for us. When John was apprehended, I fled into the Judean desert along with Simon and Andrew, the fishermen, and two others, Philip and Nathanael. We hid there for a week. Even when journeying here to Nazareth, I cut through Samaria to avoid Aenon. I'm being watchful."

"And Judas? Lavi believes he became one of John's disciples, too. What do you know of my brother?"

"He joined us late last fall. After John's arrest, he went to Tiberias in search of news. He promised to come here as soon as he could."

"Judas is coming?"

"I asked him to meet me here. There are plans I wish to discuss with him . . . about the movement."

What could he mean? The movement was in disarray. It was over. Jesus was home now. We would go back to the way it had been. I gripped his hand. I had the sense of something awful coalescing around me. "What plans?"

There were squeals at the doorway and three of the children—Judith's two girls and Berenice's youngest boy—charged into the workshop in a game of chase. Jesus caught the smallest in his arms and swung him about. When he'd given them each a twirl, he said, "I'll tell you everything, Ana, but let's seek a quiet place."

He led me across the courtyard and through the gate. As we left the village and descended into the valley, I smelled the citrus harvest that signaled the arrival of spring. He began to hum.

"Where are we going?" I asked.

"If I tell you, it will not be a surprise." His eyes were alight. Traces of his playfulness with the children still clung to him.

"As long as you're not taking me to the fields to consider the lilies, I'll go willingly."

His laugh was like a clapper bell, and I felt the months of our separation fall away. When we took the road that led to the eastern gate of Sepphoris, I knew we were going to the cave, but said nothing, wishing him to have his surprise, wanting the lightheartedness to last and last.

We walked through the balsam grove, through the thick, piney smell to the outcrop of rock. My heart did a little stag leap. There it was. It had been ten years.

When we stepped inside the cave, I looked toward the back where I'd once buried thirteen scrolls and my incantation bowl, and even now, they seemed buried to me, languishing in the bottom of my cedar chest. But he was here and I was here—I would lament nothing.

We sat in the opening. I said, "Tell me everything, as you promised."

His eyes searched mine. "Hear me to the end before you judge."

"All right, I'll hear you to the end." What he would say would change everything—I knew this indelibly.

"After I'd been with John for two months, he came to me one morning and said he believed God had sent me, that I, too, was God's chosen. Soon after, I began to baptize and preach alongside him. Eventually he moved north to Aenon, where he could slip easily into Decapolis out of Antipas's reach. But he wanted to reach the whole country and he asked me to remain in the south to preach his message of repentance. A small number of the disciples stayed with me—Simon, Andrew, Philip, Nathanael, and Judas. Multitudes came—you cannot imagine the crowds.

People began to say John and I were the two Messiahs." He drew a deep breath and I felt it blow warm on my face.

I could see where he was leading, and I didn't know if I wished to follow. He'd brought me here to the place of our beginnings, but only later would I think of the snake biting its tail, how the beginning becomes the end that becomes the beginning.

"The movement spread like floodwaters," he said. "Now, though, with John in prison, it has been silenced. I cannot let it die."

"You mean to take it up on your own?" I said. "It will become *your* movement now?"

"I'll go forth in my own way. My vision differs from John's. His mission was to prepare the way for God to throw off Roman rule and establish his government on earth. I hope for this, too, but my mission is to bring God's kingdom into the hearts of people. The masses came to John, but I will go to them. I'll not baptize them as he did, but I'll eat and drink with them. I'll exalt the lowly and the outcast. I'll preach God's nearness. I'll preach love."

He'd first told me of his vision of God's kingdom here in this cave . . . the feast of compassion where everyone was welcome. "God has surely chosen you," I told him, and I knew it to be true.

He pressed his forehead to mine and left it there. I think of it still, those moments, that leaning upon each other, the tent our lives made together. Then he rose and walked a few paces. I watched him standing there, bladelike, resolute, and felt overcome by it all. There would be no turning back.

He said, "After Salome's wedding in Cana, I will announce myself at the synagogue in Nazareth, then Judas and I will go to Capernaum. Simon, Andrew, Philip, and Nathanael are waiting for me there, and I know of others who may join us—the sons of Zebedee, a tax collector named Matthew."

I stood. "I will come with you, too. Where you go, I will go." I meant those words, but they sounded strangely ill-fated in my ears and I could not account for it.

"You may come, Ana. I have no qualms about women joining us. All are welcome. But there will be difficulties—traveling from village to village with nowhere to lay our heads. We have no patrons or money with which to feed and clothe ourselves. And it will be dangerous. My preaching will set the priests and Pharisees against me. Already there are those who say I'm the new John who'll rally resistance to Rome. This will certainly reach the ears of Antipas's spies. He will see me as a messiah who stirs revolution just as he did John."

"And he'll arrest you, too," I said, feeling fear spread through me.

At this most unlikely moment, the crooked grin appeared on his face. He sensed my fear, and wishing to break its spell, he said, "Consider the lilies of the field. They are not anxious, yet God takes care of them. How much more will he take care of you?"

xxxi.

In the days after Jesus's return, I disappeared into preparations for our departure. Yaltha and I washed her few paltry garments and hung them to dry on pegs in the storeroom. I beat her sleeping mat and sewed a leather cord to it so she could strap it on her back. I filled waterskins, wrapped salted fish, cheese, and dried figs in strips of clean flax, and stuffed her travel pouch full.

I re-stitched our sandals, laying down an extra piece of leather inside. Jesus fashioned new walking staffs out of olive limbs. He insisted we take only one extra tunic each. I packed two along with a small batch of medicinal herbs, then sat awhile, clutching the preventatives that kept me from pregnancy. I wondered if we would ever have a private place to lie together once we'd left here, then tucked what I could fit of the preventatives into the pouch.

I took care to help Mary as she went about her chores, if only to spend time with her. Almost half of her family was leaving—Salome, Jesus, me, and Yaltha—and though she pretended cheerfulness, her sorrow seeped through as she watched Jesus carve the staffs, trying to keep the tremble from her chin, and as she embraced Salome, blinking tears. She baked honey cakes for us. She patted my cheek, saying, "Ana. Dear Ana."

"Take care of Delilah," I said to her. "Keep Judith away from her."

"I will care for your goat myself."

Lavi asked if he could come with Jesus and me when we left, and I didn't refuse him. "You're a free man now," I told him. "If you come with us, it will be as a follower of Jesus, not a servant." He nodded, perhaps half understanding what following Jesus meant. He kept the leather bag with my hoard of coins strapped to his chest even when he slept. When Jesus had spoken to me at the cave of the need to finance his ministry, I'd determined to become his patron. The drachmae left over after paying Apion's bribe would fund him for many months, perhaps a year. I knew, though, if he learned how I'd obtained the money, he might refuse it. What snares my falsehoods were. I would have to layer lie upon lie to find a way to keep my patronage anonymous.

THE DAY BEFORE we were to return to Sepphoris to meet Apion, I woke with a rolling sensation in my stomach. I could not eat.

"I fear I will never see you again," I said to Yaltha.

We were standing beside the wall in the storeroom, where she'd drawn her charcoal calendar, and I saw she'd marked tomorrow, the sixth of Nisan, with her name and the word *finished*, not in Greek, but in Hebrew. She saw me staring at it. "*We* aren't finished, child. Only my time here in Nazareth."

The thought of parting from her, from Mary and Salome, had become a leviathan ache in my chest.

"We will find each other again." She sounded assured.

"How will I know where you are? How will I get news from you?" Letters were sent by paid couriers who traveled by ship, then by foot, but I would leave soon with Jesus for an itinerant life and it seemed unlikely a letter would ever reach me.

"We'll find each other," she repeated. This time she only sounded cryptic.

I went about my work, unconsoled.

Near the middle of the afternoon, Yaltha and I were beneath the olive tree cutting barley stalks, when looking up, I saw Judas at the gate. I lifted my arms in greeting, as Jesus loped across the courtyard to meet him.

The two men came toward Yaltha and me like brothers, their arms draped about each other's shoulders, yet there was something boding in Judas's face—I saw it immediately: the tightly pulled smile, his eyes shining with dread, the deep breath he took just before he reached me.

He kissed Yaltha's cheeks, then mine.

We sat in patches of shade and sun flecks, and when the pleasantries were over, I said, "Must you always bring troubling news?"

Judas's effort at pretense fell away then. "I wish it were not so," he said and looked away, delaying, and neither Jesus, nor Yaltha, nor I broke the silence. We waited.

He turned back and fixed his gaze on mine. "Ana, Antipas has ordered your arrest."

Jesus looked at me, his face gone still, and in a moment of strangeness and disbelief, I smiled at him.

The kitchen steward and the ivory sheet. Antipas has learned of my complicity. Fear came then, blood rushing up to fill my ears, the wild galloping in my body. *This cannot be.*

Jesus slid closer so I could feel the solidness of him, his shoulder against mine. "Why would Antipas arrest her?" he said calmly.

"He accuses her of treachery in the escape of Phasaelis," Judas said.

"The palace steward who smuggled Ana's warning to Phasaelis confessed its contents."

"You are certain of this news?" Yaltha asked Judas. "Is your source reliable?"

Judas scowled at her. "I wouldn't have alarmed you if I didn't think it was true. Tiberias is still rife with gossip about Phasaelis. They say the soldiers who took her to Machaerus were put to death along with two of her servants, all of them accused of conspiring. And there is much talk of a warning message carried to Phasaelis on a food tray. I knew this to be Ana's ivory tablet."

"But that's gossip. Do you assume her arrest based on gossip?" Yaltha demanded, and I could see the news had stunned her, too, for she refused to believe it.

"There is more, I'm afraid," Judas said, a glint of exasperation in his voice. "I heard of an old woman named Joanna, who was Phasaelis's attendant."

"I know her," I said. "She was married to Antipas's head steward, Chuza." I remembered her hovering about the first time I met Phasaelis. How young I'd been. Fourteen. Betrothed to Nathaniel. *You are no lamb, and I, too, am no lamb.* I glanced at Jesus. Was he remembering Chuza and the day he'd incited the crowd to stone me? I'd often wondered if we would be married if not for that terrible man.

"Chuza is long dead," Judas went on. "But Joanna lives among the servants at the palace, partially blind and too old to be of much use, but she's counted among those who now serve Herodias. She saved herself by condemning Phasaelis and swearing an oath of loyalty to Herodias. When I found her sitting outside the palace walls, she recanted both, saying she knew of Phasaelis's plot and would have fled with her if she had been younger and had her sight." He turned to Yaltha. "It was Joanna who told me about the kitchen steward's confession and of Antipas's intention to arrest Ana. She heard it from Herodias's own lips."

Around us the ordinary world went on: the children at play, James and Simon hewing wood in the workshop, Mary and my sisters-in-law kneading dough near the oven. The day in its courses. My breath hovered painfully over a flame at the back of my throat. "Joanna is certain Antipas will act?"

"He will act, Ana; there's little doubt of it. King Aretas is mobilizing for war to avenge his daughter. Her escape has set off a cataclysm and Antipas lays blame on everyone who abetted his first wife, including you. To make matters worse, Herodias learned that her new husband was once fascinated by you . . . that he commissioned the mosaic of your face. Joanna told me this as well, and I suspect it was she herself who divulged the information to Herodias as a way of gaining her favor. Herodias is pressing Antipas to arrest you as he did John. I tell you, she will see it done."

Jesus had been unaccountably silent. He covered my hand with his and squeezed. He and Judas had been displeased when I'd sent the warning to Phasaelis. I tried now to imagine myself not sending it. I couldn't. With that realization, the fear began to leave my body. There was an incongruous peace in my helplessness, in the knowledge that what was done was done and could not be undone, and even if I could change it, I wouldn't.

"I'm sorry," Judas said to me. "I should never have agreed to deliver your message."

"I don't wish to question the past," I said.

"You're right, little sister. We must think of the future and do so quickly. Joanna believed Antipas's soldiers would be coming for you in a matter of days. I walked here quickly, but Antipas's soldiers will come on horseback. They may have been dispatched by now. There's little time."

Jesus sat forward. I expected him to say we should go and hide in the Judean hills, as he'd done when John was arrested. It would mean great difficulty, and who knew how long we would have to remain out there in that forsaken wilderness, but what choice was there?

He spoke with firm, measured words. "You must go to Alexandria with your aunt."

The day was warm, lemon-yellow light brimming, and still a chill swept over me. "Couldn't we hide in the wilderness as you did before?"

"You will not be safe even there," he said.

Desperation took hold—I'd been nearly six months without him and the thought of separating again was excruciating. "We could go together to Syria, to Caesarea Philipi, to Decapolis. Antipas has no jurisdiction in those places."

Jesus's eyes were afloat with sadness. "My time has come, Ana. I must take up my ministry in Galilee in the wake of John's movement. It cannot wait."

Alexandria.

"It will be temporary," Jesus said. "You should remain in Egypt with your uncle Haran until Antipas's anger and vengeance has cooled. We'll send a letter to you there when it's safe to return."

I stared at him, finally stammering, "But . . . but that could be . . . that could be months. A year, even."

"I hate to think of being separated from you," he said. "But you will be safe, and I can carry on my ministry. When you return, you can join me."

Yaltha placed her hand on my cheek. She said, "Your husband is right. Tomorrow we'll go to Alexandria, you and I. Jesus has his destiny. Let him fulfill it. You have your destiny, too. Is this not what Sophia wanted all along?"

LAVI JOINED OUR CONCLAVE beneath the olive branches and we sat for what seemed like hours, conspiring. The plan was sealed. At daybreak, Judas would walk with us to Sepphoris, deliver us to Apion, then travel on with us to Caesarea to see us safely aboard the ship to Alexandria.

Jesus had wanted to escort us, but I'd been adamant. "I do not want you to miss your sister's wedding," I told him. It was only days away. "Nor do I wish to prolong our goodbye. Let's say farewell here in the place where we've spent these eleven years together."

I spoke the truth to my husband, but not all the truth. Convincing Apion to take me to Alexandria—and Lavi as well, for he'd begged to accompany us and I meant to bargain for his passage, too—would require another act of bribery and I didn't wish Jesus to witness it.

When we finally dispersed from beneath the tree, I pulled Judas aside, into the storeroom, and told him about trading Mother's jewelry for coins. He made no grimace of disapproval—my brother had stolen plenty from the rich to fund his sedition.

"I'm certain Apion will consent to take me and Lavi to Alexandria for a bribe of two thousand drachmae," I said. "If so, that will leave us with three thousand. Jesus needs a patron to finance his ministry. I wish to divide the remaining money between myself and him. The amount could fund his work for months, perhaps the entire time I'm away. I want you to safeguard his portion, Judas, and you must never tell him where it came from. Promise me."

He balked a little. "How will I explain it? He will press me to know his patron."

"Tell him it's someone in Tiberias. Tell him Joanna sent the coins out of gratitude for our part in saving her mistress. Tell him it's anonymous. I don't care, only don't reveal my part in it."

"He's my friend, Ana. I believe in what he's doing. Jesus is our best hope to find freedom from Rome. I don't wish to start out lying to him."

"I hate lying to him, too, but I fear he won't take the money otherwise."

"I'll do as you ask, but let it be known, when it comes to you, I'm too indulgent."

"One more thing, then," I said. "You must write to me. Set aside some of the coins to purchase parchments and hire messengers. Send me news of Jesus and summon me as soon as it's safe to return. Swear it."

He hugged me to him. "I swear it."

xxxii.

I dug my incantation bowl from the bottom of the cedar chest, where it had lain neglected and fallow for years. It was the size of a dough bowl, too large for my travel pouch, but I would not leave it behind. Nor my scrolls. When the silver coins were emptied from the large pouch, I would slip the bowl and the scrolls into it. Until then I would carry them in my arms.

I gazed at the wool sack of potsherds on which I'd penned the verses of grief for Susanna. They would have to stay behind.

The afternoon had given way to evening dark. Out in the courtyard, hushed voices. From the doorway, I could see Jesus and his family. In the sky, one lone star, a puncture of light.

"Your wife has acted recklessly," I heard James say. "Now she will bring Antipas's soldiers to our door."

"What are we to say to them?" Simon said.

Jesus clasped a hand on each of their shoulders—that way he had of reminding them they were all brothers. "Tell them the woman they seek no longer lives here. Tell them she has left me and gone away with her brother; we don't know where."

"You would have us lie to them?" James asked.

Jesus's suggestion that they prevaricate about my whereabouts surprised me, too.

Mary had been standing on the periphery, but she stepped before James and Simon. "What Jesus would have you do is help him preserve the life of his wife," she said sharply. "You will do as he asks of you!"

"We must do as our conscience requires," said Simon.

Salome made a whimpering sound. A sigh, a cry? I couldn't tell.

"Let us drink some wine and talk together," Jesus said.

I closed the door. In the stillness, a great heaviness came over me. I lit the lamps. Jesus would be back soon. Hurriedly, I cleansed my face and hands, donned a clean white garment, and smoothed my hair with oil fragrant with cloves.

Yaltha's words returned to me: *You have your destiny, too.* They stirred the old longings in me, the terrible need for my own life.

I reopened my chest and retrieved the last of the oven ink, half-full and thick with gum, then pulled a reed pen from my travel pouch. Cross-writing in quick, tiny letters between the lines of my old prayer, I wrote a new prayer inside my incantation bowl.

Sophia, Breath of God, set my eyes on Egypt. Once the land of bondage, let it become the land of freedom. Deliver me to the place of papyri and ink. To the place I will be born.

xxxiii.

I woke before daybreak with my head burrowed in the crook of Jesus's neck. His beard brushed my forehead. Heat radiated from his skin with the scent of wine and salt. I didn't move. I lay in the dark and drank him in.

The light came slow and limping, never fully arriving. Overhead, thunder—a splintering sound, then another and another, the sky timbers cracking. Jesus stirred, making a soft, droning noise with his lips. I thought he would get up then and pray.

Instead, he said, "Little Thunder, is that you I hear?" And he laughed.

I forced a lilt into my voice, teasing him back. "It's me, Beloved. I'm roaring at the thought of leaving you behind."

He turned on his side to face me and I felt that he saw deep inside me. He said, "I bless the largeness in you, Ana."

"And I bless yours," I told him.

Then he rose and, opening the door, stared toward the valley with the same deep, pure gaze he'd cast on me. I went to stand beside him and looked in the same direction as he, and it seemed for an instant I saw the world as he did, orphaned and broken and staggeringly beautiful, a thing to be held and put back right.

Parting was fully upon us now. I wished with all my being that we might have gone on together.

We ate in silence. After I dressed and made myself ready for the journey ahead, I opened the goatskin pouch that held the red thread. It was fragile, the thinnest of filaments, but I would wear it this day for him. He helped me tie it onto my wrist.

The family waited in the courtyard. I embraced each of them before Jesus walked with me to the gate, where Judas, Yaltha, and Lavi waited. The drizzle had stopped, but the sky was sodden.

We didn't linger with goodbyes. I kissed Jesus's mouth. "May this severing not cut us apart, but bind us together," I said. And holding my bowl and my scrolls to my chest, I set my face toward Egypt.

ALEXANDRIA

LAKE MAREOTIS, EGYPT

28–30 CE

i.

We sailed into the great harbor of Alexandria after eight days of turbulent seas. Though our ship—a vessel that bore Egyptian corn to Caesarea and returned to Alexandria with olives—had hugged the coastline, the waves had left me unable to keep down food or drink. Throughout the journey, I had lain curled on my mat belowdecks and thought of Jesus. At times, my distress at traveling farther and farther away from him was so great, I wondered if my sickness wasn't from the pitch of the sea at all, but from the pain and tumult of leaving him.

Still weak and nauseated, I forced myself to leave the ship's hull for my first glimpse of the city I'd dreamed about since Yaltha first began telling me stories of her greatness. Standing beside my aunt, I inhaled the foggy air and drew my coat to my neck, the clamor of the mainsail snapping ferociously over our heads. The harbor swarmed with ships— large merchant ships like ours, and smaller, fleet galleys.

"There!" said my aunt, pointing into the gloom. "There's Pharos, the great lighthouse."

When I turned, I was met by a spectacle I couldn't have imagined. On a small island facing the harbor, a massive tower of white marble rose in three grand tiers toward the clouds, and at the top, a magnificent blaze of light. Even the Temple in Jerusalem couldn't compare to it.

"How do they make such a light?" I murmured, too awed to realize I'd spoken the thought aloud.

"The fire is reflected by massive bronze mirrors," Yaltha replied, and I saw in her face the pride she felt for her city.

A statue crowned the pinnacle of the lighthouse dome, a man pointing skyward. "Who's that?" I asked.

"Helios, the Greeks' sun god. See? He's pointing to the sun."

The city brimmed along the waterfront, shining white buildings that stretched into the distance. My nausea forgotten, I stared transfixed at one of them that jutted out into the harbor, a dazzling edifice that seemed to float on the water's surface. "Behold," Yaltha said, watching my face. "The palace of the royals. I once told you about the queen who lived there—Cleopatra the Seventh."

"The one who went to Rome with Caesar."

Yaltha laughed. "Yes, that, among other things. She died the year I was born. I grew up hearing stories of her. My father—your grandfather—said she would write on nothing but papyrus made in our family's workshops. She proclaimed it the finest papyrus in Egypt."

Before I could take in the news that Cleopatra had made reference to my family, an imposing columned structure loomed up. "That's one of the temples to Isis," Yaltha said. "There's a grander one near the library known as Isis Medica that houses a medical school."

My mind had become dizzy with wonder. How alien this place was, how gloriously alien.

We grew silent, letting the city slide past like the contours of a dream, and I thought of my beloved, of how far I was from him. By now he would've attended Salome's wedding in Cana and departed for Capernaum to assemble his followers and start his ministry. The memory of him standing at the gate when I departed brought a twist of pain. I longed to be with him. But not in Galilee. No, not there . . . *here*.

When I looked again at Yaltha, her eyes were misted, whether from wind, happiness, or her own twist of pain for Chaya, I couldn't say.

When we disembarked, Apion hired a flat-roofed litter for the four of us with curtained windows and cushioned seats, pulled by two donkeys. We bobbed along the Canopic Way, the main corridor of the city, a cobblestone street so wide it could've fit fifty litters side by side. The street was lined on either side with red-roofed buildings and people milling about—women with uncovered heads, and girls, not just boys, trotting behind their tutors with wooden tablets hitched to their waists on cords. Catching sight of a brilliantly hued Egyptian woman, winged and kneeling, painted inside a portico, I made an exclamation of surprise, and Yaltha leaned to me and said, "Winged Isis. You'll see her everywhere." We came upon a line of horse-drawn chariots driven by men in helmets, who, Apion informed us, were on their way to the hippodrome.

A resplendent-looking pediment suddenly protruded in the distance. My heart gave a lurch. I couldn't see the building's facade, but the roof seemed to preside over the city. "Is that the great library?" I asked Yaltha.

"It is," she said. "We will go there, you and I."

During our voyage my aunt had described how the library's half million scrolls were meticulously cataloged and arranged, all the texts in existence in the entire world. She'd told me of the scholars who lived there, how they'd determined the earth was round and measured not only its circumference, but its distance to the sun.

And we would go there.

IT WAS NOT UNTIL our litter arrived at Haran's house that my excitement turned to apprehension. I had lied to Apion, insisting Haran had sent a letter giving his permission for Yaltha to come. How could my deceit possibly remain undiscovered? What if Haran refused to take us in? I couldn't be elsewhere—Judas would send his letters to Haran's house.

Before we'd boarded the ship in Caesarea, I'd made certain that Apion conveyed to my brother exactly how the dispatches should be addressed. "Haran ben Philip Levias, Jewish Quarter, Alexandria," he'd said.

"Is that all that's needed?" I asked.

"Your uncle is the wealthiest Jew in Alexandria," he said. "Everyone knows where he lives."

At this, Yaltha dispensed a grunt of derision, causing Apion to cut his eyes toward her.

She will have to hide her bitterness better than this, I thought, as we stepped into Haran's palatial house. How would she find Chaya without Haran's help?

My uncle looked like my father: lumpy bald head, large ears, thick chest, and beardless. Only his eyes were different—less curious and with a hawkish, preying quality. He met us in the atrium, where an oculus streamed light from the ceiling. He was standing directly beneath it in an unrelenting white shine. I could find no shadow in the room. This struck me as an ominous sign.

Yaltha approached him slowly with her face downcast. I was shocked to see her enact an elaborate bow. "Esteemed brother," she said. "I've come home humbled. I beg you to receive me." I shouldn't have worried; she knew very well how to play this game.

He glared at her, arms folded. "You've come unbidden, Yaltha. When I sent you to our brother in Galilee, it was with the understanding you would not return."

Haran turned to Apion then. "I gave you no authority to bring them here."

The revelation of my deception had come sooner than I'd anticipated.

"Sir, forgive me," Apion said, his mouth sputtering words. "The younger woman said . . ." He glanced at me, sweat forming on his temples, and I saw his dilemma. He feared that if he accused me, I would expose the bribes he'd taken.

Reading the situation, Haran said, "Is it possible, Apion, that you were bribed? If so, hand the money over to me now and I'll consider keeping you as my treasurer."

It came to me that I should save him. It appeared we would be cast out either way, and I decided to risk everything to win Apion's friendship.

I stepped forward. "I am Ana, the daughter of Matthias. Don't blame your employee for bringing us here. We gave him no bribe. Rather I led him to believe you'd sent a letter with consent for us to come and stay with you. His only fault was having faith in my word."

Yaltha glanced at me, uncertain. Lavi shifted on his feet. I didn't look at Apion, but I heard the out-breath that escaped his lips.

Haran said, "You stand here and confess you are in my house out of *trickery*?" He broke into laughter, and there was not a hint of derision in it. "Why have you come here?"

"As you know, Uncle, my father is dead. My aunt and I had nowhere else to go."

"Have you no husband?" he asked.

I should've anticipated such an obvious question, but it caught me by surprise. I hesitated too long.

"Her husband sent her away," Yaltha said, rescuing me. "She's ashamed to speak of it."

"Yes," I muttered. "He turned me out." Then, lest Haran inquire what terrible thing I'd done to deserve my expulsion, I quickly continued, "We traveled here with our guardian because you are my father's eldest brother and our patriarch. My trickery came from my desire to come here and serve you. I ask your forgiveness."

He turned to Yaltha. "She's shrewd, this one—I cannot help but like her. Now. Tell me, long-lost sister, why have you returned after all this time? Don't tell me that you, too, have come hoping to serve me—I know better."

"I have no wish to serve you, it's true. I wished to come home, that's all. I've been in exile for twelve years. Is that not long enough?"

His lips curled. "So, you've not returned in hopes of finding your daughter? Any mother would wish to be reunited with a lost daughter before she dies."

He was not just ruthless, but perceptive. I told myself I should never underestimate him.

"My daughter was adopted long ago," Yaltha said. "I forfeited her. I have no false hope of seeing her again. If you wish to tell me her whereabouts, I would welcome it, but I've made my peace with our separation."

He said, "I know nothing of her whereabouts, as you fully know. Her family insisted on a legal agreement that prevents us from having any contact with them."

"As I said, she's gone," Yaltha reiterated. "I didn't come for her, only for myself. Let me come home, Haran." How contrite she looked, how convincing.

Haran stepped away from the harsh shaft of light and paced, hands clasped behind him. He gave Apion a wave of dismissal and his treasurer nearly broke into a run as he left the room.

My uncle stopped in front of me. "You will pay me five hundred bronze drachmae for each month you stay under my roof."

Five hundred! I was in possession of fifteen hundred Herodian silver drachmae with no idea how that translated into Egyptian bronze. We needed the money to last up to a year, not just for rent, but for passage home.

"One hundred," I said.

"Four hundred," he countered.

"One hundred fifty and I will serve you as a scribe."

"A scribe?" He snorted. "I have a scribe."

"Does your scribe write Aramaic, Greek, Hebrew, and Latin . . . all four?" I asked.

"Does he create lettering and scripts so beautiful people attribute even greater import to the words?" said Yaltha.

"You do these things?" Haran said to me.

"I do."

"All right. One hundred fifty bronze drachmae and your services as a scribe. I require nothing further except that neither of you leave this house."

"You can't mean to confine us here," I said. This was a blow worse than the cost of his rent.

"If you require goods from the market, your guardian, as you call him, can do your bidding."

He faced Yaltha. "As you know, charges of murder do not expire. If I learn that either of you have left the house or made inquiries about your daughter, I'll make sure you're arrested." His face hardened. "Chaya's family doesn't want your meddling, and I won't risk them suing me because of it."

He clanged a tiny gong and a young woman, not Jewish, but a long-necked Egyptian with heavily lined eyes, appeared. "Show them to the women's quarters and put their guardian with the servants," Haran told her, then abruptly left us.

We followed behind her, listening to the shuffle of her sandals on the tile, watching her black hair swish back and forth. We were, it seemed, to be captives here.

"Does Haran not have a wife we could appeal to?" I whispered to Yaltha.

"She died before I left Alexandria. I don't know if he took another," she whispered back.

The servant girl stopped before a doorway. "You will reside here," she said to us in broken Greek, then added, "He has no wife. No one lives beneath this roof but Haran and his servants."

"What good ears you have," I said.

"All servants have good ears," she replied, and I saw Lavi grin.

"Where are Haran's sons?" Yaltha asked.

"They manage his lands in the Nile Delta." She motioned to Lavi and sauntered off, swaying hair, swaying hips. He gazed at her with parted lips, before fumbling after her.

MY SLEEPING CHAMBER was separated from Yaltha's by a sitting room that opened onto a courtyard garden—a tiny forest of date palms. We stood in the doorway looking out at it.

"Haran doesn't trust you," I said. "He knows exactly why you're here."

"Yes. He knows."

"But it's strange, isn't it, that he goes to such lengths to keep you from Chaya. Even confining us to the house. What harm would it be for you to see her? Perhaps there is some legal agreement with her family, but I wonder if he conceals Chaya from you only to punish you. Could his need for vengeance be as strong as that?"

"The rumors surrounding my husband's death were a disgrace for him—his own sister believed to be a murderer. He lost business over it. He lost favor in the city. He was shamed. He never got over it, and he has never stopped blaming me. His need for revenge is bottomless."

We stood there silent a few moments, and I thought I saw something come into her face, some awareness. She said, "What if Haran conceals Chaya not only out of vengeance, but to hide some wrongdoing of his own?"

My skin prickled. "What do you mean, Aunt?"

"I'm not sure," she said. "Time will tell us."

Out in the center of the garden, a little pond overflowed with blue lotus. *At least we have lodging here*, I thought.

While Yaltha settled herself, I stepped outside and went to kneel beside the pond. As I examined the odd way the lotus grew from the mud at the bottom, I heard footsteps. Turning, I found Apion standing behind me. "I'm grateful," he said. "You rescued me at your own expense."

"I could do no less."

He smiled. "So, niece of Haran, what is it you want from me?"

"Time will grant us an answer," I said.

ii.

I spent my mornings in Haran's small scriptorium making copies of his business records. "A fool possesses one copy," he'd said. "A wise man, two."

My uncle owned his father's lucrative papyrus fields, the transactions of which were acutely boring—contracts, deeds, accounts, receipts. Mountainous piles of dullness. Fortunately, he still sat on the council of seventy-one elders that oversaw Jewish affairs in the city, which provided me with far more engaging documents. I copied a wonderful array of lurid complaints about pregnant widows, daughters-in-law found not to be virgins, husbands beating wives, wives deserting husbands. There was an oath from a woman charged with adultery who swore her innocence in such insistent terms it made me smile, and another from a rabbi's wife claiming a male bath attendant had scalded her thighs with hot water. Most amazing of all was a daughter's petition to give her own self in marriage rather than allow her father to do it. How dull Nazareth had been.

I wrote on the most beautiful papyri I'd ever beheld, white, close-grained, polished sheets, and I learned how to gum them together to create rolls twice as long as I was tall. Haran's other scribe was an elderly man named Thaddeus who had sprigs of white hair in his ears and ink stains on his fingertips, and who fell asleep each day holding his pen.

Emboldened by his naps, I abandoned my work as well and resumed writing my stories of the matriarchs while he slept. I didn't fear Haran's sudden appearance, for he spent his days flitting about the city, if not attending council meetings, then business at the synagogue or Greek games at the amphitheater, and when he was home, we stayed clear of him, taking meals in our quarters. It was only necessary that I produce slightly more copies than slow, snoring Thaddeus. In this way, I composed the stories of Judith, Ruth, Miriam, Deborah, and Jezebel. I tucked the scrolls inside a large stone jar in my room, adding them to the others.

I spent the afternoons in our guest quarters, idling endlessly and fretting for my beloved, whom I pictured wandering about Galilee speaking openly with lepers and harlots and mamzers of every sort, calling for the mighty to be brought low, all of this in the presence of Antipas's spies.

In order to distract myself from my fears, I started filling the time by reading my stories to Yaltha and Lavi. Yaltha had grown increasingly quiet and morose since our arrival, downcast, it seemed, over our inability to seek Chaya, and I hoped my stories might lift her from her misery as well. They did seem to cheer her, but it was Lavi who reveled most in them.

He appeared unexpectedly one day at our door. "May I bring Pamphile to hear your stories?" he said.

I thought at first he'd asked because of the flair I gave to my readings. In my effort to draw Yaltha out, I'd made little performances out of them, not dancing the stories as Tabitha used to do, but enlivening them with actions and dramatic articulations. My rendition of Judith slicing off the head of Holofernes had brought gasps from Lavi and Yaltha both.

"Pamphile?" I said.

"The pretty Egyptian girl," Yaltha offered. "The house servant."

I gave Lavi a knowing grin. "Go, fetch her and I'll read."

He dashed toward the door, then stopped. "I wish you to read the story of Rachel, whose face was more beautiful than a thousand moons, how Jacob labored fourteen years to marry her."

iii.

Yaltha sat in the elaborately carved chair in our sitting room, a perch she'd taken to occupying day in and day out, often with her eyes closed, her hands rubbing together in her lap while she wandered off somewhere in her thoughts.

We'd been caged in Haran's house through the spring and summer, unable to visit the great library, a temple, an obelisk, or even one of the little sphinxes that perched on the harbor wall. Yaltha hadn't mentioned Chaya in weeks, but I guessed that was who she thought of while musing and fidgeting in the chair.

"Aunt," I said, unable to bear our helplessness any longer. "We came here to find Chaya. Let's do so even if we defy Haran."

"First of all, child, that's not our only purpose in being here. We also came to keep *you* from being tossed into Herod Antipas's prison. If we stay long enough, we should at least succeed at that. As for Chaya . . ." She shook her head and the sad, remote look returned to her face. "That is harder than I thought."

"As long as we're confined here, we'll never find her," I said.

"Even if we were free to roam the city . . . without Haran to point us in Chaya's direction, I wouldn't know where to begin."

"We could ask about her in the markets, the synagogues. We could . . ." My words sounded pathetic even to me.

"I know Haran, Ana. If we're caught venturing beyond these walls, he will make good on his word and renew the charges against me. Sometimes I think he wants me to violate his terms so he can do just that. *I* will be the one imprisoned, and you and Lavi will be turned onto the street—where would you go? How would you receive word from Judas that it's safe to return?"

I went to sit on the leopard-skin rug at her feet, letting my cheek rest against her knee, and gazed sideways at a row of water lilies frescoed across the wall. I thought of the mud walls in Nazareth, the dirt floors, the mud-and-straw roof that had to be fortified against the rains. I'd never minded those humble things, but I couldn't say I missed them either. What I missed was Mary and Salome stirring pots. My goat following me around the compound. And Jesus, always Jesus. Each morning, upon opening my eyes, it would break over me afresh that he was far away. I would imagine him rising from his mat and repeating the Shema, his prayer shawl draped about his shoulders as he wandered off into the hills to pray, and missing him would become so great that I, too, would rise, then lift my incantation bowl and sing the prayers inside it.

Sophia, Breath of God, set my eyes on Egypt. Once the land of bondage, let it become the land of freedom. Deliver me to the place of papyri and ink. To the place I will be born.

Knowing that we both prayed at the morning hour each day was like a tether binding us, but I lifted my bowl for another reason, too. I longed not only for him, but for myself. How, though, could anyone be born while quarantined in this house?

As I sat there, staring at the lilies on the wall, an idea came to me. I sat up and looked at Yaltha. "If there's any reference to Chaya in this house, it could be buried somewhere in Haran's scriptorium. He has a large upright chest there. I don't know what it contains, only that he takes care to keep it locked. I could try to search through it. If we aren't free to leave, I can at least do that."

She didn't respond, her countenance didn't change, but I could tell she was listening.

"Search for an adoption transaction," she said. "Look for anything that might help us."

iv.

The next morning when Thaddeus's eyelids thickened and his chin dropped to his chest, I slipped into Haran's study and searched for the key that unlocked the cabinet at the back of the scriptorium. I came upon it easily, poorly hidden in an alabaster jar on his desk.

When I opened the cabinet, the doors screeched like lyre strings plucked wrongly, and I froze as Thaddeus roused a bit, then settled back to sleep. Hundreds of scrolls were stacked tightly into compartments, row after row, their round ends staring at me like a wall of unblinking eyes.

I guessed—correctly, it would turn out—that I'd discovered his personal archives. Were they arranged by subject, year, language, alphabet, or some mysterious means known only to Haran? With a glance at Thaddeus, I slid out three scrolls from the top left compartment and closed the cabinet without locking it. The first one was a certification in Latin of Haran's Roman citizenship. The second implored a man named Andromachos to return Haran's black female donkey that had been stolen from his stable. The third was his will, leaving all of his properties and wealth to his oldest son.

Each morning thereafter, I retrieved the key and removed a handful of scrolls. Thaddeus's naps typically lasted slightly less than an hour, but fearing he might wake precipitously, I allowed myself only half that time to read, making certain to mark the outside of each document I'd completed with a small dot of ink. Long manuscripts of philosophy were mixed with letters, invitations, commemorations, and horoscopes.

Nothing, it seemed, was left unrecorded. If a wee beetle ate a single leaf off a papyrus plant in his field, he wrote a lament that required the sacrifice of *three* plants. My progress was slow. At the end of two months, I'd read through only half the documents.

"Did you find anything of interest today?" Yaltha asked one afternoon when I returned to our rooms. Always the same question. Of all the emotions, hope was the most mysterious. It grew like the blue lotus, snaking up from muddy hearts, beautiful while it lasted.

I shook my head. Always the same answer.

"Beginning tomorrow I'll go with you to the scriptorium," she said. "Together, we can go through the scrolls much faster."

This surprised, pleased, and troubled me. "What if Thaddeus wakes and finds you poring over Haran's documents? It's one thing for him to find me with an unauthorized scroll—I can claim I have it by mistake, that it was misplaced. But you—he could go straight to Haran."

"Thaddeus won't be a concern."

"Why not?"

"Because we will serve him one of my special drinks."

I ARRIVED IN THE SCRIPTORIUM the following morning with cakes and beer, a drink the Egyptians consumed at all hours as if it were water or wine.

I set a cup before Thaddeus. "We deserve refreshment, don't you think?"

He tilted his head, uncertain. "I don't know if Haran would—"

"I'm sure he won't mind, but if so, I'll tell him it was I who arranged it. You've been kind to me, and I wish to repay you, that's all."

He smiled then and lifted his cup, and I felt a paroxysm of guilt. He *had* been kind, always treating my mistakes with patience and showing me how to repair errors by cleaning dribbles of ink with a bitter fermented liquid. I suspected he knew that I pilfered papyrus for my own purposes, yet he said nothing. And how did I repay him? I deceived him

with a draft Yaltha had concocted with the aid of Pamphile and a seda-
tive distilled from the lotus flower.

His oblivion was quick and miraculous. I dumped out the beer in my
own cup through the window in Haran's study, and when my aunt appeared, I already had the cabinet unlocked. We unraveled scroll after
scroll, securing them with reading spools, and read side by side at my
desk. Yaltha was an uncommonly noisy reader. She made constant vibrating sounds, *hmms, ooos,* and *acks,* suggesting she'd stumbled upon
some stupefaction or frustration.

We read through a dozen or so scrolls, unable to find any mention of
Chaya. Yaltha left at the close of an hour—that was all the time we
thought we could risk. Thaddeus, however, went on sleeping. I began to
stare at his inert form to be sure he was breathing. His breaths seemed
shallow and too far apart, and I was vastly relieved when he woke, bleary,
yawning, his hair splashed up on one side of his head. He and I both
pretended, as usual, not to notice that he'd been indisposed.

Later, finding Yaltha back in our rooms, I said, "You and Pamphile must
restrain yourselves when dousing his drink. Half the measure will do."

"Do you think him suspicious of the beer?"

"No, I think him well rested."

v.

On a spring day, midway through the month the Egyptians called
Phamenoth, Yaltha and I were sitting beside the pond, she reading
Homer's *Odyssey,* which was copied onto a thick codex, one of the more
precious texts in Haran's library. I'd brought it to her with Thaddeus's
permission, hoping it would fill her afternoons and distract her mind
from Chaya.

Our clandestine hours in the scriptorium had lasted through the fall
and winter. After the first month, Yaltha limited her visits to once a week

in order to ward off any suspicions Thaddeus might have—there was only so much beer we could bring him. Our efforts had also been slowed when Haran suffered a stomach ailment and did not leave the house for several weeks. Nevertheless, we'd recently finished perusing every scroll in the locked chest. We knew more about Haran's personal dealings than we cared to. Thaddeus was fat with beer. And we'd discovered nothing that suggested Chaya had ever existed.

I lay back in the grasses and stared at shredded bits of cloud and wondered why Judas hadn't written to me. It normally took three months for a courier to bring a letter from Galilee. We'd been in Alexandria for twelve. Had Judas hired an unreliable courier? Or perhaps something calamitous had happened to the courier along the way. It seemed possible Antipas had given up his search for me long ago. I dug my fingernails into the soft pad of my thumbs. Why had Jesus not sent for me?

On the day my husband told me he would take up his ministry, he'd leaned his forehead against mine and closed his eyes. I tried now to picture it . . . to picture him. Already his features had dimmed a little in my mind. It terrified me, this slow disappearing.

Pamphile stepped into the courtyard, bringing our supper. "Would you prefer to eat here in the garden?"

I sat up, the image of Jesus scattering, leaving me with a sudden, sharp aloneness.

"Let's eat here," Yaltha said, setting aside her book.

"Has there been a letter today?" I asked Pamphile. She'd agreed to alert me to the arrival of a courier, but even so, I queried her about it daily.

"I'm sorry, no." She gave me an inquisitive look. "This letter must be very important."

"My brother promised to send word when it's safe for us to return to Galilee."

Pamphile stopped abruptly, wobbling her tray. "Would Lavi return with you?"

"We couldn't travel without his protection." I realized too late that I'd spoken without thinking. Lavi had lost his heart to her, but it seemed she'd lost hers to him as well. If she knew the letter meant Lavi's departure, would she conceal it from me? Could I trust her?

She poured wine into Yaltha's cup, then mine, and handed us bowls of lentil and garlic stew. "If Lavi returns with me," I said, "I'll make certain he has money to buy passage back to Alexandria."

She nodded without smiling.

Yaltha frowned. I had no trouble reading her face: *I understand you wish to secure her loyalty, but will there be money for such a promise?* Other than the sum I'd set aside for our return, there were only enough drachmae to pay Haran's rent for four more months, no more.

When Pamphile had departed, Yaltha's spoon thudded against her bowl. I, myself, could find no appetite. I lay back once more upon the earth, closed my eyes, and searched for his face. I could not find it.

vi.

I pressed five drachmae into Lavi's palm. "Go to the market and purchase a travel pouch made of wool, one that will hold my scrolls." I led him to the stone jar in my sleeping chamber, pulled out the scrolls one by one, and spread them across my bed. "As you see, our old leather pouch is no longer large enough."

His eyes moved over my stockpile.

"There are twenty-seven of them," I said.

Afternoon light was falling from the small window, pale green from the palms. I stared at the scrolls, at years and years of begging and scrounging for the privilege of writing—every word, every ink stroke hard-won and precious, and I felt something flood through me. I don't know if I would call it pride. It was more of a simple awareness that somehow I'd done this. I felt amazed suddenly. Twenty-seven scrolls.

During the year we'd been here, I'd completed my narratives of the matriarchs in the Bible, and also written an account of Chaya, the lost daughter, and Yaltha, the searching mother. I took it to my aunt before the ink had fully dried. Upon reading it, she said, "Chaya is lost, but her story isn't," and I felt that my words were a balm for her. I re-created the verses of grief for Susanna that I'd written on the potsherds I'd left behind in Nazareth. I couldn't remember all of them, but enough to satisfy me. I wrote the tale of my friendship with Phasaelis and her escape from Antipas, and finally of the household in Nazareth.

Lavi looked up from the pile of stories. "Does the new pouch mean we'll be traveling soon?"

"I'm still awaiting the letter telling me it's safe to enter Galilee. I wish to be ready when it comes."

I was in need of a larger pouch, it's true, but my motive in sending Lavi into the city was also ulterior. I was considering how to broach the matter when he said, "I wish to marry Pamphile."

I blinked at him, startled. "And does Pamphile wish to be your wife?"

"We would marry tomorrow if we could, but I have no means to care for her. I will have to find employment here in Alexandria, for she will not leave Egypt."

He meant to remain here? I felt the bottom dropping from my stomach.

"And when I find work," he said, "I'll make a request of her father. We can't get a license without his sanction. He's a vinedresser in the village of Dionysias. I don't know if he would give his consent to a foreigner."

"I can't imagine her father would refuse you. I'll write a commendation for you, if you think that would help."

"Yes, thank you," he said.

"I need to know—will you still return to Galilee with us? Yaltha and I cannot travel alone; it's too dangerous."

"I won't abandon you, Ana," he said.

Relief flowed through me, then pleasure. I didn't think he'd ever addressed me as Ana, not even after I'd pronounced him to be a free man. It seemed not just an act of friendship, but a quiet declaration of his autonomy.

"Don't worry, I'll find the money for your passage back to Alexandria," I said, but the words had scarcely left me before I realized I had the money already. Letter or no letter from Judas, we had no choice but to leave when the money was depleted. We could simply depart earlier, *before* I was required to pay the last month's rent. The surplus would pay Lavi's passage.

"Now, go quickly to the market," I said. "Go to the one near the harbor."

"That is not the closest, nor the largest. It would be better—"

"Lavi, this is most important. I need you to also go to the harbor. Look for a ship from Caesarea. Seek out those who arrive on it—merchants, seamen, anyone. I wish for news of Antipas. It's possible he's no longer even alive. If he's ill or dead, we can return to Galilee with peace of mind."

I PACED ABOUT OUR QUARTERS while Yaltha read, pausing now and then to offer some commentary on Odysseus, who exasperated her by taking ten years to get home to his wife after the Trojan War. She was no less annoyed with Penelope, who waited for him. I felt a remote kinship with Penelope. I knew a great deal about waiting for men.

In the courtyard, the day was taking its leave. Lavi's knock, when it finally came, landed with faint, rapid thuds. When I opened the door, he didn't smile. He looked clenched and wary.

I hadn't *really* expected to learn that we were free of Antipas—what was the chance the tetrarch had died in the course of a year? But I hadn't imagined the intelligence Lavi gathered might be adverse.

He removed a generously sized pouch of gray wool from his shoulder and handed it to me. "The price was three drachmae."

As he settled cross-legged on the floor, I poured him a cup of Theban wine. Yaltha closed the codex, marking her place with a leather cord. The lamplight flickered and snapped.

"You have news?" I said.

He looked away, the hoods pulled low over his eyes. "When I got to the harbor, I went up and down the moorings. There were ships from Antioch and Rome, but none from Caesarea. I could see three ships beyond the lighthouse approaching, one with crimson on its sail, so I waited. As I thought, it was the Roman cargo ship from Caesarea. It carried some Jewish pilgrims returning from Passover in Jerusalem, but they wouldn't speak with me. A Roman soldier chased me—"

"*Lavi*," I said. "What did you learn?"

He looked into his lap and continued. "One of the men on board didn't appear as rich as the rest. I followed him. When we were safely from the docks, I offered him the other two drachmae in exchange for news. He was eager to take them."

"Did he have word of Antipas?" I asked.

"The tetrarch is alive . . . and grows worse in his ways."

I sighed, but the news was not unexpected. I retrieved the wine jug and refilled Lavi's cup.

"There's more," he said. "The prophet that Judas and your husband followed . . . the one Antipas imprisoned . . ."

"Yes, John the Immerser—what about him?"

"Antipas executed him. He cut off the Immerser's head."

His words collected in my ears and lay there, puddles of nonsense. For a minute, I didn't move or speak. I heard Yaltha talking to me, but I was far away, standing in the Jordan River with John's hands lowering me beneath the water. Light on the river bottom. A floor of pebbles. The silent floating. John's muffled voice calling, *Rise to newness of life.*

Beheaded. I looked at Lavi, a sick churning inside me. "The servant you spoke with—is he certain of this?"

"He said the whole country spoke of the prophet's death."

Some truths seemed insoluble, stones that couldn't be swallowed.

"They say Antipas's wife, Herodias, was behind it," Lavi added. "Her daughter performed a dance that pleased Antipas so much he promised whatever she asked. At her mother's urging, she asked for John's head."

I covered my mouth with my hand. The reward for a beautiful dance: a man's severed head.

Lavi watched me, his expression grave. He said, "The servant also spoke about another prophet who was going about Galilee, preaching."

I felt my heart scurry up into my throat.

"He heard the prophet preach to a great multitude on a hillside outside Capernaum. He spoke of it with awe. He said the prophet lashed out at hypocrites and proclaimed it was easier for a camel to pass through the eye of a needle than for a rich man to come into the kingdom of God. He blessed the poor, the meek, the outcast, and the merciful. He preached love, saying if a soldier forces you to carry his pack one mile, carry it two, and if you're struck on one cheek, turn the other one. This servant said the prophet's following is even greater than the Immerser's, that people spoke of him as a Messiah. As King of the Jews." With that, Lavi fell quiet.

I fell quiet, too. The wooden door onto the courtyard was flung wide onto the Egyptian night. I listened to wind shake the palm fronds. The dark, tumbling world.

vii.

As Yaltha parted the veils that encircled my bed, I shut my eyes, feigning sleep. It was past the midnight hour.

"I know you're awake, Ana. We will talk now." She carried a beeswax candle, the light flickering under her chin and onto the bony ledge over her eyes. She rested the holder on the floor and the choking sweetness of the wax filled my nostrils. As she squeezed beside me onto the pillows, I turned on my side, away from her.

Since Lavi's news seven days ago, I'd been unable to speak of John's gruesome death or of my terror that his fate would become my husband's. I couldn't eat. I'd slept little, and when I did, I dreamed of dead messiahs and broken threads. Jesus on the hillside, sowing his revolution—that was a good thing, and I couldn't help but feel pride in him. The purpose that had burned in him for so long was finally being realized, yet I was filled with a deep and immutable dread.

At first, Yaltha left me to my silence, believing I needed time alone, but now here she was, her head on my pillow.

"To avoid a fear emboldens it," she said.

I said nothing.

"All shall be well, child."

I reared up then. "Will it? You cannot know that! How can you know that?"

"Oh, Ana, *Ana*. When I tell you all shall be well, I don't mean that life won't bring you tragedy. Life will be life. I only mean you will be well in spite of it. All shall be well, *no matter what*."

"If Antipas kills my husband as he did John, I cannot imagine I will be *well*."

"If Antipas kills him, you'll be devastated and grief-stricken, but there's a place in you that is inviolate—it's the surest part of you, a piece of Sophia herself. You'll find your way there, when you need to. And you'll know then what I speak of."

I laid my head against her arm, sinewy and tough like herself. I couldn't grasp what she was saying. I fell into a dreamless sleep, a black chute that had no bottom, and when I woke, my aunt was still there.

. . .

As we took our breakfast the following morning, Yaltha said, "We must talk about this plan of yours to return to Galilee." She dipped her bread into the honey and pushed it into her mouth, dribbling the nectar onto her chin, and I felt my appetite return. I tore a chunk from the wheat loaf.

She said, "You fear for Jesus's safety—I fear for yours."

A slate of brightness had formed beside us on the floor. I gazed at it, wishing some magic scribble of light would appear telling me what to do. Returning was dangerous, perhaps as much now as when I'd first fled, but my need to see Jesus had become urgent and insurmountable.

"If there's a chance Jesus is in danger," I said, "I want to see him before it's too late."

She leaned forward, her eyes softening. "If you return to him now, I'm afraid it would make Antipas more inclined to snatch Jesus as well."

I hadn't considered this. "You think my presence might endanger him further?"

She didn't answer, but looked at me and lifted her brows. "Don't you?"

viii.

I'd not shown up in the scriptorium all week, but I appeared that morning resolved to carry on for now in Alexandria. I slid onto the stool at my desk, which, I noticed, had been cleaned, the yellow wood gleaming, smelling of citrus oil.

"You've been missed," Thaddeus commented from across the room.

I smiled at him and set to work copying a petition from a woman who asked for the tax on her grain stocks to be reduced, something about her crops failing to receive irrigation from the year's flood—a most lackluster entreaty. I was glad, though, to give my mind something to contemplate besides my own worries, and as the morning passed, I became lost in the mindless, rhythmic movement of my hand as it formed letters and words.

Thaddeus stayed awake, perhaps a little animated by my return. Near noon, catching me glance at him over my shoulder, he said, "May I inquire, Ana—what was it that you and your aunt were searching for in the scrolls?"

I stared at him dumbly. Heat shot through me. "You knew?"

"I enjoyed my sleep, and I thank you for it, but I did wake now and then, if only barely."

How much had he actually seen? It crossed my mind to tell him that Yaltha had been in need of tasks to fill her time and was assisting me with my work, nothing more, but the words reached the precipice of my tongue and stalled. I didn't want to lie to him anymore.

I said, "I took the key that unlocks the cabinet. We read the scrolls inside it hoping to find some record of Yaltha's daughter."

He stroked his chin, and for an awful moment, I thought he might go straight to Haran. I jumped up, forcing myself to speak calmly. "I'm sorry for our deceit. I didn't wish to involve you in what we were doing in case we were discovered. Please, if you could forgive me . . ."

"It's all right, Ana. I have no grudge against you or your aunt."

I felt myself unclench a little. "You won't report this to Haran?"

"Goodness, no. He's been no friend to me. He pays me little, then complains of my work, which I find so tedious I take naps to escape it. Your presence, though, has brought a certain . . . liveliness." He smiled. "Now, what record were you seeking?"

"We sought anything that might tell us where her daughter could be. Haran gave her out for adoption."

Neither Thaddeus nor any of the servants had been in Haran's employ back then—Yaltha had been careful to inquire about this when we'd first arrived. I asked if he'd heard the rumors about my aunt.

He nodded. "It was said she poisoned her husband and Haran sent her to the Therapeutae in order to save her from arrest."

"She poisoned no one," I said indignantly.

"What's her daughter's name?" he inquired.

"Chaya," I told him. "She was two years old when my aunt last saw her."

He squinted, tapping his fingers against his temple as if to dislodge some memory. "That name," he muttered more to himself than to me. "I know I've seen it written somewhere."

My eyes flared wide. Was it too much to think he knew of her? He'd presided over the scriptorium and its contents for nine years. He knew more about Haran's business than anyone. I wanted to go over and tap the other side of his head, but I remained waiting.

He got up and walked in a circle about the room and had started a second loop when he stopped. "Oh," he said. A look passed over his face. Dismay, I thought. "Come with me."

We slipped into Haran's study, where Thaddeus retrieved a locked wooden box that sat unobtrusively on a low shelf. It was painted on top with an image of the falcon-winged Goddess Nephthys, guardian of the dead, a detail Thaddeus kindly provided. He produced a key from a peg beneath Haran's desk and slipped it into a keyhole, then lifted the lid to reveal a cluster of scrolls, perhaps ten or twelve of them. "This is where Haran conceals documents he wishes to keep secret."

He sorted through the scrolls. "Soon after I began working for Haran, he had me make copies of all the scrolls in the box. If I remember rightly, there's a death notice in here of a girl named Chaya. Hers was an unusual name; it remained with me."

The blood left my head. "She's dead?"

I sank down into Haran's grand chair, taking a slow breath as Thaddeus opened a papyrus on the table before me.

> To the Royal Scribe of the Metropolis from Haran ben
> Philip Levias of the Jewish Council.
>
> I attest that Chaya, daughter of my sister, Yaltha,
> died in the month of Epeiph of the 32nd year of the
> Emperor Augustus Caesar. As her guardian and
> kinsman, I request that her name be entered among
> those who have died. She is not default in the
> payment of taxes being the age of two years at the
> time of her death.

I read the notation twice, then pushed it back to Thaddeus, who perused it quickly. He said, "The laws do not require notification of the death of a child, only of an adult male who is taxable. It's done, but rarely. I recall thinking it odd."

Chaya is dead. I tried to picture myself standing before Yaltha, saying the words, but even in my imagination, I couldn't say them.

He replaced the scroll and locked the box. "I'm sorry, but it's best to know the truth."

So shocked was I, so choked with dread at passing on this horrific news, I wasn't at all sure knowing was best. Right then, I preferred to go on living in uncertainty, imagining Chaya alive somewhere.

I FOUND YALTHA walking about the garden. I watched her from the doorway for a while, then strode toward her, trying to steady myself.

As we sat at the edge of the pond, I told her about the death notification. She looked at the sky, where there was not a bird or a cloud, then dropped her chin to her chest as a sob broke from her lips. I wrapped my arms about her caved-in shoulders, and we sat like that for a long time, quiet and dazed, listening to the garden. Birds chirping, the rustle of lizards, a tiny zephyr in the palms.

ix.

Days passed in which Yaltha sat and stared into the garden through the open door of the sitting room. I woke one night to check on her and there she was, gazing out at the dark. I didn't disturb her. She was griev-ing in her own way.

I returned to bed, where sleep came and with it a dream.

A great wind rises. The air fills with scrolls. They fly about me like white and brown birds. Looking up, I see the falcon Goddess Nephthys streak across the sky.

I woke with the dream still in my body, filling me with lightness, and what came into my mind was the wooden box in which Haran stored his secret documents. It was as if in my dream Nephthys had escaped from her confinement on the lid, as if the box had been thrown open and all the scrolls set free.

I lay very still and tried to remember everything about those mo-ments when Thaddeus showed me the box—the key, the creak in the lid as he lifted it, the cluster of scrolls inside, reading the death notice twice. Then, in my memory, I heard Thaddeus say, *The laws do not require noti-fication of the death of a child, only of an adult male who is taxable. It's done, but rarely. I recall thinking it odd.*

The statement had seemed irrelevant at the time, but I wondered now why my uncle had taken the extra precaution of declaring Chaya dead if it wasn't required. Why had it been so important to record it? And something else came back to me: she'd only been two when she'd died. Was it not strange that her life had ended so soon after Yaltha had been sent away?

I bolted up.

I was waiting in the scriptorium when Thaddeus arrived. "I must look once more inside the locked box in Haran's study," I told him.

He shook his head. "But you've seen the death notice. What more is there?"

I thought better than to tell him about the dream or my feeling that something was amiss. I said, "My uncle has already left to conduct his business in the city. It will be safe enough."

"It's not Haran I'm worried about, but his personal servant, the one with the shorn head." I knew which one he meant. He was said to grovel before Haran, as well as snoop for him—anything to ingratiate himself.

"We'll be quick," I promised, and gave him my most pleading look.

He sighed and led me to the study. I counted nine scrolls inside the box. I unraveled one and read a harsh repudiation of Haran's second wife for failing in her oath of fidelity. The second scroll was a settlement of their divorce.

Thaddeus watched me, his eyes roving toward the door. "I don't know what you're looking for, but it would be prudent to read faster."

I didn't know what I was looking for either. I smoothed open a third scroll, anchoring it on the desk.

> Choiak, son of Dios and a keeper of camels in the
> village of Soknopaiou, his wife having died and left
> him toil and suffering, does hand over his two-year-
> old daughter, Diodora, to a priest of the Temple of Isis
> for the sum of 1,400 silver drachmae.

I stopped reading. My mind began to reel a little.

"Have you come upon something?" he asked.

"There's mention of a two-year-old girl." He started to question me further, but I held up my hand, signaling him to wait as I continued to read.

The purchaser, who is granted anonymity by virtue of his status as a representative of the Goddess of Egypt, receives Diodora into his legal ownership and from this day will possess, own, and have proprietary rights over the girl. Choiak henceforth has no power to take back his daughter and through this sale agreement, written in two copies, gives his consent and acknowledges payment.

Signed on behalf of Choiak, who knows no letters, by Haran ben Philip Levias, this day in the month of Epeiph, in the 32nd year of the reign of the illustrious emperor Augustus Caesar.

I lifted my head. Heat crept from my neck into my face, a kind of astonishment. "*Sophia*," I whispered.

"What is it? What does it say?"

"The two-year-old belonged to a man named Choiak, a destitute father whose wife died. He sold his daughter as a slave to a priest." I glanced again at the document. "The girl's name was Diodora."

I rummaged in the box for Chaya's death certificate and placed the

two documents side by side. Two-year-old Chaya. Two-year-old Diodora. Chaya died and Diodora was sold in the same month of the same
year.

I didn't know if Thaddeus had arrived at the same supposition as I
had. I didn't take the time to inquire.

x.

I found Yaltha napping soundly in the chair beside the door to the courtyard, her mouth open and her hands folded high on her chest. I knelt in
front of her and softly called her name. When she didn't rouse, I gave
her knee a shake.

She opened her eyes, frowning, her forehead wrinkling up. "Why did
you wake me?" she said, sounding annoyed.

"Aunt, it is good news. I found a document that may give us a reason
to hope Chaya is not dead."

She sat straight up. Her eyes were suddenly bright and churning.
"What are you talking about, Ana?"

Please, don't let me be wrong.

I told her about my dream and the questions it had stirred, compelling me to return to Haran's study and reopen the box. As I described
the document I'd found inside it, she stared at me, mystified.

I said, "The girl who was sold into bondage had the name Diodora.
But don't you think it's peculiar that both Chaya and Diodora were the
same age? That one died and the other sold as a slave in the same month
of the same year?"

Yaltha closed her eyes. "They are the same girl."

The certainty in her voice startled me. It impelled and excited me,
too. "Think of it," I said. "What if it wasn't some poor camel keeper who
sold a two-year-old girl to the priest, but Haran himself?"

She gazed at me with sad, stunned wonder.

"And afterward," I continued, "Haran concealed what he'd done with a notice of Chaya's death. Does this seem possible to you? I mean, do you think him capable of this?"

"I think him capable of anything. And he would have good reason to cover up the deed. The synagogues here condemn selling Jewish children into slavery. Haran would be removed from the council if this was discovered. He could be cast out of the community altogether."

"Haran wanted people to believe Chaya was dead, and yet he told you she'd been adopted. I wonder why. Do you think he wanted you to leave Alexandria believing she was loved and cared for? Maybe there's a speck of kindness in him somewhere."

Her laugh was bitter. "He knew how anguishing it would be for me to have a daughter out there who was lost to me. He knew it would haunt me all my days. When my sons died, the grief was an agony, but with time I reconciled myself to it. I've never reconciled myself to losing Chaya. One moment she seems within reach and the next moment she's in an abyss I can never find. Haran was pleased to offer me this special brand of torture."

Yaltha leaned back in the chair and I watched her anger fade and her eyes soften. She let out an extravagant breath. "Did the document record the name of the priest who bought the girl, or what temple he served?" she asked.

"It mentioned neither."

"Then Chaya could be anywhere in Egypt—here in Alexandria or as far as Philae."

Finding her suddenly seemed impossible. I could tell by the disappointment in my aunt's face that she thought so, too.

She said, "It's enough that Chaya is alive."

But, of course, it wasn't.

xi.

One morning shortly after I'd arrived in the scriptorium, Haran's servant appeared at the door. He made a little bow in my direction. "Haran wishes to see you in his study."

During the many months we'd been here, I'd never been summoned by Haran. In fact, I'd rarely seen him, having passed him no more than two dozen times as I moved between the scriptorium and the guest quarters. I'd paid his rent requirements to Apion.

It's a curiosity how the mind alights first on the worst scenario. I immediately thought Haran must have discovered I'd been prying into his locked cabinet and box of secrets. Wheeling about on my stool, I looked at Thaddeus, who seemed as surprised and disconcerted as I. "Shall I come with you?" he asked.

"Haran asked only for the woman," the servant said, shifting about impatiently.

My uncle sat in his study, elbows propped on his desk, one fist balled into the other. He glanced up at me, then refocused his attention on an array of scrolls, pens, and ink vials scattered around him, making me wait. I didn't think his servant had seen my intrusions, but I couldn't be sure. I replanted my feet.

Minutes passed. "Thaddeus tells me your work is satisfactory," he said. Finally. "As such, I've decided to waive your rent requirement. You may stay for now as guests, not boarders."

Guests. Prisoners. There was little difference.

"Thank you, Uncle." I tried to smile at him. It helped immensely that he had a dab of ink on the side of his nose, which he'd placed there with his smudged finger.

He cleared his throat. "I leave tomorrow to inspect my papyrus crops and workshops. I travel to Terenouthis, Letopolis, and Memphis and expect to be away for four weeks."

We'd been shut up in this house for nearly a year and a half, but here it was—*sweet freedom*. It was all I could do to keep from breaking into song and dance.

"I've bidden you here," he said, "to advise you in person that my absence does not change our agreement. If you or my sister leave the house, you will forfeit your right to remain here and I will have no choice but to renew the charge of murder against you. I've instructed Apion to watch you. He will report your movements to me."

Sweet, sweet, sweet freedom.

FINDING NO TRACE OF YALTHA in our rooms, I hurried to the servants' quarters, where she sometimes retreated. I found her there with Pamphile and Lavi, hunched over a game of senet, moving her ebony pawn over the board, trying to be the first player to pass into the afterlife. The game had become a salve, a way to distract herself, but her disappointment about finding Chaya still hung over her like a small cloud I could almost see.

"Aghhh!" my aunt cried, landing on a square that symbolized bad fortune.

"I'm in no hurry for you to reach the afterlife," I said, and the three of them looked around, surprised to see me.

My aunt grinned. "Not even this paltry afterlife on the game board?"

"Not even that one." I slipped beside her and whispered, "I have welcome news."

She flipped her pawn onto its side. "Since Ana has requested that I not visit the afterlife today, I must withdraw from the game."

I led her to a private spot near the outdoor kitchen and told her what had just transpired.

The corners of her mouth twitched. "I've been thinking. There's one person who would have known about Haran's deception and that's Apion's father, Apollonios. He was Haran's treasurer before Apion, but also his confidant, doing his bidding. It's likely he was involved in the matter."

"Then we'll go and find him."

"He will be old now," she said. "If he's alive at all."

"Do you think he would help us?"

"He was always kind to me."

"I'll approach Apion when the time is right," I told her and watched her tilt back her head and drink in the spaciousness of the sky.

xii.

Apion was in the small room he called the treasury, writing numbers onto a piece of lined parchment. He looked up at my approach. "If you've brought money for your rent, Haran has done away with the requirement."

"Yes, he told me himself. I'm here to ask for the favor you owe me." I tried to look modest, to be the kind of genial person one is eager to grant favors.

He sighed audibly and laid down his pen.

"I understand my uncle has placed Yaltha and me under your watchful eye while he's away. I would like to respectfully request that you forgo this onerous task and leave us to ourselves."

"If you plan to venture out of the house against Haran's wishes and expect me to say nothing to him, you are mistaken. It puts me at risk of losing my position."

"It seems taking undisclosed bribes also puts you at risk," I said.

He rose from the table. His dark curls glittered with oil. I caught the scent of myrrh. "You threaten me then?"

"I only ask that you look the other way while Haran is away. My aunt and I have been here more than a year and have seen nothing of the greatness of Alexandria. Are a few excursions too much to ask? I don't wish to go to Haran about the bribes you took from me, but I will."

He studied me, seeming to weigh my threat. I doubted I would follow through with it, but he didn't know that. I held his gaze. He said, "I'll ignore your goings and comings, but once Haran has returned, my debt to you will be paid. You must give me an oath you will extort me no further."

"Extort is a harsh word," I said.

"It's also the correct word. Now swear before me that your uncle's return will be the end of it."

"I swear it."

He sat down again, dismissing me with a flick of his wrist. I said, "May I ask, is your father still living?"

He looked up. "My father? Why is this of interest to you?"

"You may recall that when I first met you in Sepphoris—"

He interrupted, his mouth tightening, "Do you mean back when you were *with child*?"

It took a moment to realize what he meant. I'd forgotten the lie I'd told him; clearly he had not. When I'd pretended I was pregnant in order to obtain from him what I needed, I hadn't known I'd be traveling to Alexandria, where the months would reveal my falsehood. I felt an embarrassed heat on my cheeks.

"Are you going to lie again and tell me you lost the child?"

"No, I confess I lied to you. I'll not do so again. I'm sorry." I *was* sorry, and yet my lie had helped win us passage to Alexandria. And my extortion, as he insisted on calling it, now offered us the freedom to roam about the city. Yes, I was sorry, and no, I was not sorry.

He nodded, his shoulders dropping. My words seemed to mollify him.

I began again. "As I was about to say . . . when we first met, I mentioned that my aunt had known your father. She was fond of him and asked me to inquire of his health."

"Tell her he's well enough, though he's grown corpulent in his old age—he lives on a diet of beer, wine, bread, and honey."

Apollonios is alive. "If by chance Yaltha wished to see him, how would she find him?"

"I don't wish to give you another reason to stray from the house, but it seems you plan to do so anyway. My father can be found at the library, where he goes each day to join the enclave of men who sit in the colonnades and debate exactly how far God is from the world—a thousand iters or seven times a thousand."

"They think God far?"

"They are Platonists and Stoics and followers of the Jewish philosopher Philo—I hardly know what they think."

This time when he flicked his wrist, I left.

xiii.

I moved along the Canopic Way as if thrust from a bow, flying ahead of Yaltha and Lavi and then having to pause for them to catch up.

In the center of the street, narrow pools of water cascaded one into the other for as far as I could see, and hundreds of copper pots filled with kindling lined the sides, waiting to be set afire at night to light the thoroughfare. The women were clad in blue, black, or white tunics cinched under their breasts with bright-colored ribbons, making me conscious of my plain Nazareth dress, dingy undyed flax. As they passed, I studied their coiled silver snake bracelets, hoop earrings with dangling pearls, their eyes lined in green and black, hair swept into knots atop their heads with a row of curls on their foreheads. I pulled my long, single braid over my shoulder and held on to it as if it were the end of a tether.

Nearing the royal quarter, I spied my first obelisk—a tall, narrow structure that jutted toward the sky. I craned my head back and studied it.

"It's a monument to a particular part of the male body," Yaltha said, perfectly serious.

I looked at it again and heard Lavi laugh, then Yaltha. I didn't say so, but I'd had no trouble believing her jest.

"They are more useful as timekeepers," she said, inspecting the long, bright black shadow the obelisk cast. "It's two hours past noon. We've tarried long enough."

We'd set out at midday, leaving quietly through the servant quarters when no one was about. Lavi had insisted on accompanying us. Aware of our mission, he shouldered a pouch containing the last of our money in case it became necessary to bribe Apollonios. Lavi had constantly implored me to slow down, and once had steered us across the street when a legation of officious-looking Roman men approached. I looked at him now, thinking of him and Pamphile—they seemed no closer to realizing their plans to marry than when he had first told me about them.

At the entrance to the library complex, I halted and drew an awed breath, my palms coming together under my chin. Before me, two colonnades stretched along either side of a vast courtyard that led to a magnificent building of white marble.

Finding my voice, I said, "I cannot seek out Apollonios until I've seen inside the library." I knew there to be ten halls containing the half million texts Yaltha had told me about. My heart was running rampant.

My aunt linked her arm in mine. "Nor I."

We wound through the courtyard, which was dense with people whom I imagined to be philosophers, astronomers, historians, mathematicians, poets . . . every kind of scholar, though they were likely ordinary citizens. Reaching the steps, I read the Greek inscription carved over the doors—"A Healing Sanctum"—and scrambled up them two at a time.

Inside, dimness hit my eyes first, followed by lamplight. A moment later the walls came alive with brightly hued paintings of ibis-headed men and lion-headed women. We moved along a dazzling corridor covered with Gods, Goddesses, solar disks, and all-seeing eyes. There were boats, birds, chariots, harps, plows, and rainbow wings—thousands of glyphs. I had the sensation of floating through a storied world.

When we arrived in the first hall, I could barely take in the sprawling room with its cubicles reaching toward the ceiling, each one labeled and stuffed with scrolls and leather-bound codices. Enheduanna's exaltation to Inanna was likely in here, as well as at least a few works by female Greek philosophers. It seemed absurd to think my own writings might be housed here one day, too, but I stood there and let myself imagine it.

As we moved from hall to hall, I became aware of young men in short white tunics dashing about, some carrying armloads of papyri, others on ladders arranging scrolls in cubicles or dusting them with tufts of feathers. I noticed that Lavi watched them intently.

"You are very quiet," Yaltha said, sidling next to me. "Is the library all you hoped?"

"It's a holy of holies," I said. And it was, but I could feel the tiny lump of anger tucked beneath my awe. A half million scrolls and codices were within these walls, and all but a handful were by men. They had written the known world.

At Yaltha's urging we turned back to search for Apollonios and the men who debated the distance to God and back. We found them seated beneath one of the colonnades, as Apion had predicted.

"He's the ample one with purple on his tunic," Yaltha said, pausing in a niche to observe him.

"How will we manage to draw him away from the others?" I asked. "Are you going to boldly interrupt him?" He was at that moment ardently debating some point.

"The three of us will proceed along the colonnade and when we draw near him, I'll call out, 'Apollonios, it is you! I'm shocked to come upon you.' He will have no choice but to come apart and speak with us."

I gave her an approving look. "What if he tells Haran of his encounter with us?"

"I don't think he'll do so, but we have no choice. He's our only way."

We did as she suggested, and Apollonios, though oblivious to our identities, left his bench and came aside to greet us. "Do you not recognize an old friend?" Yaltha asked. "I'm Yaltha, the sister of Haran."

A pained expression entered his face, passing quickly, followed by a gush of pleasure. "Ah, yes, I see now. You've returned from Galilee."

"And I brought back my niece, Ana, the daughter of my youngest brother." His gaze swept over me, then over Lavi, prompting her to introduce him as well.

The old treasurer bestowed a surplus of smiles on us, his belly so rotund he was forced to bend backward from his waist as a counterbalance. I could smell the cinnamon oil on him. "Do you reside with Haran?" he asked.

"We had nowhere else," Yaltha said. "We've dwelled with him more than a year and today is the first time we've left his house, a freedom we've been able to seize only because he's away from the city. He forbids us to leave the house." She feigned a look of distress, or perhaps it was real. "I trust you won't tell him we slipped out?"

"No, no, of course not. He was my employer, but never my friend. I find it remarkable, though, that he isolates you from the city."

"He does so to prevent me from asking about my daughter, Chaya."

He looked away from her to a crinkling of clouds overhead, frowning, arching back his spine, his fists bored into the small of his back. He knew something.

"I cannot be too long on my feet," he said.

The four of us made our way to a pair of benches near his fellow debaters, the old man grunting heavily as he sat. "You've returned here to seek your daughter?"

"I'm growing old, Apollonios. My wish is to see her before I die. Haran will tell me nothing of her whereabouts. If she's alive, she's a woman of twenty-five now."

"I may be able to help you, but first I must have your word and that of your niece and your friend that you won't reveal how you've come to know what I'm about to tell you. Especially to Haran."

We reassured him quickly and he suddenly appeared pale and breathless, sweat and oil beading in the folds of his neck. He said, "I've wished many times I could relieve myself of this burden before I die." He shook his head, pausing for far too many minutes before continuing. "Haran sold her to a priest who served in the temple of Isis Medica here in Alexandria. I myself recorded the transaction."

Having confessed, he sank back, seemingly exhausted, his head resting on the great orb of his body. We waited.

"I've wished for a way to repay you for my part in it," he said, unable to meet Yaltha's gaze. "I did as Haran asked and I came to regret it."

"Do you know the name of this priest or where Chaya might now be?" Yaltha asked.

"I made it my business to know. For all these years, I've kept abreast of her from a distance. The priest died some years ago—he freed her before his death. She was raised as an attendant in the healing precinct of Isis Medica. She serves there still."

"Tell me," Yaltha said, and I saw the effort in her face to remain composed, "why would Haran choose to sell my daughter? He could have given her in adoption like he falsely told me he did."

"Who can decipher Haran's heart? I only know he wanted to be rid of the child in a way that would leave no trace. An adoption would have required triple documents, one for Haran, one for the adopted parents, and one for the royal scribe. And the parents would've been named, unlike the priest, who could be kept anonymous."

He pushed himself up from the bench. "When you go to Isis Medica, ask for Diodora. It's the only name Chaya knows. She was raised as an Egyptian, not a Jew."

As he turned to leave, I said, "The men in the library who wear the white tunics and climb the ladders . . . who are they?"

"We call them librarians. They keep the books ordered and cataloged and retrieve them for scholars at the university. You will see them running at great speed delivering them. Some of them sell copies to the public. Others assist the scribes in procuring inks and papyri. A fortunate few are sent on expeditions to purchase books in distant lands."

"Lavi would make an excellent librarian," I said, looking at my friend to judge his reaction. He straightened. From pride, I thought.

"Does the position pay well?" Lavi asked.

"Well enough," Apollonios said, suddenly wary and surprised, it seemed, that Lavi spoke to him directly. "But the positions are hard to acquire. Most are passed from father to son."

"You said you wished to repay me for your part in Haran's sin," Yaltha said. "You can do so by obtaining this employment for our friend."

Flustered, Apollonios opened and closed his mouth several times before saying, "I don't know—it would be difficult."

"You have much influence," Yaltha said. "There must be many people who owe you favors. Securing the post for Lavi won't make up for selling my daughter, but it would repay your debt to me. It will make the burden of guilt you've carried lighter."

The old man glanced at Lavi. "He would start as a low-paying apprentice and the training is rigorous. He must be able to read Greek. Can he do that?"

"I read it," Lavi said. This news astonished me. Perhaps he'd learned to read Greek in Tiberias.

"Yes, then, I'll do what I can," Apollonios said.

As the old man left, Lavi whispered to me, "Would you teach me to read Greek?"

xiv.

I was happy for Yaltha and for Lavi, as well—one had located a daughter and one had found possible employment—and the memory of being inside the library glowed inside me, but my mind went to Jesus, as it did almost every hour of every day. *What are you doing now, Beloved?* I could see no resolution to our separation.

Crossing the city on our way back to Haran's, we came upon an artist painting a portrait of a woman's face on a piece of limewood. The woman sat before him in a small public courtyard, adorned in her finery. A little crowd of bystanders had gathered to watch. As we joined them, I remembered with a sickening roll in my stomach the hours I'd spent posing for the mosaic in Antipas's palace.

"She's posing for a mummy portrait," Yaltha explained. "When she dies, the image will be placed over her face inside the coffin. Until then, it will hang in her house. It's meant to preserve the memory of her."

I'd heard of Egyptians putting odd articles into their coffins—food, jewelry, clothes, weapons, a myriad of things that might be needed in the afterlife—but this was new to me. I watched as the artist painted her face life-size and perfect on the wood.

I sent Lavi to inquire what a mummy portrait costs. "The artist says it's fifty drachmae," Lavi reported.

"Go and ask if he will paint mine next."

Yaltha gave me a surprised, half-amused look. "You wish to have a mummy portrait for your coffin?"

"Not for my coffin. For Jesus."

Perhaps also for myself.

THAT NIGHT I PLACED the portrait on the table near my bed, propping it beside my incantation bowl. The artist had painted me as I was, ornament-less, wearing the worn tunic, a plain braid dangling over my shoulder and wisps of hair loose about my face. It was just me, Ana. But there was something about it.

I took the picture in my hands, holding it up to the lamp to study it more closely. The paint gleamed in the light and the face I saw seemed like that of a newfound woman. Her eyes looked out levelly. Her chin was raised in a bold tilt. There was strength in her jaw. The corners of her lips were lifted.

I told myself that when I returned to Nazareth and saw Jesus again, I would make him close his eyes, then place the portrait in his hands. He would look at it with awe, and I would tell him with feigned seriousness, "If there should be another threat of my arrest and I'm sent once more to Egypt, this will ensure you won't forget my face." Then I would laugh and he would laugh.

XV.

Standing at the door to the lotus garden, I listened to the evening sky creak and rumble. All day the heat had been like a viscous film coating the air, but now suddenly wind gusted and rain poured down, black needles rattling the date palms and pummeling the surface of the pond, and then dissipating almost as quickly as they came. I stepped out into the darkness, where a bird, a wagtail, sang.

For the past three weeks, I'd spent my mornings in the scriptorium teaching Lavi to read Greek instead of attending to my usual duties. Even Thaddeus had joined in the tutoring, insisting that our student begin by copying the alphabet over and over on the back of old, discarded parchments. I was careful to destroy the evidence of his lessons lest Haran discover it on his return. Pamphile burned so many alphas, betas, gammas, and deltas in the kitchen, I told her there'd never been a more scholarly oven in all of Egypt. By the second week, Lavi had memorized the inflections of the verbs and nouns. By the third he was locating verbs in the sentence. Very soon he would be reading Homer.

Most afternoons, Yaltha and I had scampered about Alexandria, roaming the markets, gaping at the Caesareum, the gymnasium, and the splendors along the harbor, and returning twice to the library. We'd visited every Isis temple in the city but one, Chaya's. Again and again I'd asked my aunt why she avoided it and each time she'd answered the same: *I'm not yet ready.* The last time I'd pestered her about it, she'd bitten off the answer and spit it at me. I'd not asked again. Ever since, I'd carried remnants of hurt, confusion, and exasperation.

The wagtail flew. The garden stilled. Hearing footsteps, I turned to find Apion approaching through the palms.

"I've come to forewarn you," he said. "A message arrived this day from Haran. He returns early. I expect him in two days."

I looked up at the sky, the moonless, starless night. "Thank you for informing me," I said without expression.

When he departed, I raced to Yaltha's bedchamber with my anger spilling over. I burst upon her without a knock. "Chaya is just across the city, yet all this time has passed and you've not gone to her. Now Apion has informed me Haran will be back in two days. I thought Chaya was the reason you came to Egypt! Why do you avoid her?"

She gathered her night shawl about her neck. "Come here, Ana. Sit down. I know you've struggled to understand my delay. I'm sorry. I can only tell you that on the day we spoke to Apollonios . . . even before we departed the library courtyard, I became possessed by the fear that Chaya may not want to be found. Why would an Egyptian woman who serves Isis want to be claimed by the Jewish mother who abandoned her? I became afraid she'd reject me. Or worse, reject herself."

I'd thought of my aunt as invincible, impervious—someone assailed by life, but somehow unmaimed by it—but I saw her suddenly as a person of flaws and bruises like myself. There was an odd relief in it.

"I didn't realize," I said. "I shouldn't have judged you."

"It's all right, Ana. I've judged me, too. It isn't as if this worry hadn't crossed my mind earlier, but I've never let it fully settle on me until now. I suppose my own need to find Chaya and make right what I'd done by leaving her didn't allow me to consider that she might turn me away. I fear losing her all over again." She paused. The candlelight wavered in an unknown breath of wind, and when she spoke again, I caught the same wavering in her voice. "I didn't consider the need she might have . . . to remain as she is."

I started to speak, but stopped myself.

"Go ahead," she said. "Speak your mind."

"I was going to repeat what you said to me, that resisting a fear only emboldens it."

She smiled. "Yes, I resisted my fear, too."

"What will you do? There's little time left."

Outside the rain had started again. We listened to it for a while. Finally she said, "I can't know if Chaya wants to be found or how finding her might change either of us, but it's the truth that matters, isn't it?" She leaned over and blew out the candle. "Tomorrow we'll go to Isis Medica."

xvi.

I stood naked on the limestone slab in the bathing room, shivering as Pamphile poured unheated water over my torso, arms, and legs. "Do you delight in torturing me?" I said, my skin rising up in tiny bumps of protest. I did truly appreciate the Egyptians' conveniences, their bathing rooms and miraculous stone-seat privies with water running beneath to flush the waste—but how hard was it to heat the bathwater?

Setting down the pitcher, Pamphile handed me a drying towel. "You Galileans have little forbearance," she said, grinning.

"Forbearance is all we *do* have," I retorted.

Back in my chamber, freshly scrubbed and flesh tingling, I donned the new black tunic I'd bought in the market, tying it snugly under my breasts with a green ribbon, then draped a red linen mantle about my shoulders. I would wear it despite the heat outside, which was atrocious. At Pamphile's insistence, I allowed her to line my eyes with a green pigment, then wrap my braid into a little tower on top of my head.

"You could pass for an Alexandrian woman," she said, leaning back to take me in. The notion seemed to please her enormously.

Alexandrian. After Pamphile left, I turned the word over and over in my head.

Stepping into the sitting room, I heard Yaltha in her chamber, singing as she dressed.

When she finally stepped into the sitting room, my breath caught. She wore her new tunic, as well, cerulean like the sea, and I saw that Pamphile had tended my aunt, too, for she had streaks of black paint beneath her eyes, and her graying hair was freshly plaited and fastened in intricate coils. She looked like one of the lion-headed Goddesses painted on the wall in the library.

"Shall we go and find my daughter?" she said.

Isis Medica appeared in the Royal Quarter near the harbor like an island unto itself. Catching my first glimpse of it from a distance, I slowed my steps to take in a complex array of walls, tall pylons, and rooftops. It was more expansive than I'd imagined.

Yaltha pointed. "See the pediment of that large building over there? That's the main temple to Isis. The smaller ones are minor temples to other divinities." She squinted, trying to make sense of the maze. "Over there—that's the healing sanctuary where Chaya attends, and behind it, not visible, is the medical school. People come from as far as Rome and Macedonia to find cures here."

"Have you ever sought a cure there?" I asked.

"No. I've been inside the walls only once and then merely out of curiosity. The Jewish citizenry doesn't go there. It's a transgression of the first commandment."

Last night I'd learned to love her weakness; today it was her daring that excited me. "Did you go inside Isis's temple?"

"Of course. I remember there was an altar there where people left little statuettes of Isis as offerings."

"And the healing sanctuary? Did you go there, too?"

She shook her head. "To enter, one must present an illness and be prepared to remain through the night. Those seeking cures are put into an opium sleep in which they dream their cure. It's said that sometimes Isis herself comes in their dreams and presents cures."

So strange was all of this, it left me speechless, but inside me, there was a kind of humming.

THE OUTER COURTYARD swarmed with people making music. Sistrums rattled and flutes piped out soft curling sounds that spiraled like ribbons through the air. We watched a line of women wind through the scarlet pillars of the colonnade, their dance like a bright flowing centipede.

Yaltha, who understood the Egyptian tongue, cocked her head and listened to their song. "They're marking the birth of Isis's son, Horus," she said. "We seem to have come on a day of celebration."

She tugged me past the courtyard and dancers, small unnamed temples, and wall reliefs painted with blue flowers, yellow moons, and white ibises, until we arrived at the main temple, a marble structure that looked more Greek than Egyptian. We stepped inside into a foggy cloud of incense. Kyphi billowed out of the censers—the smell of wine-soaked raisins, mint, honey, and cardamom. Around us, a sea of people strained their necks for a glimpse of something at the far end. "What have they come to see?" I whispered.

Shaking her head, Yaltha led me to a low niche in the rear wall and we climbed up to stand inside it. I swept my eyes over the top of the crowd, and it was not some*thing* the throng craned to see, but some*one*. She stood erect in a robe of yellow and red with a black sash from her left shoulder to her right hip. It was covered in silver stars and red-gold moons. On her head, a crown of golden cow horns.

I'd never seen anyone so mesmerizing. "Who is she?"

"She would be a priestess of Isis, perhaps the highest of them. She wears Isis's crown."

The doll-like statuettes Yaltha had mentioned were heaped on the floor around the altar like mounds of washed-up shells.

The priestess's voice came suddenly like a cymbal clap. I leaned toward Yaltha. "What is she saying?"

Yaltha translated. "O lady Isis, Goddess of all things, you bring the sun from rising to setting and light the moon and the stars. You bring the Nile over the land. You are the lady of light and flames, the mistress of water . . ."

I began to sway with her monotonic chant. When it ended, I said, "Aunt, I'm glad you allowed your fears about finding Chaya to thwart you for so long. If we'd come any sooner, we would've missed this great spectacle."

She looked at me. "Just take care not to fall off the niche and break your skull."

An attendant in a white tunic made her way to the altar, holding a bowl of water, taking feather steps as she labored to keep the liquid from spilling over the sides. The priestess took the bowl and poured the libation over a colorfully painted statue of Isis that stood on the altar. The waterfall splashed over the Goddess, spilling onto the floor. "Lady Isis, bring forth your divine son. Bring forth the rising of the Nile . . ."

When the ceremony ended, the priestess left the chamber through a narrow door at the back of the temple, and the multitude moved toward the entrance. Yaltha, however, made no effort to climb down from the wall niche. She stared straight ahead with rapt concentration. I called her name. She didn't answer.

Gazing in the direction she stared, I saw nothing unusual. Only the altar, the statue, the bowl, the attendant drying the wet floor with a cloth.

Yaltha stepped down and strode against the crowd, as I scurried behind. "Aunt? Where are you going?"

She stopped a few paces from the altar. I had no understanding of what was happening. Then I looked at the attendant, who was lifting herself from the dried floor, her dark hair like brambles.

In a voice so muffled I almost didn't hear it, Yaltha said, "Diodora?"

And her daughter turned and looked at her.

DIODORA LAID HER CLOTH on the altar. "Do you have some need of me, lady?" she asked in Greek. She bore a startling resemblance to me, not only in the kinks and whorls of her hair, but in the black eyes too large for her face, the small pursed mouth, the tall thin body like a gathering of willow boughs. We looked more like sisters than cousins.

Yaltha stood transfixed. Her eyes moved over her daughter as if she were not flesh and bone, but air and apparition, a visage she'd half dreamed. I saw her lip quiver ever so slightly, the commotion of a bee's wing. Then she threw back her shoulders, as I'd seen her do a hundred times. Seconds passed, ceaseless seconds.

Give her an answer, Aunt.

"I wish to speak with you," Yaltha said. "May we find a place to sit?"

Uncertainty wrinkled Diodora's face. "I'm only an attendant," she said and took a step backward.

"Do you also serve in the healing sanctuary?" Yaltha asked.

"That's where I attend most often. Today, I was required here." She picked up the cloth and wrung it out in the bowl. "Have I attended you there in the past? Do you wish to seek another cure?"

"No, I didn't come for healing." Later I would think Yaltha was wrong about that.

"If you have no need of me then . . . I'm tasked with removing the offerings. I must see to it." She hurried away, disappearing through the door at the back.

"I didn't think she could be so beautiful," Yaltha said. "Beautiful and grown and very much like you."

"She's also puzzled," I said. "I'm afraid we made her ill at ease." I moved close to my aunt. "Are you going to tell her?"

"I'm trying to find a way."

The door opened and Diodora emerged carrying two large empty baskets. She slackened her pace when she saw we were still there, the two peculiar strangers. Without acknowledging us, she knelt and began placing the Isis figures into a basket.

I lowered myself beside her and picked up one of the crudely fashioned carvings. Up close, I saw it was Isis cradling her newborn son. Diodora cast a sideways glance at me, but said nothing. I helped her fill both baskets. In my soul, I was a Jew, but I closed my fingers around the statuette. *Sophia*, I whispered to myself, calling the figure by the name I loved.

When all the offerings had been gathered, Diodora rose and looked at Yaltha. "If you wish to speak with me, you may do so on the portico of the birth house."

THE BIRTH HOUSE was a shrine to honor the motherhood of Isis. The small columned building sat near the courtyard, which was still and quiet now, the dancing women gone.

Diodora led us to a cluster of benches on the portico and sat facing us, her hands clasped tightly and her eyes shifting from Yaltha to me. She must have known that something momentous was about to occur— it seemed perched in the air over our heads like a bird about to swoop. A hundred birds.

"My heart is full," Yaltha told her. "So full it's difficult for me to speak."

Diodora tipped her head to the side. "How is it that you know my name?"

Yaltha smiled. "I once knew you by another name. Chaya. It means life."

"I'm sorry, lady, I do not know you or the name Chaya."

"It's a long, difficult story. All I ask is that you allow me to tell it to you." We sat a moment with the rustling in the air, and then Yaltha said, "I've come over a great distance to tell you that I'm your mother."

Diodora touched her hand to the gully between her breasts, just that small gesture, and I felt an unbearable tenderness come over me. For Diodora and Yaltha and the years stolen from them, but also for myself and Susanna. *My* lost daughter.

"And this is Ana, your cousin," Yaltha said.

My throat thickened. I smiled at her, then mirrored her gesture, placing my hand to my breasts.

She sat terrifyingly still, her face as unreadable as the alphabet ash we'd created in the oven. I could not imagine myself hearing such a thing as she'd just heard. If she lashed out in mistrust or grief or anger, I wouldn't have blamed her. I almost preferred such reactions to this strange, inscrutable quiet.

Yaltha continued in measured sentences, sparing Diodora nothing as she relayed the details of Ruebel's death, the murder accusations against her, and her eight-year exile with the Therapeutae. She said, "The Jewish council decreed if I left the Therapeutae's precincts for any reason, I would be given a hundred strokes by cane, mutilated, and exiled to Nubia."

This I'd never heard. Where was Nubia? Mutilated how? I slid closer to her on the bench.

When she'd finished the entire story, Diodora said, "If what you say is true and I am your daughter, where then was I?" Her voiced sounded small, but her face was like an ember.

Yaltha reached for Diodora's hand, which she quickly drew back.

"Oh, child, you were little more than two years old when I was sent away. Haran swore to keep you well and safe in his household. I wrote letters to him, inquiring of you, but they went unanswered."

Diodora frowned, rolling her eyes to the top of a column crowned with a woman's head. After a moment she said, "If you were sent to the Therapeutae when I was two and remained there eight years . . . I would've been ten when you left them. Why didn't you come for me then?" Her fingers moved in her lap as if counting. "Where have you been the last sixteen years?"

As Yaltha struggled for words, I spoke. "She has been in Galilee. She's been with me. But it's not as you think. She didn't regain her freedom when you were ten, but she was banished once again, this time to her brother in Sepphoris. She had hoped to reclaim you and bring you with her, but—"

"Haran told me he'd given you out for adoption and he would not reveal your whereabouts," Yaltha said. "I left then—I felt I had no choice. I thought you were cared for, that you had a family. I had no knowledge Haran had sold you to the priest until I returned to Egypt over a year ago to search for you."

Diodora shook her head almost violently. "I was told my father was a man named Choiak from a village somewhere in the south, that he sold me out of destitution."

Yaltha placed her hand on Diodora's and once again Diodora yanked it away. "It was Haran who sold you. Ana has seen the document of sale, in which he disguised himself as a poor camel keeper named Choiak. I didn't forget you, Diodora. I longed for you every day. I returned to find you, though even now my brother threatens to revive the old charges of murder if I should seek you out. I ask your forgiveness for leaving. I ask your forgiveness for not coming sooner."

Diodora dropped her head onto her knees and wept, and we could do nothing but let her. Yaltha stood and hovered over her. I didn't know whether Diodora was grieved or comforted. I didn't know whether she was lost or found.

When she ceased weeping, Yaltha asked her, "Was he kind to you, your master?"

"He was kind. I do not know if he loved me, but he never raised his hand or his voice to me. When he died, I grieved for him."

Yaltha closed her eyes and blew out a little breath.

I had no intention of saying anything, yet I thought of my parents and Susanna, whom I'd lost, and of Jesus, my family in Nazareth, Judas, and Tabitha, who were all so far away, and I felt no assurance that any of them would be restored to me. I said, "Let us be more than cousins. Let us be sisters. The three of us will be a family."

Light was falling in bright bands across the colonnade, and she squinted up at me and said nothing. I felt I'd said a foolish thing, that I'd trespassed somehow. At that moment, someone called her name from a distance, singing it. "Diodooora . . . Diodooora."

She leapt up. "I've neglected my duties." She wiped her face with the sleeve of her tunic, then pulled on her tight, stoic mask.

"I don't know when I can come again," Yaltha said. "Haran returns from his travels tomorrow and as I said, he forbids us to leave his house. We will find a way somehow."

"I do not think you should return," she said. She walked away, leaving us there on the portico of the birth house.

Yaltha called out to her, "Daughter, I love you."

xvii.

The following day in the scriptorium in Haran's house, I listened to Lavi read from the *Iliad* in starts and stops, finding it difficult to stay focused. My mind wandered to Diodora and to the things spoken in the birth house. I kept seeing her walk away from us.

"What will we do?" I'd asked Yaltha during the long walk from Isis Medica back to Haran's.

"We'll wait," she'd replied.

With effort I turned my attention back to Lavi as he faltered over a word. When I attempted to prompt him, he held up his hand. "It will come to me." It took an entire minute. "Ship!" he cried, beaming.

He was in a happy, though somewhat nervous mood. Earlier that morning a courier had arrived with news that he'd been granted the position at the library. His apprenticeship would begin on the first day of the following week.

"I've made a vow to finish reading Achilles's adventures before my employment," he said, lowering the codex. "My Greek is not yet perfected."

"Don't be concerned, Lavi. You read Greek quite well. But yes, finish the poem—you must find out who prevails, Achilles or Hector."

He seemed to bask in my praise, sitting up taller. "Tomorrow I will go to Pamphile's father to ask for a settlement of marriage."

"Oh, Lavi, I'm glad for you." His nervousness, I realized, was not merely about his reading skill. "When do you hope to wed?"

"There's no betrothal period here as there is in Galilee. Once her father and I draw up the settlement and sign it before witnesses, Pamphile and I are considered married. She gave me a portion of her wages and I purchased a shabti box as a gift for him. I will not ask for a bride price. I hope these things will be enough to conclude the contract tomorrow."

I walked to Thaddeus's desk and gathered up a stack of papyrus sheets, the costliest and finest in Egypt. "You may offer him these as well. It seems an appropriate gift from a librarian of the great library."

He hesitated. "Are you sure? Will they be missed?"

"Haran has more papyrus than exists in all of Sepphoris and Jerusalem combined. He won't miss these few sheets."

As I thrust them into his arms, there was a shuffling at the door. The servant who did Haran's bidding was standing there.

"Our master has just returned," he said, his eyes traveling to the papyri.

"Does he have need of me?" I asked, more haughtily than I should have.

"He asked me to inform the household of his return, that is all."

Once again we were in captivity.

WAITING WAS AN INSUFFERABLE ENDEAVOR. One sat, one dithered, one stirred a pot of questions. I fretted over whether we should accept Diodora's rejection or find a way to return to Isis Medica. I pressed Yaltha to set a course, but she persisted in her waiting, saying if the pot was tended long enough, the answer would bubble to the surface. A week passed, however, and we seemed no closer to resolving the matter.

Then one day with the sun dangling low above the rooftops, Pamphile broke in upon Yaltha and me in the sitting room, breathless from hurrying. "A visitor has arrived asking for you," she said. I imagined it was the long-awaited courier bearing a letter from Judas—*Come home, Ana. Jesus bids you to come home*—and my heart began to thump.

"She waits for you both in the atrium," Pamphile added.

I knew then who it was. Yaltha nodded at me. She knew, as well.

"Where's Haran?" Yaltha asked.

"He has been away all afternoon," Pamphile answered. "He hasn't yet returned."

"Bring the visitor to us here and say nothing of her presence to any-one but Lavi."

"My husband hasn't returned either." She let the word *husband* slide slowly from her tongue. The marriage settlement had been signed as Lavi had hoped.

"Be certain to alert him when he arrives. Ask him to wait in the gar-den out of sight. When our visitor leaves, we'll need him to slip her out through the servant quarters."

"Who is she?" Pamphile asked, alarm appearing on her face.

"There's no time to explain," Yaltha said and waved her hand impa-tiently. "Tell Lavi it's Chaya. He'll know. Now, hurry."

Yaltha opened the door onto the garden, allowing hot air to invade the room. I watched her preparing herself, smoothing her tunic, taking deep, concentrated breaths. I poured three cups of wine.

Diodora hesitated at the threshold, peering inside before she entered. She wore a rough-weave brown mantle about her white tunic and had pinned back her hair with two silver ornaments. Her eyes were painted with malachite.

"I didn't know if I'd see you again," Yaltha said.

When Diodora stepped inside, I quickly closed the door, which had an iron lock on the inside and on the outside, but we had no key to se-cure it. I reminded myself that Haran had not come to our rooms in all the time we'd been here. Why would he do so now?

Standing in the middle of the room, Diodora looked thin and child-like. Did she know how dangerous this was? Yet there was a beautiful irony in her being here; the girl he'd gone to such lengths to be rid of was in his house, beneath his roof, under his nose. It was a revenge so hidden and precise, I wanted to laugh. I offered her the cup of wine, but she refused it. I took mine and drank it in four swallows.

As Yaltha seated herself, I gave Diodora the bench and settled on the floor, where I could look into the garden to watch for Lavi.

"The news you brought me was a great shock," she said. "I have thought of nothing else."

"Neither have I," said Yaltha. "I'm sorry I thrust so much on you at once. I'm not known for subtlety. My delicate side wore away many years ago."

Diodora smiled. It was the first time we'd seen her do so and it was like a little dawn had broken over the room. "I was glad at first that you stayed away from Isis Medica as I asked, but then . . ."

When she said nothing further, Yaltha responded, "I wanted to go back if only to see you from afar, but I felt I should honor your wishes. I'm happy you've come."

"I remembered what you said about your brother confining you here. Even if you decided to ignore my wishes, I didn't know if it would be possible for you to leave. So, I've come to you."

"Weren't you concerned you might encounter Haran?" I asked.

"Yes, but I conceived a story in case I came upon him—I was relieved not to need it."

"Please, tell us."

She undraped a pouch from her shoulder and extracted a bronze bracelet carved with the head of a vulture. "I planned to show him my bracelet and say, 'One of your servants may have left this behind in the healing sanctuary at Isis Medica. I've been sent to return it. Would you kindly let me speak with one of them?'"

Her story was shrewd—but it bore flaws Haran was too clever to miss. He would know Diodora was an attendant at Isis Medica. And look at her—she was the image of me.

"And when you spoke with the servant, what did you plan to say?" I asked.

She reached into the pouch once more and removed a small ostracon. "I planned to beg her, servant to servant, to deliver it to Yaltha. There's a message on it to . . . to my mother."

She lowered her eyes. The word *mother* hung in the air, golden and unmissable.

"You read and write?" I asked.

"My master taught me."

She handed the ostracon to Yaltha, who read its six words aloud. "I beg you to come again. D."

Out in the garden, I could see the last orange clamor of the sun. Haran would return home soon, yet we lit all the lamps and talked, even laughed. Yaltha asked her daughter about her work in the healing sanctuary and Diodora told of bleedings, sacred baths, and the intoxicating plants that induced dreams. "I'm one of only two attendants who write down the petitioners' dreams when they wake. My master taught me to read and write so I could have this high position." She amused us for a short while with accounts of the more preposterous dreams she'd recorded. "I take my dream recordings to the priest, who deciphers their meanings and prescribes cures. I know not how he does it."

"And do these cures work?" I asked in bafflement.

"Oh yes, almost always."

I glimpsed a movement in the garden and saw Lavi treading through the spiky palm shadows. Catching my eye, he lifted his forefinger to his lips and concealed himself behind the foliage near the open door.

"Do you live within the temple precinct?" Yaltha was asking.

"Since my master died when I was sixteen, I've had a bed in the temple domicile with the other attendants. I'm free now and make a small wage."

We went on asking questions while she basked in the genuineness of our attention, but after a while she begged Yaltha for knowledge about the two years they'd spent together before being separated. My aunt told her stories about her fear of crocodiles, her favorite lullaby, how once she'd dumped a bowl of wheat flour on her head.

"You had a little wooden paddle doll," Yaltha told her. "A brightly painted one I found in the market. You called her Mara."

Diodora sat up very tall, her eyes widening. "Was her hair made of flax threads with an onyx bead on each end?"

"Yes, that was Mara."

"I still have her! She's all I have from my life before I was bought by my master. He said I arrived clutching her. I didn't remember her name." She shook her head. "Mara," she repeated.

In this way, she took the bits and pieces Yaltha offered and began to piece them into a story of who she was. I'd stayed very quiet, listening— they seemed to inhabit a realm of their own. But after a while, Diodora noticed my reserve and said, "Ana. Tell me of yourself."

I hesitated a moment before telling her about her family in Sepphoris— Father, Mother, and Judas—but said what I could, leaving out a great deal. I described Jesus and my heart pined so badly that I resorted to tales of Delilah standing in the water trough, just to have the relief of smiling.

Darkness came, and in that softening, Diodora turned to Yaltha. "When you told me who you were, I didn't know if I should believe it. That you could be my mother . . . it seemed impossible. But I saw myself in you. Deep inside, I knew who you were. After I heard your confession, bile rose in me. I told myself, she left me once, now I will leave her, so I walked away. Then you called me daughter. You called out your love." She went and knelt beside Yaltha's chair. "I cannot forget that you left me. That knowledge will always remain in a corner of me, but I wish to let myself be loved."

There was no time to ponder or rejoice in what she'd said. The door flew open. Haran stepped into the room. Behind him, the obsequious servant.

xviii.

Yaltha, Diodora, and I stood and edged together, shoulders touching, as if to make a tiny fortress. "Since you didn't knock, I assume you've come on a matter of urgency," Yaltha said to Haran, sounding remarkably restrained, but when I looked at her, she gave the impression of little bolts of lightning flashing around her head.

"I was told you received a visitor," he said. His eyes were fixed on Diodora. He searched her face, curious, but as yet unseeing, and I realized that was all he knew—*a visitor*.

"Who are you?" he asked, coming to stand before her.

I was desperately searching for some scenario to explain her presence—something about Diodora being Pamphile's sister who'd come regarding Lavi's marriage. We shall never know if my fabrication might've convinced him, or if Yaltha, who was also readying to speak, might've distracted him, for just then Diodora pulled the vulture bracelet from her pouch and offered her clumsy story, too frightened to grasp that it made little sense now. "I'm an attendant at Isis Medica. One of your servants left this behind in the healing sanctuary at Isis Medica. I've been sent to return it."

He glanced at the cups of wine and gestured toward Yaltha and me. "And are these the servants who left the bracelet?"

"No, no," she sputtered. "I was only inquiring if they knew who it belonged to."

Haran was looking at Yaltha now, a burning, triumphant look. His gaze returned to Diodora. He took a step closer to her. He said, "Chaya, I see you're back from the dead."

We stood motionless, as if blinded by an inexplicable burst of light. Even Haran did not move. The room was silent. There was only the smell of the oil lamp, a cold tingling in my arms, heat shoving through the courtyard door. I looked out toward the garden and saw Lavi's crouched shadow.

It was Yaltha who broke the thrall. "Did you really think I would not seek out my daughter?"

"I thought you smarter and more prudent than to try," he answered. "Now I shall ask *you*: Did you think I wouldn't fulfill my promise to go to the Romans and have you arrested?"

Yaltha gave him no answer. She glared at him, defiant.

I, too, had a question, but I didn't voice it: Would you like it known, Uncle, that you declared your niece dead, then sold her into slavery? The disgrace of it would cost him. He would be thrust into scandal, public shame, and banishment, and I saw that this was his deepest fear. I decided I would remind him of what was at stake, but delicately. I said, "Won't you have mercy on a mother who only wants to know her daughter? We don't care how Chaya came to belong to the priest at Isis Medica. That was long ago. We'll say nothing of it to anyone. We care only that she is reunited with her mother."

"I'm not so great a fool as to trust three women to hold their tongues and certainly not the three of you."

I tried again. "We don't wish to reveal your sins. Indeed, we'll return to Galilee and you will be rid of us."

"Would you leave me behind again?" Diodora cried, turning to her mother.

"No," said Yaltha. "You would come with us."

"But I don't wish to go to Galilee."

Oh Diodora, you are not helping.

Haran smiled. "I'll grant that you're clever, Ana, but you won't persuade me."

He was, I realized, driven as much by revenge as by his fear of disgrace.

"Besides, I'm afraid you'll be unable to go anywhere. It has been reliably reported to me that you've committed a theft."

Theft? I tried to make sense of what he'd said. Observing my confusion, he added. "It's a crime to steal papyrus."

I lifted my eyes to the servant in the doorway. I could hear Yaltha breathing, a quick raspy sound. Diodora cowered against her.

"Charge me, if you must," Yaltha said. "But not Ana."

He ignored her and went on speaking to me. "The punishment for stealing in Alexandria can be as harsh as for murder. The Romans show little mercy, but I will do my best to have you spared the flogging and mutilation. I will plead for both of you to be exiled to western Nubia. There's no return from there."

I could hear nothing but the heartbeat in my head. It grew until the entire room pounded. My grip on the world loosened. I'd not been clever. I'd been reckless and full of hubris, thinking I could outwit my uncle . . . steal and deceive without consequence. I preferred to be flogged and mutilated seven times over rather than sent to this place of no return. I must be free to go back to Jesus.

I looked at my aunt, whose silence puzzled me—why didn't she rail at him? But my voice, too, had disappeared into the dark of my throat. Fear sloshed in my belly. It seemed impossible that I'd fled Galilee to avoid arrest only to be charged in Egypt.

Haran was speaking to Diodora. "I will allow you to return to Isis Medica. But it's on the condition that you never speak of this night, nor of your origins, nor of me and this house. And you will not attempt to seek out Yaltha and Ana. Give me your oath and you may go." He waited.

Diodora's eyes trailed to Yaltha, who nodded at her. "I give my oath," she said.

"If you break it, I'll learn of it and bring charges against you, as well," he said. He believed her to be a fragile girl, one he could browbeat into obedience. Right then, I didn't know if he'd appraised her rightly or wrongly. "Leave now," he said. "My servant will see you out."

"Go," Yaltha told her. "I'll come to you when I can."

She hugged her mother, then stepped through the doorway without looking back.

Haran strode across the room and yanked the door to the courtyard closed. He slid the horizontal bolt into the post and locked it with a key tied to a cord around his tunic. When he turned to us, his face had mellowed some, not from lack of resolve, it seemed, but from weariness. He said, "You'll be confined here tonight. In the morning, I'll hand you over to the Romans. It's regrettable it came to this."

He left, closing the main door behind him. The outside bolt slid into place with a soft thud. The key turned.

I RAN TO THE COURTYARD DOOR and knocked, gently at first, then louder. "Lavi is in the garden," I told Yaltha. "He's been hiding there." I called out through the thick, impenetrable door, "Lavi . . . Lavi?"

No sound returned. I went on beckoning him for several moments, slapping my palm against the wood, absorbing the sharp stings. Finally, I gave up. Maybe Haran had ensnared him, too. Crossing the room, I shook the handle on the main door, as if I could wrest it free of its hinges.

I paced. My mind was whirling. The windows in our sleeping rooms were too high and too narrow to climb through, and calling for help seemed useless. "We have to find a way out," I said. "I will not go to Nubia."

"Conserve your strength," Yaltha said. "You will need it."

I slid onto the floor beside her with my back against her knees. I looked from one locked door to the other, a sense of futility gathering in me. "Will the Romans really punish us merely on the word of Haran?" I asked.

Her hand came to rest on my shoulder. "It seems Haran means to swear his case to the Roman court instead of the Jewish one, so I'm unsure, but I suppose he'll set forth witnesses," she said. "Ruebel's old friends from the militia will be eager to say I poisoned him. Tell me, who saw you take the papyri?"

"Haran's obnoxious servant."

"Him." She made a grunt of disgust. "He will take pleasure in bearing witness against you."

"But we will deny their accusations."

"If we're allowed to speak, yes. We won't give up hope, Ana, but neither should we allow our hope to be false. Haran has Roman citizenship, as well as the ear of the Roman prefect of Alexandria. He commands an important business and is one of the highest-ranking members of the Jewish council. I, on the other hand, am a fugitive and you are a foreigner."

My eyes began to burn.

"There's also the possibility my brother could bribe the court authorities."

I lowered my head to my knees. Fugitive. Foreigner.

Tap, tap.

We looked in unison at the courtyard door. Then came the clatter of a key.

The key pegs found the pins in the lock and Pamphile stepped inside, followed by Lavi, who held up an iron key tied with a piece of identifying parchment.

I threw my arms around each of them. "How did you come upon the key?" I asked, keeping my voice low.

"Haran has two for each door," Pamphile said. "The extra ones are kept in a pouch that hangs on a wall in his study. Lavi was able to read the labels." She beamed at him.

"You heard Haran's threats?" I asked him.

"Yes, every word."

I turned to Yaltha. "Where will we go?"

"I know of only one place where Haran wouldn't trespass," she said. "We'll go to the Therapeutae. Their precinct is sacred among the Jews. We'll be safe there."

"They'll take us in?"

"I spent eight years there. They'll give us a haven."

Since the moment Haran had locked us in, the world had pitched side to side like a ship, but I felt it settle now into an immense rightness.

"The community sits on the shore of Lake Mareotis," Yaltha said. "It will take us nearly four hours to walk the distance. Perhaps longer in the darkness—we'll have to carry a lamp."

"I'll see you there safely," Lavi said.

Yaltha gazed at him—a frown, a twist to her mouth. "Lavi, you can't continue to stay in Haran's house either."

Pamphile looked like the ground had opened beneath her. "He cannot leave here."

"He'll be in danger if he stays," Yaltha said. "Haran will naturally assume Lavi helped us escape."

"Then I will leave, too," she said. "He's my husband now."

I touched her arm. "Please, Pamphile, we need you to remain here at least a while longer. I'm still awaiting the letter that will tell me it's safe to return to Galilee. I can't bear to think it would come and I wouldn't know of it. I need you to watch for it and when it arrives, to see that it gets to us. It's selfish of me to ask this of you, but I beg you. Please."

Lavi said, "We have told no one of our marriage for fear Haran would dismiss Pamphile from his employ." He looked at his wife of only a week. "He wouldn't suspect you of being involved in their leaving."

"But I don't wish to be separated from you," she said.

Lavi spoke gently to Pamphile. "You know as I do that I can't remain here. The library has a domicile for the librarians who aren't married. I will stay there and I wish you to remain here until Ana's letter comes from Galilee. Then I will find us lodging together."

I'd been away from Jesus for one year and six months. An eternity. He was traveling about Galilee without me, preaching that God's kingdom was near, while I, his wife, was far away. I sympathized with Pamphile, but her severance from her husband would be an eye blink in comparison to mine.

"It seems I'm given no choice," she said. Her words brimmed with resentment.

Lavi slit open the door to the garden and peered out. He handed the key to Pamphile. "Return the key before it's discovered missing. Then unbolt the door in the servant quarters that leads outside. If anyone questions you about our whereabouts, tell them you have no knowledge of it. Behave as if I've betrayed you. Let your anger be known." He kissed her cheeks and nudged her out the door.

I worked swiftly to squeeze my possessions into my two travel pouches. My scrolls filled one entirely, leaving me to stuff the other with clothing, the mummy portrait of my face, the little bag that contained my red thread, and what was left of our money. Once again, I would leave carrying the incantation bowl in my arms.

xix.

When Skepsis, the old woman who led the Therapeutae, looked at me, I felt swallowed by her stare. She reminded me of an owl, perched there on the edge of a bench with her piercing gold-brown eyes and white feathery hair ruffled from sleep. Her squat body was hunched and still, but her head swiveled from me to Yaltha as she listened to my aunt explain how we came to be standing in the vestibule of her small stone house in the middle of the night, begging for sanctuary.

THROUGHOUT OUR LONG, exhausting trek from Alexandria, Yaltha had schooled me in the community's strange workings. "The members are divided into juniors and seniors," she'd explained. "The juniors aren't necessarily the youngest members, as you would think, but rather the newest. I wasn't thought of as a senior until I'd been with them for seven years."

"Are the juniors and seniors seen as equals?" I'd asked. If there were a hierarchy, I would most certainly be at the bottom of it.

"Everyone is seen as equal, but the labor is divided differently between them. The community has its patrons, including Haran, so I suppose they could hire servants, but they don't believe in them. It's the juniors who grow and prepare and serve the food, tend the animals, build the houses—whatever labor is required, the juniors do it, along with their spiritual work. I used to work in the garden in the mornings and return to my solitude in the afternoon."

"The seniors have no work at all?"

"They've earned the privilege of devoting all of their time to spiritual work."

We trudged past sleeping villages, vineyards, wine presses, villas, and farms, Lavi walking ahead of us holding the lamp and relying on Yaltha to call out directions. I marveled that we didn't get lost.

She said, "Every forty-ninth day, there's an all-night vigil filled with feasting, singing, and dancing. The members work themselves into a state of ecstasy. They call it a sober drunkenness."

What manner of place *was* this?

Nearing the reedy shores of Lake Mareotis, we grew quiet. I wondered if Yaltha was remembering when she'd arrived here before, freshly torn from her daughter. It was no different this time. I watched the moon bob on the water, stars floating everywhere. I could smell the sea just over the limestone ridge. I felt the mix of fear and elation I used to get long ago waiting at the cave for Jesus to appear.

At the nadir of the night, we turned off the road onto an exceptionally steep hill. Up on the slope, I could make out clusters of flat-roofed houses.

"They're small and simple," Yaltha said, following my gaze. "Each one has a little courtyard, a room for sleeping, and what they call a holy room for spiritual work."

It was the third time she'd used the odd phrase. "What is this spiritual work?" I asked. After ten years of daily toils in Nazareth, it was hard to envision sitting around in a holy room.

"Study, reading, writing, composing songs, prayer. You'll see."

Just before we reached the tiny gatehouse, we stopped and Lavi handed us the travel pouches he'd carried. I dug inside mine for a handful of drachmae. "Take these," I said. "When the letter from Judas arrives, have Pamphile hire a wagon and make her way to us as quickly as she can."

"Don't worry—I will see to it."

He lingered a moment, then turned to leave. I caught his arm. "Lavi, thank you. I think of you as my brother."

The night obscured his face, but I felt his smile and reached out to embrace him.

"Sister," he said, then bid Yaltha goodbye and turned to make the long journey back.

One of the juniors was keeping watch in the gatehouse. He was a skinny man, who balked at first to let us in. His job, as he said, was to keep out thieves, charlatans, and wayfarers, but when Yaltha told him she'd once been a senior member of the Therapeutae, he'd leapt to do her bidding.

Now, standing in Skepsis's house, listening to Yaltha elaborate on why I stole the papyri, I wondered if I would have the chance to experience any of the things my aunt had described. She'd already explained that we'd fled Galilee to avoid my arrest. I tried to read Skepsis's expression. I supposed she was considering the persistent way trouble seemed to follow me around.

"My niece is an exceptional scribe and scholar, more so than any man I've known," Yaltha said, finally offsetting my shortcomings with praise.

Skepsis patted the bench beside her. "Come and sit beside me, Yaltha." She'd implored her to do so earlier, but Yaltha had refused, pacing as she'd recounted her reunion with Diodora and Haran's threats.

Yaltha sighed heavily now and sank onto the bench. She looked haggard in the lamplight.

Skepsis said, "You've come to us out of desperation, but that alone is not a reason to take you in. Those who dwell here do so out of love for a quiet, contemplative life. They come to study and to keep the memory of God alive. Can you say you're here for those reasons as well?"

Yaltha said, "When I was sent here before, you took me in rather than let me be punished. I'd left my daughter behind and I was grieving. I spent much of my time imploring you to help me find a way to leave. My happiest day was when you struck a deal with Haran that allowed me to go to Galilee . . . though it took you long enough—eight years!" Skepsis chuckled. "I feel now as I did then," Yaltha continued. "I won't lie and say I've come here for the noble reasons you mention."

"I can say it, though," I declared.

They turned to me with startled expressions. If I could've peered into my old copper mirror at that moment, I believe I would've witnessed the same surprise on my own face. "I've come with the same desperation as my aunt, but I've arrived with all the things you said are necessary to dwell here. I've come with a love for the quiet life. I wish nothing more than to write and study and keep the memory of Sophia alive."

Skepsis scrutinized the pouch on my shoulder stuffed with scrolls, the ends of which protruded from the opening. I was still clutching my incantation bowl, holding it tightly to my abdomen. I'd not taken time during our escape to find a cloth to wrap it in and the white surface was grimy from where I'd set it down in the reeds in order to relieve myself.

"May I see the bowl?" Skepsis asked. It was the first time she'd addressed me.

I handed it to her, then watched her lift the lamp to the opening and read my inmost thoughts.

Skepsis handed back the bowl, but not before cleaning the sides and bottom of it with her hem. "I can see from your prayer that the words you spoke to us a moment ago are true." Her eyes shifted to Yaltha. "Old friend, because you accounted for your and Ana's sins, holding nothing back, I know you are honest in all else. As always, I know where you stand. I will give you both refuge. I require one thing from Ana in return." She turned to me. "I require that you write a hymn to Sophia and sing it at our next vigil."

It was as if she'd said, *Ana, you shall climb to the top of the cliff, sprout wings, and fly.*

"I know nothing about composing a song," I blurted.

"Then how fine it is that you'll have this chance to learn. Someone is required to write a new composition for every vigil and the songs have become sadly alike and unadventurous. The community will be glad to have a fresh hymn."

A hymn. To Sophia. And she wished me to perform it. I felt both petrified and captivated. "Who will teach me?"

"You will teach yourself," she said. "There won't be another vigil for forty-six days—you have ample time."

Forty-six days. Surely I would not still be here.

xx.

The first two weeks I moved through my days as if wandering about in some languorous trance. Hours of solitude, prayers, reading, writing, antiphonal singing, philosophy lessons—I'd dreamed of such pursuits, but the sudden flood of them conjured the sensation of walking around without my feet touching the ground. I had dreams of floating, of ladders stretching into the clouds. I would sit in the holy room of the house and stare half-seeing, digging my nails into the pads of my thumbs to feel the flesh of myself. Yaltha said my untethered feeling derived from the simple shock of being here.

Soon thereafter, Skepsis assigned me to the animal shed, which quickly cured me. Chickens, sheep, and donkeys. Manure and urine. Grunting and mating. The insect blizzard at the water trough. Hoof-churned dirt.

It even came to me that these things might be holy, too, a sacrilege I kept to myself.

ON THE FIRST COLD DAY after our arrival, I lugged the water vessel down the hillside to gather water for the animals from the spring near the gatehouse. The summer inundation, when the Nile floods, was over and cool winds were sweeping in from the sea on one side of the ridge and up from the lake on the other, creating a little maelstrom. I wore a shaggy goatskin cloak supplied by one of the juniors, which was so impossibly large it dragged on the ground. By my count we'd been here five and a half weeks. I tried to determine what month it would be in Galilee—Marcheshvan, I thought. Jesus would not yet be in his woolen cloak.

He hovered constantly in my thoughts. When I woke, I would lie there and picture him rising from his sleeping mat. When I ate the first meal of the morning, I imagined him breaking his bread in that unhurried way of his. And on those days, as I listened to Skepsis teach the symbolic way of reading our Scriptures, I saw him on the hillside Lavi had told us about, preaching to the multitudes.

As I descended the path, I came upon the hall where the forty-ninth-day vigils took place. The vigil was in eight days, and though I'd spent hours trying to write a song, I'd made no progress. I made up my mind I would inform Skepsis she should abandon all expectations of me either composing or performing one. She wouldn't be pleased, but I couldn't believe she'd send me away.

There were thirty-nine stone huts scattered across the hillside, each designed for one person, though most of them held two. Yaltha and I shared a house, sleeping side by side on reed mats. Skepsis offered to restore Yaltha to her senior status, but my aunt had refused in order to work in the garden. She spent her afternoons in our minuscule courtyard, sitting under the lone tamarisk tree.

Now that I'd found my equilibrium again, I liked having the holy room to myself. It had a wooden writing board and a stand on which to unfurl a scroll, and Skepsis had sent papyrus and inks.

Reaching the spring, I squatted on the ground to fill my vessel. When I heard men's voices in the gatehouse, I paid little attention—peddlers often came and went, the woman selling flour, the boy bearing sacks of salt—but then I caught certain words: "The fugitives are here. . . . Yes, I'm certain of it."

I set down the vessel. Pulling the shaggy cloak to the top of my head, I crept on all fours toward the voices until I dared edge no closer. The junior who kept the gatehouse was nowhere in sight, but one of the seniors was there speaking with two men who wore short tunics, leather sandals laced to their knees, and short knives at their belts. It was the garb of the Jewish militia. "My men will keep vigil along the road in case they attempt to leave," the taller one said. "I'll send word to Haran. If you have intelligence for us, you may leave your missives at the gatehouse."

It wasn't a surprise Haran had found us, only that it'd taken him so long. Yaltha and Skepsis devoutly believed he wouldn't defy the sanctity of the Therapeutae by sending someone inside to apprehend us. "The Jews of Alexandria would most assuredly turn against him," Skepsis had said. I didn't feel as confident.

When the soldiers departed, I hugged the ground and waited for our betrayer to pass by on his way back up the hill. He was a thin, bent man with eyes like dried grapes, the one called Lucian, who was second in seniority to Skepsis. When he was out of sight, I recovered the water vessel and rushed to the garden to inform Yaltha.

"That snake Lucian was Haran's spy when I was here before," she said. "It seems he hasn't improved with age. The man has fasted too much and been celibate too long."

. . .

TWO DAYS LATER, I glimpsed Skepsis and Yaltha hurrying toward me in the animal shed.

I'd been gathering green grasses to feed the donkeys. I set down the rake.

Without bothering to greet me, Skepsis lifted a parchment. "This arrived today from Haran. One of the soldiers who guards the road delivered it to the gatehouse."

"You know about the soldiers?" I said.

"It's my business to know what threatens our peace. I pay the salt boy to bring me news of them."

"Read it to her," Yaltha said.

Skepsis scowled, not used to being ordered about, but she complied, holding the parchment at arm's length and squinting:

I, Haran ben Philip Levias, faithful patron of the Therapeutae for two decades, write to Skepsis, the community's esteemed leader, and ask that my sister and niece, who are presently under the Therapeutae's guardianship, be relinquished into my care, where they will be accorded every concern and favor. By delivering them to the men who encamp nearby, the Therapeutae will continue to enjoy my loyal generosity.

She dropped her hand as if the weight of the parchment had tired her. "I've sent him a message, refusing his request. The community will, of course, lose his patronage—his threat is clear enough. It will mean a little more fasting, that's all."

"Thank you," I said, saddened we would cause any privation at all.

She tucked the message inside her cloak. As I watched her walk away, I understood that she was the only one standing between us and Haran.

I would write the song.

xxi.

The library was a small, cramped room in the assembly house, teeming with scrolls that lay about on the floor, on shelves and tables, and in wall niches like piles of scattered firewood. I stepped over and around them, sneezing at the dust. Skepsis had told me there were songs here that bore inscriptions of both lyrics and melody, even Greek vocal notations, but how was I to find them? There was no catalog. Nothing was sorted. My animal shed had more order and my donkeys' fur less dust.

Skepsis had warned me about the disarray. "Theano, our librarian, is old with a weakness that makes it impossible for him to walk," she'd said. "He hasn't tended the library in more than a year and there's been no one willing or able to take his place. But go and search for the songs— they'll be instructive."

It struck me now she'd had another motive. She was hoping I would become her ad hoc librarian.

I cleared a space on the floor, setting the lamp well away from the papyri, and opened scroll after scroll, finding not just Scriptures and Jewish philosophy, but works by Platonists, Stoics, and Pythagoreans; Greek poems; and a comic play by Aristophanes. I set about organizing the manuscripts by subject. By late afternoon I'd categorized more than fifty scrolls, writing a description of each one, as they did at the great library in Alexandria. I swept the floor and sprinkled the corners with eucalyptus leaves. I was brushing the mint-honey smell from my palms

when the marvel happened, the one that had been coming all day, unbe-
knownst to me.

Footsteps. I turned to the door. There, in the broken light, stood
Diodora.

"You are *here*," I said, needing to verbalize what I saw but couldn't yet
believe.

"So she is," said Skepsis, stepping from behind her into the room.
Her old eyes sparked with delight.

I drew my cousin to me and felt her cheek wet against mine. "How
did you come to be here?"

She glanced at Skepsis, who pulled a bench from beneath the table
and lowered herself onto it. "I sent a message to her at Isis Medica and
asked her to come."

"I didn't know what had become of you and my mother until I got
her letter," Diodora said, still gripping my hand. "When you didn't return to Isis Medica, I knew something had befallen you. I had to come
and see for myself that you're both well."

"Will you remain with us long?"

"The priestess has given me leave for as long as I wish."

"You will share the house with Ana and Yaltha," Skepsis said. "The
sleeping room is just wide enough for three beds." Tucking stray pieces
of hair behind her ears, she studied Diodora. "I asked you to come so
you could be near your mother and she near you, but I also asked for
myself. Or, I should say, for the Therapeutae. We have need of you here.
Some of our members are old and sick and there's no one to tend them.
You're accomplished in the art of healing. If you remain with us, we
would benefit from your care."

"You wish me to live among you?" Diodora said.

"Only if you wish a quiet, contemplative life. Only if you wish to
study and keep God's memory alive." These were the same words she'd
spoken to Yaltha and me the night we'd arrived.

"But yours is the God of the Jews," Diodora said. "I know nothing of him. It's Isis I serve."

"We will teach you about our God and you will teach us about yours, and together we'll find the God that exists behind them."

Diodora gave no answer, but I watched a light come into her face.

"Does Yaltha know you're here?" I asked.

"Not yet. I only just arrived and Skepsis wished you to accompany us."

"I would not have you miss Yaltha's face when she sees who has come," Skepsis said. Her eyes pored over my neat, methodical stacks of scrolls. "I pray we shall soon have a healer *and* a librarian."

YALTHA HAD FALLEN ASLEEP sitting on the bench in the courtyard beside our hut with her head leaning against the wall. Her arms were crossed over her thin breasts, her lower lip fluttering with each puff of breath. Seeing her at rest, Skepsis, Diodora, and I paused.

"Should we wake her?" Diodora whispered.

Skepsis strode over and shook her shoulder. "Yaltha . . . Yaltha, someone is here."

My aunt opened one eye. "Leave me be."

"What do you think, Diodora?" Skepsis said. "Should we leave her alone?"

Yaltha started, looking past Skepsis to where Diodora stood near the entrance.

"I think we should leave her alone," I said. "Go back to sleep, Aunt."

Yaltha smiled, motioning for Diodora to come and sit next to her. When they'd said their greetings, she summoned me, as well. As I sank down on the other side of her, she looked at Skepsis. "My daughters," she said.

xxii.

Diodora and I followed a zigzagging footpath to the top of the limestone cliffs that rose behind the Therapeutae community. Sunlight lay across the summit and the rocks were shining white as milk. Scampering through the few remaining poppies, I was possessed by the ebullient feeling of being set free. I didn't like to think I could be happy with Jesus so far away and his circumstances unknown to me, yet I felt it—happiness. The realization brought a twist of guilt.

"Your countenance has fallen," said Diodora. She'd been trained to observe the body and little escaped her notice.

"I was thinking of my husband," I said. I told her then about the circumstances of our separation and how much it grieved me to be away from him. "I'm awaiting a letter telling me it's safe for us to return."

She came to a standstill. "*Us?* Do you believe Yaltha will leave and go back?"

I stared at her, silence gnawing around us. The night she'd come to Haran's house, she'd become distressed when Yaltha had spoken of returning to Galilee, and she'd made it plain she had no wish to go there with us. Why had I said anything about leaving?

"I don't know if Yaltha will leave or stay," I told her, realizing it was true. I didn't know.

She nodded, accepting my honesty, and we continued on more subdued. Reaching the crest ahead of me, she took in the vista and swept her arms open. "Oh, Ana. Look!"

I hastened the last few steps and there before me was the sea. The water stretched all the way to Greece and Rome, glittering striations of blue and green, ripples of white. Our Sea, the Romans called it. Galilee was a million fathoms away.

Finding a cranny protected from the winds, we sat, squeezed together between the rocks. Since Diodora's arrival she'd been effusive, telling us about her days growing up at Isis Medica. She'd asked questions as well, eager for stories about us. Our whispered talks on our sleeping mats had left me yawning and heavy-eyed the next day. But it was worth it. She was telling me now about Theano, whose illness prevented him from tending the library. "He has a weakness of the heart. It will give out soon."

Listening as she gave an all too vivid account of the bodily complaints she'd heard, I began to feel I should return and set to work on the hymn to Sophia. The forty-ninth-day vigil was tomorrow night and I sat idle on a rock while Diodora spoke of foot ulcers. "It surprises me," she said. "After all the years I spent at Isis Medica, I do not yet miss it."

"What about Isis? Do you miss her?"

"There's no need for me to miss her. I carry her inside me. She is everything." She continued speaking for many minutes, but I heard nothing more. I felt the song I would write quicken to life inside me. I didn't know how to go on sitting there.

I stood. "We must go."

She threaded her arm around mine. "The day we met, you said, 'Let us be more than cousins. Let us be sisters.' Do you still want that?"

"I wish it even more now."

"It's my wish, too," she said.

AS WE DESCENDED THE PATH, I spied a figure beneath the eucalyptus tree where I collected my aromatic leaves. He wore the white tunic and shaggy cloak of the Therapeutae, but I couldn't identify him. Treading farther, I lifted my hand to shield the sun and saw it was the spy, Lucian.

"It's late in the day," he said as we came nearer. "Why aren't you engaged in study and prayer?"

"We could ask the same of you," I said, assailed by the uneasy feeling he'd been waiting for us.

"I've been at prayer here beneath the tree."

Diodora bristled. "And we've been at prayer up there on the cliffs." I gave her an approving look.

"The rocks up there are treacherous and there are wild animals," he said. "We would all be saddened if you came to harm."

His face had such a quiet malevolence that I looked away. He seemed to be threatening us, but I was unsure how. "We feel safe enough there," I told him and attempted to pass. The words *She is everything* were like a fire in me. I had no time for him.

He stepped to block the path. "When you are in need of a walk, it would be safer to travel down the hill and along the road to the lake. There are solitary places on the shore that are as beautiful as the sea. I will be glad to show you."

Ah. That was it. The lake lay down the hill and across the road, just beyond the protection of the Therapeutae's precinct.

I said, "The lake sounds like a pleasant place to pray. We'll go there another time. Right now we have duties to attend."

He smiled. I smiled back.

"Don't attempt to go to the lake," I told Diodora when we were some distance away. "You've just met Lucian, Haran's spy. He means to lure us onto the road, where the militia wait to arrest us. The boy who brings the salt said the soldiers stop everyone who passes from the west, looking for an old woman with a drooped eye and a young woman with unruly curls. They could easily mistake you for me."

My words sobered her.

When we arrived at our hut, we found Yaltha sitting in her spot in the courtyard reading a codex from the library. Seeing her, Diodora said quietly to me, "It isn't merely a question of whether Yaltha will choose to go to Galilee or stay in Egypt, is it? It's whether any of us will be able to leave at all."

She'd spoken my fear out loud.

. . .

LEAVING DIODORA AND YALTHA in the courtyard, I cleansed my hands and face in preparation to enter the holy room and write the hymn that was burning a hole in my heart. I set the lamp on the table and poured ink into the palette.

I dipped my pen.

xxiii.

The forty-ninth-day vigil began the next day at sunset. I arrived late to find the dining hall ablaze with lamps, the seniors already reclined on their couches, eating. The juniors were hauling about platters of food. Diodora was at the serving table replenishing a tray of fish and hen eggs. "Sister!" she cried as I approached. "Where have you been?"

I held up the scroll that contained my opus. "I was finalizing the words of my hymn."

"Lucian has been inquiring of your whereabouts. He has twice pointed out your absence to Skepsis."

I picked up a serving bowl of pomegranate seeds. "It is good of him to miss me."

She smiled and rolled her eyes at her platter. "I've refilled it four times. Let us hope they leave a morsel for us."

Though Yaltha had been designated as a junior, I noticed Skepsis had allowed her to recline on one of the couches reserved for seniors. Lucian left his couch and stood before Skepsis. "Yaltha should be serving us alongside the other juniors," he said angrily, his voice carrying across the room.

"Anger is effortless, Lucian. Kindness is hard. Try to exert yourself."

"She shouldn't be here at all," he persisted.

Skepsis waved her hand. "Leave me to eat in peace."

I looked at Yaltha, who was biting a turnip, unfazed.

When the banqueting wore down, the community made their way to the opposite end of the room, where a waist-high partition ran along the center with benches on each side, women to the left, men to the right.

I sat on the last bench with Yaltha and Diodora. "Get comfortable," Yaltha told us. "You'll be here the rest of the night."

"All night?" Diodora exclaimed.

"Yes, but you will not lack for entertainment," Yaltha said.

Coming behind us and overhearing, Skepsis said, "Our gathering is not entertainment, as Yaltha well knows—it's a vigil. We watch for the dawn, which represents the true light of God."

"And we will sing ourselves into a stupor before it arrives," Yaltha said.

"Yes, that part is true," Skepsis conceded.

Skepsis began the vigil with a lengthy discourse, about what, precisely, I couldn't say. I gripped the scroll on which I'd written my hymn. My song suddenly seemed too audacious.

I heard Skepsis call my name. "Ana . . . come, offer your hymn to Sophia."

"I call my hymn 'Thunder: Perfect Mind,'" I told her when I reached the front of the room. Someone struck a timbrel. As the drumbeat began, I lifted my scroll and chanted.

I was sent out from power . . .

    Be careful. Do not ignore me.

    I am the first and the last

    I am she who is honored and she who is mocked

    I am the whore and the holy woman

    I am the wife and the virgin

    I am the mother and the daughter

I stopped and looked at their faces, glimpsing both wonder and be-wilderment. Diodora was watching me intensely, her hands tucked under her chin. A smile moved on Yaltha's lips. I felt all the women who lived inside me.

> *Do not stare at me in the shit pile, leaving me discarded*
> *You will find me in the kingdoms . . .*
>
> *Do not be afraid of my power*
> *Why do you despise my fear and curse my pride?*
> *I am she who exists in all fears and in trembling*
> *boldness*

I paused once more, needing to find my breath. The words I'd sung seemed to swirl over my head. I wondered where they had come from. Where they would go.

> *I, I am without God*
> *And I am she whose God is magnificent . . .*
>
> *I am being*
> *I am she who is nothing . . .*
>
> *I am the coming together and the falling apart*
> *I am the enduring and the disintegration . . .*
> *I am what everyone can hear and no one can say*

I sang on and on, and when the hymn was ended, I walked slowly back to my place.

As I passed the benches, a woman rose to her feet and then another, until everyone was standing. I looked uncertainly at Skepsis. "They are telling you that you are Sophia's daughter," she said. "They are telling you she is well pleased."

I remember the rest of that night only vaguely. I know we sang without ceasing, first the men, then the women, blending finally into a single choir. The sistrums shook and the goatskin drums beat. We danced, pretending to cross the Red Sea, wheeling and counterwheeling, exhausted and delirious, until dawn came and we turned east and faced the light.

xxiv.

One afternoon, near the end of winter, Skepsis arrived unexpectedly in my holy room with swatches of leather, papyri, a measuring rod, needles, thread, wax, and a huge pair of scissors. "We're going to turn your scrolls into codices," she said. "A bound book is the best way to ensure your writing endures."

She didn't wait for my consent, which I would have given a hundred times over, but she set about spreading her bookmaking wares across the table. The scissors were identical to the ones I'd used to cut Jesus's hair the day I'd told him I was with child.

"With which scrolls do you wish to begin?" she asked.

I heard her, but I could not stop looking at the long bronze scissor blades. The remembrance of them caused a toppling sensation in my chest.

"Ana?" she said.

Shaking my head to clear the memory, I retrieved the scrolls that contained my stories of the matriarchs and placed them on the table. "I wish to begin at the beginning."

"Watch carefully and learn. I'll show you how to make the first book, but the rest you must do yourself." She measured and marked the scrolls and the leather cover. When she cut them, I closed my eyes, remembering the sound of the shears, the feel of his hair in my fingers.

"See, I did not injure a single one of your words," she said when she was done, seeming to mistake my preoccupation as concern over her cutting skills. I did not correct her. Holding up a blank page of papyrus, she added, "I've cut an extra page so you may write a title on it." Then she began to sew the pages together inside the leather covers.

"Now," she said. "What is it that troubles you, Ana? Is it Haran?"

I hesitated. I had poured out my fears and longings to Yaltha and Diodora, but not to Skepsis. I said, "When spring comes, it will be two years since I've seen my husband."

She smiled slightly. "I see."

"My brother promised to send a letter when it was safe for me to return to Galilee. There's a servant in Haran's house who will bring it to me, but Haran will prevent my leaving."

It seemed impossible that the Jewish militia was still posted on the road after all these months; their encampment had become a permanent outpost.

Skepsis pushed and pulled the needle, using a little iron hammer to force it through the leather. She said, "The salt boy tells me the soldiers have built a small stone hut in which to sleep, as well as a pen for a goat, and they've hired a local woman to cook their meals. It's a testament to Haran's patience and need for revenge."

I had heard these things from Yaltha. Hearing them again left me even more disconsolate.

"I don't know why the letter hasn't come," I said. "But I don't feel I can tarry here much longer."

"Do you see how I'm making a backstitch to make a double knot?" she asked, all of her attention refocused on the book. I said nothing more.

When the codex was completed, she placed it in my arms. "If your letter comes, I'll do what I can to help you leave," she said. "But it will sadden me to see you go. If your place is in Galilee, Ana, so be it. I only wish you to know that this place will be here if you desire to return."

She left. I looked down at the codex, this thing of wonder.

XXV.

Then came a day balmy with spring. I had just finished turning the last of my scrolls into books, a task I'd worked on for weeks with an exigency I couldn't explain. Now, alone in the house, I surveyed the stack of codices with relief, then amazement. Perhaps my words would endure now.

Yaltha had left the house to visit the library, and Diodora was off caring for Theano, who lay at death's threshold. Skepsis had already ordered his coffin to be constructed—a simple box of acacia wood. Earlier, while watering the animals, I'd heard the insistent hammering in the woodworking shop.

Eager to show Diodora and Yaltha my collection of codices, I hurried to complete one last task before they returned. I filled the palette with ink and inscribed a title onto the empty page in each book, blowing the ink gently to dry it.

The Matriarchs

The Tales of Terror

Phasaelis and Herod Antipas

My Life in Nazareth

Lamentations for Susanna

Jesus, Beloved

Yaltha of Alexandria

Chaya: Lost Daughter

The Ways of the Therapeutae

Thunder: Perfect Mind

Remembering Enheduanna, who signed her name to her writing, I reopened the books and signed mine: Ana. Not Ana, daughter of Matthias, or Ana, wife of Jesus. Just Ana.

There was only one codex I didn't sign. When I lifted my pen to *Thunder: Perfect Mind*, my hand would not move. The words in the book had come from me, but also from beyond me. I closed the leather cover.

Awe took hold of me as I arranged the books inside the wall niche, then placed my incantation bowl on top. As I stepped back and took them in, Yaltha entered the room.

Pamphile was at her side.

xxvi.

My eyes flashed to the goatskin pouch in Pamphile's hand. She held it out to me without a word, her face tense.

I took the pouch and fumbled with the knot on the leather tie, my fingers fat as cucumbers. Prying open the drawstring, I peered inside at a scrolled parchment. I wanted to snatch it out and read it that moment, but I loosely retied the pouch. Yaltha looked at me, understanding, it seemed, that I wished to be alone when I read it, away even from her.

"A courier arrived with it three days ago," Pamphile said. "I hired a wagon with a donkey as soon as I could. Apion thinks I'm visiting my family in Dionysias. I led him to believe my father had fallen ill."

"Thank you, Pamphile. You have done well."

"It's Lavi you should thank," she replied, her face hardening. "He's the one who insisted I remain at Haran's all these months and wait for your letter. If it'd been left to me, I would've departed there long ago. I think my husband is more loyal to you than to me."

I didn't know how to respond to this—I thought she might be right. "Is Lavi well?" I asked, hoping to divert her.

"He's happy with his work at the library. His superiors heap praise on him. I go to him whenever I can—he rents a small apartment now."

Every moment the letter remained unopened was an agony, but I owed it to her to listen.

"Did you see a colony of soldiers on the road near the gatehouse?" Yaltha asked.

"Yes. I've seen these same kind of soldiers in Haran's house. One comes each week to see him."

"Do you know what they speak about?" I asked.

She glared at me. "Do you expect me to listen at the door?"

"I wish you to do nothing that puts you in danger."

"You should be prepared when you pass back by the soldiers," Yaltha said. "There's no danger to you, but they inspect everyone going east, searching for me and Ana. You'll be stopped. If asked, say you have no knowledge of us, that you came to sell papyrus."

"Sell papyrus," she repeated, then glowered at me again. "I didn't know I would have to tell more lies for you."

"Only one more, and only if asked," I said.

"I wish this to be over," she said. "Now that your letter has come, I only want to leave Haran's employ and go live with my husband."

I tightened my fingers on the letter's pouch. *Be patient, Ana*, I told myself. *You have waited so long—what are a few more minutes?*

"What news do you have of Haran?" Yaltha asked her.

"The morning after you left, his shouting could be heard through the house. He searched your rooms in a rage, looking for some sign of where you'd gone. The man ripped bedcovers and shattered water pots. Who do you think was charged to clean it up? Me, of course. He plundered the scriptorium as well. I found scrolls across the floor, spilled ink, a broken chair."

"Did he suspect you of aiding us?" I asked.

"He was content to lay the blame on Lavi, but not before he interrogated me and the rest of the servants. Even Thaddeus wasn't spared." She balled her fists and mimicked Haran. "'How did they manage to flee? Did they turn into smoke and float under the locked door? Did they fly out the window? Which of you unlocked the door?' He threatened to have us flogged. It is only through Apion's intervention that we were spared."

It was plain how much she'd suffered under Haran's roof separated from Lavi. "I'm sorry," I said. "You've been a brave and true friend." I pulled the bench toward her. "Here, rest. I'll return shortly. Yaltha will bring you food and water. You will stay the night with us."

I walked self-consciously from the house, past the assembly hall, the woodworking shop, the clusters of houses, the animal shed, forcing myself not to break into a run. As I passed the eucalyptus tree, I quickened my pace, then took flight up the escarpment toward the cliffs.

Finding a boulder midway up, I sat with my back against it, letting the strength of it hold me. My heart was in an uproar. I took a breath, opened the pouch, and pulled out the parchment.

> Dearest Sister,
> I trust you received my earlier letter explaining why it was not safe for you to return.

My mouth parted. Judas had written before—why had I not received it?

The danger to you in Galilee has not fully passed, though it has lessened. Antipas is fully consumed by his lust to be named King of the Jews by Rome.

Last week we came into Judea on our way to Jerusalem where we will remain through Passover. Antipas has no rule here. Come to us with all haste. Sail with Lavi to Joppa and make your way to Bethany where we lodge at the home of Lazarus, Mary, and Martha.

The kingdom is close at hand. Vast throngs of people in Galilee and Judea now hail Jesus as the Messiah. He believes the fullness of time is upon us and he wishes you by his side. He compelled me to tell you that he is safe. I, though, must warn of dangers. The people are emboldened by the appearance of a Messiah and there is much talk of revolution. Jesus teaches each day in the Temple and the Jewish authorities set spies upon us the moment we enter the gates. If there is unrest, the Temple guard will most certainly arrest him. Jesus continues to believe God's kingdom can come without swords. But I am both a Cynic and a Zealot. I only know we cannot let this moment pass. If it is necessary, I will do what I must this Passover to ensure the masses rise up and overthrow the Romans at last. The sacrifice of one for many.

As I write, I sit in Lazarus's courtyard where your friend Tabitha is playing the lyre, filling the air with the sweetest of music. Jesus has gone to the Mount of Olives to pray. He

has missed you, Ana. He bids me give you his love. We
await you.
    Your brother,
    Judas
    10th day of Shebat

Judas's words slammed into me. *I will do what I must this Passover . . .*
The sacrifice of one for many. What did he mean? What was he trying to
tell me? I began to breathe very fast, like I'd run a great distance. My
head churned with confusion. I turned the parchment over, wishing he
might have explained himself on the back, but it was devoid of words.

I reread the letter. This time different pieces of it whirled up, broken-
off words. *He wishes you by his side . . . He bids me give you his love . . . He*
has missed you. How had I endured these two years without him? I
pressed the letter to my breast and held it there.

I tried to calculate time. Judas had written the letter early this past
winter, seven weeks ago. Passover in Jerusalem was fourteen days away.
I stuffed the parchment into the pouch and scrambled to my feet. *I must*
get to Jerusalem, and quickly.

xxvii.

Yaltha stood alone in the courtyard. I thrust the letter into her hand, not
asking Pamphile's whereabouts. As she read, I watched her face, noticing
the flare of surprise toward the end. "Finally, you'll go to your husband,"
she said. I waited for her to say more, but that was all.

"I must find a way to leave in the morning."

Would she not mention Judas's strange message about ensuring the masses rise up? Behind her the light was sinking. Golden-brown scintillas drifting far below over the lake. "What does my brother mean by the sacrifice of one for many?" I asked. "What is he saying?"

I watched her step beneath the branches of the tamarisk tree and become pensive. Her need to deliberate filled me with unease.

"I think I already know what he means," I said quietly. I'd known before I'd finished the letter, but I couldn't bear to acknowledge it right then. It had seemed impossible that my brother would go so far, but as I stood with Yaltha beneath the tree, I pictured the child whose father was murdered by the Romans and whose mother was sold into slavery, the boy who swore to avenge them, and I knew—yes, he would go that far.

"*Judas*," Yaltha hissed. From the corner of my eye I saw a tiny green lizard dart up the stone wall. "Yes, of course you know what he means. You know him better than anyone."

"Please say it. I cannot."

We sat on the bench and she placed her hand at my back. "Judas means to have his revolution, Ana. If Jesus doesn't bring it about peaceably, Judas means to ignite it by force. The surest way to incite the masses is for the Romans to execute their Messiah."

"He will deliver Jesus to the Romans," I whispered. Saying the words, I felt like I was falling off the edge of the world. During the time we'd been in Egypt, I'd stored away a thousand tears, and I let them loose now. Yaltha pulled my head to her shoulder and let me sob my fear, helplessness, and fury.

The deluge went on for several minutes, and in the aftermath, I experienced a great calm. I said, "Why would Judas be so brazen as to reveal his intention to me?"

"That is hard to know. Confessing to you may have been a way of alleviating his guilt."

"When it comes to overthrowing the Romans, Judas feels no guilt."

"He may have been trying to find the boldness to go through with it. Like throwing your money bag over a wall to ensure you'll climb over."

She was doing her best to humor my need to understand at least some part of Judas's warped design, but I realized how futile it was. "I'll never understand any of this," I said. "And right now, it doesn't matter. It only matters that I get to Jerusalem." I stood and peered over the wall toward the road, another anxiety taking over—Haran and his soldiers.

At that same moment, Skepsis and Diodora entered the courtyard. "Theano has died," Skepsis announced. "Diodora and I have just finished preparing his body—"

"Has something happened?" Diodora interrupted, noticing my reddened eyes. Or perhaps it was the taut, menacing air.

I picked up Judas's letter and read it to them, then tried my best to elucidate Judas's plan. Diodora, who knew nothing of Jewish messiahs and radical Zealots, seemed utterly mystified. She enfolded me in her arms. "I'm happy you will see your husband, but I am sad you will leave us." She turned to her mother. "Will you go, too?" she asked in an unassuming way, but her face betrayed her fear.

"I'll remain here," Yaltha said, looking past Diodora to me. "Having found Diodora, I cannot leave her again. I'm getting too old to make the journey anyway, and Egypt is my home. I'm content here among the Therapeutae. It will grieve me to be separated from you, Ana, but I cannot leave."

I felt a crumpling inside, but I refused to let my disappointment show. I said, "I understand, Aunt. Your decision is as it should be."

Shadows had begun to darken the edges of the courtyard, and Diodora went into the house for a lamp, though I had the feeling she left out of kindness, not wanting me to see her joy.

She returned with a look of confusion on her face. "The woman sleeping inside—she's the servant in Haran's house who showed me to your quarters."

"Yes, Pamphile," Yaltha said. "She delivered the letter from Judas. She was weary. I helped her with some chamomile."

We settled around the glowing circle of lamplight and I posed the question that loomed over everything. "How will I get past the soldiers?" I looked at their faces—I had no answer. They stared back—they had no answer either.

"Is there no way to leave here except by the road where the soldiers stand guard?" Diodora asked. "Is there a footpath that skirts around them?"

Skepsis shook her head. "We are hemmed in by the cliffs. The road is our only way of leaving, and the soldiers are positioned too close to the gatehouse to miss anyone who comes and goes from here."

"Could you disguise yourself somehow?" Diodora asked. "As an old woman? You could cover your head and use a crutch."

"I doubt they'd be fooled by that," said Yaltha. "It's far too risky. But . . ."

I prodded her. "What is it? We must consider everything."

"Pamphile will leave tomorrow. The wagon she arrived in is large enough for you to hide in the back." She glanced at Skepsis, shrugging uncertainly. "What if we concealed her beneath the sacks that store the vegetable seed?"

"The soldiers always search the carts that bring flour and salt," Skepsis said. "They would search Pamphile's wagon, too."

They grew quiet. A thin, gray hopelessness crept into the air. I didn't want them to give up. It was true I no longer believed in the God of rescue, only the God of presence, but I believed in Sophia, who whispered bravery and wisdom in my ear day and night, if I would only listen, and I tried now to do that, to listen.

What I heard was hammering. Faint, but so clear I thought for a moment Pamphile had wakened and was rapping on the door from inside the house. The realization that the sound resounding in my head was actually a memory startled me. I knew instantly what that memory was.

I'd heard it that morning while watering the animals. It was the hammering from the woodworking shop as Theano's coffin was being built.

The sound formed into an idea. I said, "There is one way for me to leave here safely, and that's inside Theano's coffin."

They sat there with blank faces.

"I would not be inside the coffin long, only until Pamphile drives the cart an ample distance past the soldiers. I will take any risk to reach Jesus, but this one puts me in the least peril. The soldiers would never think to open the coffin."

"That is true," Diodora said. "Violating the dead is a serious offense. One can be put to death for opening a tomb."

"And for Jews, a corpse is unclean," I added. I tried but was unable to read Yaltha's expression. She must have thought my idea was elaborately strange. "I believe it is the very boldness of the notion that will cause it to work," I continued. "Do you think differently, Aunt?"

She said, "I think the idea of you riding away in Theano's coffin is absurd, but it's also ingenious, Little Thunder."

My eyes rounded—no one had ever called me Little Thunder but Jesus. I received the name from her like a charge. *Go, be boiling clouds and lightning spears and sky-splitting roars.*

"Now," she said. "Let's imagine how you will accomplish this insane act."

All of us turned pointedly to Skepsis, who was studying the trails of blue on the back of her hands. None of this could be done without her. I was proposing we confiscate Theano's coffin, requiring another one to be swiftly constructed for him. Furthermore, if Skepsis entered into the deception, she would deceive the whole community.

"Lucian is our biggest concern," she said. "If he suspects it's not Theano in the coffin, he'll convey his suspicions to the soldiers, and Ana is certain to be discovered." She fell quiet, mulling further. When she lifted her face, her eyes were doing their owlish dance. "Theano's wish was to be buried here on our grounds, but I'll put out word that he wished to be buried in his family's tomb in Alexandria. This is quite typical for our wealthier members. Of course, Theano's family is not rich, but they would have enough for a mud-brick tomb, I'm sure. I'll tell everyone that the servant who delivered the letter—what was her name?"

"Pamphile," I answered, amazed at the intricacies she was working out. Until this moment, Lucian had not received a thought from me.

"I'll explain that Pamphile was sent from Theano's family to bring his body to Alexandria. This should resolve the matter."

"It should also put an end to the outpost of soldiers at our gate," said Yaltha. "If Ana is no longer here, there will be no need for the soldiers."

"What about you?" said Diodora, looking at Yaltha. "Haran would still wish to arrest you."

Skepsis lifted a finger. I knew this to be a good sign. "When Ana is well away, I'll address the community, stating she has returned to her husband in Galilee and Yaltha has taken the vows to remain part of the Therapeutae for life. It will not take Lucian long to put this news in Haran's ear. I think Haran will be relieved to have a legitimate reason to put an end to all this."

"My brother will at least be thrilled to no longer pay the soldiers from his own money bags. The only reason he has kept the outpost going this long is so not to be perceived as backing down."

I admired the scheme that had just come into being and feared in equal measure that it would fail.

Diodora said, "What will we do with poor Theano during all of this?"

"That will be easy. We'll keep him concealed in his house until Ana is gone," Skepsis said. "Then we three, along with Gaius, our carpenter, will give him a proper burial without Lucian's knowledge."

It sounded anything but easy.

"And Gaius is trustworthy?" Yaltha asked.

"Gaius? Most certainly. When I leave here, I'll ask him to begin work this very night on a second coffin and to create two small holes in one of them for breathing."

That detail sent a shudder through me. I imagined the tight, airless space and wondered for the first time if I could go through with this.

"The community has been notified to gather at the first hour tomorrow to say the prayers for the dead for Theano," Skepsis said. "You should be among us, Ana."

"When will she be placed in the coffin?" Diodora asked. Her eyes were wide and worried, and I thought she was feeling the tight, airless space, too.

"After the prayers, Ana, you slip away to the woodworking shop, where Gaius will lightly nail you inside the coffin. Four short nails, no more. I'll instruct him to place an awl in the wagon for Pamphile, but also one inside the coffin so you may pry the lid yourself. Then he and his helper will load you onto the wagon. Meanwhile, I will keep Lucian occupied."

Yaltha held out her knotty hands to me and I took them. "I'll go with Ana to the woodworking shop to make certain everything is done as prescribed," she said.

"I'll go, too," Diodora said. "We want no danger to come to you, sister."

A noise came from within the house. Then footsteps. Pamphile called, "Yaltha? Ana?"

"I tell you," I said, "the greatest danger to me is Pamphile refusing to open the lid!"

Yaltha laughed. She was the only one to understand my uneasy jest.

xxviii.

At first, Pamphile seemed agreeable to our well-laid plan, but when I told her Lavi must travel with me to Judea, she rolled out her lower lip and folded her arms over her chest. "Then I will not do it."

Behind me, I heard Yaltha, Skepsis, and Diodora sigh with one accord. For the past half hour, the three of them had been like a small Greek chorus, offering refrains and harmonious sighs while I tried my best to convince Pamphile to join our subterfuge. We were crowded into the holy room, which had grown thick with the smell of palm oil from the lamps. Yaltha had left the door open to the courtyard, but the little room was stifling. A trickle of sweat darted between my breasts.

"Please, Pamphile," I pleaded. "My husband's life may depend upon your answer. I must get to Jerusalem and stop my brother."

"Yes, so you said."

She enjoys this, I thought, *this power she holds*. "It's too dangerous for me to travel alone," I said, feeling the words like stones in my mouth. "Without Lavi I won't be able to go!"

"Then you must find someone else," she said.

"There *is* no one else."

"This needs to be settled quickly," Skepsis interjected. "If you are leaving here by coffin, I must alert Gaius right away. And Pamphile must come with me and stay at my house for the night. Otherwise, some will wonder why a servant from Theano's family would lodge with you."

Yes, please, take her.

I tried again. "If you're worried Lavi may not return to Alexandria, I assure you I have enough money to purchase his passage back. I'll show you, if you like."

"I don't care to see your money. I trust that you would send him back."

"Then what is it?" Diodora asked.

Pamphile's eyes shrank. "I have already lived apart from my husband for five months because of you. I don't intend to do so any longer."

I did not know how to get through to her. She was lonely for her husband. How could I blame her? I glanced helplessly at Yaltha, who stepped past me, closer to Pamphile, in order to make some last effort. I remember thinking: *We've come to the split in the river.* I felt, whether or not it was true, that my life would be decided now. It would rush one way or go the other.

Yaltha spoke with uncommon gentleness. "Did you know that Ana has been apart from her own husband for two years?"

I saw it then—a softening in Pamphile's face.

"I'm sorry for the months you were separated from Lavi," I told her. "I know the pain of it. I know what it's like to lie in bed and ache for your husband, to wake up and feel his absence." Even as I said these things, I felt Jesus moving around the edges of my vision like a lost dream.

She said, "If Lavi left, how long would he be gone?"

A smidgen of hope. "Three weeks, perhaps. No more."

"And what will become of his position at the library? Will they receive him back?"

"I correspond with a scholar there," said Skepsis. She was thumping her finger impatiently on the table. "I'll make certain your husband is given leave."

Pamphile dropped her arms to her sides. "Let it be as you wish," she said.

I COULD NOT SLEEP that night, even with Yaltha's chamomile. My thoughts spun. It was the deep of night, but I rose from my mat and stole past Diodora and Yaltha, who were making quiet slumbering sounds.

Standing in the darkened holy room, I felt the finality of being here. My large woolen travel pouch sat on the table, stuffed full. Diodora and Yaltha had watched in silence as I'd packed it. It contained the pouch that held my red thread, Judas's letter, the mummy portrait, money, two tunics, a cloak, and undergarments. I'd left the new black-and-red Alexandrian dress for Diodora. I would have no use for it anymore.

I could hardly bear to look at the niche where my ten codices were stacked in a beautiful leaning tower with my incantation bowl perched on top. It wasn't possible to take them with me. I might've carried a second bag and squeezed in five codices, maybe six, but something inexplicable inside me wished the books to remain all together. I wanted them here among the Therapeutae, where they might be read and preserved and perhaps cherished. I moved about the room, telling everything goodbye.

Yaltha's voice came from the doorway. "I will safeguard your words until you return."

I turned to her. "I will likely never return, Aunt. You know that."

She nodded, accepting what I'd said without questioning it.

"After I leave, place my writings in the library with the other manuscripts," I said. "I'm ready now for others to read them."

She came and stood close to me. "Do you remember the day in Sepphoris when you opened your cedar chest and showed me your writings for the first time?"

"I've not forgotten it, nor will I ever forget it," I said.

"You were something to be reckoned with. Fourteen years old and full of rebellion and longings. You were the most stubborn, determined, ambitious child I'd ever seen. When I saw what was inside your cedar chest, I knew." She smiled.

"Knew what?"

"That there was also largeness in you. I knew you possessed a generosity of abilities that comes only rarely into the world. You knew it, too, for you wrote of it in your bowl. But we all have some largeness in us, don't we, Ana?"

"What are you saying, Aunt?"

"What most sets you apart is the spirit in you that rebels and persists. It isn't the largeness in you that matters most, it's your passion to bring it forth."

I gazed at her, but could not speak. I went down on my knees; I don't know why, except I felt overcome by what she'd said.

She placed her hand on my head. She said, "My own largeness has been to bless yours."

xxix.

The coffin lay on the floor in the middle of the woodworking shop smelling of fresh wood. Yaltha, Diodora, and I gathered beside it and stared somberly into the empty cavity.

"Don't think of it as a coffin," Diodora advised.

"We mustn't delay," Gaius said. "Now that the prayers for Theano are over, members will be lining the path, wanting to proceed behind the wagon as far as the gatehouse. We can't risk one of them wandering nearby and finding you. Quickly, now." He gripped my elbow as I stepped into the coffin. I stood there a moment before sitting, unable to think of the wooden box as anything other than what it was. I told myself just not to think at all.

Diodora bent and kissed my cheeks. Then Yaltha. As my aunt hovered over me, I tried to memorize her face. Gaius placed the travel pouch at my feet and the awl in my hand. "Hold on to it." I lay back and looked up into the bright room. The lid slid over me. Then darkness.

The coffin juddered as Gaius hammered in four nails, causing my head to knock against the bottom. In the stillness that followed, I became aware of two thin beams of light. They reminded me of the fine strands of a spider's web lit with sunlight and dew. I turned my head and found the source, a tiny perforation on each side. My breathing holes.

The coffin was lifted with a jerk. Unprepared for it, I let out a small cry. "You'll have to stay quieter than that," Gaius said, his voice sounding far away.

As they carried me outside, I braced for another jolt, but the coffin slid smoothly into the wagon. I couldn't tell when Pamphile climbed in, maybe she was there already, but I heard the donkey bray and felt the lurch of the cart as we started down the hill.

I closed my eyes so as not to see the coffin's lid, which was a hand's breadth from my nose. I listened instead to the rumble of the wagon, then to the muffled singing that began to follow us. *Don't think, don't think. It will be over soon.*

When we made a sharp turn north, the singing receded into the distance and I knew we'd passed the gatehouse and turned onto the road. Moments later, one of the soldiers shouted "Halt!" and the wheels on the cart ground to a stop. The beat of my heart came so hard, I imagined the sound of it streaming out through the air holes. I was afraid to breathe.

The soldier addressed Pamphile. "We were told a man among the Therapeutae died. Where are you taking him?"

It was difficult to hear her answer. "To his family in Alexandria," I believed she said.

Relief surged through me. I thought we would be waved on now, but the cart didn't move. The soldiers' voices drew closer, seeming to move to the back of the cart. A thread of panic began to unravel in me. My eyes flew open, met by the lid of the coffin. I drew a pant and shut them again. *Don't move. Don't think.*

We lingered an interminable time for reasons I could not deduce. Then I heard one of them say, "There's nothing back here but the coffin."

Suddenly the wagon staggered forward.

We plodded on and on, jostling along the rutted road for much longer than seemed necessary. Pamphile had been instructed to stop the cart when the soldiers were out of sight, preferably along a lonely stretch, and free me. The heat inside the coffin had concentrated. I took the awl and knocked against the side of the coffin. I didn't know whether people might be about, but I no longer cared. I forced the end of the awl beneath the lid and attempted to pry it upward, but there was not enough room inside for my arms to lift up or press down. I rapped harder on the side. "Pamphile!" I screamed. "Stop now and free me!"

The wagon traveled on for some minutes more before she brought it to a stop.

I heard the split of wood as she pushed her awl under the lid and wrested the coffin open. There was a dazzling rush of light.

LAVI AND I SET SAIL for Judea on the fifth of Nisan.

JERUSALEM

BETHANY

30 CE

i.

As Lavi and I arrived outside Jerusalem, the slopes of the Kidron Valley came into view lit with a thousand pilgrim campfires. Funnels of pale smoke drifted across the night sky, thick with the smell of roasted lamb. It was the thirteenth of Nisan. Passover.

I had hoped to reach the home of Lazarus, Mary, and Martha before nightfall, early enough to eat the festival meal with Jesus. I sighed. The meal would be over by now.

Lavi and I had suffered one excruciating delay after another. First, the sea winds deserted us, slowing our ship's arrival. Then, on foot from Joppa, we had difficulty finding food due to the crowds, forcing us to detour to out-of-the-way villages to buy bread and cheese. We were obstructed for hours in Lydda by Roman soldiers attempting to control the clogged road to Jerusalem. Throughout, I'd practiced in my head what I would say to Judas, reassuring myself he would listen. I was his little sister; he loved me. He'd tried to rescue me from Nathaniel. He'd taken my message to Phasaelis against his own wishes. He would listen and then abandon this madness that would have him betray Jesus.

As I gazed at the hillside, the urgency I felt inside made it difficult to breathe.

Lavi said, "Do you need to rest?" We'd been walking since daybreak.

"My husband and my brother are just beyond this valley," I said. "I will rest once I see them."

We walked the last stretch to Bethany in silence. Had I not been so weary, my feet might've broken into a run.

"The lamps in the courtyard are still burning," Lavi said as we reached the house of Jesus's friends, and now, my friends, too. He pounded on the gate, calling out that Ana, wife of Jesus, had arrived.

I expected to see Jesus hurrying to let us in, but Lazarus came. He looked well, not nearly so yellow and pallid as when I'd seen him before. He greeted me with a kiss. "Come, both of you."

"Where is Jesus?" I said.

His feet slowed, but he walked on into the courtyard, as if he hadn't heard. "Mary, Martha," he called. "Look who's here."

The sisters rushed from the house, throwing their arms open. They seemed shorter, their faces rounder. They greeted Lavi with the same warmth they'd once bestowed on Tabitha. Thinking of her, I looked about, but she, too, was nowhere to be seen. I did notice a stack of sleeping mats piled beside the outer wall. Folded on top of them was a worn flaxen cloak.

"You and Lavi must be famished," Martha said. "I'll bring what's left of the Passover meal."

As she hurried off, I went and picked up the cloak. It bore my poor, uneven weaving. I held the garment to my face—it was filled with his scent. "This belongs to Jesus," I said to Mary.

She smiled in that serene way of hers. "It's his, yes."

"And this as well," said Lavi, holding up a staff made of olive wood, the one Jesus had carved while sitting beneath the tree in the compound in Nazareth.

I took it, wrapping my fingers around the wood, feeling the smooth, polished place his hand had worn.

"Jesus and his disciples have been staying with us for some time," Mary said, nodding at the mound of bed mats. "They spend their days in the city and return in the evening to sleep in the courtyard. This past week, each time Jesus came through the gate, he would ask, 'Has Ana come?' You seemed very much on his mind." She smiled at me. I bit hard into my lip.

"Where is he?" I asked.

"He observed Passover in Jerusalem with his disciples."

"Not here with you?"

"We expected them to share the meal with us, but Jesus changed his mind only this morning, saying he would take Passover alone with his disciples in the city. I admit, it did not please Martha. She'd prepared enough for the lot of them, and I can attest they eat a great deal." She laughed, and it came out all wrong, high-pitched and uneasy.

"Was Judas among them?"

"Your brother? Yes. He hardly left Jesus's side, except. . . ."

I waited, but she did not continue. "Except?"

"It's nothing. It's just that yesterday when Jesus and the others returned from the city, Judas was not with them. I heard Jesus ask Peter and John if they knew his whereabouts. It was quite late when he finally appeared, and even then he kept to himself. He ate alone over there in the corner." She pointed across the courtyard. "I thought he didn't feel well."

I doubted this odd behavior of Judas's was nothing, as she'd suggested, though I couldn't have said what it meant. I was still clutching Jesus's staff and his cloak, gripping them so tightly I became aware of an ache in my fingers. Relinquishing the items onto a bench, I walked to the gap in the courtyard wall and looked west toward Jerusalem. "Shouldn't Jesus have returned by now?"

Mary came and stood beside me. "It's his custom to pray on the Mount of Olives each evening, but even so, he's long overdue." Her face was shadowed, but I saw something there, something more than dismay at his lateness. I saw dread.

"Ana?" The voice came from across the courtyard, one I'd not heard in seven years.

"Tabitha!" I cried, running toward her even as she ran to me. We clung to each other for a long while, her ear pushed against my cheek. We spoke no words, but swayed together—a kind of dance. I closed my eyes, remembering the girls who had danced blind.

"I cannot believe you are here," she said. "You must never go away again." The words came out slow, measured, thick-tongued, as if they were too cumbersome for her mouth, but every syllable was there.

"You speak with clarity!" I said.

"I've had many years to practice. The tongue is an adaptable creature. It finds a way."

I took her hands and kissed them.

Martha appeared then, carrying a tray of food, followed by Lazarus with a sloshing pitcher of wine. While Lavi and I cleansed our hands, Mary bid Tabitha to fetch her lyre and play for us. "You have never heard such music," she told me.

I wanted to hear Tabitha play, I truly did, but not right then. Right then I wanted the four of them to tell me about my husband—the things he'd said and done. I wanted to know about the danger he was in that no one would speak of. I watched Tabitha dash away and said nothing.

Mary was right about one thing—I'd never heard such music. Quick, daring, even funny, the song was about a woman who cut off her torturer's beard as he slept, causing him to lose his powers. Tabitha danced as she strummed, twirling about the courtyard, graceful as ever, and I thought how much she would love the Therapeutae's forty-ninth-day rituals. All that endless music and dancing.

When she finished, I set down the nugget of bread I was about to dip in my wine cup and embraced her yet again. She was breathless, her face flushed bright. "Only yesterday I played my lyre as your husband and his disciples ate. I will not forget what Jesus said to me when I finished my song. He said, 'Each of us must find a way to love the world. You have found yours.' He's very kind, your husband."

I smiled. "He's also very insightful—you have indeed found yours." *The most wounded thing in us always finds a way*, I thought.

I could see in her eyes there was more she wished to confide. "Tabitha," I whispered. "What is it?"

"For most of the years I've been here, I've earned coins by weaving widows' garments, a portion of which I give to Martha for my keep. With the rest of it, I bought a jar of spikenard."

I wrinkled my forehead, wondering why she would buy such an expensive perfume, then remembered how we'd once dabbed it on each other's foreheads and made a covenant of friendship.

"The scent held pleasant memories for me," she said. "Yesterday, though, after Jesus spoke so kindly to me, I fetched it and anointed his feet. I wanted to thank him for what he'd said to me, and the spikenard was all I had." She glanced behind her at the others, who couldn't help but hear her. She lowered her voice. "What I did angered your brother. He chastised me, saying I should've sold the ointment and given the money to the poor."

Judas, what happened to you?

"Did Jesus fault him?" I asked, knowing the answer.

"He told Judas to leave me alone, that I'd done a beautiful thing. He said it sharply, and Judas departed in a temper. Oh, Ana, I fear I've caused a rift between them."

I covered her hands with mine. "The rift was already there." It had, I realized, always been there, buried deep within their differing visions of how to establish God's kingdom.

I returned to my plate, but I could no longer eat. I looked at Mary, Lazarus, and Martha. "Will you tell me now what troubles you? I know Jesus is in danger. Judas wrote of it in his letter. Tell me what you know."

Lazarus shifted on the bench between his two sisters. He said, "Jesus has gained much fame, Ana. People believe him to be the Messiah, King of the Jews."

"I heard of this while I was in Alexandria," I said, almost relieved that he'd said nothing new. "It concerned me as well. Herod Antipas has spent his life trying to become King of the Jews. If word of this reaches him, he'll retaliate."

Silence. Discomfiture. None of them looked at me.

"What is it?" I demanded.

Mary nudged her brother. "Tell her. We should hold nothing back."

Laying down the lyre, Tabitha caught one of the strings on her finger, the sound like a small whimper. I motioned her to the seat beside me and we sat pressed together.

"Antipas already knows the people call Jesus King of the Jews," Lazarus said. "There's not a soul in Jerusalem who hasn't heard of it, including the Romans. But the governor, Pilate, is an even greater threat than Antipas. He's known for his brutality. He will crush any threat to peace within the city."

I shivered, and not from the cold seeping into the night air.

"Last Sunday, Jesus rode into Jerusalem on a donkey," he said. "There's a prophecy that the Messiah king will come into Jerusalem humbly, sitting on an ass."

I knew the prophecy. We all knew the prophecy. That Jesus had done such a thing rendered me speechless. It was a blatant acceptance of the role. But why did this shock me? I thought of the epiphany he'd had when he was baptized, the revelation that he must act, how he'd gone off with John the Immerser.

"The crowds followed after him," Lazarus was saying. "They were shouting 'Hosanna, blessed is he who comes in the name of the Lord.'"

"We were there," Mary added. "The people were carried away with jubilation, believing they would soon be delivered from the Romans and that God's kingdom would be ushered in. You should have seen them, Ana. They broke branches off the trees and strew them in his path. We walked behind him with his disciples and joined in ourselves."

If I'd been there, would I have tried to stop him or blessed the fierce need that drove him? I didn't know; I honestly didn't know.

Lazarus walked to the wall gap, just as I'd done a short while before, and stared across the valley toward the city as if trying to divine where in the web of narrow, twisting, fevered streets his old friend was. We watched him: his back to us, hands clasped behind him, the relentless way he rubbed his fingers. "Jesus has proclaimed that he is a Messiah," he said, turning toward us. "He did it believing God will act, but it wasn't only a religious statement. It was a political one. That's what worries me most, Ana. Pilate knows the Jewish Messiah is meant to overthrow Rome—he will take it seriously."

All this time Martha had said nothing, but I saw her sit straighter on the bench and draw a breath. She said, "There is one more thing, Ana. The day after Jesus announced himself on the donkey, he returned to Jerusalem and—tell her, Mary."

Mary gave her a rueful look. "Yes, he returned to the city and started a . . . a commotion in the Temple."

"It was more than a commotion," Martha said. "It was a riot."

Mary sent her another look of exasperation.

"What do you mean, a riot?" I asked.

"This time, we were not there," Mary said. "But the disciples said he became angry over the corruption of the money changers and the men who sell the animals for sacrifice."

Martha broke in. "He upended their tables, scattering coins, and kicked over the seats of the pigeon sellers. He shouted that they'd turned the Temple into a den of thieves. People scrambled to pluck up the coins. The Temple guard was summoned."

"He wasn't harmed, was he?"

"No," said Mary. "Surprisingly, the Temple authorities didn't apprehend him."

"Yes, but Caiaphas, the high priest, is set against him now," Lazarus said. "I don't like to admit it, but Jesus is very much in danger."

Tabitha leaned into me. We sat for several moments before I could ask the question. "Do you think they will arrest him?"

"It's hard to say," Lazarus answered. "The mood in the city is volatile. Pilate and Caiaphas want nothing more than to be rid of him. Jesus could easily start a revolt."

"I cannot believe that's his wish," I said. My husband was a resister to Rome, but not a violent one. He was not like my brother.

"I wondered about his intention," Lazarus said. "He seemed to purposely provoke the authorities. But that same night, he stood right here where I'm standing now and told his disciples that whatever happened they would not take up the sword. Judas challenged him, saying, 'How do you expect to free us from Rome without a fight? You speak of love—how will that rid us of Rome?' I know he's your brother, Ana, but he was angry, almost hostile."

"Judas is a Zealot," I said. "The Romans murdered his father and sent his mother into slavery. His whole life has been about seeking vengeance." Even as I said this, I marveled that I made excuses for him. He meant to overthrow the Romans even if he had to hand Jesus over to spark a revolution. There would never be enough excuses for that. Fury surged into my chest. I said, "How did Jesus answer him?"

"He did so sternly. He said, 'I've spoken, Judas.' That silenced him."

For a moment I considered pulling Judas's letter from my travel pouch and reading it to them, but it would do nothing but alarm them more.

Lazarus rested his hand on Martha's shoulder. He said, "This morning before Jesus left for Jerusalem, I implored him to spend Passover in a quiet fashion and to keep hidden. He agreed. If the authorities seek to arrest him, they will have to find him first."

They would have no trouble finding him if Judas intervened to help them. The thought lifted me to my feet. "Should we not go and find him ourselves?"

"Go to Jerusalem? Now?" said Martha.

"Mary said he sometimes prays in the Garden of Gethsemane," I said. "We might find him there."

"It's almost the second watch of the night," she argued.

Lavi had been slumped against the wall, nearly invisible in the shadows of the house, but he stepped forward now. "I will go with you."

"It's foolish to venture into the valley at this hour," Lazarus said. "It seems Jesus has decided to spend the night on the hillside. He'll return in the morning."

Mary took my arm. "Come, you're weary. Let's get you to bed. Martha prepared you a fresh mat in Tabitha's room."

"I'll leave at daybreak," I said, sending Lavi a grateful smile, then let myself be led away, stopping to retrieve Jesus's cloak. I would sleep in the folds of it.

ii.

I woke late, well past dawn. I felt for Jesus's cloak beside me on the mat, then sat up and slipped it over my tunic.

Moving across the room, I glanced at Tabitha, trying not to wake her. I bent over the basin and splashed a palmful of water across my face, then delved through my few belongings until I found the little pouch with the red thread. I wrapped it about my left wrist, laboring to knot it with my other hand.

Lavi was waiting for me in the courtyard. If he wondered at my wearing Jesus's mantle, he didn't say so. Nor did he mention the hour. He handed me a piece of bread and a hunk of cheese, which I ate hungrily.

"How will we find him?" Lavi whispered.

"We'll begin at the Garden of Gethsemane. Perhaps he slept there."

"Do you know where this garden is?"

"It's at the foot of the Mount of Olives. Last night Tabitha told me of a path that leads there from the village."

I must've looked racked with worry, for he gave me a searching look. "Are you all right, sister?"

Sister. The word caused me to think of Judas. I didn't know how to go on being sister to him. I wanted to answer Lavi that I was well and he shouldn't worry, but I sensed there was some great portending darkness out there.

"Brother," I said, my voice cracking a little.

I stood and walked to the gate.

"We will find him," Lavi said.

"Yes, we will find him."

As we descended the slope, the sun climbed into thick clouds. Everywhere pilgrims were waking beneath the olive trees, the whole hillside seeming to undulate. We walked rapidly, quietly. The hymn I'd written to Sophia began to sing in my ears.

> *I was sent out from power . . .*
> *Be careful. Do not ignore me.*

> *I am she who exists in all fears and in trembling boldness*

IN THE GARDEN, I dashed through the trees, calling Jesus's name. No one answered. He did not step out of the gnarling shadows and open his arms, saying, "Ana, you've come back."

We wandered through every part of the garden. "He's not here," Lavi said.

I came to a standstill, the frantic feeling still going in my chest. I'd been so sure I'd find him here. All night, as I'd wandered in and out of sleep, my mind had pulsed with images of this garden at the foot of the Kidron.

Where is he?

In the distance, I could see the Temple protruding beyond the city wall, casting its white dazzle in the air, and next to it the towers of Antonia, the Roman fortress. Lavi followed my gaze. "We should go and search in the city," he said.

I was trying to imagine where in the vast maze of Jerusalem he could be—the Temple courts? the Pool of Bethesda?—when I heard someone moaning. The sound was deep and guttural, coming from the trees behind us. I started toward it, but Lavi stepped in my path. "Let me go and be certain there's no danger."

I waited as he ventured into the grove, disappearing behind an outcrop of rocks. "Ana, come quickly," he called.

Judas sat on the ground hunched over his knees, rocking back and forth, making a godforsaken sound. "Judas! My Lord and my God, what has happened?" I knelt and placed my hand on his arm.

His crying ceased with my touch. He spoke without looking up. "Ana . . . I saw you . . . from a distance. I didn't mean to draw your attention. . . . Do not look at me . . . I cannot bear it."

A sudden coldness formed inside me then. I shot to my feet. "Judas, what did you do?" When he didn't answer, I shouted, "*What did you do?*"

Lavi had kept a tactful distance, but he was beside me now. I didn't take time to explain what was happening, but stooped once more in front of my brother, fighting to drive the fear and outrage from my throat. "Tell me, Judas. *Now.*"

He looked up and I saw it in his eyes. "You handed Jesus over to the Romans, didn't you?"

I'd meant to hurl the accusation, wanting it to strike him like a slap, but the words came out in a whisper, floating into the quietness like a moth or a butterfly, its wings a thing of incomprehension. Judas squeezed his hand into a fist and struck himself hard in the chest. There was a leather pouch filled with silver coins opened beside him on the ground; he grabbed it and flung the money into the trees. I watched, breathless, as the coins fell to the ground and lay there glinting like the shed scales of some grotesque creature.

"I didn't hand him to the *Romans*." He was composed, but compelled now to recite every recrimination against himself. The scorpion-tail scar beneath his eye rippled up and down with his jaw. "Last night, I, his friend and brother, turned him over to the Temple guard, knowing *they* would hand him to the Romans. I led the guard here where I knew Jesus would be. I kissed his cheek so the soldiers would know who he was." He pointed to a spot in front of him. "That's where Jesus stood when I kissed him. Just there."

I looked at the place where he'd pointed—brown dirt, tiny white rocks, the imprint of sandals.

He kept talking in his tortured, calm voice. "I wanted to give the people a reason to revolt. I wanted to help bring God's kingdom. I thought it was what he wanted, too. I believed if I forced his hand, he would see it was the only way, that he'd resist the soldiers and lead the uprising, and if not, that his death would inspire the people to do so themselves."

Violence. Uprising. Death. Ridiculous, meaningless words.

"But do you know what Jesus said to me when I kissed him? He saw the soldiers coming behind me with their swords drawn and he said, 'Judas, would you betray me with a kiss?' Ana, you have to believe me— I didn't know until that moment what I'd done, how I'd misled myself. I'm sorry." He dropped his head onto his knees. The moans came again.

Now he was sorry? I wanted to throw myself at him and claw the skin from his face.

"Ana, please," Judas said. "I don't expect you to understand what I've done, but I'm asking you to do what I cannot—forgive me."

"Where's my husband?" I said. "Where did they take him?"

He closed his eyes. "They took him to Caiaphas's house. I followed them. At dawn they delivered him to the western palace. It's where the Roman governor resides when he's in Jerusalem."

The Roman governor, Pilate. The one Lazarus had called brutal. I searched for the sun, hoping to guess the time, but the sky had solidified into a gray murk. "Is Jesus still there?"

"I don't know," he said. "I couldn't bear to remain and learn his fate. The last I saw him, he was standing on the porch at the palace before Pilate."

"The palace—where is it?"

"It's in the upper city, near Mariamme's Tower."

I bolted, Lavi chasing after me.

"Ana! . . . Ana!" Judas called.

I didn't answer.

iii.

We entered Jerusalem through the Golden Gate, crossing the Court of the Gentiles and plunging into the tight, twisting streets bloated with Passover pilgrims. I looked west for a glimpse of Mariamme's Tower. Smoke from the Temple altar hung overhead in a thin, drooping canopy, infused with the revolting smell of burned animal entrails. I could see nothing.

We threaded our way through the masses in the upper city with excruciating slowness. *Move. Move. Move!* A desperate, anxious feeling battered against my breast. "There!" I cried. "There's the tower." It jutted up from the corner of Herod's palace into the stench and haze.

We turned a corner, then another, careening into a host of people lining the street and the rooftops above it. I wondered if we'd blundered upon a stoning. I looked for some poor woman accused of adultery or thievery crouched alone on the street—I knew the terror of it. But the crowd did not seem stirred to anger. They appeared dazed, grieved, possessed by an unnatural quiet. I didn't know what was happening, nor did I have time to inquire. I pushed through them toward the street, determined to reach the palace and gain news of Jesus.

As I reached the edge of the crowd, I heard horse hooves, then a bone-scraping noise as if some heavy object was being dragged over the street stones. "Make way!" a voice shouted.

Glancing about for Lavi, I spotted him some distance behind me. "Ana," he called. "Ana, stop!" It was not possible to stop—he must know this.

I stepped into the street. I saw everything then. The Roman centurion on the black horse. The firebird plumes on his helmet, the splash of red they created in the grayness. Four soldiers on foot, the flap of their capes, the puncturing jabs their spears made overhead as they marched. A man staggered behind them in a filthy, bloodstained tunic, bent beneath the weight of a large, roughly hewn timber. One end of the plank rested on his right shoulder; the other end dragged on the street behind him. I watched for long, stupefied moments as the man labored to hold up the beam.

Reaching me, Lavi grabbed my arm and swung me toward him, away from the street. "Don't look," he said. His eyes were like the spear tips.

I felt the wind rise, a hollow, whooshing sound. Lavi went on saying words. I no longer heard him. I was remembering the timbers that stood erect on the stark little hill just outside Jerusalem, the hill they called the Place of the Skull. Lavi and I had seen them only yesterday as we'd approached the city after our long trek from Joppa. In the dusk, they'd appeared like a little forest of dead trees amputated at the neck. We knew them to be the upright beams of the crosses on which the Romans crucified their victims, but neither of us had said it.

The bone scrape on the street intensified. I turned back to the sad procession. *The soldiers are taking the man to the Place of the Skull. He's carrying the crossbeam.* I studied him closer. There was a familiarity about him, something about the shape of his shoulders. He lifted his head and his dark hair parted to reveal his face. This man was my husband.

"Jesus," I said quietly, speaking to myself, to Lavi, to no one.

Lavi tugged my arm. "Do not be a witness to this, Ana. Spare yourself."

I wrenched free, unable to tear my eyes from Jesus. He wore a cap plaited out of the thorn twigs used to kindle fires. He'd been flogged. His arms and legs were a mass of torn skin and dried blood. A howl formed in my belly and pushed into my mouth. It came without sound, just a violent spasm of pain.

Jesus stumbled, and though he was at least twenty arm lengths away from me, I reached out to catch him. He fell hard onto one knee and wavered there as a puddle of blood oozed around it. Then he collapsed, the crossbeam thudding onto his back. I screamed, and this time it split the stones.

As I started toward him, Lavi's hand clamped my wrist. "You cannot go to him. If you impede these men, they will not hesitate to kill you as well." I jerked my arm, twisting to free myself.

The soldiers were shouting at Jesus to get up, prodding him with the shafts of their spears. "Get up, Jew! Get to your feet." He tried, pushing onto his elbow, then dropped back onto his chest.

My wrist burned from Lavi's grip. He would not relent. The centurion climbed down from the black horse and kicked the crossbeam off Jesus's back. "Leave him be," he ordered his men. "He can carry it no farther."

I hardened my eyes. "Release me now or I shall never forgive you." Lavi dropped his hand, and I charged into the street, past the soldiers, keeping my eye on the centurion, who paced the edge of the crowd with his back to me.

I knelt beside Jesus, possessed now by an eerie calm, by a self barely known to me. Everything receded into the distance—the street, the soldiers, the noise, the city walls, the people craning to watch—the whole pageant of horrors abating until there was nothing there but Jesus and me. His eyes were closed. He didn't move or seem to breathe, and I wondered if he was already dead. He would never know I was here, but I was relieved for him. Crucifixion was barbarous. I rolled him gently onto his side and a breath floated up.

"Beloved," I said, bending close.

He blinked and his gaze found me. "Ana?"

"I'm here . . . I've come back. I'm here." A drop of blood trickled over his brow, pooling in the corner of his eye. I took the sleeve of my cloak, *his* cloak, and dabbed it. His eyes lingered on the red thread on my arm, the one that was there at the beginning and would be there at the end.

"I will not leave you," I said.

"Don't be afraid," he whispered.

Far away I heard the centurion command a bystander to step forward and carry the crossbeam. Jesus and I didn't have long. In these last minutes, what did he most want to hear—that he'd been seen and heard in this world? That he'd accomplished what he'd set out to do? That he'd loved and been loved?

"Your goodness will not be forgotten," I told him. "Not a single act of your love will be squandered. You've brought God's kingdom as you hoped—you've planted it in our hearts."

He smiled, and I saw my face in the dark gold suns of his eyes. "Little Thunder," he said.

I cupped my hands about his face. I said, "How I love you."

We lingered only a second longer before the centurion returned and jerked me upward. He flung me to the side of the street, where I stumbled into a man who put out his hand to keep me from falling, but I fell nonetheless. As Lavi appeared and helped me up, I looked back at Jesus, who was being roughly hefted to his feet. His eyes lighted on mine before he trudged forward behind the large man chosen to carry the crossbeam.

As the procession began again, I noticed that the strap on one of my sandals had broken when I fell. I stooped and removed both shoes. I would go to my husband's execution as he did. Barefoot.

iv.

I called out in Aramaic, "I'm here, Beloved. I'm walking behind you." The centurion twisted in his saddle and looked at me, but said nothing.

Most of the spectators had hastened ahead of us toward the Gennath Gate that led to Golgotha, too impatient to wait on the man who was taking one slow, agonizing step after another. Glancing behind me, I saw that the few who'd remained to walk with him were women. Where were these disciples of his? The fishermen? The men? Were we women the only ones with hearts large enough to hold such anguish?

All at once a cluster of women joined me, two on my right, two on my left. One took my hand, squeezing it. I was startled to see she was my mother-in-law. Her face was wet and shattered. She said, "Ana, oh, Ana." Next to her, Mary, the sister of Lazarus, tilted her head at me and sent me a steadying look.

At my other side, a woman slid her arm about my waist and gave me a wordless embrace. *Salome.* I grasped her hand and pulled it to my chest. Beside her was a woman I'd never seen before, with copper hair and flashing eyes, whom I guessed to be the age of my mother when I last saw her.

We walked pressed together, shoulder to shoulder. As we left the city gate and the hill of Golgotha came into view, Jesus halted, staring up at the little summit. "Beloved, I'm still here," I said.

He lurched forward, moving against the swell of wind.

"My son, I am here also," cried Mary, her voice shaking, the words shredding apart as they left her lips.

"And your sister walks with you as well," Salome said.

"It is Mary of Bethany. I, too, am here."

Then the unknown woman called, "Jesus, it's Mary of Magdala."

As he climbed the slope, toiling to lift his feet, I quickened my pace and drew closer behind him. "The day we gathered our daughter's bones, the valley was full of wild lilies. Do you remember?" I called out the words loudly enough for him to hear, hoping not to draw the soldiers' attention. "You told me to consider the lilies, that God takes care of them and will surely, then, care for us. Consider them now, my love. Consider the lilies." I wished for something beautiful to fill his mind. I wished for him to think of our daughter, our Susanna. He would be with her soon. I wished for him to think of God. Of me. Of lilies.

When we reached the top of Golgotha, the man who'd carried the crossbeam laid it down beside one of the uprights and Jesus stood gazing down at it, swaying a little. We women were allowed no farther than a small knoll twenty or so paces from him. A putrid smell pervaded the air, and I wondered if it was the accumulation of all the atrocities that had ever transpired here. I pulled my scarf across my nose. My breaths came in small gulps.

Don't look away. Terrible things will happen now. Unbearable things. Bear it anyway.

Beside me the others moaned and wept, but I didn't join them. Later, alone, I would wail and fall to the ground and beat the emptiness with my fists. Now, though, I choked back my anguish and fastened my eyes on my husband.

I will think only of him. I will give him more than my presence; I will give him the full attention of my heart.

That would be my parting gift to him. I would go with him to the end of his longings.

I watched the soldiers strip Jesus of his tunic and shove him to the ground, pinning his forearms to the crossbeam with their knees. The executioner probed the underside of Jesus's wrist, searching for the hollow space between the bones, though I could not understand then why the soldier pushed his fingers into that soft place like a woman who rummages in her bread dough for some small, dropped object. He raised his hammer and drove a nail through that small opening into the wood. The cry that left Jesus sent his mother to her knees, but somehow I went on standing there, muttering "*Sophia. Sophia. Sophia,*" as the other wrist was probed and the nail driven.

The crossbeam was lifted up and its notch fitted onto the upright. Jesus writhed a moment and kicked the air as the crossbeam fell into place with a jolt. The soldiers gathered his knees together, bending them slightly, and then with studied precision, arranged his right foot over his left. A single nail was pounded through them both. I don't remember that he made any sound. I remember the vicious, hollow thud of the hammer and the wail it set off in my head. I closed my eyes, feeling I was abandoning him by retreating into the dark behind my lids. The wail slapped like waves against the inside of my skull. Then came the sound of laughter, far away and strange. I forced my eyes open, allowing in a painful slat of light. A soldier was nailing a pinewood placard above Jesus's head and finding merriment in it.

"What does it say?" Mary of Magdala asked.

"Jesus of Nazareth, King of the Jews," I read. It was written in Hebrew, Aramaic, and Latin lest anyone miss their mockery.

From behind us, someone shouted, "If you're the King of the Jews, save yourself."

"He helped others—can't he help himself?" cried another.

Salome slid her arm around Mary's waist and drew her mother to her side. "May God take him quickly," she said.

And where is *God,* I wanted to scream. Wasn't he supposed to establish his kingdom now? And the people—why didn't they revolt as Judas had expected? Instead, they jeered at Jesus.

"If you're the Messiah, come down from the cross and save yourself," a man yelled.

Indignant, I whirled about to rebuke the rabble and glimpsed my brother standing alone on the edge of the hill. Seeing that I'd caught sight of him, he stretched out his hands to me, pleading, it seemed, for mercy. *Ana, forgive me.* I stared, astonished by the sight of him, by how misguided he'd been, by how callous his zeal and sense of righteousness had become.

I searched myself for the fury I'd felt toward him earlier, but it had left me. I tried to summon it, but it had retreated at the sight of him standing there so lost and bereft. A premonition swept through me that I would not see Judas again. I crossed my hands over my chest and nodded at him. It was not forgiveness I sent. It was pity.

As I drew my eyes back to Jesus, he struggled to lift himself up in order to take a breath. The sight nearly broke me. After that all sense of time left me. I didn't know whether minutes passed or hours. Jesus went on heaving himself up and gasping for air.

Thunder rumbled on and off over the Mount of Olives. Salome and the three Marys knelt on the dirt and intoned the psalms, while I watched Jesus from the dark, sorrowful doorway of my heart, and uttered not a word. From time to time, Jesus muttered something, but I couldn't hear what he said. He seemed far away and alone. Twice I tried to go to him and both times the soldiers forced me back. A man also attempted to approach Jesus, calling, "Jesus, master," and he, too, was turned away. I looked back once for Judas. He was gone.

At midafternoon the soldiers, bored with the slowness of his dying, left their posts and squatted some distance from the cross, where they began to throw dice. I did not hesitate. I broke into a run. As I stood beneath the cross, the closeness of him shocked me. His breath rasped and raked through his chest. His legs rippled with spasms. Heat and sweat were streaming from his body. I reached for the timber, then drew back my hand, repulsed by it.

I took a deep breath and gazed up at him. "Jesus." His head slumped toward his shoulder and I saw he was looking at me. He didn't speak, nor did I, but I told myself later that everything that had ever passed between us was present then, that it was hidden somewhere among the suffering.

Mary rushed to him, followed by the others. She wrapped her hands about her son's feet like she was holding a tiny bird that had fallen from its nest. I wrapped my hands about hers and then the other three women did the same, our hands like the petals of a lotus. Not one of us wept. We stood there mute and full and held up that flower for him.

The soldiers did not tear themselves from their game of knuckle-bones to chase us away.

They no longer seemed to care we were there. We watched Jesus's eyes grow glassy and distant. I felt the moment come, the severing. It was gentle, like a touch on the shoulder.

"It is finished," Jesus said.

There was a sound like a rush of wings in the blackish clouds, and I knew his spirit had left him. I imagined it like a great flock of birds, soaring, scattering, coming to rest everywhere.

v.

We prepared Jesus for burial by the flicker of two oil lamps. Kneeling on the cave floor beside his body, I felt oddly numb. How could this be my husband?

I looked at the other women in the tomb as if observing them from a corner of the sky. Mary, his mother, was cleansing his feet and legs while the others sang the songs of lament. Their faces were smeared and wet, their voices bounding and rebounding off the cave walls. A towel and a ewer of water sat beside me, waiting for me to join them in readying him for burial. *Pick up the towel. Pick it up.* But gazing at it, I was seized with panic. I understood that if I took hold of the towel, if I touched Jesus, I would fall from my niche in the sky. His dying would become real. Grief would swallow me.

My eyes wandered to the stacks of bones at the back of the cave neatly separated into skulls, ribs, long bones, short bones, fingers, toes—countless dead people mingled together in a morbid communion. No one who'd been buried here, it seemed, had the means to purchase an ossuary to hold their bones. *This* was a pauper's tomb.

We were fortunate to have any tomb at all. Rome's custom was to leave a crucified man hanging on the cross for weeks, then toss his body into a pit to finish decaying. Jesus would've suffered that abomination except for the goodness of a stranger.

He'd been no older than Jesus and adorned in an expensive robe and finely dyed blue hat. He'd approached us moments after a soldier thrust a spear into Jesus's side to ensure his death. The act had sickened and appalled me, and I swung away, turning my back on the gruesome scene, almost careening into the man. His eyes were red and weighted.

He said, "I've located a tomb not far from here. If I can convince the centurion to turn over Jesus's body, my servants will take him there."

I eyed him. "Who are you, sir?"

"I'm one of Jesus's followers. My name is Joseph. I come from Arimathea. You women must be his family."

Mary stepped forward. "I'm his mother."

"And I'm his wife," I told him. "Your kindness is welcome."

He bowed slightly and strode off, tugging a money bag from his sash. He placed a denarius in the centurion's palm. I watched it grow into a column of silver.

When he returned to us, he held out more denarii. "Go into the city and purchase what you need to prepare the body. But you must hurry. The centurion wishes to hand over the body quickly." He glanced up into the half-light. "And he has to be buried before sunset. The Sabbath will be upon us soon."

Salome scooped the coins from his hand, and grabbing Mary of Bethany by the hand, she pulled her down the hillside. "We'll wait for you here. Be quick!" he called after them.

Now, in the cave, the lamp flames darted. Light spattered across Jesus's skin. *His skin. His.* I reached out and touched it. I let my fingers brush the inside of his elbow. Then I dampened the towel and wiped the dirt and blood from his hands, arms, chest, and face, from the coils of his ears and the creases in his neck, all the while falling and falling, slamming into myself, into the boundless pain.

We rubbed his skin with olive oil, then anointed him with nothing but myrrh. It had been the only sweet spice Salome had been able to obtain in the city at the late hour, and this had dismayed Mary. "When the Sabbath ends," she said, "we'll return to the tomb and anoint him more properly with cloves and aloe and mint."

I watched Salome draw a broken wooden comb through his hair. I'd witnessed his slaughter and not a tear had crossed my cheeks, but I cried in silence now at the comb passing through his locks.

Mary of Magdala grasped the edges of the shroud and drew it slowly down the length of him, but in that last instant before his face was gone from me, I bent and kissed both his cheeks.

"I will meet you in the place called Deathless," I whispered.

vi.

That evening Martha turned the Sabbath meal into the funeral feast, but no one cared to eat. We were sitting on the damp courtyard tiles, huddled beneath a canopy. All around us were the coming dark and the plop of rain drizzle . . . and silence, a great stunned silence. No one had spoken of Jesus since we'd left the tomb. We had squeezed through the cave opening, where Lavi waited for us, heaved the stone across it, and left our voices inside. Then we'd walked slowly to Bethany, shocked, weary, mute with horror—I, still barefoot, and Lavi, carrying my sandals.

I looked at them now—Mary and Salome; Lazarus, Mary, and Martha; Mary of Magdala, Tabitha, and Lavi. They stared back with solemn, devastated faces.

Jesus is dead.

I wished for Yaltha. For Diodora and Skepsis. I forced myself to picture them beneath the tamarisk tree beside the little stone hut. I tried to see the bright, white cliffs at the top of the hill, and Lake Mareotis shining at the foot of it like a piece of fallen sky. I managed to hold all of this in my mind for several moments before the ghastly memories pushed their way back in. I didn't know how the rubble inside me could ever be put back together.

As the night drew around us, Martha lit three lamps and set them in our midst. All of their faces shone suddenly, cheeks and chins the color of honey. The rain finally stopped. Far away, I heard the mournful call of an owl. The sound caused a pressure in my throat and I realized it was the need to fashion a story. To call into the blackness like the owl.

I broke the silence. I told them about the letter Judas had sent summoning me home. "He wrote to me that Jesus was in danger from the authorities, but I know now that most of that danger came from Judas himself." I hesitated, feeling a mix of disgust and shame. "It was my brother who led the Temple guard to arrest Jesus."

"How do you know this?" exclaimed Lazarus.

"I encountered him this morning in the Garden of Gethsemane. He confessed it to me."

"May God strike him down," Martha said with fierceness. No one refuted her. Not even I.

I watched their sharp, appalled expressions, how they struggled to comprehend. Mary of Magdala gave her head a shake, the amber light catching in her hair. She lifted her face to me, and I wondered if she knew why I'd not traveled with my husband through the villages and towns around Galilee as she'd done. Were the circumstances of my exile known among his followers? Was *I* known among them?

"It's impossible that Judas would betray Jesus," the Magdalene said. "He *loved* him. I traveled with the disciples for months. Judas was devoted to Jesus."

I bristled. I may not have been there for Jesus's ministry, but I knew my brother. I responded tersely. "I know very well that Judas loved Jesus; he loved him like a brother. But he hated Rome far more."

A look crossed her face, something crestfallen, and my annoyance vanished. Even then I knew I'd snapped at her out of envy, resentful of the freedom she'd had to follow Jesus around the countryside, while I'd been trapped in Haran's house.

"I shouldn't have spoken harshly," I told her. She smiled and the skin wrinkled around her eyes in that way that makes a woman beautiful.

There came another silence. My mother-in-law placed her hand on my arm, her fingers brushing past the bloodstain on the sleeve of Jesus's cloak. She had aged deeply in the two years I'd been gone. Her hair was silvering and her face had begun to change into an old woman's—the plump, sagging cheeks, eyelids slumped onto her lashes.

She rubbed my arm, meant to comfort, but her fingers woke the smells inside the cloak's fabric. Sweat, cook smoke, wine, spikenard. The scents, so sudden and alive, unleashed a bitter pain inside me, and I understood that I'd spoken to them about Judas because I couldn't bear to speak about Jesus. I feared it. I feared the power it had to unlock pain from common places.

There was so much, though, to be said, to be understood. I shifted, straightened. "I was on my way to the palace this morning when I came upon Jesus in the street carrying the crossbeam. I know nothing about how he came to be condemned or why he wore those dreadful thorns on his head." I looked at the women who'd climbed Golgotha with me. "Were any of you there when he was brought before Pilate?"

Mary of Magdala leaned toward me. "We were all there. When I arrived, a large crowd had already gathered on the pavement and Jesus was standing above us on the porch where the Roman governor pronounces his judgments. Pilate was questioning him, but from where I stood, it was impossible to hear what was said."

"We could not hear him either," said Salome. "Though for most of it Jesus remained silent, refusing to answer Pilate's questions. You could tell this aggravated Pilate. Eventually he shouted for Jesus to be taken to Herod Antipas."

At the mention of Antipas's name, fear, then hate blazed up in me. Jesus and I had been forced apart for two years because of him. "Why would Pilate send Jesus to Antipas?" I asked.

Mary of Magdala said, "I heard some in the crowd say Pilate would prefer Antipas to pronounce the verdict and save him from blame in case people revolted and blood was shed. He could be recalled to Rome over an outcome like that. Better to wash his hands of it and let the tetrarch do it. We waited on the pavement to see what would happen, and sometime later, Jesus returned with the thorn crown on his head and a purple cape about his shoulders."

Salome said, "It was awful, Ana. Antipas had costumed Jesus like that to mock him as King of the Jews. Pilate's soldiers were bowing to him and laughing. I could see that he'd been flogged—he could hardly stand, but he kept his head lifted the whole time and didn't flinch at their ridicule." Her face was radiant with the urge to cry.

"Who condemned him to die—Antipas or Pilate?" asked Lazarus, clasping and unclasping his hands.

"It was Pilate," said Mary of Magdala. "He addressed the crowd saying it was the custom during Passover to release one prisoner. I cannot tell you how my hope leapt at this. I thought he intended to set Jesus free. Instead he asked the crowd who it should be, Jesus or someone else. We women had arrived at the palace separately, but by this time, we'd found one another and we shouted Jesus's name as loudly as we could. But there were many followers present of a man named Barabbas, a Zealot held in Antonia's Tower for insurrection. They screamed his name until that was all that could be heard."

The knowledge that Jesus might've been saved at the end, but wasn't, staggered me. If I'd been there . . . if I'd left my bed earlier . . . if I'd not delayed in the Garden of Gethsemane, I would've been there to fill the air with his name.

"It happened so fast," Mary said, turning to me. "Pilate pointed his finger at Jesus and said, 'Crucify him.'"

I closed my eyes to keep out the picture that tortured me most, but the image could move through walls and eyelids and every conceivable barrier, and I saw my beloved nailed to the Roman timbers, trying to lift himself up to take a sip of air.

Was this what it was like to grieve a husband?

A memory came to me, a small one, a foolish one. "Mary, do you remember when Judith traded Delilah for a bolt of cloth?"

"I remember it well," said Mary. "I'd never seen you so distressed."

I looked at the others, wanting them to understand. "You see, I had charge of the animals and Delilah was more than a goat; she was my pet."

"Now she's become *my* pet," said Mary.

I felt a momentary elation—Delilah was still there and being pampered. "Judith hated the goat," I said.

"I think what she hated was how much you loved it," Salome added.

"It's true Judith liked me only slightly better than Delilah, but for her to take the goat to Sepphoris and trade her without telling me—I'd not expected it. When I confronted her, she argued that the cloth she'd acquired was fine linen, better than she could weave, and that James had recently brought home a new, younger goat, making Delilah unnecessary."

Everyone must have wondered why I was telling them this. They listened and nodded in an indulgent way. *The aftermath of tragedy is strange*, their expressions said. *Her husband has just been crucified—let her say whatever peculiar thing she needs to say.*

I continued, "Jesus arrived home the same day Judith traded the goat, after a long, exhausting trek from Capernaum, where he'd worked all week. He found me distraught. It was late afternoon and he'd not eaten, but he turned around and walked all the way to Sepphoris and bought Delilah back with the coins he'd earned that week."

Mary's eyes glittered. "He came through the gate carrying Delilah on his shoulders."

"Yes, he did!" I exclaimed. "He brought her back to me."

I could still see him, grinning as he strode toward me across the compound, Delilah bleating wildly, and the picture was as vivid to me as the one of him crucified. Leaning my head back, I breathed as deeply as I could. Overhead, a ragged blanket of clouds. The moon somewhere, hidden. The owl had flown away.

Mary said, "Tell them the rest of it."

I hadn't intended to say anything further, but I was glad to do as she said. "The following week, Judith dyed her new, fine linen and hung it in the courtyard to dry. I often allowed Delilah to leave the cramped animal pen and wander free in the courtyard as long as the compound gate was locked. I never dreamed she would eat Judith's cloth. Delilah, however, ate every bit of it."

Mary laughed. Then we all laughed. There was a vast relief in it, as if the air had grown more spacious. Was laughter grieving, too?

Martha poured the last of the wine into our cups. We were exhausted, devastated, wishing for the numbness of sleep, but we went on sitting there, reluctant to part, our togetherness like a refuge.

. . .

IT WAS NEARING the midnight watch when a voice called from the gate. "It's John, a disciple of Jesus."

"*John!*" cried Mary of Magdala, leaping up to accompany Lazarus to the gate.

"What urgency could bring him here so late at night and on the Sabbath?" said Martha.

John stepped into the glow of our lamps and peered around the circle of faces, his eyes lingering on me, and I realized I'd seen him before. He'd been one of the four fishermen who'd traveled home with Jesus from Capernaum all those years ago and talked in the courtyard late into the night. Young, gangly, and beardless then, now he was a broad-shouldered man with thoughtful, deep-set eyes and a beard that curled under his chin.

Studying him closer, I realized I'd also seen him earlier today on Golgotha. He was the man who'd approached Jesus as he hung on the cross and who, like me, had been turned back by the soldiers. I offered him a sorrowful smile. He was the disciple who'd stayed.

He settled himself on the courtyard tiles while Martha muttered absently about the empty wineskins, finally setting a cup of water before her guest.

"What has brought you here?" asked Mary of Bethany.

His gaze shifted to me and his face turned grave. Wedged between Mary and Tabitha, I reached for their hands.

"Judas is dead," John said. "He hanged himself from a tree."

vii.

Shall I confess? Part of me had wished my brother dead. When Judas had turned Jesus over to the Temple guard, he'd breached some sacred boundary in me. I'd offered him that gesture of pity as he'd stood in the distance on Golgotha, but in the aftermath, it was mostly hatred I felt.

In those blank, bewildered moments, as Mary and Salome and the others waited for me to respond to the news of Judas's death, it occurred to me that Jesus would attempt to love even the lost, murderous Judas. Once, when I'd ranted to him about some slight Judith had done to me and declared my loathing of her, he'd said, "I know, Ana. She is difficult. You don't have to feel love for her. Only try to *act* with love."

But he was Jesus, and I was Ana. I wasn't ready to let go of my animosity toward Judas. I would do so in time, but right now it saved me. It left less room inside for pain.

The silence went on too long. No one seemed to know what to say. At last, Mary of Bethany said, "Oh, Ana. This day is a desolation for you. First, your husband, now your brother."

Something about these words caused a flash of indignation. As if Jesus and Judas could be mentioned in the same sentence, as if the loss I felt over them could be compared—but she meant well, I knew that. I stood and smiled at them. "Your presence has been my only solace this day, but I'm overcome now with weariness and will retire to sleep." I bent and kissed Mary and Salome. Tabitha rose and followed me.

I curled onto the mat in Tabitha's room, but could find no sleep. Hearing me toss about, my friend began to play her lyre, hoping to draw me into sleep. As the music moved through the darkness, grief rose in me. For my beloved, but also for my brother. Not for the Judas who betrayed Jesus, but for the boy who pined for his parents, who endured our father's rejection, who took me with him when he walked in the Galilean hills, and who always took my part. I mourned the Judas who gave my bracelet to the injured laborer, who burned Nathaniel's date grove, who resisted Rome. *Those* were the Judases I loved. For them, I buried my face in the crook of my arm and cried.

viii.

When I woke the following morning, the sky was white with sun. Tabitha's mat was empty and the smell of baking bread floated everywhere. I sat up, surprised at the lateness, forgetting for a single, blissful moment the ruin of the previous day, and then all of it returned, winding itself around my ribs until I could barely breathe. Once again, I wished for my aunt. I could hear the women out in the courtyard, their soft, droning voices, but it was Yaltha I wanted.

I stood at the doorway, trying to imagine what she would say to me if she were here. Several minutes passed before I allowed myself to remember that night in Alexandria when Lavi brought news of John the Immerser's beheading and I'd been overwhelmed with the fear of losing Jesus. "All shall be well," Yaltha had told me, and when I'd recoiled at how trite and superficial that sounded, she'd said, "I don't mean that life won't bring you tragedy. I only mean you will be well in spite of it. There's a place in you that is inviolate. You'll find your way there, when you need to. And you'll know then what I speak of."

I pulled on Jesus's cloak and stepped outside. My feet were tender from walking barefoot on the stones of Golgotha.

Lavi squatted near the oven, packing his travel pouch. I watched him layer bread, salted fish, and waterskins inside it. With all that had happened, I'd forgotten he was leaving. The ship we'd arrived on would sail back to Alexandria in three days. In order to be on it, Lavi would set out for Joppa early tomorrow morning. The realization jarred me.

Mary, Salome, Martha, Mary of Bethany, Tabitha, and Mary of Magdala were gathered in the shade near the wall overlooking the valley. Even though the Sabbath would not end until sunset, Tabitha appeared to be mending something and Martha was kneading dough. I doubted Tabitha cared about the Sabbath law forbidding work, but Martha seemed devout about these things. When I joined them, sitting on the warm ground beside my mother-in-law, Martha said, "Yes, I know. I'm committing a sin, but I find consolation in baking bread."

I wanted to say, *If I had ink and papyrus, I would gladly sin along with you.* Instead, I gave her my most commiserative smile.

Peering at Tabitha, I saw that she was sewing my sandal.

Mary said, "We'll return to the tomb tomorrow after first light to finish anointing Jesus. Mary and Martha have provided us with aloe, cloves, mint, and frankincense."

I'd said what felt like my final goodbye to Jesus the day before when I'd kissed his cheeks in the tomb. It unsettled me to think of repeating the wrenching process of leaving him again, but I nodded.

"I trust one of you remembers where the tomb lies," she said. "I was too distraught to take notice and there were many caves there and about."

"I believe I can find it," said Salome. "I was careful to observe the way."

Mary turned back to me. "Ana, I think that you, Salome, and I should remain here in Bethany for the seven days of mourning before we depart for Nazareth. I'll need to seek out James and Judith in Jerusalem and learn their wishes, but I'm sure they'll agree. Would this suit you?"

Nazareth. In my mind, I saw the mud-baked compound with the single olive tree. The tiny room where I'd lived with Jesus, where I'd birthed Susanna, where I'd hidden away my incantation bowl. I pictured the little storage room where Yaltha had slept. The hand loom on which I'd woven reams of poor cloth and the oven where I'd baked loaves of scorched bread.

The air grew very quiet. I felt Mary's stare. I felt all their stares, but I didn't look up from my lap. What would it be like to live in Nazareth again, but without Jesus? James was now the eldest, the head of the family, and it occurred to me he might decide to find me a new husband, as he had for Salome when she became a widow. And there was the threat of Antipas. In his letter, Judas had written that the danger to me in Galilee had lessened, but not fully passed.

I pushed to my feet and walked a short distance from them. There was a feeling in me like rising water. It broke over me, finally, leaving behind the thing I knew, but didn't know. Nazareth had never been my home. *Jesus* had been my home.

Now, with him gone, my home was on a hillside in Egypt. It was Yaltha and Diodora. It was the Therapeutae. Where else could I write with abandon? Where but there could I tend a library and animals both? Where else could I live by the utterances of my own heart?

I breathed in, and it felt like a small homecoming.

Across the courtyard, I saw Lavi securing the opening of his travel pouch with a leather strap. The fear of disappointing Mary, of hurting her, of missing her, hurtled through me.

She called to me, "Ana, what is the matter?"

I walked back and sat beside her. She said, "You do not mean to return to Nazareth, do you?"

I shook my head. "I will return to Egypt to live out my days with my aunt. There's a community there of spiritual seekers and philosophers. I will live among them."

I said it gently, but without apology, then I waited for what she would say.

She spoke with her lips close to my ear. "Go in peace, Ana, for you were born for this."

Those ten words were her greatest gift to me.

"Tell us about this place where you'll live," said Salome.

I felt barely composed, astonished suddenly that I would be leaving so quickly, and I was anxious to alert Lavi and begin packing my own provisions, but I did my best to enlighten them about the Therapeutae, the community that danced and sang all night every forty-ninth day. I described the stone huts scattered across a hillside, the lake at its foot, the cliffs at the top, and beyond them, the sea. I told them about the holy room where I'd written my own texts and preserved them in codices, the library I was trying to restore, the song to Sophia I'd written and sung. I talked on and on, and I felt the longing in me for home.

"Take me with you," a voice said.

We all turned and looked at Tabitha. I wondered if she'd spoken in jest, but she stared at me with utmost seriousness. I didn't know how to answer.

"Tabitha!" Martha admonished. "You've been like a daughter to us all these years, yet on a whim you want to abandon us for a place unknown to you?"

"I do not know how to explain it," Tabitha said. "I feel like I, too, am meant to be there." Her voice was thickening, syllables starting to blunt and fall away. She looked slightly frantic to make her realization understood.

"But you can't just leave," said Martha.

"Why can't she?" I asked. The question arrested Martha.

I looked at Tabitha. "If you're serious about going, you must know that life within the Therapeutae is not only singing and dancing. There's work, fasting, study, and prayer." I didn't mention Haran and the Jewish militia who'd sought to arrest me. "You must also possess a desire for God," I told her. "Otherwise you won't be admitted. I would be wrong not to tell you these things."

"I wouldn't mind finding God in this place," Tabitha said, calmer now, her words intact again. "Could I not seek him in music?"

Skepsis would welcome her; I was sure of it. She would admit her based on that last question Tabitha had posed. And if not, she'd admit her for me. "I can think of no reason you can't come with us," I said.

"Do you have money for the ship's passage?" asked Martha. Practical Martha.

Tabitha's eyes widened. "I used all the money I had to buy the spikenard."

I calculated quickly in my head. "I'm sorry, Tabitha, I only have enough drachmae for Lavi's passage and my own." Why hadn't I thought about this before I encouraged her?

Martha made a noise, a little harrumph that sounded like triumph. "Well, it's fortunate, then, that I have the money." She smiled at me. "I don't know why she can't just leave if she chooses."

My sandal lay in Tabitha's lap, repaired and ready for the long walk to Joppa. She handed it to me, then rose and embraced Martha. "If I had more spikenard, I would bathe your feet," Tabitha told her.

THE NEXT MORNING, Lavi, Tabitha, and I slipped from the house before dawn, while the others still slept. At the gate, I looked back, thinking of Mary. "Let's not say goodbye," she'd told me the evening before. "We shall surely see one another again." She'd said this without artifice, with a believing hope so earnest, I thought it might be true. We would, though, never see each other again.

The moon was at its ebb, no more than a faint, curving crust of light. As we followed the path into the Hinnom Valley, Tabitha began to hum, unable to hide her joy. She had tied her lyre onto her back, where its curled arms peeked over her shoulders like a pair of wings. The happiness of home-going was in me, too, but it was lodged beside my sorrow. This was the land of my husband and my daughter. Their bones would always be here. Every step away from them was a pain in my heart.

Walking along Jerusalem's eastern wall, I begged the darkness to last until we passed the Roman hill where Jesus had died, but the light broke just as we approached, a sudden, harrowing brightness. I let myself take one last glimpse of Golgotha. Then I turned my gaze toward the hillsides in the distance where Jesus was buried, where the women would come soon to wrap him in sweet spices.

LAKE MAREOTIS, EGYPT

30–60 CE

i.

Tabitha and I found Yaltha in the garden, bent over a row of spindly plants. Absorbed in her work, she didn't notice us. She smeared her fingers across her tunic, leaving two trails of dirt, an act that filled me with inexplicable gladness. She was fifty-nine now, but she looked almost youthful kneeling in the sunlight among all these green-growing things, and I felt a surge of relief. She was still here.

"Aunt!" I called.

Seeing me, and then Tabitha, running toward her through the barley plants, she opened her mouth and dropped back onto her heels. I heard her exclaim in typical fashion, "Shit of a donkey!"

I tugged Yaltha to her feet and hugged her to me. "I thought I would never see you again."

"Nor I, you," she said. "Yet here you are after only a few weeks away." Her face was a jumble of elation and confusion. "And look who you've brought with you."

As she embraced Tabitha, a shout came from behind us, higher on the slope. "Ana? Ana. Is that you?" Looking back toward the cliffs, I saw Diodora racing down the path with a basket jostling in her arms, and I knew she'd been up there collecting motherwort. She reached us breathless, her hair sprung from her scarf into a riotous fan around her face. She swung me about, sending the spiky-leaved herbs flying.

When I introduced her to Tabitha, she said a priceless thing that Tabitha would remember all her life: "Ana has told me of your bravery." Tabitha said nothing in response, which I imagined Diodora perceived as shyness, but I knew her silence was about the severed tongue in her mouth, her fear of sounding senseless.

Tabitha helped Diodora gather the spilled herbs, and all the while, Yaltha waited to ask the question, the one I dreaded. I looked out across the hillside, searching for the roof of the library.

"What has brought you back, child?" Yaltha said. Her face looked grave and stony. She'd already guessed the reason.

"Jesus is dead," I said, feeling how my voice wanted to splinter apart. "They crucified him."

Diodora let out a cry that I felt inside my own throat. Yaltha took my hand. "Come with me," she said.

She led us to a little knoll not far from the garden, where we sat beside a cluster of brush pines that had been sculpted into outlandish shapes by the wind. "Tell us what happened," Yaltha said.

I was weary from travel—we'd trekked for two and a half days from Bethany to Joppa, sailed another six to Alexandria, then jostled for hours in a donkey-pulled wagon that Lavi had hired—but I told the story, I told them everything, and like before with the women in Bethany, it took some of the brightness from my pain.

When the story was spent, we fell silent. Far down the escarpment I could just make out a slice of blue lake. Nearby, one of my goats was bleating in the animal shed.

"It was a relief to see that Haran's soldiers are no longer encamped on the road," I said.

"They disbanded not long after you left," Yaltha said. "It happened exactly as Skepsis predicted: Haran was quickly informed that you'd

returned to your husband in Galilee and that I'd taken the vows to remain among the Therapeutae for life. Shortly after that, the outpost was
abandoned."

Returned to your husband in Galilee. The words were like little cleavers.

I noticed Tabitha open and close her fists, as if coaxing the bravery
Diodora had spoken about. Then she spoke for the first time. "Ana said
the outpost would likely be deserted, but Lavi would not take chances.
He insisted we wait in the closest village while he rode on alone to be
certain. Only then did he return for us." She spoke slowly, molding the
sounds in her mouth.

As she'd spoken, though, a new concern had clamored at me. "Won't
Lucian inform Haran I'm back?" I asked Yaltha.

Yaltha pressed her lips together and pondered this for the first time
herself. "You're right about Lucian. He will most certainly inform Haran
you're back. But even if Haran decides once again to seek our arrests, he
would have a hard time convincing the soldiers to return. Before you
left, there were rumors of their discontent. They'd grown weary searching passersby and receiving little pay for it. And Haran is bound to resist
doling out more of his money to them." She laid her hand on my knee.
"I think his revenge will go no further. But either way, we're safe here
with the Therapeutae. We can wait to venture beyond the gatehouse
after Haran dies. The man is older than me. He can't live forever." A
wicked grin formed on Yaltha's face. "We could always write a death
curse for him."

"I'm very good at composing them," said Tabitha, who may or may
not have grasped our lack of seriousness.

"I took the vows," Yaltha said. "I'm one of them for life now."

I would never have expected this. She'd spent so much of her life
rootless, exiled to places not of her choosing. Now *she* chose. "Oh, Aunt,
I'm glad for you."

"I took them, too," said Diodora.

I said, "I will do so as well."

"And I," said Tabitha.

Yaltha smiled at her. "Tabitha, dear, in order to take the vows, you'll need to be here for more than five minutes."

Tabitha laughed. "Next week, then," she said.

We rose finally to walk down the hill to find Skepsis and inform her of our return, but we paused first, listening to a bell clang in the distance. Wind was pouring down the cliffs, bringing the smell of the sea, and the air glowed with the saffron light that came sometimes on cloudless days. I remember this small interlude as if it were a sacred occasion, for I looked at the three of them poised before the brush pines and I saw that we had somehow shaped ourselves into a family.

ii.

In the middle of the afternoon, twenty-two months, one week, and a day after Jesus's death, rain thundered onto the library roof, waking me from a strange and unintended sleep. My head felt full and fuzzy, like it was stuffed with heaps of newly shorn wool. Lifting my cheek from my writing desk, I looked about—where was I? Gaius, who'd once nailed me into a coffin, had recently built a second room onto the library so I would have a scriptorium and space for cubicles to hold the library's scrolls, but in those first muddled seconds of waking, I didn't recognize the new surroundings. I felt a flicker of panic inside, and then of course, my whereabouts in the world returned.

Later, I would think of my old friend Thaddeus, who'd slept every day in the scriptorium in Haran's house, practically curled up on top of his desk, napping out of boredom and for a time from Yaltha's spiked beer. I, however, could only blame my somnolence on the passion that had driven me to work late into the night for weeks making copies of my

codices. Two copies for the library and another that could be dissemi-
nated.

I pushed the bench back from my desk and shook my head, trying to
clear the drowsy aftereffect, but the cobwebs clung to me. As I'd slept,
the room had darkened and chilled, and I pulled Jesus's cloak around my
shoulders, drew the lamp closer, and turned my attention back to my
work. My codex, *Thunder: Perfect Mind*, lay open on the desk, and beside
it was the copy I'd been making of it on a fresh sheet of papyrus. Skepsis
planned to send the copy to a scholar at the library in Alexandria with
whom she corresponded. I'd taken extra care with the lettering and
added my small flourishes, but my chevrons and spirals were wasted. A
large, messy ink smear gaped at me from the middle of the papyrus, the
place where my face had rested on the manuscript when I'd fallen asleep.
The last lines I'd written were barely legible:

> I am the whore and the holy woman
> I am the wife and the virgin

I rubbed my finger across my cheek and the tip of it came back with a
smear of ink. It seemed ironic, sad, beautiful, almost purposeful that *I am
the wife* had been smudged onto my skin. For nearly two years, I'd worn
my grief for Jesus like a second skin. In all that time, the pain of his
absence had not diminished. The familiar burning came to my eyes, followed by that sense I often got of wandering inside my heart, desperately
searching for what I could never find—my husband. I feared my grief
would turn to despair, that it would become a skin I couldn't shed.

A great tiredness came over me then. I closed my eyes, wanting the
dark, empty void.

I woke to silence. The rain had quieted. The air seemed weighted and still. Looking up, I saw Jesus standing across the room, his dark, expressive eyes staring at me.

I drew in my breath. It took several minutes before I could speak. I said, "Jesus. You've come."

"Ana," he said. "I never left." And he smiled his funny, lopsided smile.

He didn't move from where he stood, so I walked toward him, stopping suddenly when I noticed he was wearing his old cloak with the bloodstain on the sleeve. I looked down, taking in the garment draped about my shoulders, his old cloak with the bloodstain on the sleeve, the one I'd worn daily for twenty-two months, one week, and a day. How could he be wearing it, too?

I tried to discern what was happening. *This is most assuredly a dream,* I thought. Perhaps an awake dream or a vision. Yet I felt the realness of him.

I went and clutched his hands. They were warm and callused. He smelled like sweat and wood chips. His beard bore traces of limestone dust. He looked as he had when we were together in Nazareth. I wondered what he thought of the ink on my cheek.

I sensed he was leaving. "Don't go."

"I'll always be with you," he said, and he vanished.

I sat at my desk a long while, trying to comprehend. Skepsis had once told me her mother appeared in her holy room three weeks after she'd died. "It's not an uncommon thing," she'd said. "The mind is a mystery."

I believed then, and still now, that Jesus's visitation was the workings of my own mind, but it was no less a miracle than if he'd been flesh and blood. His spirit returned to me that day. He was no longer lost to me.

I removed his cloak, folded it neatly, and tucked it into an empty cubicle. I said aloud to the shadows in the room, "All shall be well."

iii.

We climb the path to the cliffs, Diodora, Tabitha, and I, walking one behind the other in the orange light. I walk at the head, holding my incantation bowl against my chest. Behind me, Diodora strikes a goatskin drum and Tabitha sings a song about Eve, the seeker. For thirty years, the three of us have lived together on this hillside.

I glance over my shoulder at them. Tabitha's hair flutters out behind her in the breezes, smooth and gray as a dove wing, and Diodora's face has become a tiny field of furrows like her mother's. We keep no mirrors, but I often see my reflection on the water's surface—the crinkling around my eyes, my hair still dark except for a streak of white across the front. At fifty-eight I can still move with quickness and ease up the steep incline, as can my two sisters, but today we walk slowly, weighed down by the bulging pouches on our backs. They are stuffed full of codices—thirty leather-bound copies of my writings. All the words I've written since I was fourteen. My everything.

Nearing the clifftops, we veer off the footpath and pick our way over rocks and wind-bowed grasses until we arrive at the spot I've selected—a little plateau surrounded by flowering marjoram bushes. I set my incantation bowl on the ground, Diodora stops drumming, Tabitha ceases her song, and we stand there, staring at two mammoth clay jars that are nearly as tall as I am, and then at two deep, round holes that have been dug side by side in the earth. I peer into one of the holes, and a mingling of elation and sadness passes through me.

We peel the heavy pouches from our backs, sighing with relief, making little grunting noises. "Did you have to write so much over the course of your life?" Diodora teases. Pointing at the little mountain of soil that was dug from the holes, she adds, "I imagine the junior who was required to dig these bottomless pits would also like an answer to that."

Tabitha circumambulates one of the clay jars as if it's the size of

Mount Sinai. "The poor donkeys who bore these Goliath jars up here would like the question answered as well."

"Very well," I say, joining in their fun. "I'll write an exhaustive answer to the question and we shall return and dig another hole, and bury that writing, too."

They groan loudly. Tabitha no longer hides her grin. She says, "Woe to us, Diodora; now that Ana is leader of the Therapeutae, we have no choice but to obey her."

We look at one another and break into laughter. I'm unsure whether it's because of the weight and volume of my books or because I have indeed become the Therapeutae's leader. At that moment, both of these things seem remarkably funny to us.

Our levity fades as we remove the codices from the pouches. We grow quiet, even solemn. The day before, I cut Jesus's cloak into thirty-one pieces. Now, sitting beside the holes dug into the hillside, we wrap the fragments of cloth around the books to protect them from dust and time, and tie them with undyed yarn. We work quickly, listening to the sea slap against the rocks far below, to the marjoram bushes alive with honeybees, the vibrating world.

When the task is done, I stare at the wrapped codices neatly stacked beside the jars and they look like they're wearing little shrouds. I shake away the image, but the worry that my work will be forgotten lingers. Earlier, I recorded exactly where the jars would be buried, writing the location on a sealed scroll that will be passed on within the community after I die. But how long before the scroll is forgotten, before the significance of what's buried fades?

I take the incantation bowl in my hands and lift it over my head. Diodora and Tabitha watch as I rotate it in slow circles and chant the prayer I wrote as a girl. The longing in it still seems like a living, breathing thing.

As I sing the words, I remember the night on the roof when Yaltha presented the bowl to me. She tapped the bone over my chest, striking it to life. "Write what's inside here, inside your holy of holies," she told me.

YALTHA FELL ASLEEP BENEATH the tamarisk tree in the courtyard four years ago at the age of eighty-five and never woke up. She had all sorts of things to say to me during her life, but at her death there were no parting words. Our last real conversation had taken place beneath that same tree the week before she died.

"Ana," she said. "Do you remember when you buried your scrolls in the cave to prevent your parents from burning them?"

I looked at her with curiosity. "I remember."

"Well, you must do so again. I want you to make a copy of each of your codices and bury them on the hillside near the cliffs." Her left hand possessed an occasional tremor and she'd become increasingly unsteady on her feet, but her mind, her glorious mind, had always been sound.

I frowned. "But why, Aunt? My work is safe here. No one is coming to burn it."

Her voice sharpened. "Listen to me, Ana. You've dared much with your words. So much that a time will come when men will try to silence them. The hillside will keep your work safe."

I simply stared at her, trying to make sense of her pronouncement. My face must have been ridden with doubt.

"You're not listening," she said. "Think what you've written!"

I scrolled through them in my head: stories of the matriarchs; the rape and maiming of Tabitha; the terrors men inflicted on women; the cruelties of Antipas; the braveries of Phasaelis; my marriage to Jesus; the death of Susanna; the exile of Yaltha; the enslavement of Diodora; the power of Sophia; the story of Isis; *Thunder: Perfect Mind*; and a plethora of other ideas about women that turned traditionally held beliefs upside down. And these were only a portion.

"I don't understand—" I broke off, because I did understand. I just didn't want to.

"Copies of your writings are gradually being dispersed," she said. "They shed a beautiful light, but they will unsettle people and threaten their certainties. There'll come a time—mark down my words, I foresee it—when men will try to destroy what you've written."

I'd always been the one who had moments of prescience, not Yaltha. It seemed unlikely she'd divined a glimpse of the future and more likely she spoke from wisdom and prudence.

She smiled, but there was a firm, urgent quality about her. "Bury your writings, so one day they can be found again."

"I promise, Aunt. I'll make certain that day comes."

"When I am dust, sing these words over my bones: she was a voice." I chant the last line of the prayer in my bowl, and together, Diodora, Tabitha, and I lower the jars onto their sides and place the codices inside, fifteen in each one.

Reaching into my pouch, I remove the mummy portrait I commissioned all those years ago as a gift for Jesus, meant to preserve my memory. The three of us stare at it a moment—my face painted on a piece of limewood board. I carried it all the way to Galilee to give him, but I was too late. I will always regret that lateness.

I fold the last remnant of Jesus's cloak around the portrait and slip it into the jar, thinking with wonder how his memory is being preserved three decades after his death. The past few years, Lavi has brought bits of news to me from Alexandria about Jesus's followers, who didn't disappear when Jesus died, but grew in number. Lavi says small groups of them have even sprung up here in Egypt, meeting in homes, telling stories about Jesus, and imparting his parables and sayings. How I would like to hear the stories they tell.

"They speak of Jesus as having had no wife," Lavi told me. That was a conundrum I puzzled over for months. Was it because I was absent when he traveled about Galilee during his ministry? Was it because women were so often invisible? Did they believe making him celibate rendered him more spiritual? I found no answers, only the sting of being erased.

We seal the lids with beeswax, and with a grand effort, lower the jars into the earth. On our knees, we rake the pebbly soil into the holes with our hands, filling them. *The codices are buried, Aunt. I've kept my promise.*

We stand, brushing away the dust, catching our breath. And it comes to me that the echoes of my own life will likely die away in that way thunder does. But this life, what a shining thing—it is enough.

The sun slips from the sky and the dark gold light rises up. I gaze into the far distance and sing, "I am Ana. I was the wife of Jesus of Nazareth. I am a voice."

AUTHOR'S NOTE

It was an October morning in 2014 when the idea struck me to write a novel about the fictional wife of Jesus. Fifteen years earlier, I'd thought of writing such a novel, but it hadn't seemed the right time, and honestly, I couldn't muster quite enough audacity then to take it on. But that day in October, a decade and a half later, the idea resurfaced with a great deal of insistence. I made a weak effort to talk myself out of it. Centuries of tradition insisted Jesus was *un*married, and that position had long been codified into Christian belief and embedded in the collective mind. Why tamper with that? But it was really too late to dissuade myself. My imagination had been captured. I'd already begun to picture her. Within minutes she had a name—Ana.

I have a habit of propping signs on my desk. This one remained there throughout the four and a half years I researched and wrote the novel:

Everything is the proper stuff of fiction.

—Virginia Woolf

The aim of the novelist is not only to hold up a mirror to the world, but to imagine what's possible. *The Book of Longings* reimagines the story that Jesus was a single, celibate bachelor and imagines the possibility that at some point he had a wife. Of course, Christian New Testament Scripture does not say he was married, but neither does it say he was single. The Bible is silent on the matter. "If Jesus had a wife, it would be recorded in the Bible," someone explained to me. But would it? The invisibility and silencing of women were real things. Compared to men in Jewish and Christian Scriptures, women rarely have speaking parts, and they are not mentioned nearly as often. If they are referenced, they're often unnamed.

It could also be argued that in the first-century Jewish world of Galilee, marriage was so utterly normative, it more or less went without saying. Marriage was a man's civic, family, and sacred duty. Typically undertaken at twenty (though sometimes up to age thirty), marriage was how he became an adult male and established himself within his community. His family expected him to marry and would have been shocked, perhaps even shamed, if he didn't. His religion dictated that he "not abstain from having a wife." Of course, it's possible Jesus defied these imperatives. There is evidence that ascetic ideals were beginning to encroach into first-century Judaism. And, too, he could be something of a nonconformist at times. But I saw more reason to think that at the age of twenty, a decade before his ministry began, Jesus did not reject the religious and cultural ethic of his time and place.

Claims that Jesus was *not* married first began in the second century. They arose as Christianity absorbed ideas of asceticism and Greek dualism, which devalued the body and the physicality of the world in favor of the spirit. Closely identified with the body, women were also devalued, silenced, and marginalized, losing roles of leadership they'd possessed within first-century Christianity. Celibacy became a path to holiness. Virginity became one of Christianity's higher virtues. Certain that the end-time would come soon, believers in the second century hotly debated if Christians should marry. Considering the accretion of such views into the religion, it struck me as not particularly acceptable for Jesus to have been married.

Perceptions like these allowed me to move outside of traditional ecclesiastical boxes and begin to imagine the character of a married Jesus.

Of course, I don't know whether Jesus was married or not. There are reasons, just as compelling, to support the belief he remained single. Unless some genuine ancient manuscript is discovered buried in a jar somewhere and it reveals that Jesus had a wife, we simply cannot know. Even then the matter would likely be irresolvable.

Yet from that first moment of inspiration to write this story, I felt the importance of *imagining* a married Jesus. Doing so provokes a fascinating question: How would the Western world be different if Jesus had married and his wife had been included in his story? There are only speculative answers, but it seems plausible that Christianity and the Western world would have had a somewhat different religious and cultural inheritance. Perhaps women would have found more egalitarianism. Perhaps the relationship between sexuality and sacredness would have been less fractured. Celibacy among the priesthood might not exist. I wondered what, if any, effect imagining the possibility of a married Jesus could have on these traditions. How does imagining new possibilities affect realities in the present?

I AM DEEPLY AND REVERENTIALLY aware that Jesus is a figure to whom millions of people are devoted and that his impact on the history of Western civilization is incomparable, affecting non-Christians and Christians both. Given that, it may be useful to comment on how I went about writing his character.

It was clear to me from the beginning that I would portray Jesus as fully human. I wanted the story to be about Jesus the man and not God the Son, who he would become. Early Christianity debated whether

Jesus was human or divine, a matter it settled in the fourth century at the Council of Nicaea and again at the Council of Chalcedon in the fifth century, when doctrines were adopted stating Jesus was fully human *and* fully divine. Nevertheless, his humanity diminished as he became more and more glorified. Writing from a novelist's perspective and not a religious one, I was drawn to his humanity.

There's no record of Jesus from the age of twelve until the age of thirty. His presence in the novel coincides in part with this unrecorded time period, with two notable exceptions: his baptism and his death. I invented the actions and words of Jesus during the unknown years the only way I could, through conjecture and reasonable extrapolation.

My portrayal of Jesus comes from my own interpretation of who he was based on my research of the historical Jesus and first-century Palestine, on scriptural accounts of his life and teachings, and on other commentaries about him. It was something of a wonder to discover that the human Jesus has so many different faces and that people, even historical Jesus scholars, tend to view him through the lens of their own needs and proclivities. For some he's a political activist. For others, a miracle worker. He's viewed as rabbi, social prophet, religious reformer, wisdom teacher, nonviolent revolutionary, philosopher, feminist, apocalyptic preacher, and on and on.

How would I fashion Jesus's character? I envisioned him in his twenties as a thoroughly Jewish man living under Roman occupation, and as a husband working to support his family, but harboring an evolving pull inside to leave and begin a public ministry. I depicted him as a mamzer; that is, one who suffers some degree of ostracism—in Jesus's case, because of his questioned paternity. I also visualized Jesus as an emerging social prophet and a rabbi whose dominant message was love and compassion and the coming of God's kingdom, which initially he viewed as an eschatological event establishing God's rule on earth, and ultimately as a state of being within the hearts and minds of people. I saw him as a

nonviolent political resister who takes on the role of Messiah, the promised Jewish deliverer. And central to the character I've drawn is Jesus's
empathy for the excluded, the poor, and outcasts of all kinds, as well as
his uncommon intimacy with his God.

It feels important to point out that the character of Jesus in these
pages provides a mere glimpse of the complexity and fullness of who he
was, and that glimpse is based on my interpretation of him, which is
woven into a fictional narrative.

THE STORY IS IMAGINED, but I've tried through extensive research to
be true to its historical, cultural, political, and religious backdrop. There
are instances, though, in which I veer from the record or from accepted
tradition for narrative purposes. The more noteworthy incidences follow.

Herod Antipas moved the capital of Galilee from Sepphoris to Tiberias somewhere around 18 to 20 CE. In the novel, this move didn't take
place until 23 CE. Sepphoris, a wealthy city of approximately thirty
thousand, was a mere four miles from Nazareth, prompting many scholars to speculate that Jesus was exposed to a sophisticated, Hellenized,
multilingual world. Scholars also conjecture that Jesus and his father,
Joseph, both of whom were builders, may have found contract work in
Sepphoris as Herod Antipas rebuilt the city during Jesus's adolescent
years. It's unlikely, though, that he would have found work on the Roman
theater, as portrayed in the novel. According to a number of archaeolo-
gists, the theater was constructed close to the end of the first century,
decades after Jesus's death. The mosaic of Ana's face in Antipas's palace
was inspired by an actual mosaic found on the floor of an excavated
mansion in Sepphoris. Known as Mona Lisa of the Galilee, it is an exquisite depiction of a woman's face that dates to the third century.

Phasaelis, the first wife of Herod Antipas, was a Nabataean princess
who covertly escaped back to her father in the Arabian kingdom of

Nabataea when she learned that Antipas planned to take Herodias as his wife. The exact year she fled is debated, but I've almost certainly pre-dated it by several years.

Christian Scripture states that Jesus had four named brothers and multiple unnamed sisters; I could only make room in the story for two brothers and one sister. My representation of James is likely harsher than he deserves, though in New Testament Scripture it does appear there was some conflict between Jesus and his brothers during Jesus's ministry. James later became a follower of Jesus after his brother's death and the leader of the Jerusalem church.

In the Scriptures, Jesus appears at the Jordan River to be baptized by John the Baptist, then immediately goes off into the wilderness, after which he begins his ministry. I've imagined, however, that after his bap-tism and retreat into the wilderness, Jesus spent some months as one of John's followers. While there's no mention of this in Scripture, there are conjectures by some scholars that Jesus was likely one of John's follow-ers and was deeply influenced by him, a premise I adopted.

Mary of Bethany is the woman named in the New Testament Scrip-ture as anointing Jesus's feet with an expensive ointment shortly before his death, an event that elicited criticism from Judas. I took the liberty of having Ana's friend Tabitha perform this act of anointing instead.

In the novel, Ana rushes to Jesus on the street when he falls beneath the weight of the crossbeam. This deviates from a long-held nonscrip-tural tradition that a woman named Veronica went to him and wiped his face when he fell.

The Gospels in the New Testament describe Jesus as arriving in Beth-any and Jerusalem in Judea the week before his death. However, in order to accommodate the timeline of the story, I had them arrive a number of weeks before the crucifixion.

I've attempted to adhere to the biblical stories of Jesus's trial, cruci-fixion, and burial, though not all of the occurrences in these stories could be incorporated. The inclusion or absence of events depends on whether or not they are witnessed or discovered by Ana, the narrator. In the novel, Ana and a group of women walk with Jesus to his execution, remain there as he's crucified, and then prepare him for burial. The Gospels give somewhat differing accounts of his death, but they all record the presence of a group of women at his crucifixion. Jesus's mother and Mary Magdalene are listed among them. Salome, Jesus's sister, and Mary of Bethany are not mentioned, but I inserted them in place of two other women who were. The scene in the novel in which the women walk with Jesus to his crucifixion is my invention.

The Therapeutae was not a figment of my imagination, but a real monastic-like community, near Lake Mareotis in Egypt, where Jewish philosophers devoted themselves to prayer and study and a sophisticated allegorical interpretation of Scripture. Thriving during the time period in the novel, the group is represented in these pages with a significant amount of factual detail. The forty-ninth-day vigils with their delirious all-night singing and dancing did indeed take place, the holy rooms in their small stone houses existed, as did female members and a devotion to Sophia, the feminine spirit of God. However, the Therapeutae's practice of asceticism and solitude was far more prevalent and intense than I describe. In the story, I refer to their fasting and solitude, but I essentially reimagine the group as more interactive and body-friendly.

The Thunder: Perfect Mind is an actual document written by an unknown author believed to be female and dated within the novel's time frame. Its nine pages of papyrus were among the famous Nag Hammadi texts discovered in 1945 in a jar buried in the hills above the Nile in Egypt. In the novel, *Thunder: Perfect Mind* is authored by Ana, who composes it as a hymn to Sophia. The passages of it that are included in the novel are from the real poem. I've read and reread this poem for two decades, awed by its provocative, ambiguous, commanding, gender-bending voice. Imagining Ana creating it as her great opus simply made me happy.

. . .

THE AUTHOR'S NOTE dwells heavily on the figure of Jesus for obvious reasons, but the story in *The Book of Longings* belongs to Ana. She wandered into my imagination and I couldn't ignore her.

I saw Ana not only as the wife of Jesus, but as a woman with her own quest—that of following her longings in pursuit of the largeness inside herself. I saw her, too, as a woman able to become not only Jesus's wife, but his partner.

The day Ana appeared, I knew one thing about her besides her name. I knew that what she wanted most was a voice. If Jesus actually did have a wife, and history unfolded exactly the way it has, then she would be the most silenced woman in history and the woman most in need of a voice. I've tried to give her one.

ACKNOWLEDGMENTS

I am grateful to the following people and resources that helped me bring Ana's story to life.

Jennifer Rudolph Walsh, my extraordinary agent and cherished friend, as well as Margaret Riley King, Tracy Fisher, Matilda Forbes Watson, Haley Heidemann, Natalie Guerrero, Zoe Beard-Fails, and Alyssa Eatherly, all invaluable members of the William Morris Endeavor team.

My brilliant editor, Paul Slovak, along with Brian Tart, Andrea Schulz, Kate Stark, Louise Braverman, Lindsay Prevette, Shannon Twomey, Britta Galanis, Allie Merola, Roseanne Serra, and the entire amazing team at Viking, all of whom have given me and this novel immense support, expertise, and enthusiasm.

Marion Donaldson and Headline Publishing, my wonderful UK editor and publisher.

Ann Kidd Taylor, my first reader, who offered me amazing feedback and insights. I would hate to write a book without her.

The many scholars whose books, lectures, and documentaries on the historical Jesus, the people, culture, religion, politics, and history of first-century Palestine and Alexandria, biblical interpretation, the Gnostic

Gospels, and women and gender in religion formed the mainstay of my research. The Biblical Archaeology Society, which provided me with excellent resources. The Great Courses for their videotaped academic lectures.

The new translation of *The Thunder: Perfect Mind* by Hal Taussig, Jared Calaway, Maia Kotrosits, Celene Lillie, and Justin Lasser, with gratitude to Palgrave Macmillan for permission to quote from it.

Scott Taylor, for exceptional business and technical support.

Terry Helwig, Trisha Sinnott, and Curly Clark, who gave me endless listening and encouragement as I contemplated the idea for this book and worked to bring it into being.

My family, children, grandchildren, and parents, who fill my life with so much goodness and love, especially my husband, Sandy, with whom I'm blessed to share my life. Since that long-ago day when I turned thirty and announced to him I wanted to be a writer, he has offered me infinite believing and encouragement . . . for this book especially.